PRAISE FOR PAUL LEVINE'S
JAKE LASSITER SERIES

"Take one part John Grisham, two parts Carl Hiaasen, throw in a dash of John D. MacDonald, and voilà, you've got Jake Lassiter."
—*Tulsa World*

"Realistic, gritty, fun."
—*New York Times Book Review*

"Lively entertainment. Lassiter is attractive, funny, savvy, and brave."
—*Chicago Tribune*

"Mystery writing at its very, very best."
—*USA Today*

"An assured and exciting piece of work. Jake Lassiter is Travis McGee with a law degree. One of the best mysteries of the year."
—*Los Angeles Times*

"Jake Lassiter is the lawyer we all want on our side, and on the page."
—*Lee Child*

CHEATER'S GAME

BOOKS BY PAUL LEVINE

THE JAKE LASSITER SERIES
To Speak for the Dead
Night Vision
False Dawn
Mortal Sin
Riptide
Fool Me Twice
Flesh & Bones
Lassiter
Last Chance Lassiter
State vs. Lassiter
Bum Rap
Bum Luck
Bum Deal
Cheater's Game

THE SOLOMON & LORD SERIES
Solomon vs. Lord
The Deep Blue Alibi
Kill All the Lawyers
Habeas Porpoise

STAND-ALONE THRILLERS
Impact
Ballistic
Illegal
Paydirt

CHEATER'S GAME

Paul Levine

HERALD
SQUARE
PUBLISHING

Cheater's Game
Paul Levine

Text copyright © 2020 by Paul J. Levine

Published by Herald Square Publishing
Cover design by www.Damonza.com
Interior Design by Steven W. Booth, GeniusBookServices.com
Author Photo by Doug Ellis, www.DougEllisPhoto.com

ISBN-13: 9781734251005

Printed in the United States of America

Maybe all you ever get for integrity is the largest kick in the ass the world can provide. Crime pays a lot better. I can bend my own rules way, way over, but there is a place where I finally stop bending them.
—Travis McGee in *The Turquoise Lament* by John D. MacDonald

In a society without shame, where faking it is making it and deceit trumps virtue, integrity is for losers and cheaters win. Fairness? Forget about it! A meritocracy? In your dreams! Earn your diploma? Why bother, when you can buy it?
—Jake Lassiter

For Sue and Joe Paterno, compassionate mentors,
loyal friends and tireless educators

PROLOGUE
Road Fury

With the recklessness of a 20-year-old who had not yet been scorched by life's wildfires, Kip Lassiter floored the Tesla X, which whooshed along the narrow road, splashing through potholes barely two feet from a murky Everglades canal.

Kip opened the windows, and a humid blast enveloped him. It had been a great morning. Twenty-five thousand in cash under the backseat. No invoice, no receipt, no howdy-do from the IRS.

Twenty-five grand for four hours' work!

And it was more fun than work. Taking the risk and getting away with it. What a rush, like being the last person standing in *Fortnite.*

Slowing down to navigate a buckled stretch of asphalt, Kip heard a discordant sound anfd glanced at his rearview mirror. A metallic blue Maserati, a growling beast, appeared in the mist a hundred yards behind. In seconds, the sports car closed the distance and pulled alongside, exhausts throbbing like symphonic horns. Kip glanced left, but the Maserati's windows were tinted a bottomless black, the driver a phantom.

Kip sped up and the Maserati kept pace, hanging there.

What? You want to race? That's cool.

His mind flashed to a video game he had played as a kid. *Road Fury*. Two cars zipping along a highway filled with hairpin turns. The goal: make the other car crash through a guardrail and fly over a cliff.

Kip punched the accelerator, and the Tesla shot ahead, but the Maserati quickly caught up. Hurtling neck and neck, the two vehicles flew past low-slung gumbo limbo trees that crowded the scarred roadway.

The Maserati's windows rolled down, and Kip immediately recognized the driver and passenger. Niles and Teague, rich-prick twins from Palm Beach, whose combined IQ wouldn't equal his.

Okay, so I punked Niles on his SAT exam. But playing chicken at high speed? Seriously?

Niles, or maybe Teague, lunged halfway out the window and shouted, "Keep your mouth shut, Lassiter!"

Oh. That's it? As if I would talk to the feds.

The Maserati moved closer, claiming the center of the narrow road. Inches apart now, the Tesla's collision warning bleated like a frightened goat. Kip's eyes darted to the road ahead. Something moving, just a low silhouette against the glare. Closer now, Kip made out a Florida panther, the color of sun-bleached saw grass.

The Maserati braked hard and fishtailed, sideswiping the Tesla. Kip fought the steering wheel, but his tires skidded off the road and chewed through a patch of swamp lilies. Out of control, the Tesla slid down the embankment and splashed into the canal.

The airbag deployed like a boxer punching Kip in the face, pinning him against his seat. Water poured through the open windows. Through the windshield, he saw fish the size of fingernails scattering in the brackish water.

Kip tasted blood and thought he heard the Tesla's horn wailing, but as the water reached his chest, he realized it was his own scream.

CHAPTER ONE
Just Who Is This Boy?

"Mr. Lassiter! Jake Lassiter!"

Milagros Soto, a court bailiff, called out to me, her voice echoing down the courthouse corridor. More urgent than necessary, I thought, for my being three minutes late for a hearing.

"Hey, Millie. Tell the judge I'll be right there."

"Hearing's cancelled. Why aren't you answering your phone?"

"I turn it off when I'm in the courthouse."

True enough. When I took the job with the Florida Bar, I started following rules I had always ignored.

"Get over to Jackson Memorial right away," she said. "It's your nephew."

I froze, my chest crushed by dread, as if my lungs had suddenly filled with mud. "What's hap...?" I couldn't get the words out.

"I don't know, Jake. Just get to the trauma center, now."

Oh, Kip! Just when you'd turned your life around. Now what?

ᕦ

Fifteen minutes later, I was double-timing through the maze of Jackson Memorial, as Gloria Sanchez, a deputy administrator, filled me in. "I don't know why, Jake, but your nephew told me not to contact you. He said you weren't related."

"Aw, jeez. I thought the kid had outgrown that."

I'd known Gloria for twenty years, and she routinely gave me access to the inner sanctum of the trauma center so I could visit clients and witnesses, circumventing the rules. A while back, when her son was a junior at Coral Gables High, I got his marijuana possession charge dismissed. *Pro bono*, of course.

A sturdy woman in her fifties, Gloria kept pace, quick on her feet. She had probably traveled the circumference of the earth on the rock-hard tile of these chilly corridors.

"When EMS brought him in, I saw the name, 'Chester Lassiter.' I remember years ago you showed me photos of the boy. So proud of how smart the little fellow was. You raised Chester, right?"

I nodded. "He goes by 'Kip.' My half-sister named him 'Chester' after her dad. She was too busy jumping bail to catch the name of the kid's father."

Gloria led me into a room where Kip lay on his back, eyes closed, cervical collar around his neck, oxygen clips in his nose, tubes and wires sprouting from his arms and chest. Crimson scratches ran down both cheeks and across his forehead, and two black eyes gave him a raccoon look. A nearby monitor blinked with his respiration, pulse rate, and blood pressure.

In her professional tone tempered with motherly compassion, Gloria told me that Kip was in intensive care because that's what they do with head trauma. The brain scan appeared normal, but that didn't rule out a moderate concussion and a whiplash injury.

The headline: Kip had driven his car into a canal, and it was difficult to tell how long he'd struggled to get out of the shoulder harness and claw his way through a window. The trauma crew had pumped a small amount of slimy water out of his stomach. No water down his airway thanks to laryngospasms, the throat sealing the trachea. Good thing because water in the lungs can lead to pneumonia.

I walked to the bed and clasped Kip's hand. Hundreds of times, I'd held him, hugged him, tousled his hair. I'd watched him grow. Taught him values. I'd marveled at his achievements and suffered at his stumbles. And now here he was, as helpless as the day he arrived at my home, my worthless half-sister shoving him out of the car. All his belongings—two filthy changes of clothes— stuffed into a Mickey Mouse backpack that looked as if Pluto had taken a dump in it.

Not a toy. Not a single toy.

He was nine with broomstick limbs, and no one had taught him how to throw or catch a ball, so we invented a game called "Ten." I'd toss him a rubber ball. If he caught it ten times in a row, he'd get a prize. A milkshake or a comic book or a pack of baseball cards. Soon he could catch it twenty or thirty times without a miss, but we still called the game Ten.

When I'd come home from court, as soon as I walked in, Kip would say, "Let's play Ten." And by then, the phrase had taken on a meaning of its own. "Let's hang out" or "Let's watch a game" or "Let's talk." Our own private code.

Now, I squeezed his hand and whispered, "Hey little guy. I'm here."

Kip didn't respond.

"Give him a couple hours for the sedatives to wear off," Gloria said.

Kip stirred and grunted in his sleep.

"Where exactly did the car go into the water?" I asked, thinking that Miami-Dade had hundreds of miles of waterways, a few not far from the hospital.

"In the Everglades," Gloria said. "Just this side of Ochopee on a Water District road north of the Trail."

That stopped me. "Way the hell out there? Who called 911?"

Gloria sighed. "I knew you'd ask, so I called the county. Male voice, a little agitated but not hysterical. Wouldn't leave a name but gave a precise description of the location. GPS coordinates. They don't get that very often."

"Did the county pick up a tower location or the caller's number?"

She shook her head. "Call was too quick. When your nephew's awake, I'm sure he'll tell you everything."

I wasn't so sure.

Kip stirred again, his eyes blinking, but he didn't awaken.

"Did the paramedics recover anything from the car?" I asked.

"One of them dived in, but just to make sure no one was in the vehicle. All we've got now is what Kip had in his pockets."

My look asked her a silent question, and her answer was to lead me to a room with two dozen small lockers. She used a master key to open one and handed me a plastic pouch containing a wallet and a passport, both still wet.

"Don't let anyone see you and put everything back." Gloria studied me a moment and asked, "Are you okay, Jake? I read in the paper that you're in that concussion study. I hope everything works out for you."

I mumbled my thanks, and she smiled at me. "You look like you could still play linebacker."

"Ha! I still weigh 235, but it's repositioned itself."

She said goodbye and left, and I opened the passport and looked at the photo. Issued eleven months ago, a sly smile on Kip's face.

But what's this?

Five trips out of the country, five stamps, each with a little green turtle.

Cayman Islands, a British Overseas Territory.

All short trips, two to four days, including one last week. *What the hell!*

Kip had never mentioned his travels.

I closed the passport and opened the wallet, which contained nine hundred eighty-seven dollars. Okay, that's more than I carry around, but so what? Kip had a small business tutoring high school students for the ACT and SAT exams.

I then pulled out a Florida vehicle registration certificate, expecting to find the paperwork for his ten-year-old Toyota Camry. Gloria hadn't mentioned the make of Kip's car, and I'd just assumed it was his old clunker. What I found was the registration for a brand-new Tesla SUV, Model X with a personalized license plate, "EZ-1600."

I drive a 1984 Cadillac Eldorado ragtop, so I'm a little behind the times. But just how the hell did Kip afford this high-tech, space-age vehicle? The Tesla title was folded inside the wallet, too. No lienholder, meaning no loan. He owned the damn thing free and clear.

As for the license plate, I knew the meaning of "1600." That had been Kip's score—perfection—on the SAT exam. So much promise. But then came the disaster his freshman year in college. An arrest, expulsion, and a humiliating trip home. And now what? The vehicle registration date was three months ago. I'd seen Kip several times since then. He had an apartment on Brickell, and on his occasional trips to my Coconut Grove house, he always was at the wheel of that old Toyota.

So, *the kid who used to tell me everything now secretly buys a luxury vehicle with cash and goes to pains to make sure I don't know.*

I pulled Kip's driver's license out of its slot and studied the photo. Sixteen when it had been taken, and he looked about twelve. Straw-blond hair falling into his eyes, a look of innocence, totally lacking in guile. I knew everything about him then. We had no secrets. Was that him in the hospital bed or had space aliens taken over his body? Maybe all parents ponder that question one time or another.

So many threads that lead...where?

Why the Cayman Islands?

And what's with the pricey Tesla at the bottom of a canal?

Who called 911?

I replaced the items in the locker and walked down the corridor toward Kip's room. I would be there when he woke up. And we would talk.

Kip. This is your Uncle Jake. It's time to get reacquainted. Let's play Ten.

CHAPTER TWO
The Doctor Is In

Melissa Gold...

Jake's phone call rocked Dr. Melissa Gold. "Oh my God, Jake! Is he unconscious?"

"Sedated. It's probably just a concussion." He paused a moment. "I guess that's a little ironic, my saying, 'just a concussion.'"

Her fiancé, Jake Lassiter, had his own history of head bangers, which may have led to brain damage. Irony there, too. If not for Jake's traumatic brain injury, they never would have met. As a neuropathologist, she treated him. As a woman, she loved him.

"I'm with a patient," Melissa said, "but I can be there in an hour."

"Maybe it's better if I talk to him alone first. We need to reconnect."

"Has he strayed that far?"

"All my fault. I've let him get away from me."

Sadness and regret were heavy in his voice. She could practically see his broad shoulders slumping. Jake had given so much of himself so unselfishly, raising Kip after his mother had abandoned him. Jake's capacity for giving, in fact, had been one of the attractions for her.

They met when she was director of the Center for Neuroscience at UCLA's medical school. He had taken her deposition in a civil suit, and there was an immediate attraction. He said he liked long, leggy women who were smart and savvy. She usually didn't like wise-guy lawyers, but there was something solid about him. A strength of character to go with that barrel chest.

In her Left Coast days, she'd dated a number of eligible bachelors. Hollywood business managers in their Zegna suits and Italian silk ties, film agents in their Brioni suits and shiny shirts with no ties, even a couple of actors (*what was I thinking?*) in torn jeans and five-day beards. The men shared one personality trait: none could pass a mirror without pausing to admire himself. Los Angeles was awash with that kind of man, a Century City Narcissus worshiping his own reflection, waiting for his next project to be greenlit. Sure, a man of towering ego liked having an attractive, professional woman on his arm, but no more than that diamond-encrusted Piaget watch.

Then she met Jake, who was effortlessly natural and without pretensions, responsive to her needs, an excellent listener, and unaware of how rare a prize he was. He was something of a throwback. At a downtown diner, he drank his coffee black with a slice of apple pie, not a cinnamon cappuccino with a passionfruit macaron. In chi-chi South Beach, he remained a brew-and-burger guy in a paté and Chardonnay world.

"Do it, Jake. Talk to him first. You know him best."

"I thought I did, but what the hell happened?" He sighed into the phone. "When he went off to college, he had such promise."

"*Has* such promise. Jake, he's twenty! Didn't you ever get into trouble at that age?"

"I was almost kicked out of Penn State for throwing a refrigerator off a fourth-floor balcony. It was a twenty-dollar bet, and I'd already emptied the refrigerator of beer, so I knew I could do it."

"Just be gentle with Kip. He's sensitive and..."

"And I'm not?"

"No, you are, but in a different way. You grew up like Huck Finn, barefoot and rowdy. I doubt Kip ever free-dived to steal lobster pots."

"Only stole the lobsters. I left the pots on the ocean floor."

"I love you, big guy."

"I love you, too, Doc. Even when you stick needles in my butt."

She worried about both Lassiter men. Kip was a mystery. Just how did a kid who got a perfect score on the SAT, who never sweated through an academically rigorous private school, get booted out of college his second semester?

But her fiancé's medical condition had become her primary focus. Once Jake had been diagnosed with a precursor to Chronic Traumatic Encephalopathy, the fatal brain disease best known for afflicting former football players, he suggested—politely and sweetly—that they put off the wedding.

"I need a definitive diagnosis," Jake had said. "I don't want you to be a young widow."

When they spoke of marriage now, it was tied to a clean bill of health. Jake was in a study she was running at the University of Miami. Would the early indications of the disease that showed up on his brain scans morph into the full-blown killer that had stricken so many of his contemporaries? Or would they discover a cure for C.T.E. itself, saving him and thousands of others? No one knew.

Their personal relationship was much more joyful. When Chloe, her best girlfriend in Los Angeles, had asked how it was going, Melissa told her, "He gets me. Respects me. It's so easy, and we mesh so well."

"And in bed?" Chloe said.

"He takes my breath away."

"New lab project. Clone him!"

All of which raised a troubling question. When could she tell Jake about the new development in her life? Certainly not today, not until Kip was safely at home. She faced an issue so common these days that it had become a cliché. How could she manage both her relationship and her career? And perhaps the biggest question of all: Would Jake uproot his life for her, as she had done for him?

CHAPTER THREE
Blizzard

I'd been sitting in a straight-back chair designed for pygmies for three hours when Kip's pale blue eyes fluttered open and focused on me. I helped him scoot into a sitting position, and he ran a hand across his face, as if checking for dents.

"Uncle Jake?"

"How you feeling, kiddo?"

"I dunno." He touched the cervical collar around his neck and wriggled his toes under the sheets.

"Are you in pain?"

He touched a spot above his right temple. "Head's pounding. That's about all."

I bent over, picked up a Styrofoam cooler and opened it.

"What's that?" he asked.

"Got something I didn't want the nurses to put in a fridge with the urine samples." I handed him a gigantic blue and red cup with a plastic spoon and fork sticking out of a cold, creamy froth.

"You brought me a Blizzard. Jumbo size." Kip gave me a smile that started as gratitude but turned frosty, like the drink.

"An *Oreo* Blizzard from Dairy Queen," I said. "Your favorite."

"Yeah. When I was nine."

Without taking a sip, he placed the cup on the elevated tray next to the bed.

"I remember the first time I took you to the D.Q. on South Dixie," I said. "You'd never had a Blizzard. You probably never had ice cream unless your mom shoplifted a Nutty Buddy from the 7-Eleven."

"Cheap wine," he corrected me. "That's what she boosted from convenience stores."

"Anyway, an hour ago, I called Tony Frontero. Remember him?"

"He owned a cab company." Kip said. "Drove you home whenever you got wasted."

"I kept Tony out of jail when he was pocketing payroll taxes. Drives an Uber now and made a special delivery for you, kiddo." I shot an admiring look at the cookie chunks floating in vanilla ice cream above the rim of the cup. "Nothing on earth like an Oreo Blizzard."

Kip studied me a moment as if he didn't know quite what to say. *Thanks, Uncle Jake* did not seem to be on the tip of his tongue.

"You know I'm a vegan, right?" he said.

"Yeah, but for old times' sake..."

"I don't eat dairy anymore. Period."

"Suit yourself." I grabbed the giant cup and slurped through the straw until my throat grew icicles. I wanted to make Kip forget all about kale and tofu and avocado toast. I wanted him to rip the Blizzard out of my hand and chug it and then demand baby-back ribs for dinner. In short, I wanted the old Kip back. The kid he used to be.

Part of parenting, I know, is allowing your children to grow up and become their own persons. To get away from your home and your influence. This part of parental self-discipline, however, is not my forté.

In theory, I got it. Kip was 20. He had his own apartment and did not give me a key. He owned an expensive SUV that I knew nothing about and traveled out of the country without telling me.

Deal with it. The kid is a grown-up. Or is he just playing one?

"Mmm," I murmured, wiping my lips. "Oreo cookies and vanilla ice cream. A heavenly treat."

"Might send you straight to heaven. Eleven hundred calories, forty-one grams of fat, and one hundred twenty-two grams of sugar."

A young nurse nametagged "Magda" walked in and checked various panels and electronic displays, a couple of which beeped and whistled as she pushed buttons. She told us the doctor would be coming around soon, and they'd be keeping Kip overnight for observation.

When she was gone I said, "How do you know all that nutritional info?"

"Three or four years ago, I looked it up."

"Amazing."

He shrugged. "I just remember stuff. It's no big deal."

"Hah! You're a genius."

"Let's not go there, Jake."

His voice was taking on an edge. Now it was *Jake*. Not *Uncle Jake*.

"Where are we not going, Kip? What subjects are off limits?"

I need a road map to avoid the path where my nephew's disapproval lurks like a pool of quicksand.

"College," he said. "In a second you'll want to dredge up what happened at Penn and where I go from here."

"I swear I wasn't thinking of that."

Okay, a white lie. Sure, I was thinking of Kip's spectacular flame-out at the Ivy League school most of my pals confuse with Penn State.

"You have tremendous potential," I said. "Untapped potential. That's all I've ever said."

He dismissed that notion with a wave of his hand, the hospital ID band sliding around his small wrist. "I don't want to talk about it."

I sighed and let us sit in silence a moment. Then I said, "Okay, you win. Tell me about the accident."

"I drove off the road."

"Did you have a blowout?"

"No."

"Fall asleep at the wheel?"

"Of course not."

"Collision with another car?"

"What other car?"

I noticed he hadn't answered the question. "I don't know, Kip. How did your car end up in the drink?"

"Jeez, Uncle Jake. Do you think I was playing *Road Fury* in real life?"

The question struck me as odd. Kip's obsession with eGames was a painful reminder of his adolescence. *Medal of Honor, League of Legends, Road Fury*. A child psychiatrist told me that the games had warped Kip's perception of reality so that he couldn't tell where fantasy ended and real life began. It took two years of therapy to kick the eGames habit. As far as I knew, Kip had hung up his saddle and stopped killing horse rustlers in *Red Dead Redemption*.

"No, I think you're over that eGame nonsense," I said.

"You're right. What happened isn't complicated. I just drove into a canal."

"In a new Tesla SUV, model X. What is that, about eighty thousand bucks?"

He snorted a laugh. "You are so yesterday," which meant "yesterday" in hipster-speak, but if I knew that, it probably didn't mean it anymore.

"With the high-performance package and the autopilot," Kip said, "you're talking north of a hundred grand. But what you really want to know is how I could afford it."

"The thought crossed my mind."

"If I tell you everything, will you back off, let me breathe?"

"I didn't know I was suffocating you."

"You didn't used to. But when you got sick…"

"I'm not sick."

"Fine. When your C.T.E. symptoms cropped up, you decided to become Parent of the Year. Like maybe you'd better do that before you croaked." He paused a moment, seeming to consider whether to fire another harpoon into the whale. "Tell you the truth, Jake, I liked you better when you were more wrapped up in yourself."

"And I liked you better, kiddo, when you were a carnivore."

"Yasss!" He laughed, a high-pitched jangle of coins. "Nice clap-back!"

Great, he enjoyed sparring with me. That was better than sullen and silent. Then I spoke the words nearly every parent has said to a child once, or maybe a million times. "C'mon Kip. Tell me what's going on with you."

He gave me a half-smile. "Okay, here's the deal. Ask me anything. I won't deflect or evade. Then when we're done, you'll get out of my grill."

"Deal." I tried hard not to wince at the coldness in his voice, the distance in his manner.

I began asking questions, and true to his word, Kip did not deflect or evade. He just lied.

CHAPTER FOUR
Launching the Child Like a Sailboat

"Good morning," he lied.

That's what popped into my head midway into our colloquy. I have cross-examined professional perjurers for twenty-five years. Kip reminded me of a witness I once questioned, a guy who fabricated every answer, even to the polite request, "Please state your name for the record."

It started well enough. Kip grinned and said, "Fire away."

"What were you doing in the Glades?"

"Collecting money Jimmy Tiger owed me for tutoring his dumb ass. He was staying at his family's fishing cabin."

"Who's Jimmy Tiger?"

Kip pushed a button on a remote, and the hospital bed groaned and propped him upright. "Jimmy was a year behind me at Tuttle."

Meaning Biscayne-Tuttle. Kip's fancy-pants private high school that sits regally on the shoreline of Biscayne Bay in Coconut Grove. Mediocre football program, but the sailing and chess teams, top-notch.

Kip continued, "Jimmy used to come over to the house. Don't you remember?"

I shook my head. The name neither rang a bell nor set off alarms. "How much did he owe you?"

Silence. I could have run the 40-yard dash while he decided what to say, and I was never fast. Surely he knew the amount, so why the delay?

"Eight hundred bucks," he said, finally.

"I guess that explains the $987 in your wallet."

Another pause. "I guess."

Kip might be able to get a perfect score on the SAT, but he was a real dunce at prevarication.

"Why didn't Jimmy send you a check?" I asked. "Or...what's that system you use?"

"PayPal." He shrugged. "Jimmy likes cash."

"So do a lot of my clients. I send them birthday cards every year. Raiford, Avon Park, Dade Correctional."

"Chill, Jake. This isn't illegal."

I chilled by finishing the icy Blizzard shake. The nurse returned and left a menu for Kip. He was hungry, and I wasn't, probably because I had just inhaled a zillion calories.

When she was gone, I shifted gears. "What's with your trips to Grand Cayman?"

Instead of answering, Kip took the oxygen clips out of his nose. "I gotta pee."

Maybe he did or maybe he just wanted to concoct an answer. He swung his feet out from under the sheets, and I grabbed his skinny left arm.

"I don't need help, Jake. Just push the cart for me, will you?"

I didn't protest that he was wobbly. If he stumbled, I could catch him with one paw. I pushed the cart that held his IV bag and opened the door to the restroom.

"I go to Cayman for business," Kip said, once inside.

I heard a tinkling. At least he wasn't lying about that.

"Dr. Ringle has a vacation house on the beach," Kip continued. "It's where we have our marketing meetings."

"Hold on. Who's Dr. Ringle?"

"Max Ringle. He's got a Ph.D. You remember Shari Ringle, right?"

"Another student at Tuttle?" I ventured.

"Boarding school at Saint Andrew's in Boca Raton." Kip walked unsteadily back into the room, and we retraced our steps. After he slid under the sheets, he continued, "The Ringles live in California, but they have houses in Palm Beach and Grand Cayman. I tutored Shari for the SAT, and now she's at USC."

"Go Trojans. Is she your girlfriend?"

"I wish. Anyhow, that's how I met her dad, who's really brilliant. He runs Quest Educational Development. You know the Latin abbreviation, right? Q.E.D."

"No, but I'm sure you do."

"*Quod erat demonstrandum.* 'Thus, it has been demonstrated.' Mathematicians use it to signify the accuracy of their proofs."

"So it's a math tutoring company?"

Kip gave me a pitying look that teachers reserve for their dimmest students. "You're being too literal. Philosophers use Q.E.D. with their propositions. You could even end a closing argument with it."

"Speak Latin? My jurors have trouble with bus schedules."

"Q.E.D. helps wealthy families get their kids into elite universities," Kip went on. "Résumé enhancement, SAT and ACT prep, even psychologists to help with test anxiety."

"'Résumé enhancement' leaves an unsavory taste. Sounds like hired hands putting a spit shine on the shoddy work of rich dullards."

"Max says we're just showing students in their best possible light."

"When you cut through the marketing bullshit, aren't rich parents just paving the road for their kids to get into fancy colleges? Meanwhile, poor parents scrape by, hoping for loans and scholarships."

"How's that different from a rich defendant hiring a top lawyer and posting bail while a poor guy stays in jail and gets the public defender?"

"Point taken." Kip had been a star on the Biscayne-Tuttle debate team and seldom lost an argument with anyone, including me.

"Somehow," I said, "I thought higher education should be a meritocracy, even when so much of society is not."

"Wake up, Jake! Survival of the fittest. Capitalism at work. And it *does* work. Max pays me very well, as my Tesla ought to prove."

"I've never heard you talk about money and material things like this, Kip. It's so..."

"Adult?"

"Avaricious."

He regarded me quizzically. "We've talked about Q.E.D. before. Don't you remember?"

"Nope."

"I worked for Max Ringle as a freelancer before I went to Philly, then I started full-time when I came home."

"Went to Philly." "Came home." Sounds so much better than getting his ass kicked out of college.

"My business cards say 'Senior Vice President, Standardized Testing.'"

"Impressive. Let's do lunch. Have your girl call my girl."

He rolled his eyes. "When I got back to Miami, do you remember my saying how I was upgrading my clients and making a lot more cheddar?"

"Can't say that I do."

"Max Ringle was the first guy to call me. He said I could make a ton of money with him and I didn't need a college degree. Bill Gates dropped out of college. So did Steve Jobs and Mark Zuckerberg."

"Don't forget Jeffrey Epstein and Ted Bundy."

"I knew you'd say something like that."

"I'm just surprised that your boss peddles such bullshit. And, frankly, this is all news to me."

He paused long enough to measure his words. The P.A. speakers informed us that Dr. Kornspan's presence was requested in the maternity ward.

"I'm worried about you, Jake."

"Right back at you."

"I bet you wish you'd never played football."

"No, but I wish I hadn't blocked that punt with my face mask." That was true, given my grade-three concussion to go along with two minutes of unconsciousness. True, too, that organized football has become organized brain damage.

"You met Jimmy Tiger at the house a couple years ago," Kip said. "Okay, so maybe you forgot him. But I told you about working with Max Ringle. Do you remember my asking your opinion about the Tesla before I bought it?"

I pointed a finger at him, as if aiming a dagger. "I'd remember the Tesla if we'd talked about it, and I don't."

"You better take some memory tests the next time you're at the concussion center."

"I don't have drain bamage," I said, repeating an old joke between the two of us.

Sure, I've been forgetful. So are lots of people my age. In conversations, the name of an actor or a movie or an old teammate slips away. I used to watch *Jeopardy* with Kip when he was a little kid. The game show places a premium not just on knowledge, but on how quickly you can retrieve that knowledge. Back in the day, my brain synapses fired at Usain Bolt speed. Now, the answer—*What is Liechtenstein?*—may come to me next Tuesday.

I can't say whether my memory lapses are the result of brain disease or the ailment we call life. Either way, I'm not as sharp. Still, there are some things I'm sure I would remember, and I had the distinct impression that Kip was gaming me.

"What about those trips to Grand Cayman?" I asked. "Did you tell me about them?"

"I'm a grown man. I don't need you to babysit me."

Grown man sounded so discordant.

I looked him dead on. "Did you get your probation officer's permission to leave the country?"

"In the practice of law, do you ever break the rules?"

"Only the little ones."

"When you were in private practice, you'd get guilty people off, but you're lecturing me about my legal responsibilities."

"I didn't get anybody off, Kip. I just forced the state to prove its case."

He laughed. "What a rationalization. And I mean the psychological defense mechanism of making excuses. Not the mathematical process of removing the square root from the denominator of a fraction."

"You win, Kip. You're the smartest guy in the room, and likely the smartest guy in any penitentiary."

"Relax, the probation department loves me. I made restitution ahead of schedule."

"A hundred thirty thousand? How?"

"I got an advance from Max."

"So you owe your boss. Is he charging you vig?"

Kip laughed and buried his face in both hands. "Vig?" he said with utter delight. "You've been representing lowlifes too long, Jake. I'm practically Max's partner. We're businessmen."

This businessman still seemed like a naive waif to me.

"Sometimes, Kippers," I said, "you exhaust me."

We were both quiet a moment. If the battle had been with bare knuckles instead of words, this is where we would be stuffing cotton up our bloody noses. I listened to the squeak of rubber soles on the tile floor outside the room. On the P.A. system, a Dr. Emery was required in the ICU. Outside the window, the sun was shining, and a breeze ruffled the fronds on a trio of queen palms.

"I'm worried about you, Kip. Or did I already say that? 'Cause I'm such a senile old bastard, maybe I forgot."

"I'm good, Jake. Really."

We had come to an impasse. He'd kept secrets from me, and I'd called him on it. He felt I was invading his personhood, and there was no way to convince him my good intentions outweighed his need for autonomy. So I gave up...for now.

I told Kip to call me whenever he was ready to be discharged. I'd pick him up. He said he would, and I didn't know whether to believe that, either.

You raise your child the best you can. You send the child into the world, like launching a toy sailboat in a pond. Except the world is not a placid pond. More often, it is a raging sea, and life a perfect storm of the unexpected crashing head-on into the unbearable. There is no way to prepare the child for such a world because your own personal crises, traumas, and failures are just that, your own. Your child, as you will belatedly learn, is not you.

CHAPTER FIVE
Money and Secrets and Lies

Melissa Gold...

Melissa watched the man she loved use a spatula to flip snapper filets on the grill. She could see the weight of the troubles on his handsome, craggy face. He lived for Kip. She knew that if his nephew was hurting, Jake felt twice the pain.

"Maybe I should have stayed at the hospital overnight," he said.

"If you slept in a chair, your back would go into spasms," she said.

"I just didn't like the way it ended today. It's as if he's rejected me in favor of his new boss. I just keep wondering how I let him drift away."

They were in the backyard of their coral rock house on Kumquat Avenue in Coconut Grove. It was where Jake—with ample help from Granny Lassiter—had raised Kip.

Jake wore running shorts and a Penn State wrestling T-shirt. He hadn't been a wrestler, but he made a point of celebrating his alma mater's numerous national championships. Melissa was barefoot and wearing a sleeveless, flowing cotton dress with a bright print design and a deep V-neck and halter straps. The night was warm and muggy, which in Miami was redundant.

"When the child becomes an adult," she said, "there's a natural separation process from the parents. It doesn't mean you did anything wrong."

Jake spooned a mixture of olive oil, garlic, lime juice, and crushed ginger over the snapper filets, and a fragrant smoke whooshed up from the white-hot charcoal. "I get that. He needs to create distance between us to feel grown up."

"To *be* grown up."

"Okay. I just worry that he's gotten too attached to this Doc Ringle, a guy I don't know but already hate."

This was a delicate subject for Melissa. Like Jake, she had never been married. Unlike Jake, she had never raised a child. He welcomed her advice, but she didn't feel fully competent in giving it.

"I tried to mark a path for Kip," Jake said, "without being a snowplow parent. You know, clearing out all the obstacles."

"You tried to prepare Kip for the road, not prepare the road for Kip."

"Exactly. But maybe I didn't do enough. Maybe I threw him into a snowdrift and said, 'Dig yourself out, kiddo.'"

The horn of the Metrorail train blared from the direction of South Dixie Highway. "That's not what you did, Jake. You're a man of integrity with a strong work ethic. You tried to teach him by example."

"And look what happened. Expelled from college and now this. I don't even know what he's doing, except it involves money and secrets and lies. It's almost as if Kip wants to flaunt how different he is from me."

She didn't know exactly what had happened at Penn. Out of embarrassment, Kip had asked Jake not to go into details.

He honored that commitment, and she honored the private relationship between the two of them. Then, as if Jake had been reading her mind, he said, "I should never have promised Kip confidentiality."

"It's your lawyer-client training. You just turned it into the uncle-nephew privilege."

"Yeah, but the fiancé-fiancée relationship should trump that. We can't have secrets from each other. I'm going to ask Kip to release me from the promise."

"Whatever you two decide is fine with me."

He cocked his head and looked at her without saying a word.

"What?" she asked.

"You're the best, Mel. You don't Wisconsin me."

"Hah, you mean *badger*. I know all about the Big 10."

Ten minutes later, they were inside the house at the kitchen table. In July, only alligators in nearby canals and the neighborhood peacocks dined al fresco, sometimes the former on the latter. Jake spooned a salsa of mango, pineapple, and papaya over the snapper, and Melissa served a green salad.

"Oh, shit," Jake groaned, frowning. "I'm a lousy mate, a horrible fiancé."

"Why would you say that?"

"All I'm doing is talking about my problems and Kip's problems. I've totally neglected you. I'm sorry."

She smiled and took a bite of the snapper, tangy with the tropical salsa. At least he recognized what he was doing. Acknowledged it. Apologized for it.

"That's okay," she said. "I knew you'd get around to me."

"So how the hell was your day? What's new in the world of neurons and synapses?"

Now was the time, she supposed. A decision had to be made. A joint decision. Her future was their future. The conversation would be about marriage and career, or in a word, life. Why, she wondered, was she nervous about it? Here was the man who returned her love as no one else ever had.

"Do you remember I told you we applied for a grant from N.I.H. to expand our clinical trials?"

"Sure, I do. Are you saying you got it? They're gonna fund you?"

"More than that. They want to take our program in-house and expand it. The C.T.E. research, the diagnostics, the clinical trials of new drugs. And get this, with a budget eight times what we requested."

"Wow! Fabulous. I'm so proud of you." His look was so wide-eyed with pleasure that it made her smile right back at him.

"They're already doing brain injury research in their institute for neurological disorders," she said. "We'd become a new division as soon as Congress funds it."

"This is amazing. We should celebrate. Champagne? Key lime pie? Both?"

He was so excited his face resembled that of a little boy, she thought. She'd seen pictures of him at twelve years old, holding up a fish he'd caught with a bamboo pole. Same thing now. Only his excitement was for her.

Before she moved to Miami to be with Jake and run the University of Miami Concussion Project, Melissa directed an early study of deceased football players in which 20 of 24 autopsies were positive for the disease. Then she pioneered neuroimaging of the brains of living ex-players—Jake included—in an effort at early detection.

"It's all you, Mel," he kept going. "You're gonna bust this disease wide open and cure it."

"Maybe, with the N.I.H. staff and time and money and some luck. Like football, there's a team involved."

He rooted around in the refrigerator, found a bottle of Dom Pérignon in the back. "Don't be so modest. They're going to name it the Gold Vaccine. You're gonna get the Nobel Prize, and I'll put on a tux, and we'll get a free trip to Sweden. Not only that, tonight we're gonna have great sex. Off-the-charts sex!"

She didn't smile at that, and he said, "What? Did I say something wrong?"

She couldn't delay any longer. "I'm a finalist to be executive director of the program."

"Of course you are. And you'll get it. So, let's celebrate and... oh." A frown crossed his face like a storm cloud scudding across the sun. "The job isn't in Miami, is it?"

"Bethesda, Maryland. So, assuming I get the position, we need to talk about what to do and come to a joint decision."

"Okay. Well. Let me see. I need to process this." Little vertical lines scrunched on his forehead as he tore the foil off the top of the champagne bottle and removed the little wire cage. "Okay, I've got it."

"That wasn't much processing."

"It's easy. If they make the offer, you can't turn it down. This is your life's work."

"Life's *work*. But not my life. My personal life is just as important, more important, really. You're more important, Jake. They can always get someone else to direct the program. I can do discrete pieces of the research like I've always done."

"They want you! They think you're the best person in the country, maybe the world."

She tried not to show just how irritated she was with him. When she had said, 'You're more important, Jake,' that was his cue. How did he miss it? He was supposed to respond in kind and say how much she meant to him. But he didn't. Meaning what? Did he want her to be a thousand miles away? Was this the easy way out for a man who really didn't want to be married? Who had *never* been married.

She crossed her arms and leveled her gaze at the man she loved. "Jake Lassiter, tell me whether you want to marry me and intend to marry me."

"Yes and yes."

"And how do you propose we do this with me so far away?"

"Didn't I say it? Wasn't I clear?"

"No and no. The last time we discussed it, you said you didn't want to be a burden to me."

"I think I said I didn't want you to be a young widow or spend the best years of your life caring for me as I drool into my oatmeal."

"Why? Do you think there any guarantees? Do you think young, healthy people don't face obstacles? And it's my choice whether I take on the risks of your future health."

"And I just said 'yes' and 'yes.'"

He twisted the champagne bottle slowly while holding the cork motionless. "Obviously, I'm moving to Bethesda with you. I want to spend my life with you. Oh, my offer of great sex tonight still stands."

She exhaled a long, happy sigh. She knew this would be a significant disruption to his life. Except for four years away at college—okay, five years—Jake had always lived in South Florida. That he so readily chose to be with her, despite the complications, reminded her why she fell in love with him.

"Great, you big blockhead. Do we have to be finished in time for *SportsCenter*?"

"No way, Doc. Our bed is *SportsCenter*."

Pop, went the champagne cork.

CHAPTER SIX
The Seductive Lawyer and the Senile Judge

"Is it my fault I'm irresistible to women?" Bert Kincaid asked.

I stayed quiet. I've practiced law long enough to know when to give a witness enough rope to hog-tie, if not hang, himself.

"Is it a crime to be a romantic?" he continued. "To wonder wistfully if this is the woman of my dreams, my one and only?"

If we were on Broadway, this is where Kincaid would have broken into song. But we were in the chambers of Judge Erwin Gridley in the mildewed old limestone monstrosity known as the Miami-Dade Courthouse.

It was the morning after Kip's accident. At 8 a.m., I had called Gloria Sanchez, who told me Kip was doing well and would be released in the afternoon. I felt myself exhale a long breath of relief. Gloria would remind Kip to call me when he was ready to leave. Meanwhile, in court, I had the unhappy duty of trying to punch the ticket of a fellow lawyer. At Melissa's suggestion, I had given up my stressful private practice for the nine-to-five job of a Florida Bar prosecutor.

"Is it a crime to woo a woman, or perhaps a few, simply because there is an 'Esquire' after my name?" Kincaid asked.

"Is he charged with a crime, Jake?" A confused Judge Gridley peered at me, fish-eyed, through his trifocals.

"No, Your Honor. This is a license revocation proceeding, and Mr. Kincaid is representing himself."

"That's what I thought!" The judge signaled a "T" with both hands. "Time out, ya'll. Don't be jumping offsides, Mr. Kincaid, and keep your feet inbounds."

The mishmash of football jargon stemmed from Judge Gridley's past as a college football official. For several decades, he spent weekdays in court, dispensing erroneous rulings, and Saturdays on the field, missing even the most egregious holding calls. Now semi-retired, he was sitting as a senior judge on Florida Bar disciplinary cases. Conveniently, judges were called "referees" in Bar proceedings. Doubtless, Judge Gridley took the assignment thinking he'd be wearing a striped shirt and tooting a whistle.

"Mr. Kincaid," I said, "you appear to admit the allegations of the Bar complaint."

Kincaid tugged at a fleshy earlobe as if deep in thought. In his late fifties, he wore his hair long and dyed shoe-polish black, which only emphasized the white saucer of bare skull on top. "Could you be more specific, Mr. Lassiter?"

"Do you admit to having sex with several female clients?"

"*No-lo con-ten-dere*," he sing-songed. "A serial seducer, I am, I am."

"Are you familiar with Bar Rule 4-8.4 prohibiting sexual relations with a client?"

"Unconstitutional! Violates my right to the pursuit of happiness."

"That's in the Declaration of Independence, not the Constitution," I said.

"Either way, our Founding Fathers were a bunch of horndogs. I saw it on the History Channel. Ben Franklin didn't just fly kites. He had babes on the side."

I lowered my tone to a stentorian bass to indicate the gravitas of my question. "Would you concede that being sexually involved with a woman in a child custody case might interfere with your professional judgment?"

"I concede nothing!" He fixed me with a glum expression. "Jeez, Jake, why are you prosecuting me anyway? You're a defense lawyer, you big galoot. You don't carry the government's water."

"Jake's no water boy," the judge agreed.

"Bert. Mr. Kincaid," I said, "let's keep this professional."

"Everyone on Flagler Street knows you have brain damage. Is that what's behind this?"

"It's a good question, Jake," the judge said. "What made you switch teams?"

Concentrate, I told myself. Stay on track!

"My doctors thought I should reduce stress," I explained, "so I gave up my private practice for a nine-to-five job."

"Too many concussions on the football field," Kincaid agreed, sympathetically.

The judge stroked the stuffed alligator head on his desk, symbol of his beloved University of Florida. Gridley was a Bull Gator Emeritus, and his last will and testament provided for his ashes to be tossed into the air at the 50-yardline of Ben Hill Griffin Stadium.

"You had no quick, Jake, but you surely could hit," the judge said.

"Never thought I'd see the day you'd go to work for those tight asses in Tallahassee," Kincaid complained, piling on.

"It gives me no pleasure to bring you before Judge Gridley," I said.

"That's me," his Honor announced, in wonderment, Balboa discovering the Pacific Ocean.

The serial-seducing lawyer and the semi-senile judge had knocked me off-kilter. It should have been easy to nail Kincaid, who had admitted to having sex with five clients, including one in a detention facility, the tryst captured on security cameras and broadcast on TMZ. In response to my petition to disbar him, he filed papers claiming that "No client ever complained about the quality of my services, legal or sexual. I am one of the rare breed of lawyers who can litigate all day and fornicate all night—and do both well."

And he says I have brain damage.

"Mr. Kincaid, do you have any legal defenses to the charges against you?" I asked.

"Sure, I do, Jake. I'm a sex addict, protected under the Americans with Disabilities Act."

Judge Gridley put his right thumb and index finger into his mouth and whistled two short blasts. "Halftime, boys. We're in recess until 3 p.m. because Jake has an appointment to get his head examined."

"It's about time, Your Honor," Kincaid said, giving me a sly grin. He grabbed his briefcase and bolted from chambers.

I gathered my files and headed for the door, but Judge Gridley stopped me. "How are you feeling, Jake?"

"Got some ringing in the ears and headaches. Minor complaints. We'll see what the brain scan shows."

He paused a moment and said, "This morning, when you came into chambers, we both said howdy, and you asked, 'How's Martha?' You remember?"

"Sure. And you said she was 'fine and dandy.' Your exact words."

"Well, Jake. I didn't know what to say. Martha passed almost three years ago."

I stood frozen. "Oh, jeez, Judge. I'm sorry. That was thoughtless of me."

"No, it wasn't. I could see you didn't remember. But the thing is, you were at Martha's funeral. I remember because you commented on her famous coconut flan."

We remained silent. The judge let me think my private thoughts, which were mostly fears about my mind turning to a pile of mud. How could I tell truth from fiction when the past shows itself, then fades away like a mirage?

C.T.E. is to former football players what black lung is to coal miners: the grim reaper cutting a swath through our fraternity. It's a progressive, neurodegenerative, incurable brain disease. My prior brain scans showed early evidence of the disease, but no definite diagnosis can be made except in an autopsy. Hah! I don't mind the blood draws, the radioactive imaging, even the spinal taps. But I damn well draw the line at an autopsy!

The judge broke the silence. "You take care of yourself, Jake. Go get your noggin looked at, and Godspeed."

CHAPTER SEVEN
The Protocol of Parenting

Melissa Gold...

Jake's bare butt was sticking out the back of his hospital gown, so Melissa slapped it.

"Ouch! What was that for?" he protested.

"You're supposed to leave your underwear on."

"Really?"

"It's a brain scan. Do you keep your brains in your underpants?"

"Well..."

She slapped his butt again. Left-handed. Where she wore the emerald-cut diamond ring Jake had given her the night he proposed while wading in the shorebreak off South Beach, a supermoon glowing overhead. Now, under the glare of fluorescent hospital lighting, they stood by a bank of lockers just outside the imaging room. Jake followed her instructions and retrieved his blue boxer shorts emblazoned with figures of roaring Nittany Lions. Other than the butt-slapping, she intended to keep the appointment professional.

Jake had already been injected with a radioactive tracer, and in a few minutes, he would undergo positron emission tomography, a PET scan. Because he'd had several others over the past three years, it would be possible to determine if the tangles of tau protein—a sticky sludge that kills brain cells—had increased, decreased, or stayed the same.

Melissa had administered a bunch of experimental treatments, from lithium and hyperbaric oxygen to protein antibodies and good old marijuana. So far, there was no cure for C.T.E. and no reliable method of either predicting its onset or the speed of its advance.

After injections of the protein antibodies a couple years ago, the tangles seemed to shrink. But Melissa's team wasn't sure because the neuroimaging equipment had improved so much, it might have been simply a more accurate picture of what previously existed. As with much of experimental medicine, the results were vague and uncertain. When Melissa ran possible scenarios through her mind, she tried to chase the scariest ones away. With Jake, she struggled to remain objective, pretending at times that he was just another patient. That seldom worked. The burden of her research, so far unfruitful, weighed on her.

I want to find a cure. I need to find a cure. For Jake and for everyone.

Melissa's current project studied the brains of former football players, cage fighters, and military personnel who had suffered head injuries, large and small. It had become well known that even sub-concussive injuries—getting your helmet slapped hundreds of times—can cause brain damage years later. The more we learn about the brain, the more concern there is about head injuries, she had told the grant committee.

"How are you feeling?" Melissa asked in her serious doctor tone.

"If you're asking as my fiancée, I'm still in the afterglow of last night. But since you're holding a clipboard, I'm guessing you're asking as my physician. Tip-top. I could do a triathlon."

"That might be a bit much."

"Drinks, dinner, and sex. Surely, you haven't already forgotten, Doc."

No, she had not. Still dreamily in her mind was the passion and heat in the tumble of sheets beneath the paddle fan *whompety-whomping* in endless circles.

"My short-term memory is fine," she said. "How's yours?"

"Apparently, it's A-OK, though I can't remember if you had three or four..."

"Can't help with your arithmetic. How's your tinnitus?"

"Three drums and a tuba short of a marching band."

"Stress level?"

"Remarkably low. Swapping criminal defendants for prosecuting my brethren of the Bar seems to agree with me."

"Good to hear. Irritability and temper?"

"I got really steamed at Kip yesterday, but I kept it under control."

"Well done. Impulse control?"

"Excellent. Not a minute ago, I resisted the urge to kiss my doctor."

"How about your long-term memory?"

"Hard to say. Kip claims he told me a bunch of things that I swear he didn't."

"You swear? Or you just don't remember if he told you?"

"An impossible question. I don't know what I don't know."

She made a notation on her paperwork. She knew Jake understated his deficits. "And your short-term memory?"

"Trick question! You already asked."

"Well done. Let's move on. Migraines?"

"Pretty much every day. They start at level three, a petite ballerina bouncing a few grand jetés inside my skull. Then up to a level nine, a herd of pachyderms pounding the pavement."

"What are you taking for the migraines?"

"You know the answer. Cannabis. All varieties. Sativa, indica, hybrids. Oils, edibles, buds, and honey. I'm an equal opportunity pothead."

Her pencil scratched a note.

"If I'm not mistaken," he continued, "you joined me last night about 10 p.m. with a particularly potent bud called Mendocino Thunderhump."

She looked around as if someone might be listening, then whispered, "It has certain psychoactive properties I find appealing and..." She lowered her voice even more. "Arousing."

So much for my professional demeanor.

"And all this time, I thought it was me," Jake said.

Over the P.A., a Dr. Prystowsky was being called to the I.C.U.

"Cannabis is also an anti-inflammatory," she said, "so it may be useful for your various joint pains." Meaning both shoulders, his right hip, his left knee and ankle, and a turf toe injury that had never healed.

"Can we get this show on the road?" he said. "I want to pick up Kip and I have to get back to court."

"We have to wait for the tracers." She checked her watch. "Ten minutes."

Her mind drifted back to last night, after their triathlon. They had talked about Jake's troubling visit to Kip's hospital room. She'd tried to convince him that his problems communicating with Kip were not that unusual. Many parents, maybe most parents, went through similar rough patches with their kids. Jake had disagreed, saying this went far deeper than missed communications.

"It's like he's a completely new person," he had said, "one I don't know and don't particularly like."

As always, she treaded carefully, aware of boundaries. She was a latecomer to Jake's household. She didn't know Kip when he was younger, so it was hard to measure the changes in him. She loved both uncle and nephew. "My boys," she called them. More than anything, she wanted the family unit—Jake and Kip and her—all in harmony. That didn't seem like too much to ask.

But for a trained scientist, the vagaries of parenthood seemed imponderable. Where was the graph with numerical constants? The protocol for diagnosis and treatment?

Last night, she had chosen her words cautiously and had spoken them gently. "I'm wondering if this might be the time to give Kip some room. Let him figure this out."

"Just the opposite. I've let him get away from me because I've been so damn involved with my own problems. What's crazy is that he thinks the opposite. That I got overly involved when I thought I might be dying. It's confusing as hell."

"We've talked about this, Jake. Hard as it is to accept, kids should achieve a healthy independence from their parents."

"You don't get it, Mel. He's hiding things. That's not independence, it's deception. And what about the Blizzard? You've taken psychiatry courses. He wasn't rejecting cows or ice cream or a milkshake." Frustrated, he raised his voice. "He was rejecting me!"

Melissa's laugh was a gentle wind chime that defused Jake's anger.

"What?" he asked. "What's so funny?"

"Jake, he wasn't rejecting you. He was expressing his sense of individuality and personhood. Sometimes a Blizzard is just a Blizzard."

CHAPTER EIGHT
Two Men in Suits

Melissa waited with me in the imaging room while the radioactive tracers traveled from my arm through my bloodstream into my thick skull and swirled around inside my brain. At least that's how I imagined it.

A young female technician wearing a smock with her embroidered name, "Lourdes Garcia," approached, saw Melissa, *la jefa*, huddling with me, and retreated to the control room. She could wait a few minutes to fry my brain.

"I had a revelation last night," Melissa said. "About us."

"Really?"

"I fell in love with you the day we met, when you took my deposition."

"It took me longer. I didn't fall for you until you said, 'This might sting a little.'"

Melissa Gold. Neuropathologist. Compassionate human being. Smart, savvy, and sexy. The future Mrs. Lassiter.

I felt lucky as hell that such a woman would fall for me. Melissa was a tall, slender woman with reddish brown hair and a sprinkling of freckles the color of paprika across her nose. Her eyes were a pale green flecked with gold. Her complexion had a rosy hue as if she'd just jogged five miles. And, oh, she was whip smart, to use one of my Granny's expressions.

Melissa had a bachelor's degree from Columbia, a medical degree from Duke, and both a Ph.D. in molecular science and a master's in neuroscience from Yale. This compares favorably with my education. I had been an indifferent student at Coral Shores High in Tavernier in the Florida Keys. We were the "Hurricanes," though why we—or the University of Miami—would celebrate killer storms was something I never could fathom. At Penn State, I did enough work to get by, though I hit the blocking sled harder than the books. And night law school was a struggle.

Now Melissa looked toward the window of the control room and caught the eye of Lourdes Garcia, who returned to the imaging room. They were ready to peek inside my brain.

Ms. Garcia helped me into the sliding tray. The hospital gown crept up my thighs, and I was glad Melissa made me put my boxers on. I'm sure that doctors invented hospital gowns to embarrass patients so completely that they'll be more amenable to following orders.

Melissa gave me one last look, and I gave her a thumbs-up. She smiled and retreated into the control room where she would watch the monitors in real-time along with the radiologist.

Ms. Garcia pushed a button, and the tray slipped into the machine with me aboard. "This always reminds me of a loaf of bread going into the oven," she said.

I thought it was more like sliding a corpse into the cooler at the morgue, but I kept quiet. Once I was inside, the monster machine began to *cuck, cuck, cuck* in those hollow percussive sounds. Insistent and loud, the way FBI agents knock on your door before battering it down.

I had declined the offer of earphones with music to help the time go faster while lying motionless inside the machine. I preferred to think, my mind floating to my unhappy confrontation with

Kip. I considered Melissa's opinion. She was crazy smart, but I thought she was wrong. This wasn't a communications breakdown or some normal separation process.

I failed the boy. In retrospect, how could I not have?

What did I know about fathering, anyway? My own father was killed in a bar fight in Islamorada when I was a kid. My mother ran off with a guy who worked on oil rigs in the Gulf. That was Chester something-or-other, who fathered my half-sister Janet, who gave birth to Kip, father unknown, but likely someone whose mug shot has been featured in various post offices. Not that the Lassiter clan was descended from the House of Windsor.

My granny raised me in the Florida Keys, basically by booting me out the screen door in the morning with a fishing pole and instructing me to bring home supper. In retrospect, that was a perfect way to be raised. I hung out with similarly lower-middle class barefoot kids on the island chain. Swimming one day on the Gulf side and the next in the ocean. Playing football on a field of crushed seashells with an ocean breeze in my face wasn't so bad, either.

But poor Kip. A vanished father. A vagabond mother, my half-sister, a serial shoplifter who fashioned herself a Bohemian rather than a fleeing felon.

The *cuck, cuck, cuck* quickened its pace, sounding now like a thousand Mauser rifles, their bolts thrown into place, *CUCK! CUCK! CUCK!*

Melissa thought that Kip was just expressing his individuality, his independence, his adulthood. I would never say this to her, but all her book-learning and medical knowledge couldn't replace one missing element. She wasn't a parent. Something else. She hadn't been there in the hospital. She hadn't seen his demeanor. She hadn't heard the sharpness of his words. And she surely didn't feel the wound, as I did.

"Wake up, Jake! Survival of the fittest. Capitalism at work. And it does work. Max Ringle pays me very well, as my Tesla ought to prove."

The words still stung. How was it possible that Kip had rejected my values so completely?

When the scan was over, with my freshly baked and possibly radioactive body out of the tray, I poked my head into the control room. Melissa and the radiologist were discussing the ligand molecules that bind to the tau and other stuff I didn't understand. The project's protocol called for three radiologists to review the scan before revealing the results, so I wouldn't get any news for a while.

I moseyed down the corridor to the lab where another technician would fill five vials with my blood for yet more tests. I then returned to the locker room, changed back into my clothes, and checked my cell phone. Kip hadn't called. His phone went down with his Tesla and was being used, if at all, by an alligator. But he could have used a hospital phone.

I called Gloria Sanchez in the trauma center.

"Your nephew was released about an hour ago," she told me.

"Damn! What'd he do, take an Uber?"

A pause, and then she said, "No, he left with two men."

"What men?"

"I'd never seen them before and didn't speak to them. Kip was in a wheelchair, which is standard procedure, and one man pushed him while the other walked alongside. The men were wearing dark suits."

"Suits with ties?" I asked.

"Yes, why?"

"It's July in Miami. Only lawyers and detectives wear suits and ties."

"I don't know who they are, Jake. I'm sorry."

I was plagued with questions that frightened me. Just what was Kip involved in? Was it so dark and terrible that he couldn't confide in me? Didn't he know that I was the one he could trust, the one he could rely on?

I wanted to scream to the heavens, scream so loud that Kip could hear me and come running home.

CHAPTER NINE
A Lard Ass and a Hard Ass

I wanted to be tracking down Kip, but at 3 p.m., with my mind elsewhere, I was back in court on Bert Kincaid's disbarment proceeding.

Kincaid called Dr. Arthur Eisenberg, a psychiatrist, to testify as an expert witness. He was a trim man in his fifties with a gray goatee and wire-rimmed glasses, which apparently is the required uniform for shrinks.

"Dr. Eisenberg, what's sex addiction?" Kincaid said.

"It's a mental disorder in which people obsessively engage in sex with multiple partners to a degree that interferes with work and relationships."

"Have you examined me with respect to this disorder?"

"Yes. We discussed your infidelity to your wife and your sexual relationships with your female clients."

"Were you able to reach any medical conclusions?"

The shrink cleared his throat and said, "Your aberrant conduct appears to be in response to dysphoric mood states, including depression and anxiety. You can't control your behavior. You're a sex addict."

Judge Gridley emitted a surprised *hmmm*-ing sound and said, "Offsides, doc! Are you saying Bert Kincaid's unzipping his trousers 'cause he can't help it?"

"Sex addiction is no more about sex than binge eating disorder is about food or compulsive gambling is about money," Dr. Eisenberg said. "The sex addict's behavior stems not from lust but from stress and depression."

"In-ter-est-ing," the judge said, chewing on the word. The judge peered over his glasses at Kincaid. "You need your shrink to say anything else, Bert?"

Meaning the judge gets the point, so let's whip this horse to the finish line.

"Your Honor, that's my case. Since I'm suffering from a disease, I'm protected by the Disabilities Act, and it would be discriminatory to disbar me."

"Jake, you want to ask the doc anything?" Judge Gridley asked.

Not really. I wanted to find out who picked up Kip from the hospital. I wanted him home, safe and sound. But I was getting paid to prosecute Kincaid, and that required beating up his shrink. Oh, pardon me, cross-examining the eminent psychiatrist.

"Dr. Eisenberg," I began, "in the extensive research I've done on you, which consists of Googling your name five minutes ago, it appears you have a pediatric psychiatry practice. Is that right?"

"Yes, it is."

"And you've written scholarly articles on mental issues of teenagers, correct?"

"That's true."

"Have you ever written about sex addiction?"

"I have not."

"Is sex addiction listed in the Diagnostic and Statistical Manual of Mental Disorders?"

A glum look settled on Dr. Eisenberg's face. "It is not."

"And isn't the D.S.M. your team's playbook?"

"Playbook?"

"The bible of your profession. The Holy Grail. The word from on high."

"It's how we make diagnoses, yes."

"Is schizophrenia in that book?"

"Of course."

"Bipolar disorder?"

"Yes."

"PTSD and antisocial personality disorder?"

"Yes."

"Anorexia and bulimia?"

"Yes."

"Even gambling disorder is in the DSM, isn't it?"

Judge Gridley piped up. "Only time gambling's a disorder is when you're losing. Like when you scored a touchdown for the wrong team, Jake, and I dropped five hundred bucks."

"Scored a safety, Your Honor," I corrected him.

"I remember. You recovered a fumble and ran to the wrong end zone."

"I got turned around." Truth was, I suffered a concussion making the tackle. I still had enough wits to scoop up the ball but not enough to head the right way.

"Wrong-Way Lassiter," Kincaid butted in, reminding me of the newspaper headline, in case I'd forgotten.

"Jake, I get your point," the judge said, his mind miraculously returning to the case. "Sex addiction ain't official. You got anything else?"

I wasn't sure. There's an unwritten rule about not asking a question on cross unless you know the answer. But I don't blindly follow rules handed down by professors who may not know their asses from the Ninth Amendment, whatever that is.

So, I went fishing. "Dr. Eisenberg, are you and Mr. Kincaid friends?"

"I wouldn't use that word."

"I'm going to take a wild stab here. Are the two of you related?"

"Yes, you could say that."

"I'd rather you did. Related by blood or marriage?"

"Marriage."

He was making me drag it out of him. "Dr. Eisenberg, is Bert Kincaid your brother-in-law?"

He didn't say "unfortunately," but his eyes revealed as much. "Yes, sir."

"So, married to your sister?"

"Yes, Audrey."

"Does Audrey work outside the home?"

"Not for many years."

"If Bert Kincaid loses his law license, will you have to support your sister?"

He sighed, looked at his brother-in-law with hang-dog regret, and said, "It's certainly possible. She's told me as much."

"I have nothing further," I said.

The judge grunted his approval. "Jake, you were a lard-ass linebacker, and you're a hard-ass prosecutor. I'm taking this under advisement, and I'll rule within a week."

Two minutes later, I was pounding down the courthouse steps—nimble as a water buffalo—when my cell phone rang. It had to be Kip, right? But caller I.D. showed "Sugar Ray," meaning Raymond Lincoln Pincher, our duly elected State Attorney.

A county bus on Flagler Street belched black smoke in my face as I answered the call. Ray skipped the preliminaries and said, "Jake, any chance you can come by the office?"

"What's this about?"

"I'll tell you when you get here."

I couldn't stop myself from asking. "Ray, did you just have a couple guys pick up my nephew?"

"Why the hell would I?"

"I have no idea."

"So, this isn't about Kip?"

"I didn't say that, Jake. It's all about him."

CHAPTER TEN
Tobacco, Rum, and Bullshit

Two men were smoking cigars and drinking rum on the rocks when I entered the office of the duly elected State Attorney, the chief prosecutor of our burg. The rum was Mount Gay Black Barrel from Barbados. The chubby cigars were Cohiba Robusto Reserva from Cuba. They were finally legal in the U.S., though the Embargo Act never stopped Ray Pincher from buying, smoking, and giving them to pals when they were still contraband.

"The Jakester!" Ray Pincher greeted me. "The guy who put the shy in shyster and took the fog out of pettifogger."

"That's getting old, Sugar Ray," I said.

Pincher motioned me toward a cushy chair in front of his shiny mahogany desk. "Jake, you know Gilberto Foyo, right?"

I nodded at the heavyset man of about 60, and he waved his Cohiba in greeting. He was the state attorney's chief investigator, a relentless, pavement-pounding gumshoe of the old school. Foyo had little use for the young prosecutors he had to assist, baby lawyers who used the office as a trampoline to private practice.

Pincher, now in his fifth four-year term as State Attorney, was a guy who knew where all the skeletons were buried, as well as who shoveled the dirt. He was one of the first African Americans elected to county-wide office in the state. We were friends and adversaries who both liked and were wary of each other. We fought each other, sometimes viciously, in court, then did favors for each other on the street.

"Ray, what about my nephew?" I asked.

"Gilberto has something for you but hold your horses."

"I got a snippet," Foyo said, "*el murmullo del viento*, a whisper in the wind. Ain't much."

"Well, what is it, for Chrissakes?" Another check mark on Melissa's "irritability" box.

"Relax, Jake," Pincher said. "Stress is bad for you. You want a Cohiba?" He opened a handsome wooden box with cigars lined up like plump little soldiers asleep in their bunks. "Gift from a happy constituent, a hundred bucks a stick."

"No to the smoke," I said, "but I'll have some rum, neat. Maybe it's a good chaser for radioactive isotopes."

Pincher poured me a drink, and I sensed the aroma of molasses and burnt oak. "Jake, how are you feeling?"

"I'm great. Ready to go three rounds with you as soon as Gilberto tells me about Kip."

Pincher laughed and shadow-boxed, left jab, right jab, left hook. "It's been bothering me, Jake. Our time in the ring. I hope it didn't contribute to your problems."

"No worries, Ray." I downed the sweet liquor in one swallow. "Getting hit in the nuts with a bolo punch doesn't cause brain damage."

In truth, Pincher had rung my bell lots of times in our sparring sessions. Pretty embarrassing, since I outweighed him by a couple kegs of beer. Of course, he had been a decent middleweight boxer in Golden Gloves, giving rise to his nickname "Sugar Ray." Boxing had been his ticket out of the Liberty City projects. Usually, the only way I could inflict damage was to put him in a headlock with my left arm and pound his face with my right fist. His response was to knee me in the groin. When we boxed, we did not invite the Marquess of Queensberry to observe.

I turned to Foyo. "Gilberto, what the hell's going on with my nephew?"

He looked toward Pincher for the go-ahead.

Pincher sailed a smoke ring into the ether and said, "We'll share information with you, and whatever you learn thereafter, you're gonna share with us."

"Jeez, Ray. Okay, just tell me about my nephew!"

Pincher nodded, and Foyo began talking. He was the point man on a joint operation of the State Attorney's office with the U.S. Justice Department. They were investigating a chain of opioid pill mills. Yesterday, Foyo paid a visit to the U.S. Attorney's Office downtown to swap files. He delivered background workups on dirty doctors, and the feds gave Foyo a stack of transcripts of wiretapped recordings.

"I start thumbing through the transcripts," Foyo said. "Meanwhile, the A.U.S.A., some Ivy League kid, is multitasking, texting his hair stylist and asking whether I play squash 'cause he just ordered a custom-made graphite racket, or some such shit. The first couple transcripts were from pharmacists he'd had under surveillance. The next one stopped me."

He opened a small notebook, the kind old-school detectives use, and read aloud. "'Covert recording of Chester Lassiter *aka* Kip Lassiter.'"

"Shit," I said.

"Instead of keeping quiet like I should have," Foyo continued, "I blurted out something like, 'What the hell's this?' The A.U.S.A. drops his cell phone and goes, 'Whoops, that's another case,' and grabs the transcript."

"Shit on a shingle," I said, elaborating on my earlier remark.

"I remember your nephew from when you used to bring him to court," Foyo said. "Quiet kid, big mop of hair falling in his eyes. Anyway, knowing that you and *el jefe* are buddies when you're not whomping the tar out of each other, I told Ray, and here we are."

"Could you tell from the transcript who Kip was talking to?"

"A guy named Max Ringle. You know him?"

"Not yet, but I will. My nephew works for him."

"We know that now," Pincher said. "Gilberto combed through Ringle's website, plugged his name into all the law enforcement databases."

"Quest Educational Development," I said.

"Right," Foyo said. "College admissions consultants. Office is in California, but they do business nationally. We've checked. No charges pending against Quest or Ringle or your nephew anywhere."

"Unless there are sealed indictments," I added.

"Got a hit on real estate, too," Foyo said. "Ringle owns a condo on the fifty-first floor of the Bahamas Club on Brickell. Assessed at $2.3 million, probably worth more."

A new headache was piling on top of an old one, and I didn't think it was the rum. "Kip lives in 5105," I said. "Told me he was renting it, didn't say from whom."

"Maybe a company perk," Foyo suggested.

"Sounds like your nephew didn't share much about his boss," Pincher said.

"He told me Ringle was brilliant, a word he's never used to describe me. It's as if Kip's found a new surrogate dad."

Quiet descended over us, along with a cloud of smoke. After a moment, I asked, "Gilberto, were you able to read anything before the A.U.S.A. grabbed the transcript?"

"Only saw one line, your nephew talking. Seemed to be answering a question. He said, 'Niles? Are you shitting me? He's dumber than a Pitt nose tackle.'"

My laugh was more rueful than joyous.

"You know this Niles?" Pincher asked.

"Nope. But I knew a couple Pitt defensive linemen. 'Dumber than a Pitt nose tackle' is an expression of mine from my days at Penn State." I drained my rum. "So, my nephew, who disregards all my good advice, picks up my stupid juvenile badassery. Ray, you ever think about the damage we do to our kids without even knowing it?"

"I've been lucky," Pincher replied. "Paulette takes after her mother."

"Any idea what your nephew is talking about?" Foyo asked.

I shrugged. "He's putting somebody down, maybe another tutor or a student. Who knows? But why would the feds record Kip? Even assuming a tutoring service could commit federal crimes, wouldn't the government use an employee to go after the owner, not vice versa?"

"Sure, that's the way the Justice Department prefers it," Pincher said. "But when they can't make a case against the big fish, it's the other way around."

"Two men in suits escorted Kip out of the hospital today," I said. "Now I'm thinking FBI agents or federal marshals."

"Most likely." Pincher blew another smoke ring and watched it sail to the ceiling. "So, this is all news to you. Your nephew didn't tell you anything or ask for your advice?"

"Why would he? He's 20 years old and knows everything."

Pincher allowed himself a knowing smile. "I got a petition from half a dozen of my youngest prosecutors," Pincher said, "demanding an espresso machine in the break room."

"Entitled Yuppie brats," Foyo complained.

"Gilberto, nobody says 'Yuppie' anymore," Pincher said.

"Try millennials," I advised.

"Or hipsters," Pincher chimed in.

"Like hippies?" Foyo asked, confused.

"I like this," Pincher said. "A black guy, a Cuban guy, and a Florida cracker sitting around, drinking booze and complaining about young people."

"I'm not a Florida cracker," I corrected him.

"Trailer park in the Florida Keys. Sorry, pal."

Foyo cleared his throat and said, "Something else popped up, Jake. In New Jersey. A sealed criminal file with your nephew's social security number attached. What's that about?"

"Kip had a little problem at the Jersey shore when he went to Penn."

"Is that all you're gonna say about it?" Pincher asked.

"I promised him I wouldn't blab all over town."

Pincher came around the desk and poured a refill of the rum. "I respect that."

"I owe you, Ray. Thanks for going beyond the call of duty... hell, for breaching some duties, to help me."

"So, you owe me one. You know me. I'll collect."

I polished off the rum. "What aren't you telling me?"

"Nothing. I just thought you'd want to know if the feds are sharpening their steak knives, and your nephew is a slice of rare tenderloin. I thought you'd be concerned."

"Concerned? I'm terrified because I have no idea what he's gotten himself into, so I'm grateful for the information."

"But...?"

"But you're a political animal, Ray. You're a pool shark who loves the double kiss bank shot."

"Whadaya mean, Jake?"

"What's your angle? What's with the tobacco, rum, and bullshit?"

"'Cause I know you. You'll twist arms. You'll break down doors. You'll find out what's going on downtown."

"You're blowing smoke, Ray, and not from the Cohiba. Why'd you have me take a blood oath to keep you informed of what I find? Why do you even care what the feds are doing?"

"Simple, Jake. If the Southern District's G-men are crapping in my backyard, I'd like to know before I step in it."

CHAPTER ELEVEN
The Bahamas Club

"Kip's in trouble," I told Melissa on the phone, as I exited the expressway onto Second Avenue downtown.

I was headed to my nephew's apartment on Brickell Avenue. I had fired up the old Eldo, top down, on this steamy summer day. Sure, I should have put up the canvas and cranked the clunky AC to high, but somehow, I found pleasure in the blast furnace of the sun baking my face. In July, Miami is hell with palm trees, or at the very least, a steamy, sweaty, muggy, and buggy purgatory that lasts until Thanksgiving.

I told Melissa about my meeting with Pincher and Foyo, and she expressed concern but remained calm, ever the professional diagnostician. "And you have no idea who the men who took Kip from the hospital were?"

"Federal agents, maybe, but I can't be sure."

"And he's never told you about any of this?"

"That's what's eating at me. I have clients who can barely read comic books, but they have the good sense to call me when a cop starts asking questions. Kip could be making incriminating statements, getting himself in deeper trouble."

"What kind of trouble?"

"No idea. There's a federal investigation. He's involved, but I don't know how. Witness. Target. Bystander. Dammit to hell!" I slammed my hand onto the hot steering wheel. "What should I do, Mel?"

"I have to think about it. I don't have the framework for this in my background."

"Yeah, but you're smart and intuitive. What's the first thing that pops into your head?"

"Your meeting with the state attorney."

"Why?"

"It seems odd for him to be poking around in federal cases."

"Completely. It's on the down-low."

"Hmm...." She seemed to be thinking that over.

Traffic was backed up from the Brickell Avenue bridge, and I was stuck. It's a drawbridge that might have been handy when steamships chugged up the Miami River and early settlers grew mangoes in what is now downtown. But it's a civic embarrassment now that traffic is gridlocked a dozen times a day. City and county taxpayers are shelling out more than $2.5 billion in principal and interest to build a ballpark—a gift to the owner of the baseball team no one cares about—but our government dunderheads can't find a way to drive one mile down Brickell Avenue in less than 20 minutes.

"I just don't understand why the state attorney is going out of his way to help you," she said.

"Aw, that's Sugar Ray. A regular Javert at work and a teddy bear after five. We go way back. Adversaries who respect who each other. He also thinks he might have scrambled my brains in the boxing ring, and he's making amends."

A snowy egret landed on the hood of the Eldo, found it too hot, and took flight, its yellow feet waving goodbye.

"I guess it's a guy thing," she said.

"Wait, I shouldn't brush you off like that. You're suspicious. Tell me what you're thinking."

"It's not complicated. Can you trust Ray Pincher?"

"I don't have a yes or no answer. I genuinely like him, but he can be devious."

"With a scientific experiment, I consider all possible conclusions. If Pincher has no skin in the game, why is he taking the risk of spying on a federal investigation?"

"He says he just wants to know what the feds are doing in his backyard. It could just be the usual rivalry between state and federal prosecutors." I thought about it a moment. "Unless Ray has a political interest in the case that he's not telling me about."

"In which case he's giving you information only to make you give him more valuable information."

"Okay, Mel, that's a good read. I'll watch Ray as closely as when he feints the left jab and sucker punches me with his right."

Having a brilliant fiancée had its advantages. If I ever tried a case again, I wouldn't mind letting her help pick the jury. I told Melissa I'd see her for dinner, then clicked off and resumed broiling. I tried Kip's cell again. By now, he might have replaced the drowned phone. But the call went straight to voice mail.

Are you in custody, Kip? Have you been charged with a crime?

No way he could handle that. He was a rabbit in a world of wolves. Not knowing where he was, fearing the worst, I felt my chest tighten as if someone were cinching it with a leather strap.

Breathe in, Jake. Deeply. Breathe out. Repeat.

Melissa taught me the relaxation technique, and now it helped a bit. The drawbridge cranked down. I watched the giant gear slowly churning, feeling like Charlie Chaplin in *Modern Times*, stuck in the maw of machinery beyond my control.

The Caddy's big engine grumbled in protest as I inched down Brickell's canyons of luxury condos and office buildings. I am old enough to remember, though barely, when the only skyscraper was the Brickell Townhouse, then an apartment building. Murf the Surf hid the gigantic Star of India sapphire in a ceiling tile there, after the legendary heist from a museum in New York.

I pulled into the curved driveway of Kip's high-rise where a spit-and-polish uniformed valet looked at my ancient Caddy as if it might soil the shiny pavers. He shot a sideways glance at the license plate, which read "JUSTICE?" Yeah, it's a question that has long plagued me. He asked if I wanted him to park it out front, for which there was a twenty-dollar surcharge. I answered in the negative and warned him against drag racing down U.S. 1.

The Bahamas House occupied a narrow sliver of real estate directly on Biscayne Bay. It was a sleek tower of steel and glass with all the amenities that Miami's urban affluents, hipsters, trust funders, status seekers, and other members of the elite aspirational class could require.

The lobby, all granite floor and twenty-foot glass wall, had the requisite coffee shop with artisanal donuts. Plugged into earphones, a few young people labored on laptops, either writing the next great screenplay or posting photos of a cappuccino whose foam resembles Kim Kardashian's butt. In the corner of the lobby, overlooking the infinity pool, bocce ball court, and cabanas, was a craft cocktail bar where the combination of celery juice and vodka seemed to be popular. A video monitor showed a display of the day's activities and announcements about the pet-walking service and an admonition against pouring champagne into the hot tub. I didn't have time for afternoon hot yoga or the evening lecture, "How to Start Up a Start-Up."

I took a speedy elevator to the fifty-first floor. No one answered my heavy-fisted knocking. The place was quiet. No neighbors in the corridor, no yellow crime scene tape on the door, no team of federal agents serving a search warrant and tossing the place.

Kip had not *given* me a key, which was different than my not *having* a key. He had asked for my help when he moved in, mostly because I could carry a cocktail table under one arm and a floor lamp in the opposite hand. While he parked a small U-Haul truck, I stopped in the concierge's office to pick up the keys. I was given three but only turned over two to Kip. What had I been thinking at the time, nearly a year ago? Something I would never say to my nephew.

Kip, I might only be your uncle and you might be an adult in the eyes of the law, but I've been acting in loco parentis *so long, I'm not going to cut you loose now.*

Now, I used my purloined key and opened the door. It had been after dark when we'd moved the furniture in, so I was startled by the blast of sunlight and endless horizon that hit me now. The floor-to-ceiling windows overlooked Biscayne Bay, Key Biscayne, and the Atlantic Ocean. In the distance, I saw a shimmering dot that had to be the island of Bimini, maybe 60 miles away across the Gulf Stream.

The old furniture I'd lugged in last year—a mix of Ikea and eBay—was gone. Sleek glass, chrome, and white leather now dominated the living room. I roamed the place. The master bedroom had a cavernous walk-in closet. Kip's casual shirts and pants hung neatly in a corner, leaving enough room for a pick-up basketball game. There was a stack of lightweight cashmere sweaters in a variety of muted colors on one shelf. A second bedroom had been converted into a study with a desk of glass and steel. No laptop, no landline phone. A matching credenza had three drawers, all unlocked.

The drawers were lined with neat, old-fashioned hanging files. So, some of Uncle Jake did rub off. I had expected that all of Kip's business materials would be on disk drives, or thumb drives, or hiding in the clouds. But no, here was a folder with a 72-page document:

"Strategies for Standardized Tests: How to Maximize Your SAT and ACT Scores. By Kip Lassiter."

I thumbed through it.

"Trust your first response."

"Don't skip answers, guess."

"Budget your time."

All legitimate. Whatever else Kip was involved in—he could be a hired assassin for all I knew—he was certainly a knowledgeable tutor of high school students.

I found a folder marked "Q.E.D. Reimbursements." Printed email receipts from various airlines. Five first-class round trips, Miami to Grand Cayman. A dozen trips from Miami to Santa Barbara, California with stops in Dallas. What's with that? Several more round-trip flights: Miami to Houston, Los Angeles, and Kansas City. All in the last year. No wonder I hadn't seen much of Kip. I wrote down the dates of each trip.

It was possible that every trip was strictly legit. Kip could be lecturing to Q.E.D. students around the country. And Grand Cayman could be, as Kip claimed, the site of marketing meetings with Max Ringle. I was pondering these thoughts when I heard someone knocking on the apartment door. "Yo, Kip! Are you in there, dipshit?"

CHAPTER TWELVE
The Twins and the Big Bully

I went to the door, stared through the peephole, and looked into the brown eye of some smart-ass with his face pressed close.

"Open up, Lassiter! I know you're in there! C'mon, Kip, you crudball!"

I yanked the door open, and everything happened fast.

The fat end of a baseball bat jammed through the doorway into my right shoulder, and I staggered back a step. Reflexively, my right hand grabbed the bat halfway down the barrel and pulled hard toward me. Hanging onto the bat and hurtling through the open door was a wiry young man with a dark mop of hair.

"Hey! What...?" His eyes opened in wide confusion.

I tore the bat loose, and with the guy off balance, threw a short left hook into his solar plexus. He made a *whoomphing* sound and fell to the floor, his throat gurgling.

Then, an optical illusion.

Even though he was on all fours on the verge of soiling the white granite floor, he was also coming through the door again. Same mop of dark hair, same white T-shirt with the logo "Palm Beach Prep Sailing." He raised his right hand and aimed a black, blunt-nosed Taser at my chest.

I ducked into a crouch and two electrode darts sailed just over my head, nearly parting my hair. I came at him straight-on, driving the top of my skull under his chin, powering up with my legs, and lifting him off his feet, driving him against the door jamb, his head snapping back into the wood with a *clunk* before he crumpled to the floor. I turned and headed back into the apartment where the same guy was just getting up.

What the hell! Was I hallucinating?

I blinked twice and realized the guy inside the apartment wore green Gucci Flashtrek sneakers with pink crystals on the cross straps. I recognized them from a story on the sports pages. They retail for about sixteen hundred bucks! The guy getting to his feet in the corridor wore gray Nike Lunar sneakers, the ones with the three-dimensional moon rock design that makes it appear you've stepped into a bucket of wet cement. I'm no expert, but I'd bet they cost well north of a grand.

So, there are two guys. Twins! With more money than brains.

I grabbed the Lunar rock kid by the scruff of his T-shirt and hoisted Gucci kid by his armpit. His slim-cut Robin egg blue pants were wet in the crotch. "What are you two pussies doing here!"

Lunar's eyes went wide. "That's so Neanderthal."

"I know the dude!" Gucci cried out. "Kip's grandfather."

"I'm his Uncle, pissboy!"

Gucci screwed up his mouth. "Your toxic testosterone is creating a hostile environment."

I tightened my grip. "You attacked me, kid. I oughta bitch-slap you silly."

The twins shrieked in unison, high-pitched *screeches* like red-tailed hawks.

"You can't use that word," Lunar said.

"What's wrong with 'silly?'" I asked.

"B-i-t-c-h." He whispered the letters, as softly as cinnamon wafting onto a latte. "Git woke, dude. It's an intimidating slur."

"Corrosive masculinity," Gucci agreed.

"Oh, man up," I said, and they shrieked again.

I tossed them both to the floor and kicked the door closed to keep them from crawling away. "What do you want with my nephew?"

The twins looked at each other, and Lunar said, "We want to know if Kip's ratting us out."

"What'd you do? Knock over a smoothie stand?"

Again, they locked eyes in some secret twin ritual. Then, Gucci said, "You tell him, Niles."

"Niles?" I blurted, speaking to the kid in the moon rock sneakers. "You're the one dumber than a Pitt nose tackle."

"Mocking my intelligence! That's so cringy."

"Just an expression, forget about it."

"I'm not saying I'm the smartest guy in school," Niles confessed.

"I get that. That's why you hired Kip to tutor you."

He laughed at me, a high-pitched cackle. "*Tutor* me? That's why I hired him to take the SAT for me."

Oh, shit! There it was. The gut punch. I must have known it was coming, or something like it, but I'd been in denial.

Niles chattered on about paying $35,000 to Kip, who then double-crossed him. I was only half listening as I considered the spider's web in which Kip was snared. He'd fallen prey to easy money. Dirty money.

He might already be indicted! But why hasn't he called me?

I had a dozen reasons why this was all my fault. If Kip lacked a moral compass, well, I had been the navigator of his life. What examples did I set? All those years taking him to court, rubbing shoulders with my felonious clients, many of whom walked free or received token punishments. Had I stunted Kip's ethical growth? Had he concluded that crime does pay? Did he wear thousand-dollar sneakers like these twin dipsticks?

"You feel me, bro?" Niles said. "Kip took my money and wangboozled me. It was a big rip."

"What are you saying? He got a lousy score?"

"The opposite! He nailed a 1560 and the College Board flagged my file."

"I don't get it."

"Last year, when I took the test, I scored an even 1000, and Kip knew it. Dr. Ringle told him to never go more than 30 percent higher than the student's prior test."

"Everybody knows that," his twin in the Gucci sneakers added.

Niles looked helplessly at his brother. "And 30 percent would be what, Teague? Like a 1250?"

Teague looked puzzled. "More like a 1325, I think."

The twins' math brain cells had apparently been divided in half at birth.

"A 1560 is asstastic," Niles said, "not fantastic. Now I gotta take the test again, with like, the Secret Service watching. I'm gonna end up at Lackawanna JUCO in Scranton, Piss-Pot-Pennsylvania instead of USC."

"I still don't get it," I said. "Why would Kip sabotage you like that?"

"Yo, Gramps. You don't know shit about Kip, do you?" Niles said.

"Because of Shari Ringle," his twin offered.

"Me and Shari hang out," Niles said, "and Kip does his creeper thing, trolling her. She's already at USC. I took a year off to travel the world and shit."

"You couldn't shit at home?" I asked

"Yadidimean, dude."

"What?"

"You know what I mean, Gramps. Dad wanted me to travel and do cultural shit. Then me and Shari would both be at USC, but she'd be a year ahead..."

"And she'd help Niles pass his courses," his brother concluded.

"But instead of scoring what he was supposed to, Kip fojangled me."

"But it wasn't smart," the brother said. "Not when a whadayacallit's looking at Ringle's company."

"A what?" I asked.

"A great jury."

"Grand jury?" I offered.

"Yeah. They're in season now."

"The grand jury's in session?" I asked.

"They subpoenaed us, and we figured Kip was talking," Niles said. "That's why we chased him down in the Glades yesterday. We didn't mean to run him into the canal."

"You two dickwads did that?"

"But I called 9-1-1," Teague said proudly. "I'm like a hero or something."

CHAPTER THIRTEEN
The Visitor

Melissa Gold...

Melissa had just gotten home from the hospital when there was a knock at the door. She peered out a window and saw Kip standing there. He had a key to the house and he also knew that the door, swollen fat with humidity, was usually unlocked and could be opened with a good shove. His waiting on the front step made him seem like a stranger, not someone who, until recently, lived here.

She opened the door and saw a black Cadillac Escalade idling in the driveway. A man in a suit and aviator sunglasses stood outside the passenger door. He removed his suit coat and loosened his tie. The day was sweltering. Another man behind the wheel still had his suit coat on. The AC must have been cranked up to frozen beef levels. Kip stood at the doorway in jeans and a T-shirt, holding a small package wrapped in shiny gift paper. She saw that he had two black eyes and scratches across his face.

"Kip, come in. Get out of the heat."

He walked inside almost shyly, and she gently hugged him. "Are you okay? I've been so worried about you."

"I'm fine. Just bumps and bruises." He handed her the package. "This is for Uncle Jake. I was saving it for his birthday, but..."

"His birthday is in December. What's going on, Kip?"

"I've got a safe place to stay. I'll let you know when I get there."

"What does that mean? Please, Kip. Wait for Jake. He'll be here soon."

"I don't have time. I've got a plane to catch."

"Where are you going?"

"Look, I'm sorry Melissa. Tell Uncle Jake not to worry. He's shook, but everything's cool. Really."

"No, it's not. Don't cut us out of your life. Not now."

She tried to make eye contact, but he was staring at the top of his sneakers. "Gotta go," he said.

"We love you. Kip..."

He headed out the door, and she followed him. The man standing by the Escalade opened the rear door, and Kip hesitated a moment. Melissa caught up and saw that his eyes were moist. "Tell Jake..." he started to say.

"Tell him what?"

He got into the backseat and, tears welling, spoke three sentences before the man in the suit closed the door. She memorized every word, as well as his tone and inflection, so she would get everything right when she told the man she loved.

CHAPTER FOURTEEN
Three Simple Sentences

When I walked into the kitchen, Melissa was squeezing limes into a tumbler with two ice cubes. She wore white linen slacks and a black silk blouse and was barefoot. I took off my lawyer's suit coat and removed my tie, which had lately begun to feel like a noose.

Usually, when I get home, I have a pint of Grolsch, the Dutch beer in the green bottle with the white porcelain stopper. Tonight, Melissa accurately guessed that I needed something stronger. She poured two jiggers of Grey Goose into the tumbler with a splash of club soda.

I leaned over to kiss her, and Melissa said, "Kip was here."

"What! When?"

"About an hour ago. I tried calling your cell, but it went straight to voice mail."

"Shit. I was at Kip's apartment, getting woke by two Gen Z idiots. Tell me everything from the moment Kip got here till he left."

I collapsed into one of the kitchen chairs. Physical and mental exhaustion. Feeling the beginning of a migraine, a sharper pain than the dull sledgehammer of the daily headache, I took a long, limey sip of the drink.

"He knocked on the door and I let him in. A black Escalade was parked in the driveway with a man at the wheel who didn't turn off the engine, either knowing Kip would be quick or to keep the A/C on, or both." Melissa pushed a few strands of hair off her forehead. "Another man, wearing a suit and tie and aviator sunglasses, stood outside the passenger door. I'd say about forty. Good haircut. I couldn't see the man behind the wheel very well."

"Government plates?" I asked.

"Georgia license plate with one of those big peaches in the center."

"That's odd. Why Georgia?" I didn't expect an answer. I was just thinking out loud.

"It was a rental," Melissa said. "I saw the Hertz sticker on the rear bumper when they pulled out."

Melissa was not only a great medical diagnostician, she would have made a highly credible witness in a murder trial.

"So, the two are from out of town and rented a pricey Escalade, probably at the airport. What else?"

"Kip brought this." From the counter, she retrieved a gift-wrapped package the size of a shirt box. "He said it's for you."

"As best you recall, what were his exact words?"

She thought a moment, while outside the neighborhood male peacock was hooting. It's an odd mating call, faking a sexual sound to attract a female peacock. When she approaches, the male rushes her and...well, mates. Despite spending most of my life unattached and haunting every after-hours joint in NFL cities, including Buffalo, I have never done this. The bull rush, I mean. The hooting I might have tried once or twice.

"He said, 'This is for Uncle Jake. I was saving it for his birthday, but...' He broke it off there."

"Like maybe he's not gonna be around in December, so here it is now," I guessed, hating the sound of it. My temples were pounding with pain.

I unwrapped a gold ribbon and tore open the plain brown wrapping paper, then lifted the lid off the cardboard box. Under two layers of decorative paper was a lightweight sweater, size XXL, in a rust color. I ran two fingers across the fabric. Softer than cashmere, maybe softer than a cloud.

Melissa looked at the label. "It's a Loro Piana. One hundred per cent vicuña."

My blank look told her to continue. "The softest, most expensive wool in the world. Comes from an animal that roams the Andes Mountains. Looks a bit like a llama."

"You're saying there's a llama look-alike shivering in the Andes so a guy in Miami can have a nice sweater. Guess I won't wear it to the gym."

"For around five thousand bucks, I think not."

"What! Is that true?"

My mature migraine was now having baby migraines, and my vision blurred.

"Five grand, more or less," she said. "It's what Axe wears on the show."

"Axe?"

She gave me a sympathetic look reserved for the clueless. "Bobby Axelrod. On 'Billions.' If you wouldn't fall asleep after dinner on Sunday nights, you'd know."

I thought of the twins and their grotesquely expensive sneakers. And now this, a lightweight sweater that was, admittedly, handsome but, likewise, obscenely priced.

I remembered Niles's taunting voice: *"Yo, Gramps. You don't know shit about Kip, do you?"*

Kip had adopted the values of other people. Not the Lassiters, one generation removed from hard-drinking, hardscrabble, bar-brawling, hand-to-mouth fishermen and trailer trash.

"Mel, do you think Kip's sticking it to me?" I asked.

"How do you mean?"

Outside, the male peacock hooted louder. A female was likely within striking distance, and he was probably saying, *"You come to the Grove often?"*

"What's Kip's message to me?" I asked. "My last gift to him was only a T-shirt, remember? And in return he gives me a five-thousand-dollar sweater."

"You spent four days designing the T-shirt, and he loved it."

I pulled up the memory. When Kip was accepted at Penn with a full ride, tuition-free, I was ecstatic. So were my pals who congratulated Kip for following his uncle's path to Penn *State*. Not being Phi Beta Kappas, they couldn't keep it straight. I played football and graduated, *cum NO laude*, at the sports powerhouse in Happy Valley. Kip was headed to the Ivy League university in Philadelphia.

"Penn. Not Penn State!" Kip yelled at my clueless friends.

It soon became a running joke, so I designed a T-shirt with pictures of Benjamin Franklin and Joe Paterno side by side with the seals of the University of Pennsylvania and Penn State. Beneath the artwork was the slogan:

Penn. NOT Penn State.

We both wore the shirts and passed them out to family friends.

I polished off the vodka and said, "What else did Kip say?"

The wind had come up, and palm fronds slapped the kitchen window. A late afternoon thunderstorm was brewing.

"He said he had a plane to catch but wouldn't say where he was going. You shouldn't worry. He's got a safe place to stay."

"What the hell does that mean?"

"Please let me finish."

"I'm sorry, Mel. Keep going."

"I walked him out to the Escalade, and he got teary-eyed. We stood there a little awkwardly. Then he said, 'Tell Uncle Jake thanks for everything.'"

Oh, shit. I know "goodbye" when I hear it.

I forced myself to concentrate, even though several Abrams tanks were doing figure eights inside my skull, occasionally firing rounds of blindingly hot white phosphorus. "Anything else?"

"I'm getting there. Just as he was getting into the backseat, he said something I made a mental note to remember. Three simple sentences."

"Okay, shoot."

"He said, 'Tell Uncle Jake I'm sorry I didn't drink the Blizzard. I love Blizzards. Always have and always will.'"

Aw, jeez.

"You understand what he's saying, don't you, Jake?"

I didn't answer, so she kept going. "You were right yesterday, and I was wrong. Kip's rejecting the Blizzard was really about you. But listen to what he just said. A complete turnaround. He loves you and always will. You get that, right?"

I would have said "Yes" if I hadn't been sobbing.

CHAPTER FIFTEEN
Storm Warning

The wind howled and the sky turned angry shades of smoky gray. I paced on the back porch as Melissa sat in an Adirondack chair with her laptop balanced on her knees. She was working and I was griping. I needed to know just where that plane Kip had to catch was taking him. Wherever it was, I would follow.

"I don't know his friends," I said. "I don't know who to call, where to go, how to find him. He could be flying to Grand Cayman—or any of those other cities I didn't know about. Or, if he's on the run, someplace new entirely."

I had given Melissa the dates of Kip's flights that had been reimbursed by Q.E.D. and she was at work on the Internet.

"The trips to Kansas City, Houston, and Los Angeles line up with either SAT or ACT exams in the last year," she said, looking up from her laptop. "This week, there are no tests in those cities or anywhere else for that matter. So, that leaves Santa Barbara and Grand Cayman."

I stopped pacing as distant lightning backlit the clouds over the Everglades to the west. "Let's find out by process of elimination."

I called information on my cell phone, then let the mechanized operator connect me. It was three hours earlier on the West Coast.

"Quest Educational Development," said a pleasant female voice.

"This is Mr. Harris. Could you connect me with Dr. Ringle?"

"Mr. Harris?" It seemed to be a question.

"Yes, Franco Harris. From Pittsburgh." I heard a keyboard clacking.

"Will Dr. Ringle know what this is in reference to?"

"Signing up my kids for some first-rate tutoring. Money's no object."

"Dr. Ringle is in conference and should be free in about an hour."

"What about Mr. Lassiter? Is he there?"

"He's not expected until tomorrow. May I take a number?"

I hung up.

California, here we come.

"I'm gonna be on the first flight tomorrow," I said.

My cell rang with the invigorating notes of the Penn State fight song. "This is Franco Harris," I said, expecting the Q.E.D. receptionist to apologize for our getting cut off.

"In your dreams," Ray Pincher said. "Franco glided when he ran. You looked like you were stomping grapes."

The clouds had turned as black as a funeral shroud, but the lightning was still so far away, I couldn't hear the thunder.

"What's up, Ray?"

"We need to talk, pal. I'm in your neighborhood. At my daughter's house."

"Gables Estates isn't my neighborhood. I'm in the South Grove with bohemians and aging hippies."

"Close enough. C'mon over." I could hear him exhale, could practically smell the pungent aroma of a Cohiba. "P-Three's been asking about you, Jake."

"P-Three" being Pincher's name for his daughter ever since she married Barry Popkin and became Paulette Pincher-Popkin. Actually, *Doctor* Paulette Pincher-Popkin, a respected OB-GYN.

"Tell me what's up," I said.

A thunderclap rattled the windows. Still no rain, but the storm blew closer.

"A county crew pulled your nephew's Tesla out of that canal," Pincher explained. "A couple of FBI agents showed up and processed the scene."

I felt a shiver of icy fear run through me. "Tell me there wasn't anything inside the car other than murky water and a couple snook."

"Plastic bag with twenty-five grand in hundred-dollar bills. The Tesla has a dent streaked with blue paint on the driver's side. Easy conclusion is that a blue car sideswiped your nephew's vehicle, sent it into the drink."

"The FBI agents told you this?"

"Aw, they wouldn't tell me I had toilet paper stuck on my shoe. Foyo talked to the tow truck driver. What do you think, Jake, a drug deal gone bad?"

"I wish."

"Why the hell would you?"

"I know how to defend a drug case."

"What then?" At this point, I expected the worst.

"I'll tell you when I see you. Ten minutes."

CHAPTER SIXTEEN
The Variance

I rounded the LeJeune Circle and headed down Old Cutler Road under a canopy of banyan trees, two green parrots circling overhead. Matching my mood, the skies to the west looked like the apocalypse, clouds billowing steely gray with black puffs like bursts of anti-aircraft fire.

Ray Pincher's daughter Paulette and son-in-law Barry Popkin lived in a mansion on Casuarina Concourse in the gated community of Gables Estates. Barry was a banker, real estate developer, and condo builder who could be credited, or blamed, for much of the Brickell Avenue canyon I had visited earlier today. He was also chairman of the Orange Bowl Committee, a board member of nearly every charity in town, and known for his philanthropy. Popkin's generosity extended to his father-in-law's reelection campaigns, to the point where Pincher's war chest scared off serious challengers.

The house sat on a full acre with 100 feet of waterfront, which was a good thing, because the yacht tied to the dock was 90 feet long. The house had a full-size pub with a bar imported from London and a giant wine cellar, which, of course, was not in a cellar, as the house was barely above sea level. I'd first been here for Paulette's wedding, a lavish affair in which Barry Popkin—a white, Jewish New Yorker—wore a red and gold silk dashiki and a matching knit kufi cap, instead of a yarmulke. Paulette was lovely in a traditional floor-length white wedding gown. Her father was dressed, as usual, in Brooks Brothers and complained loudly about the reception food, which included both latkes and chitlins, and the thunderous Jamaican steel band, whose drums could probably be heard in Jamaica.

"I blame Michael Jordan for making it cool to be black," Pincher told me that day.

The double wrought iron gates, wide enough for a herd of elephants, were open, so I eased the Eldo into a driveway of pink and gray granite pavers and parked adjacent to a regulation-size basketball court. As I approached the court, a skinny teenager with the unlikely name of Moses Pincher-Popkin took a jump shot twelve feet from the hoop.

Clang. Off the back of the rim.

A tall, muscular African American man wearing University of Miami shorts and a muscle-tee rebounded and snapped a pass directly at Moses's chest. If he hadn't bobbled the ball, Moses could have leapt and fired in one smooth motion. But nothing was smooth about Moses's moves.

No *clang* of the rim, as this shot was an air ball, tickling the bottom of the net. The rebounder snagged it with one hand and whipped it back to Moses. He caught the ball cleanly but didn't leave his feet. Taking three seconds to line up his shot, he squinted and fired. The ball hit the backboard and banked in.

"Attaboy, Moses!" the rebounder encouraged him. "Keep that elbow under the ball."

Moses was Ray Pincher's grandson, Paulette and Barry's boy. If I remembered correctly—and these days, who knows—Moses was between his junior and senior years of high school. The kid was scrawny, 5' 10? and maybe a buck-forty, with olive skin and vaguely African American features.

I opened a gate and walked onto the court. "Hey Moses, do you remember me?"

He shot me a wide smile that had none of the guile or mischief of his grandfather. "You're Wrong-Way Lassiter, grandpop's friend."

Oh, thanks a lot, Ray. Score one time for the wrong team, and I have to carry that name my whole life.

"Thanks for reminding me, Moses." I nodded hello to the man. "You're Dominique Barkley. I saw you play for the Heat."

"Long time ago. Nice to meet you."

"You never scored a bucket for the wrong team, did you?"

He laughed. "I'm an assistant coach at U.M. now. Mr. Popkin hires me as a shooting coach for Moses."

I didn't ask how that was going, and Dominique didn't offer his opinion.

"I'm trying to make varsity," Moses said.

"Ransom Everglades?" I asked, figuring the ritzy place was not only close but prestigious.

"No way. Dad doesn't believe in private schools, even though he went to Andover and Harvard. I'm at Palmetto. He says if it was good enough for Jeff Bezos, it's good enough for me."

"Much tougher competition to make the team." I shot a look at Dominique Barkley, and he nodded. I didn't say what I was thinking.

Kid, your dad might have named you after Moses Malone, and you might be half African American, but you're gonna get eaten alive in tryouts by kids who play on asphalt courts with chain-link nets.

"One-on-one, Jake? Game of twenty-one?"

The voice came from behind me. Approaching was Ray Pincher, monogrammed sleeves rolled up on his custom-made shirt, Italian silk tie at half-mast.

"Or a quick game of HORSE," I said. "Fifty bucks a letter, like the old days."

"Later. Walk with me, pal." Then, over his shoulder, "Eyes on the rim, Moses! Don't follow the flight of the ball. Dominique, how are his mechanics coming?"

"Getting better, Mr. Pincher," Barkley reported, diplomatically.

As we rounded the corner heading toward the dock, Pincher whispered, "My son-in-law pays Dominique two hundred bucks an hour to teach Moses to flip his wrist to get the backspin right. But the kid's a klutz. Poor Barry thought he might get my fast-twitch muscle fibers. And I thought with Paulette's height, Moses might be taller."

"Got his dad's genes. What's Barry, five eight?"

"Six feet if he's standing on his wallet."

We both laughed at that. Pincher loved his son-in-law but also loved razzing him. We parked ourselves on a bench on the dock and admired the *Variance*, Popkin's motor yacht, named for his skill at winning zoning changes that let him build high-rises with woefully insufficient parking. It was a sleek tri-deck with six staterooms for guests and another five cabins for crew.

"Okay, Jake. Your turn."

"At what?"

"Like we agreed in my office. You gotta share everything you get. I told you about the twenty-five thousand bucks in the Tesla. So, your turn."

"Ray, you don't have to treat this like the Treaty of Versailles."

"My legal training," he offered as an excuse.

I thought about Melissa's misgivings. Just what was Pincher's angle? "You don't have a dog in this hunt, do you, Ray?"

"Only my antipathy for the Justice Department and its minions, thick as mosquitoes on a sweaty neck."

The wind picked up, rippling the waterway and squeezing the *Variance* into the rubber fenders that cushioned the big boat from the dock.

Because I couldn't think of a good reason not to, I spent the next few minutes telling Pincher what I knew. I told him about the twins who couldn't swing a baseball bat, aim a Taser, or take a standardized test without hiring a ringer. I told him that Kip was on his way to California to see his boss, Max Ringle.

Pincher listened quietly, a priest in a confessional, as I admitted that Kip took SAT and ACT exams for pay in Houston, Kansas City, and Los Angeles. My tone was as regretful as if my nephew's misdeeds were my own.

"My turn," Pincher said when I had finished. "One more tidbit. It's hearsay on hearsay, so who knows what it's worth. It's what the tow truck driver told Foyo he overheard the FBI agents saying."

"I'm listening."

A horn blasted, and a Hatteras Sportfish in the forty-foot range chugged up the waterway, beating the storm back to dock. Two bare-chested men on the flybridge waved to us in that merry way of neighboring seafarers, and we waved back.

"The FBI approached your nephew, asking him to cooperate in an investigation of Max Ringle, and he told them to shove it."

"Oh, shit. When did this happen?"

"No idea."

"Those twins I told you about seemed to think a grand jury is meeting now, and this would corroborate it."

"Jesus, Jake, why didn't you mention that?"

"It...It...I'm not sure."

"Did it slip your mind?"

"Maybe."

And it had. I wasn't lying. Another check mark in the wrong column of Melissa's questionnaire.

Short-term memory? "Sketchy."

"Somehow, Ray, I let Kip get away from me." I felt like a mourner at a funeral, filled with regrets for words unsaid, things undone, and the knowledge that it was too late for amends. "He's strayed so far, and I've been clueless."

"Jesus, Jake! This isn't your fault. You gave everything you had to that boy."

"I don't know, Ray." Something was tickling my brain, something about grand juries and federal prosecutors. Not a lost memory, but a legal question that hadn't occurred to me in the hours since I learned the source of Kip's new wealth.

"Ray, let's assume rich parents are paying Kip to take their kids' tests."

"Safe assumption."

"I haven't done the research," I said, "but I don't know any statute on point. Nothing that expressly prohibits what Kip's doing."

"Right, insofar as 'expressly prohibits' goes. There's no standardized test security law, or whatever Congress would deem to call it."

"So, what Kip has done is unethical and immoral and a lousy thing to do. I get all that. But if a grand jury is investigating, what the hell is the crime?"

CHAPTER SEVENTEEN
Postcards from Hawaii

"I'll tell you how the feds would answer your question," Pincher said.

But before he could, his daughter Paulette appeared, carrying a tray with a bottle of tequila and three leaded crystal glasses. "Welcome, Jake," she said with a wide smile. "Forgive my father for his terrible manners. Has he even offered you a drink?"

"Nah. Usually, he plies me with fancy cigars and sweet rum, then picks my brain."

"Would it be presumptuous of me to think you might like some sipping tequila?" She poured from the bottle into the three glasses.

"Presume away, Paulette. You know me well."

When she was done pouring, Pincher examined the bottle. "Casa Dragones 16. Small batch sipping tequila. *Bottela Número 001*. The first bottle. Did Barry buy the distillery?"

"Not yet, Dad."

Paulette wore a white physician's smock. A statuesque woman with carved cheekbones, she seemed tired around the eyes. She ran a women's health clinic in Liberty City, a neighborhood untouched by the gentrification of nearby Wynwood and the Design District.

Paulette often spent late nights and weekends delivering babies, and she seldom billed her patients.

"Jake, when are you going to marry that wonderful fiancée of yours?" Paulette asked.

"Soon, before she changes her mind. You'll get the first invitation, just like that bottle of tequila."

Paulette and Melissa, both high achievers with nimble minds and sharp senses of humor, had hit it off immediately. When their crazed schedules permitted, the two physicians had lunch together.

Paulette sipped at her tequila and said, "Please thank Melissa for sending me those studies about the brains of teenagers not being fully developed."

"Will do," I responded.

"I use the data when I tell tenth-grade girls that they might not want to have sex quite yet. When they ask why, I tell them it's because in three or four years you'll look back and say, 'I can't believe I let that lame-ass bone me.'"

I laughed and asked, "Does that work?"

Paulette shrugged. "Not so much. That's why I pass out condoms like party balloons and birth control pills like jelly beans. You gotta cover all the bases."

We all took long pulls on the tequila, smooth and mellow, liquid sunshine on the way down.

"I saw Moses shooting hoops," I said. "Boy's sprouting up."

Paulette glanced toward the house. "Barry hopes he can make the high-school team." She tipped her glass in my direction. "I just hope he passes calculus." She got to her feet. "I'd better see how the cook is doing. Jake, will you join us for dinner?"

Pincher butted in. "P-Three, please tell me it's not fried chicken and okra again."

"And sweet potato pie," she replied, cheerily. "Barry's deep into his ethnic identity program."

"Then why aren't we having matzoh ball soup?"

Paulette turned to me. "Jake, how about it?"

"Thanks Paulette, but Melissa is waiting for me," I said.

"Jake, is that you?" A male voice came from overhead.

I looked up and saw the pink, cherubic face of Barry Popkin at the balustrade of the second-floor balcony. "Yo, Barry!"

He was wearing what looked like a silk doo-rag in a floral print with a tail that fell halfway down his back. "I'd join you, Jake, but I'm taking my Swahili lesson."

"Lord, have mercy," Pincher grumbled.

"Another time, Barry," I said. "Gotta go."

"Nenda kwa amani ndugu yangu," Popkin called out. "Go in peace, my brother."

Pincher pointed a finger at his son-in-law. "If you tell Alexa to play any of that hip-hop shit at dinner, I'm gonna throw her electronic ass in the ocean."

"Got it, Pop. Strictly the Supremes and Sinatra tonight."

Popkin went back inside to practice his Swahili, and Paulette left us alone on the dock. I said to Pincher, "You were about to give me a lesson in federal jurisprudence. Just how does the Justice Department make something a crime when there's no law on the books? What statute will they use?"

"Probably mail fraud. That's the grab-bag when the feds don't have anything else. You smack that piñata, all kinds of goodies spill out."

"Honestly, I don't see it."

"It's simple. Assume I go to Hawaii, and I send you a postcard, saying, 'Jake, having a wonderful time, wish you were here.' But I'm lying. I'm having a lousy time, and I don't want to share the beach with you. The feds would say that's mail fraud."

"That's absurd," I said.

"Or, I send the same postcard to five friends. The feds would call that racketeering."

"C'mon, Ray. The racketeering statute is for organized crime and street gangs."

"Maybe that's what Congress intended. But the Justice Department has its own ideas. Let's say I buy a shaved ice stand on my Hawaiian vacation, then flip it for a big profit. I put the money in a bank, then decide I don't like that bank, and I split the dough up among three other banks. Now, the feds say I'm money laundering."

"Aw, you're going way too far."

"I'm stretching things. But not as much as you'd think."

I let that settle in and concluded that my old friend and adversary was probably right. When the federal government decides to come after you, they'll find the weapon, and it won't be a pea-shooter.

I stood and took a last look at the Pincher-Popkin mansion. "You must be very proud, Ray. She's really something."

"From the Liberty City projects to Gables Estates in two generations. Is this a great country or what?"

"Can you forgive me, Ray, for being a little jealous?" I asked.

He got to his feet and jabbed a finger into my chest. "Don't be feeling sorry for yourself, Jake."

"I can't help it. Look how Paulette turned out and how Kip..." I let it hang there.

"Dammit, Jake! Life's not over for him. You're a defense lawyer. What have you argued all these years? Second chances and redemption. My advice, if your nephew is indicted, get him damn good counsel. And not you."

"If you're thinking I'm brain-dead, I'm not!"

"Your medical condition is only part of it. You're too close to him. You can't be objective, and if the feds offer a deal, you gotta be able to divorce yourself from your love of the boy."

"I'll consider your opinion."

"No, you won't! Do you know what Roy Black says about being a trial lawyer?" Pincher asked, referring to the dean of Florida criminal defense lawyers.

"Says a lot of things. Been working his magic for fifty years."

"Roy says you leave a little bit of yourself behind in every case. Not that you want to, but that the practice of law demands it."

"True enough. There's a lot of me smeared on courtroom floors."

"How much you got left, Jake? You're in no condition to handle a federal trial."

"So, you're saying I should turn over Kip's life to another lawyer?"

"Hell, yes! Doing this yourself is suicidal, a kamikaze mission. You want to die with your boots on?"

I considered that as if it were a plea deal. "If I have a heart attack in closing argument and the jury acquits my nephew, I'd consider that a win."

Pincher gave me his exasperated look. "Your skull is so thick, I don't know how you got brain damage. How are you going to prep for trial? How big is your staff?"

"That's a pretty personal question."

"C'mon, Jake! How many associates do you have? How many paralegals?"

"In round numbers, zero. You know damn well I gave up my office when I took the job with the Bar."

"So how are you going to manage a federal case where you have to brief every motion? Who's going to do your research, your writing?"

"I can handle it."

He made a scoffing sound. "How many cases have you had in federal court?"

"State or federal, it's the same game. A contact sport. I buckle my chin strap and hit somebody."

"Dammit! How many federal cases, Jake?"

"I pled a guy to tax evasion and a couple drug dealers when that was a thing."

"I'm not talking about pleas. I'm talking about jury trials."

"I had one securities fraud trial back in the day."

"What do you know about securities law?"

"Nothing. I represented a co-defendant and rode Ed Shohat's coattails."

"And what was the verdict?"

I tried to dig up the memory, but it was an itch in the back of my mind that I couldn't scratch. "It was a long time ago, Ray."

"Ah, jeez, the one federal trial you took to verdict, and you can't remember. What are you gonna do when the government buries you in documents? Ten thousand pages, a hundred thousand pages, half a million, a blizzard of paper!"

A jagged bolt of lightning flashed over the bay, followed by a cacophonous thunderclap that I felt in my teeth. The darkened sky opened and, at long last, the deluge poured down in great slanting torrents. I closed my eyes and raised my head to the storm, raindrops pelting me so hard they stung my face. Pincher, soaking wet, hadn't moved. He was still looking at me, his expression one of puzzlement.

"A kamikaze mission," I declared.

"Yeah, Jake, that's what I just said."

"Maybe you're right, Ray, but those bastards sunk a lot of ships."

CHAPTER EIGHTEEN
Kiss Kiss, Pet Pet, Bam Bam

Melissa Gold...

Melissa was removing a baking dish from the oven when Jake walked in the door.

"Smells great, Mel." He picked up a bottle of tequila from the counter. "Margarita grouper?"

"Your favorite." She had marinated the fish filets in a mixture of tequila, lime juice, and orange liqueur, with a touch of olive oil and garlic. Now, she spooned a sauce of tomato, jalapeno, onion, and brown sugar over the cooked fish.

As she put on the finishing touches, Jake told her about Ray Pincher's advice to hire a lawyer for Kip.

She knew Jake wanted her input, but hesitated before asking, "What lawyer will care about Kip as much as you do?"

"Exactly. Pincher doesn't get it. I've prepared my entire life for this. To put everything on the line, to defend someone I love. I've got to be the one."

She looked at him, feeling a warm flood of emotions for this oversize man she loved. "I know you'll do the right thing for Kip. You always have."

He dipped a fork into the baking dish, stole a chunk of the grouper, tasted it, and smacked his lips with approval. "And how was your day?"

"Strange," she said. "There's a problem with appropriations for the C.T.E. program."

"What's the problem?"

"Apparently, NFL lobbyists are whispering in congressmen's ears that they don't like the program's mission statement."

"Why? Are they against saving lives?"

"They think the statement overly emphasizes football and by participating in the study, the NFL will look like it's trying to make amends for killing former players."

"Those bastards! The owners have always had an aversion to the truth, just like the tobacco companies. If they were honest, they'd change their name to the National Brain Damage League. They like to boast about their billion-dollar class-action settlement for C.T.E. victims, but they always forget to say it's to be paid over sixty-five years and doesn't cover everybody."

"What I'm hearing is the NFL wants hockey, boxing, and martial arts prominently mentioned in the mission statement."

"Can you do that?"

"We intend to study traumatic brain injuries in several sports, so it's no big deal to change the wording."

"Great."

"But that's a smokescreen, not the real problem."

He looked at her a moment, waiting.

"I have a friend at N.I.H. who's in the loop," Melissa continued. "The league claims the program will be biased because I'm the one who wrote the protocols and will likely be running the show."

"Biased how?" Before she could answer, he asked, "Because of me? Because you're my fiancée?"

She shrugged. "They know you're one of the former Dolphins with symptoms of C.T.E., and you're an outspoken critic of the league. The NFL suits think I can't be objective."

"Damn them! Who are they to question your integrity?"

"When you petitioned for higher pensions benefits for retired players...well, you upset the powers that be on Park Avenue."

"Bastards! I spoke up because of the NFL's discrimination. Pensions for guys who retired before 1993 are half that of current players. We have no 401(k)'s, no annuities, and no health insurance, like the younger retirees get. It's an outrage! And to punish you for what I say and do, that's beyond the damn pale."

"My friend tells me to give it time," she said. "I have allies who are trying to help."

"Why does the NFL even get a vote? When Congress appropriates money for the FBI, they don't ask the Mafia for permission."

"We need the league's cooperation to get their medical records. That's really the starting point."

"Okay, okay." Jake seemed to be calming down after blowing off steam. "We'll give it time. But we're not gonna let them shitcan your project or veto you. We'll fight."

She loved the way he leapt to her defense, ready to curse out or punch out anyone who threatened her. A few old-fashioned male virtues were still...well, virtues.

"Your support means a lot to me," she said.

"And you're everything to me, Mel. You know that, right?"

She smiled at him, this protective teddy bear of a man she loved. "Let's eat dinner, and then show me just what you mean."

☙

After dinner and showers, it was spooning time in the Lassiter bedroom. Jake's arms were wrapped around Melissa and her curves were tucked into the angles of his body. Whoever invented spooning should get a Nobel Peace Prize, she thought. They gave one to Henry Kissinger, and as far as she knew, he never did anything to make people feel warm and loved.

"Jake the Cuddler," Melissa had said, the first time they drifted off to sleep this way.

Tonight, Jake was whispering in her ear, her hair tickling his nose, one hand playing gently on the slope of her hip. Usually, the whispers were sweet and romantic, the prelude to friction and heat. Tonight, the talk was more like a summary of the nightly news. Jake told her about Pincher's theory of the lying postcards, that a crime is whatever the Justice Department says it is. She told Jake she'd booked him on an early morning flight to Los Angeles. He told her how much it hurt that Kip didn't turn to him when he got in trouble. She told Jake to wear the obscenely expensive sweater to show that he wanted to reestablish his bond with Kip. The symbolism wouldn't be lost on him.

"I love the way you're always looking under the hood," Jake murmured.

"Checking your oil?"

"Analyzing the psychological underpinnings. You're better at it than I am."

"We're a great team." After a quiet moment, she said, "Why do you suppose you never got hitched?"

"You mean why didn't I have a starter marriage in my twenties?"

"Or your thirties or forties. And don't say, 'Because I never met anyone like you.'"

"That's a given. But I also looked at my friends and saw marriage as trench warfare, sort of like World War I. Fight like hell to gain ten yards of turf, then retreat to the cold, wet trench. Grab your rifle, stick your head up, take a few wild shots, duck down again. Once in a while, there's a cease-fire, like the Germans and the Brits at Christmas singing 'Silent Night' from one trench to another. The next day, more shooting."

"Wow, that's a pessimistic view of marriage, if ever I've heard one."

"But that's not us. Never will be."

He hugged her more tightly, the spoons even closer together now.

"I love being in your arms," she said. "You make me feel safe."

They were quiet for a long moment. They listened to the paddle fan rotating above the bed. Outside, a nighttime breeze slapped palm fronds against the bedroom window.

"Before I forget," Jake said, "Paulette thanks you for sending her those studies of adolescents and their immature brains."

"Happy to do it."

"Mel, I wouldn't mind reading the data myself."

"Hmm, why?" she asked, sleepily.

"If Kip is charged, maybe there's something in there for me. That he didn't have criminal intent, it was just a risk-taking adventure."

She stirred under the sheet. Nothing like a neuroscience issue to awaken her. "If you're saying that Kip is a thrill junkie, doesn't his profit motive hurt your case? Seems to me it would hold more weight if Kip hadn't been paid so handsomely."

"You'd make a great prosecutor," Jake whispered in her ear.

"That doesn't sound like a compliment," she whispered right back.

"Sure, it is. You'd be the sexiest prosecutor I know. I wouldn't mind if you locked me up right now. Life without parole." His lips brushed her neck and she purred. One of his hands cupped one of her breasts and his other hand traced the dip and curve where her hip ski-sloped to her waist.

"Is this foreplay?" she asked, "or are you just proving you're ambidextrous?"

"Both?" he ventured, cautiously.

"Your flight is at six-forty-five a.m."

"Which is why my foreplay is double-handed, sort of eight-play."

"Why didn't you say so, slugger? You want a *bon voyage* kiss kiss, pet pet, bam bam?"

"Bam bam...bam. Sure."

She turned to face him, their noses inches apart. Who would kiss whom first? She elected to be the one. Long and slow. Then he kissed back, and in a few moments, the bed creaked from below and there was heaving and sighing above.

CHAPTER NINETEEN
The Hubris of the Young

I put on jeans, running shoes, and that thin, soft, rust-colored sweater Kip had given me. Melissa insisted on driving me to the airport. Just another one of her gestures of care and affection, tenderness and love. It was beyond the call of duty, leaving the house at 4:45 a.m. But here she was, sans makeup, that sprinkle of freckles making her look like a college coed.

We were stopped at the traffic light at Douglas and U.S.1 when I said, "Let me tell you about the trouble Kip got into when he was at Penn."

"You don't have to."

"Yes, I do. No secrets."

"You promised Kip."

"You can better advise me if you know his past, so I'm changing the rules."

When the light turned green and we headed north on Douglas, I told Melissa the story.

"Kip's smarts came back to haunt him," I explained. "His test scores placed him in upper-level math courses. In his second semester, he's hanging out with upperclassmen in something called nonlinear dynamics. He's a whiz, and they like him. Maybe he's their kid mascot. They're all poker players and they teach him Texas Hold 'Em. He's fascinated, learns the ratio method and percentage method of figuring pot odds. First, he plays video poker to sharpen his skills, and, as you'd expect, he's damn good. Then he starts playing with his new pals for low stakes."

"I think I see where this is going," Melissa said, as we passed *Calle Ocho* in the predawn traffic. "He gets addicted to poker and flunks out."

"He didn't have time to get addicted. This was a one-shot deal. A trip to Atlantic City to hit the casinos."

"Don't you have to be 21 to get into a casino?"

"Hang on, Mel. I'm getting to that. At the last minute, this kid Taylor backs out because he's got to study. He and Kip have the same color hair and look enough alike that..."

"Taylor gives Kip his driver's license."

"And his American Express Centurion card."

"The black titanium card? A college kid?"

"His old man runs a hedge fund. They have a mansion in Greenwich plus a two-story penthouse on Central Park South. Anyway, Taylor was staking Kip, who had maybe sixty bucks in cash. He told Kip they'd split the winnings."

"What if Kip lost?"

We passed the darkened Mel Reese golf course. Just a few blocks from the airport now.

"Kip says they never even considered the possibility of losing."

"The hubris of the young," Melissa said, nailing it, as usual.

"So, this car full of guys drives to the Jersey shore. And now Kip's not playing against college kids. Some are professionals. This is their full-time job, and they know the math as well as Kip does. They also know poker psychology, which requires assessing your opponents. That comes from experience that Kip doesn't have. Maybe worse, he's also playing against the bus crowd, rank amateurs who know nothing. They bet when they shouldn't and pull cards out of their ass when they should have folded on Fourth Street."

"So how much did Kip lose?"

Melissa parked the car in front of the first set of doors at the American Airlines terminal. A hotel van pulled alongside and discharged its sleepy passengers.

"Oh, he won. At first. Says he was up about thirty-seven thousand dollars."

"Wow. But he didn't quit while he was ahead, did he?" She lowered her forehead and pretended to pound it onto the steering wheel, a universal gesture of *"Oh shit!"*

"Right. Now, it's about three a.m., and he's on a losing streak. So he uses that credit card, buys stacks of hundred-dollar chips. Bets too much on bad hands and too little on good ones, bluffs big while sweating big, chases lost money, and, of course, when he has a dead solid perfect hand, he loses on a bad beat."

"Is that where the other player gets lucky?"

"Makes a ridiculous bet and wins. Long story short, Kip loses an all-in pot while he's holding four sixes because some yahoo who's holding a pair of queens gets kissed by stardust when the other two regal ladies turn up on Fourth and Fifth Street. The odds of any hand beating four sixes, according to Kip, are one in one-hundred-seven-thousand. To do it like that, it just doesn't happen."

৵৹

A uniformed airport cop, a broad-shouldered woman in her thirties wearing a shiny black duty belt, rapped on the driver's window and motioned for Melissa to move the car. Melissa lowered the window and said, "Just another minute, officer."

"One minute, you got," she said, and walked on.

"How much did Kip lose?" Melissa asked.

"All told, one hundred twenty-nine thousand, four hundred ninety-eight dollars."

She gasped. "On a credit card?"

"The Centurion card has no limit. But when it hit a hundred grand, Taylor's father gets a fraud alert that wakes him up. He calls Taylor, who panics and says he must have lost the card. Taylor frantically calls Kip and tells him what happened, and if anyone asks, he's gotta say he borrowed the card without permission because if he tells the truth, his old man will pull him out of school and make him sell commodities, which is akin to capital punishment in that zip code. Meanwhile, the old man calls the casino, which was named in the fraud alert. Casino security and two local cops grab Kip, who says he's using the card without Taylor's knowledge."

"Admitting he committed a crime."

"Grand larceny, identity theft, unauthorized use of a credit card, and forgery."

"Oh my God."

The airport cop appeared at the window again and yelled, "Move it," even though there were plenty of open spots in front of the terminal.

I grabbed my carry-on and opened the passenger door, buying another few seconds. "I got him into pre-trial intervention as a first-time offender, but he had to plead nolo to one count. It all goes away, record expunged, if he completes probation. But a person on probation is like a gymnast on the balance beam. You don't have to fall off to lose points. A wobble from the straight and narrow and you go to jail."

"Last warning!" the cop yelled.

"One second, please," I pled, one foot on the pavement, the rest of me still inside the car. I turned to Melissa. "Maybe I didn't do enough for him after all this happened. Maybe I didn't make it clear that he had to be ultra-cautious, instead of so damn reckless." I exhaled a long sigh. "There's no probation this time. There's only prison."

"Thanks for telling me all this," Melissa said. "It means a lot to me."

"No more secrets," I promised.

"You're the best, Jake. You're real in every sense of the word."

"And we're closer every day. Pulling together for a common purpose."

She rewarded me with a warm smile. "and remember this. He may have lost his way, but he's not a lost cause."

We kissed, and I stepped out of the car.

"Hold it right there, sir," the cop said, sternly.

I looked at my watch. Not late, yet. "What have I done, Officer?"

"Place your bag on the sidewalk and your hands at your side where I can see them."

Melissa had driven away, unaware that I was being rousted. The cop approached me warily.

"If you're gonna strip-search me," I said, "I gotta warn you. I'm ticklish."

"That's a handsome sweater, sir."

"Thank you. It's vicuña."

"Is it now?"

"Unless that's an endangered species, in which case it's polyester. Look, it's a Loro Piana, if that means anything."

"Oh, it does. We have a problem with counterfeit Loro Piana sweaters. Customs confiscated half a dozen containers last week."

"You're not going to take my sweater, are you?"

"Do you have a receipt?"

"It was a gift."

"Uh-huh. Keep your hands at your side and bend forward so I can reach the label."

"Is that really necessary? I have a plane to catch."

"I'm not asking again." She fingered the call button on the radio mic clipped to her chest, as if she might seek reinforcements, a SWAT team, maybe.

I did as I was told. She pulled up the neck of the sweater and examined the label. "One hundred percent vicuña," she said. "With the tilde over the 'n.' The knock-offs omit the tilde." She let go and smoothed the fabric. "You're good to go, sir."

"Thank you, Officer."

"Have a safe trip."

I grabbed my bag and nodded my thanks.

"And may I say, sir, the sweater looks very nice on you."

CHAPTER TWENTY
Public Shame

A young woman with two-tone lacquered fingernails checked me in at the American Airlines counter. She allowed as how my rust-colored sweater matched my eyes, which I took to mean they were bloodshot. The gate agent, a portly man, said he wished he could wear a sweater like that, but he didn't have the shoulders and his paunch would only be accentuated. And the flight attendant stationed at the doorway of the Boeing 777 asked if the sweater was cashmere, but I set her straight about those wild vicuñas and their tildes in the Andes.

I had paid full fare for business class in the wide-body jet because coach seats cause my back to go into spasms. With the full recliner, I dozed off and on during the flight. Each time I awoke, Kip was on my mind.

Just when did I lose him? When did he go from basking in the warmth of my care to running from it?

Melissa had repeatedly told me this was all part of the normal process of the child becoming an adult. "All parents lose their children when they cease being children," she said. But criminal charges in New Jersey and now possible federal charges at home are not normal. And Kip's emphasis on money, on acquisitiveness, well, that was foreign to me.

I wasn't an angel growing up, wild and rowdy in the Florida Keys. Fueled by cheap beer and raging testosterone, I'd crept onto docks after midnight to take boats for joyrides. I'd dived for spiny lobster in other people's traps and gotten into fistfights with punks from Homestead High.

At Penn State, I was into football, girls, and classes...in that order. I joined a student thespian group and played Big Jule in "Guys & Dolls," my performance marred by bruising Nathan Detroit's vocal cords when lifting him from the stage with one hand.

Somehow, I got through my youth relatively unscathed. Why hadn't Kip?

ↄ

At LAX, I rented a Mercedes SUV and was speeding down a steep hill on the 101 just outside Camarillo when my cell rang.

"Got a minute, Jake? Erwin Gridley here. I want to run something by you."

"What's that, Judge?"

"Bert Kincaid and his wandering pecker."

"Judge, you know we can't talk about the case without Bert's presence."

"Jeez, when did you start crossing the t's and dotting the i's?"

"Not sure. Maybe when I got a job with the Florida Bar."

The judge's laugh seemed to scoff at me. "Funny you should mention that. I was researching what punishment to dole out to Bert, and what do I come across? The Florida Bar vs. Jacob Lassiter."

"Yes, sir. Long time ago, the Bar hauled my ass to Tallahassee for a public reprimand in front of the state Supreme Court."

"You punched out a client. Kincaid diddled a few. Seems to me your violation is greater, which is why I'm considering the lesser punishment of a private reprimand."

"Double secret probation? A don't-do-it-again letter? The Bar can't agree to that."

I was on flat land now, broad expanses of lettuce fields on both sides of the freeway, arms of irrigation devices rotating like airplane propellers, shooting mist into the air.

"You're pretty high and mighty for a guy who's lucky to still have his license."

"Mine was a heat-of-anger deal. Not premeditated and it only happened once."

All true. I had just won a date-rape case because I'd gotten a bottle of roofies suppressed on an illegal search. My client joked about putting me on retainer for next time, now that he had his get-out-of-jail card. I broke his jaw with one punch. Then I went on a three-day bender and nearly quit the practice. After that, when people asked my occupation, I'd say I worked in the *so-called* justice system.

"Bert Kincaid repeatedly abused the attorney-client relationship," I said. "A confidential, private reprimand won't stop him."

Traffic backed up heading into Oxnard. I merged into the fast lane, which, at the moment, was going twenty miles an hour.

"Tell me about it, Jake. What was it like, standing in front of the Supremes, getting a tongue-lashing in open court?"

"The biggest humiliation of my life."

"Convince me then. Can public shame change a man?"

The judge was asking about me and, of course, about Kincaid, but I was thinking about Kip. When he was arrested in Atlantic City, I protected him from public shame. Swept it under the rug. Got the file sealed, and, until today, I'd never told a soul. If I'd been more forthcoming, if I'd dealt with his conduct openly, if I'd gotten him into therapy, could I have kept him from a far more serious run-in with the law?

I hadn't answered, so Judge Gridley asked again. "Jake, you there? Was your public shaming enough?"

"The Bar thought it was. I took anger management classes and never had another complaint. When I applied for the prosecutor's job, they seemed impressed with my rehabilitation. Sort of like a former addict who becomes a drug counselor."

"That's it, then. I'll give Bert Kincaid a public reprimand and trust he'll change his ways."

"Sure, judge. Sure."

Truth be told, I no longer cared about Kincaid and his punishment. All my operative brain cells were focused on Kip. Experiencing shame isn't what changes a person, I thought. You need to deal with the wayward conduct itself. You need to accept responsibility. You need to rely on loved ones for support. You need to do a dozen things Kip would resist, but that wouldn't stop me from trying.

CHAPTER TWENTY-ONE
The Subjunctive Mood

A few minutes after hanging up with Judge Gridley, I passed through the seaside town of Ventura, jagged mountains to my right, the ocean to my left, sparkling in the afternoon sun. My cell phone rang again. Caller ID didn't show a name, just an 805-area code and a number that meant nothing to me. I answered with an inquisitive "Hello?"

"Is that Franco Harris?"

"Kip! Great to hear your voice. I guess the receptionist told you I called."

"I'm surprised you didn't say 'immaculate reception-ist.'" He drew out the word, in case I didn't catch the reference to Franco Harris's improbable winning touchdown in a playoff game.

"How are you feeling, Kip? Are you okay?"

"I'm fine, Uncle Jake. Minor aches, a little stiffness."

Uncle Jake. Okay, I'm liking that. The warmth in his voice, too.

"I want to see you, kiddo. We need to talk."

"I'm guessing you're on your way to Santa Barbara."

"Maybe thirty minutes, depending on traffic."

Just then, an eighteen-wheeler with signage proclaiming it was loaded with fresh fish moved into my lane, and I tap-tapped the brakes.

"Hey, thanks for the sweater," I said.

"You like it?"

"I'm wearing it. It's a real chick magnet."

"You can't say 'chick' anymore, Uncle Jake."

"Why? Is it offensive to poultry? Listen, I met the twins, Dumb and Dumber. We gotta talk about this so-called tutoring you're doing."

"I know how you think, Uncle Jake, but don't worry. I'm not gonna be busted or anything."

"Who were those two guys in suits who picked you up from the hospital and chauffeured you around town?"

"Our lawyers."

"Who's 'our?'"

"Max Ringle and me. They're L.A. lawyers. Expensive and first-rate."

"Listen, kiddo. Any lawyer of Ringle's isn't yours. What the hell were they doing in Miami?"

"The FBI is trying to subpoena me, and Max thought I should stay under wraps. I flew here last night on Max's jet. Pretty cool."

Max's lawyers. Max's jet. Max's thoughts.

At least he was talking to me. But he was so blinded by Ringle's money that he couldn't see past the glare.

Traffic cleared a bit, and my Mercedes sailed along, easing through a slight bend in the freeway at Mussel Shoals, a scenic spot overlooking a line of oceanfront homes.

"Did you talk to the FBI without a lawyer?" I asked.

"You gotta chill, Uncle Jake. Max has an opinion of counsel that says everything we do is kosher."

"Yeah?"

"Max asked the top law firm in L.A. to look at our business. They say it's really ingenious, and even though it's a little hinky, it's not illegal because there are no specific laws covering it."

"Really? Ray Pincher says the Justice Department doesn't give a shit what your lawyers say."

"C'mon, Jake. You and Sugar Ray are old school. Max says that relying on a legal opinion is a solid defense to a criminal charge."

Once again, I had become "Jake," a doddering old fool, and Max was Kip's trusted mentor.

"That's true in very limited circumstances. I want to see that legal opinion."

"Fine, when we sit down with Max, ask him for it."

"I want to meet with you alone first."

"Why?"

"Your interests aren't aligned with his. He's the big fish, and you have to consider cooperating with the feds, if it's not too late."

"No way! I'm not gonna flip on Max. That'd be like me flipping on you."

Oh, that puts a pretty fine point on it.

"And Max would never flip on me," he continued. "We're pretty much partners."

"You didn't answer my question. Did you talk to the FBI?"

"A couple losers in baggy suits came up to me six months ago, making threats, telling me I should wear a wire and implicate Max."

Six months! I could have helped you, Kippers. But now?

"I wouldn't talk to them. A few weeks ago, they came around again, saying it was my last chance. I should voluntarily appear before a grand jury. I told them to voluntarily kiss my ass."

"Why the hell didn't you tell me about this six months ago?" I demanded, my voice picking up volume.

"Because I knew how you'd react. Jake, I know you mean well..."

Sometimes you can hear a "but" roaring toward you, like a train whistle blaring around the bend.

"But I'm a grown man. A businessman. That's hard for you, I get that. But I don't need to be babied. And, frankly, you're not my real father."

Ouch! The unintended cruelties inflicted by the ones you love.

"That's right, Kip. I *chose* to be your father."

"You sound like you regret it."

"Not true, dammit! Not for a moment."

"So why didn't you adopt me? Why are you still my *un-cle*?"

And why, Kip, are you dishing out heartache to the one person in the world who would do anything for you?

"I filed the adoption papers years ago, and you know that. I needed your mother's signature unless I could prove she was dead. All I could prove was that her last known address was a jail in Shreveport. She was getting cash refunds from Target on merchandise she'd shoplifted. What could go wrong with that brilliant scheme? Time passed, and I didn't think the formalities mattered that much. I considered you my son in every respect. I still do."

He kept quiet, and I continued, "I'm sorry, Kip, if I let you down."

For a moment, there was no sound but the whistle of tires on the pavement and a buzz on the line. Then, Kip said, "Even if I were your son..."

"Yeah?"

"Did you notice I used the subjunctive mood? 'If I were...' Because I'm not your son. There's always a subjunctive mood question on the SAT."

"Wherever you're going with this, just spit it out."

"Even if I were your son, at this point in my life, I'm capable of making my own decisions. I'm not mad at you for looking out for me. But your point of view is skewed."

"I have no idea what that means."

"Not everyone who makes a lot of money is a crook or a fraudster. Max Ringle has created a brilliant business plan, and he's recognized my talents and is happy to share the wealth."

What could I say? That you're young and foolish and you don't know that the big beautiful world out there is often a world of hurt?

"Jake, I want you to be happy for me," he continued. "For my climbing the mountain so fast."

"I promise I will be, as soon as I'm convinced you're not walking off a cliff."

"I won't be doing this forever. As soon as I have enough capital, I'm going to open my own chain of tutoring businesses. Strictly legit. And I'll help poor kids pro bono."

"You'd be surprised how many of my clients were only going to pull one more heist."

"I'm not a criminal, Jake."

I didn't want to argue the point, so I kept quiet. The Mercedes was cruising through Summerland, a quaintly named village a few minutes from Santa Barbara, according to my GPS companion. My back was stiff from the cross-country flight and the drive up the coast. My head hurt from a lifetime of noggin-banging and my current shitload of stress.

"Okay, Kip, let's stop jawing at each other. I'm just a few miles out of town and I'm dying to see you."

"I'm glad you're here," Kip said, cheerily, as if we hadn't just been hurling grenades at each other. "We're having a reception at Max's house for our feeders. I'll give you the address."

"Feeders?"

"Financial planners and stockbrokers who send us clients. We're celebrating after landing a couple Chinese billionaire families. You wouldn't believe what they pay to get their kids into colleges here."

Kip kept talking about Max's wonderful and splendid and profitable business. I exited the freeway and started driving up the gentle slope of San Ysidro Road in the ritzy suburb of Montecito.

When Kip's upbeat monologue was over, I couldn't help myself. "With the FBI on your trail, why the hell are you celebrating?"

"Jeez, Jake. Like I said, you gotta chill."

"You know how Franco Harris made that immaculate reception?"

"Duh. We only watched it on 'Greatest Plays' about a hundred times."

"How'd Franco score? Why wasn't he tackled?"

"He ran down the sideline and no one caught him."

"There's more to it. Franco's just a rookie out of Penn State, youngest player on the field, kind of like you at Q.E.D. The game appears lost. Steelers are down by a point. Twenty-two seconds left, fourth and ten from their own forty-yard line. Terry Bradshaw scrambles for his life, tries to hit Frenchy Fuqua deep over the middle, but Jack Tatum karate chops the ball. It should fall to the ground for an incompletion."

"But Franco drifts out of the backfield as a safety-valve receiver," Kip said. "I know. Everybody knows."

"He kept running even after the ball went over his head toward Fuqua. So, Franco's in the perfect spot to scoop the ricochet off his shoe tops before it hits the ground."

"Yeah, sure," Kip said. "Play 'til the whistle blows. You taught me that."

"Four Raiders could have made the tackle, and it would have been game over. Jimmy Warren, a cornerback, was busy congratulating Tatum. Linebacker Gerald Irons was watching Fuqua on the ground, not following the path of the ball. Linebacker Phi Vilipiano did a lazy job covering Franco out of the backfield."

"I get your point or maybe two points. Franco didn't give up on a play that seemed doomed, and the Raiders started celebrating early."

"Exactly! And six months ago, the FBI thought they could use you to put a case together against Ringle. When you said no, did they give up? Game over?"

"Apparently not."

"Then last week the same agents ask if you'd voluntarily appear before a grand jury, right?"

"Yeah, I told you that."

"And the feds have subpoenaed the twins. Meaning the grand jury is in session and the FBI is already presenting evidence to establish probable cause and return indictments. So, if I were you—and note my use of the subjunctive mood, because I am not you—I would damn sure not start celebrating quite yet."

CHAPTER TWENTY-TWO
The Battle for Kip

I turned right on East Valley Road, and then left on Park Lane, continuing to climb the mountain past gated estates perched high enough for clear views of the harbor and ocean. There was little traffic, other than gardeners in their pickup trucks and dog groomers in their vans. It was a street that spoke of quiet money and secluded lives. I stopped in front of a gated palace that made Barry Popkin's mansion look like a starter home in Hialeah.

The front gates were light wood and dark metal thirty feet high. A brass plaque on the guardhouse built of gray stones said *Casa de la Sabuduría.* "House of Wisdom." A tad pretentious, but if you own an estate with both ocean and mountain views, well, maybe you can crow about how smart you are. I stopped at the guardhouse and was greeted by a uniformed man with a clipboard.

He asked for my name and told me I was the first to arrive for the festivities. He said that Lance would take me to the main house in a golf cart. I got out of the Mercedes, stretched and swung from side to side, easing the pain in my lower back. All those years tackling large, moving objects compresses the spine as well as concusses the brain.

Lance wore a black suit, white shirt, and black tie. With his close-cropped hair and aviator sunglasses, he looked in shape and ex-military. A guy about thirty-five who seemed thin—until you noticed the oversize wrists and the neck strung with cables. Special Forces would not have surprised me.

Before we got in, he took out a metal detector wand and ran it over me.

"Anything metallic on you?" he asked.

"Does titanium in a shoulder and knee count?"

"No, sir." He gave me a tight little smile. "I've got some in my spine, and it never sets off the equipment."

I figured he'd gotten his spare parts in a far more important and courageous manner.

It was a five minute ride along two rows of towering oak trees. We emerged in front of a sprawling house in the Mediterranean style with an orange barrel tile roof. The house sat high on a mesa with a dandy view of the ocean and the Channel Islands. Two smaller buildings, likely guest cottages, sat farther down the slope, their tiled roofs barely visible.

"Dr. Ringle and Mr. Lassiter are on the terrace," Lance said.

"Do I get a roadmap?"

"I'll escort you, sir."

Lance took me through the house at a fast pace. Lots of dark woods and large windows overlooking the sea. High ceilings crosshatched with heavy beams that might have been salvaged from Clipper ships. We passed a piano room and a game room with the requisite billiards table, pinball machines and free-standing video arcade games. I paused at the doorway, and Lance had no other choice but to also stop.

"What's that?" I pointed at what looked like a 100-inch wall-mounted television screen. Ten feet in front of the screen were two pods containing cushioned chairs astronauts might use on a space mission, plus computer keyboards, headsets, and various control panels and remotes.

"EGame consoles," Lance answered. "High tech ones, the kind they use in arenas for championship matches."

"Does my nephew play?"

"Kip Lassiter? He's the best. *Fortnite, Call of Duty, World of Warcraft*. No one can beat him, not even Dr. Ringle."

We resumed walking and passed a theater with perhaps twenty cushy chairs and lots of plush red velvet inside.

"Lance! Lance!"

The woman's voice came from behind us. We stopped and turned. A barefoot young woman padded toward us, her full lips pouting. Her toenails were painted a color that might be called midnight blue. She was lithe and tanned with chestnut hair pulled back into a ponytail, and she wore a gold thong bikini and enormous red-framed sunglasses, each lens shaped like a heart. "Lance, what the hell's wrong with the sauna?"

"Nothing, Ms. Ringle," he replied politely.

"Really! My nipples nearly froze to death!"

I stared at the ceiling, both too chivalrous and too old to look for proof of her assertion. Lance, bless his security man's heart, did the same.

"You have to pre-heat it," Lance said. "It'll take about six minutes to get to 175 degrees, just the way you like it."

"Six minutes! Who's got six minutes?"

Lance didn't answer. She took off the big sunglasses, cocked her head, and studied me a moment. "You're Kip's dad."

"Uncle. But yes, he's mine. You must be Shari."

"He says you're brain-dead."

"A little dinged. Just a fender bender."

"Kip's adorkable."

"You mean adorable?"

"No. A combo platter. Adorable dork."

"Ah. I get it."

"And he's savage smart."

"He is that."

"You don't seem anything like him."

"Well...what can I say?"

"Kip's a clout chaser who wants to be part of the fam, but to be dead-A, he's so cringy that's it's awks."

"My thoughts, exactly," I said, not understanding a word.

"But he's in my squad. I couldn't have gotten into USC without him." She put her weight on one leg and shot her hip, model style. "I'm a drama major."

"I bet you're very good at it."

"I hate college. Why do I have to learn Spanish? To talk to my maid? I'm only there because Daddy makes me. Did you know Kim Kardashian never went to college? And she's, like, a billionaire. She's my role model."

"Shoot for the moon, I always say."

"I'm a social media influencer."

I was quiet a moment, and she asked, "You don't know what that is, do you?"

"Sure, I do. You're on Chap Snatch and What's Up?"

"You're kidding, right? I do a vlog sponsored by NoBurn, the suntan lotion company. I'm the prime model, so I gotta keep my tan." She spun around to give me a view of her coppery back and butt. "And I have 105,000 Instagram followers."

"That's a lot. About the capacity of Beaver Stadium."

"That's nothing! How many followers do you think Kim Kardashian has?"

"I don't know, maybe two beavers. A couple hundred thousand."

"Are you stoopy? More like 130 million!"

While I wondered if that could be true, she replaced her sunglasses, waved goodbye, and sashayed down the corridor, wiggling just a tad more than necessary.

Lance and I exited the rear of the house onto a loggia with a seating area around a fireplace, where logs blazed, preparing for the bone-chilling moment when the current 70 degrees plummeted to 67. I'm not being pissy about that. Floridians love fireplaces. We just wish we needed them. We love mountains, too. But we're long on coastline, short on mountains, and big on envy.

Lance and I emerged onto a shaded terrace that overlooked a garden with a dozen rows of rose bushes. Past the garden were tiled steps that led down to a grassy lawn the size of a football field. A bar with a white-coated bartender was set up at one end of the terrace. Below was an infinity lap pool about fifty yards long. If you were swimming laps, the pool would appear to be endless, merging with horizon, which is to say, the Pacific Ocean.

Kip and Max Ringle, wearing identical thin, dark blue zip-up hoodies and jeans, stood at the bar. Thanks to Melissa showing me a website called "Dress Like a Billionaire," I knew those were the Loro Piana bomber hoodies worn by Bobby Axelrod, the shady hedge fund antihero of "Billions." Cashmere, smooth as a baby's ass, about $2,300, according to what I'd read. The hoodie announces to the world that you idolize a hedge fund zillionaire who tiptoes so close to the line that his shadow ought to be in prison.

Ringle had added one accessory to his outfit that Kip, thankfully, had not. A red silk scarf casually tossed around his neck like Snoopy, about to fly his Sopwith Camel into battle against the Red Baron. If you ask me, the scarf didn't go with the hoodie, but my knowledge of fashion is stuck in a time warp of bell-bottom jeans and tie-dyed T-shirts, or are those back in style?

Ringle long-legged it toward me across the wide expanse of terrace, his scarf flapping behind him. He was just over six feet tall and lanky. He had a full head of hair, grayish white like a seagull with yellow nicotine streaks, and it was combed forward, Julius Caesar style. His handsome angular face was deeply tanned and deeply lined, and when he smiled at me, he had two rows of perfect white teeth—or crowns—that shined like headlights from that tanning hide complexion.

"Jacob!" he called out. "Jacob Lassiter! At long last!"

Ringle was as ecstatic as if I were his long-lost brother, just rescued from a desert island. He extended a hand. We shook, vigorously, thanks to his enthusiasm. "I'm Dr. Maximilian Ringle. Call me Max."

"Call me Jake. Nice to meet you."

"Love your sweater! God, I wish I had your chest." He shot a look at Kip, who was taking his time joining us. "He's bigger than I imagined."

Kip moseyed my way, and I threw my arms around him and squeezed. His return hug was less enthusiastic, but it was still a hug. He still had a pair of purplish black eyes and scratches on his face from where the airbag had smacked him. "Kippers," I said. "I'm so damn happy to see you."

"Same here, Jake." A tone as formal as the evenly spaced rows of roses in the garden.

"We're drinking gin rickeys," Ringle said. "Perfect to slake your thirst, eh?"

"Slake," Kip said. "From the Old English 'slacian,' meaning 'to mitigate or moderate.'"

"Ha! There he goes," Ringle said. "Does he do that with you, Jake? I say a word, and the lad gives me its etymology."

"From the Greek," Kip said. "*Etumologia.*"

Ringle laughed, just delighted with his protégé or maybe his prodigy. I'm not as good with words as my nephew.

"I guess your word game has replaced Ten," I said.

Ringle raised his silvery eyebrows, as if asking a question, and Kip explained, "When I was a kid, Jake used to toss me a ball until I caught it ten times in a row."

"Ah so," Ringle said. "Must be that athletic training of yours, Jake. Mindless repetition, eh?"

"I'll have that gin now," I said.

Ringle gave a hand signal to the bartender, who caught it, though he was a good fifty feet away. The three of us sat in tasteful, cushioned outdoor furniture, Ringle giving me the best ocean view. After the bartender brought my first drink and their refills, I got right to the point. "I'm concerned about Kip."

"Why?" Ringle said. "Because some government scribblers making civil service salaries are sniffing around?" He dismissed that idea with a wave of his hand. "We're legitimate. Ninety percent of our business is no different than other college consulting firms."

"I'm betting it's that other ten percent the government is fussing about."

"Our only sin is making too much money." His perfect teeth gave me a high-beam smile. "You'd be astonished to learn how much some parents will pay to get their children into prestigious universities."

"Go ahead. Astonish me."

"Say you're a Chinese billionaire." Ringle swirled his glass, ice cubes clinking. "You own factories that sell to the West. You admire America, and you want your children to attend Harvard or Yale or Stanford. You come to us."

I sipped at my drink. "What would this billionaire pay?"

"Whatever I ask, and I'll tell you why. I've spent twenty years nourishing contacts at our finest universities. I've knocked on all the doors. The front door is the standard admission route. Apply blindly over the Internet, take your tests, and hope for the best. Good luck with that."

He flashed a look at Kip, who nodded his approval. They shared a disdain for those suckers lined up at the front door.

"Then there's the back door," Ringle said. "You have four generations of alumni in your family, and your grandfather gave a five-million dollar gift that bought a small structure on campus, a covered bicycle rack or a bus stop. Maybe that will get your kids in, and maybe it won't."

"Why do I think there's one more door?" I asked.

"The side door. It's where we enter, and we guarantee admission."

"How can you possibly do that?" I asked.

Ringle polished off his drink and whispered, "Trade secret."

Kip said, "The guarantee is why we can charge whatever the parents can afford."

"Which is?" I asked.

"Maybe for a family in Bakersfield, it's only $30,000 for résumé enhancement, essay preparation, and immersive test strategies. But for that billionaire Chinese family, they might happily pay five million."

I let out a long whistle. "I hope you throw in a Harvard sweatshirt with that." I finished my gin rickey, and before I put the glass on the table, the bartender delivered another, perfectly chilled and perfectly tart. "Let's follow that money," I said. "What happens to the five million?"

Ringle tapped his temple with an index finger whose nail was manicured and polished. "That information is locked in here."

A cool breeze stirred the rose bushes in the gardens below us and chilled the terrace. My $5,000 sweater kept me at room temperature, but I wondered how those shaved vicuñas made it through the winters in the Andes.

"What else would you like to know?" Ringle asked.

"I saw your game room and its fancy eGame consoles. Kip, are you blowing battleships out of the water these days?"

"Aw, jeez, Uncle Jake."

"Let me intervene," Ringle said. "Kip has told me that when he was younger, he overindulged."

"Let's not sugarcoat," I said. "He was addicted. It took over his life."

"Jake, I have a master's in social work and a Ph.D. in psychology. Before I founded Q.E.D., I was an addiction counselor to adolescents at a prominent rehab facility in Orange County. Alcohol, opioids, gambling. I don't believe Kip was addicted in the clinical sense. Still, bearing in mind your concerns, I've limited his time to three hours of play every other day. About the length of a football game, is it not?"

He had an answer for everything, I thought. Best not to underestimate the guy. He was such a slick con man, he could sell a boy's band to the rubes in River City.

"Let me tell you something else about your nephew," Ringle said. "He's a stand-up guy."

"Do you want to elaborate?"

"Kip told me about his problem in Atlantic City."

Whereas he made me give a blood oath of Omertà.

"He took the rap for that rich kid from Greenwich," Ringle continued. "Most young people would have caved. That told me I could trust Kip completely. That if I was loyal to him, he would be loyal to me, even when external forces applied extraordinary pressure. I know the FBI came to him and asked him to wear a wire, and he told them to shove it up their tight asses."

Both Ringle and Kip shared a laugh, nodding at each other inside their smooth hoodies. I felt left out of the party.

So bizarre. Wasn't it only yesterday I was teaching Kip how to field sharply hit ground balls without closing his eyes? Now, he had adopted a new coach. Someone wealthier, smarter, and more ambitious than his old Uncle Jake. A player in a world I knew nothing about.

Kip likely imagined a future where he would own an adjacent villa on that Grand Cayman beach. Meanwhile, stuffy old Uncle Jake figured they'd be sharing adjacent prison cells.

Through all the fog, a realization was dawning, an island peeking out of the mist. I had misjudged Kip. It went back to when he had taunted me with those hurtful words that kept surging back like a relentless incoming tide: *"Wake up, Jake! Survival of the fittest. Capitalism at work."*

I had thought he was merely echoing Max Ringle. But there was more to it. That was who Kip had become. Ringle had somehow found this innocent, brilliant waif and conned him into becoming his unethical and avaricious clone.

In the battle for Kip, I was being routed by the enemy. But the war had just begun.

CHAPTER TWENTY-THREE
The Golden Key

The three of us were still drinking gin rickeys, and the sun was performing its nightly trick of sinking toward the Pacific Ocean, streaking a thin band of clouds with shades of orange and purple. A uniformed catering crew was setting up platters of salmon and shrimp and iced mounds of caviar with various cheeses and fruits.

Lifestyles of the rich and infamous.

"Do you have any other questions about our little business?" Ringle's smile was a humble brag. He didn't mean "little" at all.

"These financial advisors you're wining and dining tonight. Your feeders. Do you pay them kickbacks for sending you clients?"

"'Kickbacks' is such an ugly word."

"So is 'prison,' but I still use it from time to time."

Ringle regarded me curiously. Just why was I pulling his chain? Simple. I yearned to provoke him. I wanted to see what was under that smooth veneer and cashmere hoodie. In my experience, when an adverse witness is angry with me, he's more likely to blurt out the truth.

"It's true, we pay the financial advisors consulting fees," he said. "If that's a breach of their fiduciary duties to their clients, it's not our concern."

"Max is expanding our Pacific Rim business," Kip added. "We're opening offices in Beijing and Taipei. Maybe Seoul, too."

"Our first step is totally immersive English language classes," Ringle said. "The Chinese students have the most difficulty with reading comprehension. Who can blame them? Can any of us speak Mandarin?"

Ringle and Kip shared a laugh over that. Oh, they were on the same page of the same script. Yeah, I was jealous, I'll admit it.

"The Chinese students are brilliant," Ringle said, "the best young minds anywhere. If we educate them here, think of the possibilities for better relations between our countries. They're the next generation of Chinese leaders."

"So, you're actually performing a public service."

"In part, certainly."

"If you're not indicted, maybe you'll get the Presidential Medal of Freedom."

Ringle studied me. "What makes you so cynical, Jake? All those years defending criminals?"

"Could be. In Florida, our main products are oranges and fraud. And maybe I'm always seeing the danger around every corner. But mostly, I'm worried about Kip."

"Then why don't you simply ask the question you've been dancing around?"

"When I examine a hostile witness, I don't begin by kicking him in the nuts. I start by complimenting his Loro Piana hoodie and maybe his Patek Philippe watch." I nodded toward his wrist. "Your stainless-steel Nautilus is more understated than the solid gold and probably keeps time just as well. Perfect accompaniment for your hoodie."

He nodded. "Now that the formalities are over, fire away."

I took a deep breath and exhaled. It was late afternoon, but with my abbreviated night's sleep, the coast-to-coast flight, and the time change, my energy was waning, and my head was pounding, drumsticks banging on tympani.

"Is Kip getting paid to take SAT and ACT exams for your clients?" I asked.

"You'll have to ask Kip. He's President of Personalized Test Enhancement, Incorporated. It's a separate division within Q.E.D."

"Separate division? What is this, General Motors?"

"My lawyers suggested a distinct corporate entity when Kip came up with the idea. The Golden Key, Kip called it. It unlocks that side door when all our more traditional methods fail."

"Let me guess," I said. "Kip is the sole officer and shareholder. You have no title and no salary. Your name doesn't appear in the corporate documents, and on the books, Kip gets all the revenue."

"He deserves it. It's his baby from A to Z. So clever, so deliciously devious. Kip is the brains of the operation, the mastermind. And he's paid accordingly."

"Max has been very generous," Kip said.

"And very insulated," I chimed in. "He's the Mafia don sipping espresso at the social club, blissfully unaware that the guys who drive his trucks are dumping bodies in the Meadowlands."

"Jesus, Jake!" Kip shot me an accusing look. "Why are you throwing shade? You're embarrassing me."

"All parents embarrass their kids. It's our job. It's how we protect you."

"You're an old burnout. Like that sheriff in *No Country for Old Men*. You just don't get it."

I processed that for a moment. Tommie Lee Jones played an aging sheriff who couldn't wrap his head around the extreme violence that had come to his doorstep. He planned to turn in his badge. What was it he said?

"I feel overmatched."

Okay, I can relate. I turned toward Ringle, my head clanging, cymbals now joining the drums. "Kip told me you were brilliant. And now I see why."

"I think he's brilliant, as well."

"Sure. Sure. We all know that. But Kip is young and reckless and hasn't learned the art of covering his ass. On the other hand, you, Max Ringle...you wear boxer shorts that are just like your wristwatch. Stainless steel."

CHAPTER TWENTY-FOUR
Sleeping with the Roses

There was simply no provoking the man. I had insulted Ringle to get a rise out of him. Instead of a heated reaction, he asked if I wanted another drink and would I like an early start on the buffet?

No and no.

"There are vegan options if you're like Kip and me," he said, pointedly.

I shook my head. They could have the sesame-ginger-tofu veggie stir-fry all to themselves. Still the gracious host, Ringle apologized for not being able to put me up for the night. The guest cottages were filled with the financial advisors who send him Chinese billionaires and Hollywood studio executives. I told him I'd seen a Motel 6 from the freeway and could backtrack and find it. He chuckled and said he'd taken the liberty of making a reservation for me at the new Miramar oceanfront hotel. A bungalow on the beach. Just sign for everything, Q.E.D. will pay for the room, which he casually mentioned was two thousand a night.

"Before you go," Ringle said, "what else do you want to know?"

"Those contacts at the fancy universities. What's the word you used? You 'nourished' them. What's that mean? Watered them like your roses down there?"

Ringle stood and turned toward the railing overlooking the perfect rows, each bush symmetrical. All those velvety reds. All those deep yellows, some with the high color of ripe peaches. And tiny, mini roses in a painter's palette of colors. The sea breeze carried their heady perfume across the terrace.

"It took two decades of trial and error to find the right people," Ringle said. "Coaches and admissions officers who aren't burdened by every rule and regulation, who see the good in our work. On a corporate balance sheet, those contacts would be priceless assets."

"Why do I think they actually have a price? And when some billionaire gives you five million bucks, a bundle goes to you, some to the university, and some to these well-fed assets."

"We earn our fees, and I make no apology for them. We enhance résumés, magnify extracurricular activities, maybe even exaggerate athletic prowess to get a leg up in admissions. Nothing illegal about that, is there?"

"I have no idea."

My headache was morphing into tinnitus with at least seventy-six trombones accompanying the drums as a marching band high-stepped inside my cranium.

"That's all I choose to say about my business," Ringle said. "However, I have no objection if Kip tells you about his business."

"His business."

As if there were a real boundary. I suspected the border between Kip's business and Ringle's company was more like the seashore. No clear delineation where the incoming tide ends and dry sand begins. But for legal purposes, there was an imaginary wall protecting Ringle and exposing Kip.

"Jake, you'll be proud of your nephew's accomplishments if you just ease up a little."

"I'll ease up when I'm confident he's not going to get indicted for tending your roses."

Ringle sighed and looked over the expanse of his property. A sunbaked man in his sixties wearing a straw hat was spraying the rose bushes from a hose, the mist rainbowing in the late afternoon sun.

"We have a computerized irrigation system that turns on when the ground is dry," Ringle said, "but Orlando insists on manually hosing the plants. He knows each bush individually and the moisture sensors do not. He pays such close attention that he knows every bud, every leaf, and every thorn. Do you follow me, Jake?"

"I think in your little fairy tale, Kip's a rose bush, you're the smart gardener, and I'm the guy who hauls manure. You think you're a better judge of Kip's needs."

"It is possible, is it not?"

"Please guys, don't fight," Kip pleaded. "It doesn't help anything."

Another easy smile from Ringle. "Quite so. Kip, please tell your uncle about your business. It's quite brilliant, albeit a bit complicated."

"I'll try to keep up," I said.

Kip shrugged his narrow shoulders and said, "I've devised two plans. One is to take the tests as an imposter, and the other is to monitor the tests as a proctor. For the first one, I make phony drivers' licenses and assume the identity of the student. That only works with the guys. For the girls, I bribe proctors to get in the door. That's only in a few cities, but I'm working on several more for next year."

It's way worse than I had thought, and my fears were bad enough.

Kip went into detail, and I caught most of what he said, though my eyes were squinted shut against the tinnitus that had taken on the timbre of pealing church bells. He told me that Q.E.D. paid a psychologist to write letters claiming that little Johnny and Susie had learning disabilities and needed extra time for their exams. That got them special rooms where Kip did his proctoring, correcting wrong answers and nailing the appropriate scores.

"That's the fun part," he said. "I do a side deal with the parents. They ask for a specific score, say 1490. If I come within five points, I get a $20,000 bonus. If I nail it, $30,000. It's like playing eGames again. Explosions. Battle music. The risk of annihilation. It's a rush."

A game? The kid thinks he's playing a game!

I turned to Ringle. "Kip told me you had an opinion of counsel saying this is legal."

"That's true. Los Angeles counsel, a deep-carpet firm. Expensive as hell."

"I need to see the opinion."

"Nothing to see. I had lunch with a senior partner at Sachs & Copeland and over appetizers at the Grill on the Alley, he told me that not every piece of fruit in the shade of the tree is a rotten apple."

"What the hell does that mean?" Ringle's bullshit was getting on my nerves, and I now figured the Ph.D. after his name stood for *Piled Higher and Deeper.*

"Not everything an overzealous prosecutor considers shady is necessarily a crime," Ringle said.

"That's not an opinion of counsel. That's a lawyer's small talk while sipping vichyssoise."

"It was tuna tartare, and if I may say so, Arthur Sachs is a much more distinguished lawyer than you. I take his word for it."

"An opinion of a counsel is a written document that lays out the facts, the law, and objective conclusions, and in very limited circumstances, it can be a defense to a crime if you've relied on it in good faith. And in my undistinguished opinion, what you got along with your tuna tartare was a pile of bullshit."

Ringle turned his attention back from his rose garden to the thorn in his side. Me, standing next to him at the railing. "Jake, you have a certain amount of street smarts, I'll grant you that."

"So what?"

"Are you comfortable in a courtroom?"

"Court is like the hammock in my backyard, except I fall asleep less often."

"When a trial turns against you, are you strong in the face of adversity?"

"I don't piss my pants when a judge holds me in contempt, if that's what you mean."

"I can always use a lawyer like you. How does a retainer of $200,000 sound?"

"Like a handsome bribe. Why would you need me?"

"Perhaps I never will. That's the purpose of a retainer is it not?"

"That, or to create attorney-client privilege for the conversation we just had, so I can't repeat it. And..."

It hit me then, a wicked punch to the gut that nearly took my breath away. How had I not seen it before? Was I already brain-dead, as Shari Ringle said?

"And what, Jake?" Ringle's expression was as composed as if sitting cross-legged in his yoga class. "Please continue."

"And when Kip is indicted, I'd be conflicted out of representing him because I'd be your lawyer!" I turned and jabbed Ringle's chest with an index finger. "You son of a bitch! The feds nailed you, didn't they?"

His face was placid, a toothy smile in place. "What in heaven's name are you talking about, Jake?"

"What is it? Income tax evasion? Mail fraud? Racketeering?" I could feel my face heating up, could hear my voice booming.

"Jake, you're acting weird," Kip said.

"Don't you see it, kiddo? He's flipped. On you!"

Ringle didn't flinch. His voice remained hardly more than a whisper. "Jake, consider your own analogy about the Mafia don. The feds didn't get John Gotti to flip on his capos. It was the other way around. They wanted Kip to get to me, not vice versa."

"They tried that and left empty-handed. What a stand-up guy, you said. But when Kip turned them down, the feds got the goods on you without his help. You're saving your own worthless hide by selling out my nephew."

From somewhere on the property, a leaf blower whined. I strained to hear Ringle, *sotto voce*, over my tinnitus and the lawn machinery.

"I would never do that," he said. "Though, to be sure, the only conduct that could arguably be considered criminal was committed by Kip. That's what my lawyer told me over dessert. Irish coffee and fudge brownie pie. Did I not mention that?"

That struck my ear like an off-key piano chord. So contradictory and so artificial, discordant and jarring. Something Ringle wanted on the record to exonerate himself and implicate Kip. My addled brain played back the conversation of the last several minutes.

"You'll have to ask Kip. He's President of Personalized Test Enhancement, Incorporated."

And...

"It's his baby from A to Z. Frankly, I'd never even thought of it. No, Kip's the brains of the operation, the mastermind."

And then Kip's admissions...

"I've devised two plans. One is to take the tests as an imposter..."

And...

"I make phony drivers' licenses and assume the identity of student..."

And...

I bribe proctors to get in the door..."

It was all there. How did I miss it? Are my brain synapses firing blanks?

I stuck my face close to Ringle's, nose to nose. "You worthless piece of slimy whale shit! You're wearing a wire right now! You're teasing a confession out of my nephew!"

"Absurd."

I grabbed each end of his red scarf and yanked hard, tightening the silk into a ligature. He brought both hands to his neck and pulled at my fingers, but he wasn't strong enough. I yanked harder and from behind me, heard Kip shriek, a not-very-manly cry. When Ringle's eyes began to bulge and he started making gurgling sounds, I let go. He coughed and hacked, and I grabbed the collar of his hoodie, lifted him off his feet, and shook him like a sack of potatoes. I yanked downward, and my big mitts ripped the cashmere down the front, the fabric hissing like an angry cat. I pulled the shredded hoodie over his head, then frisked him, patting his armpits, turning him around, checking his back, then yanking down his jeans.

"You've gone insane!" Ringle sputtered, helpless in my grip.

"Jesus, Jake! Stop!" Poor Kip, eyes wide, jaw slack, maybe on the verge of tears.

Ringle tried to wriggle free, so I braced my right forearm against his Adam's apple. With my left hand, I patted his groin, found no extra parts, then checked his butt. No mic, no transmitter, no recording device.

Shit.

I heard footsteps behind me. I turned in time to see Lance, his suit coat unbuttoned, coattails flapping as he ran toward me. I released Ringle, spread my legs to shoulder width, and bent my knees, bouncing on my toes, ready to ward off any blow and deliver my own.

When he was six feet away, Lance launched himself, spun in the air, a wondrous 180 degrees, and executed a picture-perfect flying back kick.

Damn, I hate karate.

Maybe ten years ago, I could have sidestepped in time. But on this day, his speed and timing and momentum were too fast for me. His front foot landed like a cannon blast high on my chest. It knocked me backward into the railing. I bounced off in time to see Lance land, cat-like, on his feet and throw a straight right fist that caught me on the jaw. I tumbled over the railing, flailing, plunging into a bush of apricot-colored mini roses. I neither smelled the flowers' sweetness nor felt their thorns, and I was unconscious before I hit the ground.

CHAPTER TWENTY-FIVE
The House of Wisdom Has Bugs

My dream was a casserole, a mishmash of mismatched ingredients.

Kip was yelling at me. Angry. I couldn't hear the words.

A woman was laughing at me. Who could that be? She might have been naked. Women in my dreams tend to be.

I heard music and singing. *"We're ever true to you, dear old white and blue."*

Wait. That's the Penn State fight song, about a hundred years old, pretty much the way I felt. It was my cell phone ringing. I fumbled through a tangle of sheets and found the damn thing.

I tried to say "hello," but mostly I just coughed and cleared my throat of phlegm.

"Jake, is that you?" Melissa's voice.

"I think so."

"Where are you?"

I considered the altogether reasonable question as I looked around the room. The ocean was visible outside a window, and the room seemed to sway. "I think I'm on a boat."

"Really? Pleasure cruise?"

From outside, I heard the unmistakable clamor of a railroad train along with its piercing whistle. It might have been my imagination, but the room seemed to shudder.

"Hold on, Melissa. It's possible I'm in a sleeper car on a train."

I examined the nightstand, which had promotional material for the Miramar Resort. An aerial shot showed railroad tracks running just behind oceanfront bungalows. "I think I'm in a hotel that costs two grand a night and has a locomotive running through the lobby."

"I hope your Mastercard isn't maxed out."

My head was beginning to clear and, oddly enough, didn't hurt, though the decibel range of my tinnitus neared triple digits. "Max Ringle promised to pay the hotel tab, but that was before I ripped his clothes off and choked him with his stupid scarf."

"Sounds like an adventure. Did you have fun last night?"

"Not so much. Why?"

"Check your email."

It took me a moment because an iPhone is not designed for an oversize thumb, especially one that got jammed in another guy's face mask and fractured at the first knuckle. In a moment, I managed to pull up an email that had been sent from my iPhone to both Melissa and me. The subject line read "Wrong-Way Lassiter." There was no text in the body. Only a photo.

Yours truly in bed. Eyes closed. Mouth open. Face scratched raw.

Oh, I failed to mention something. In the photo, my head rested comfortably between two bare breasts. Not large breasts. Not small breasts. Just a dandy matching pair of perky breasts that showed suntan lines stopping slightly above and below the nipples. The kind of tan a woman would get if she's wearing a bikini. The woman's face was not visible.

Applying the powers of reasoning that made Sherlock Holmes legendary, I said, "I think that's Shari Ringle, daughter of Max, object of Kip's affections, and a proud USC Trojan who hates school."

"I was glad to get the picture. When you didn't call, I thought you'd been kidnapped, and first thing in the morning, here's proof of life, though not much life."

"Look, I know that you know that I wouldn't..."

"Oh, stop, Jake. Of course I know. Your loyalty is your primary personality trait."

"Really?"

"Part of your charm is you don't realize that what you do naturally, without even thinking, is so honorable. And that starts with your loyalty to friends, to family, to me."

"Tell that to Kip."

"He knows it. Deep inside, he knows." She was quiet for a moment. "Where is he now?

"I assume with his new mentor, a guy so twisted he could stand in the shadow of a corkscrew. And Kip doesn't see it. The kid may be brilliant, but he has no street smarts. That's what I failed to teach him."

"C'mon, Jake. You don't teach street smarts. You learn them in the streets. Give him time."

"He doesn't have time. There's a freight train coming, and he's tied to the tracks." Doubtless, I was thinking about this posh hotel with its choo-choo trains.

"Tell me about yesterday."

I told her everything, from the gin rickeys to Ringle's perfidy, to getting kicked by a mule and plummeting ass-over-elbows into thorny rose bushes. And while I had no memory of it, I assumed that Lance the karate champ had trundled me down the hill to the hotel for my snooze and photo shoot.

"So, you strip searched your host but didn't find a wire." She had just a touch of disapproval in her voice.

"I wasn't thinking clearly. Now I see it. He didn't have to wear a wire. It's his house. *Casa de la Sabuduría.*"

"House of Wisdom? Oh, brother."

"Ringle wasn't wearing a wire under his cashmere hoodie because he let the FBI bug his house."

"You're sure?"

I propped myself onto one elbow but wasn't quite able to get out of bed. "I'm betting the terrace has three mics and two cameras. Everything Kip said was recorded and filmed. And believe me, he made admissions against interest that any judge would let into evidence."

"And you know the place was wired, how?"

"I just know it! Ringle was playing for an audience, and that means the FBI and Justice department prosecutors. Kip's going to get indicted, and the government is going to play the tape, and..."

"And...?"

"There's no way I can win the case."

I fell back onto the bed, still feeling last night's gin and maybe the kick, too. Melissa was quiet a moment, and I knew she was trying to figure a way to say something I wouldn't like, but in a manner that was caring and loving.

"Jake, you know that one symptom of C.T.E. is paranoia, right?"

"Right. And irritability. That's a big one."

"I just wonder," she said, softly and sweetly, "if given a framework of several possible explanations, your mind is pushing you to go for the most hurtful and injurious. Kip develops a closeness with his boss, and you feel abandoned and betrayed. The man's business is under investigation, and you leap to the conclusion that Kip is a target. Then, based on your assessment of the way Ringle spoke, you're certain he knew he was being recorded, but it turns out he wasn't wearing a wire. Finally, you believe the government wants Ringle, the boss, to testify against Kip, his employee, when logic and experience dictate that the opposite would be true."

"Dammit, Mel!" I boomed through the phone, proving my point about irritability. "You weren't there! And frankly, you don't have the background for this. I don't tell you how to test neurons or whatever the hell it is. And you can't tell me how to read a room, how to tell when someone is lying or posturing or setting me up. I've cross examined Hall of Fame liars for so long I can smell the stink of perjury from across the room, and yesterday it smelled like Max Ringle's roses."

"Well there," she said, just as sweetly and softly, "someone woke up on the wrong side of a couple tits this morning."

I let out a long, sad regretful sigh. "I'm sorry. That was...I don't know...really shitty of me. I'm not sure why I said that."

"Apology accepted. Now what?"

So quick to forgive, I thought. There I was, taking out my frustration and anger on the one person in the world who gave me unconditional love. Maybe it was the brain damage, or maybe that was a handy excuse, and I was just a total asshole. I remembered Granny's advice to Melissa: *"You're way too good for the rapscallion, and I oughta know. I raised him from a pup."*

I reached for the pitcher of water on the nightstand. That's when I saw the handwritten note on hotel stationery. It was on the floor next to the bed.

Jake,
Stay out of my life.
Kip.

I read the note to Melissa, my eyes filling with tears, my throat constricted as if being strangled. I could barely get the words out. "It's over, Mel. Kip's gone."

"You're caught in the moment, Jake, and can't see beyond it. Kip's not gone. Not forever, anyway. But if your instincts are right about the trouble he's in, he needs you more than ever, both as his parent and as his defender, and there's no one on earth who can do either one as well as you."

CHAPTER TWENTY-SIX
An Ear to the Keyhole

An hour later, disregarding Kip's instructions, I called the 805 number that appeared on my cell when he reached me on the 101. Once, twice, three times. Voice mail, each time. No return calls.

Later that day, numbed by the sense of loss, fearful of Kip's uncertain future, I drove to LAX and caught the redeye back to Miami. I rolled into the house just as Melissa was leaving for the hospital. Before heading out the door, she examined a bruise the color of a ripe eggplant on my chest where Lance had mule-kicked me. She gently rubbed some cannabis balm on the bruise. I don't know if the fragrant ointment helped the healing process, but it felt good to be touched. Melissa's fingers lingered on my skin. She understood my pain was more than skin-deep.

Life returned to a sort of artificial normalcy. I went to work at the Bar office, came home, ate dinner, made love to Melissa. Hanging over my head were storm clouds that neither gave way to rain nor cleared to a sunshiny day. A sense of foreboding pervaded every activity. Where was Kip? What disaster lay ahead for him?

On my third day back, I cooked thick ribeye steaks on the grill in the backyard, and we sat on the porch in the humid evening, eating and swatting mosquitoes. I was drinking a Grolsch beer while Melissa sipped at her Chardonnay.

"Any news from N.I.H. about the C.T.E. program?" I asked.

She shook her head. "Like they say in those war movies, it's quiet out there. Too quiet."

I gave her a sheepish look. "Well, I made a couple calls."

"Oh, no Jake. You didn't."

"Very discreet. I'm still friends with the old Dolphins' team physician. Back in the day, he sat on the NFL's Health and Safety Committee. I called him, and he called a colleague at Yale Medical School who's on the league's Head, Neck and Spine Committee. You were right about team owners trying to blackball you. They're backing a Dr. Jason Jeffries to run the program."

She shrugged. "I've never heard of him."

"Jeffries is a nonpracticing M.D. who's also a biomechanical engineer. He was deputy director of the helmet safety study the league did a couple years ago." I popped the porcelain top on a second bottle of Grolsch. "The NFL praised his research and banned a dozen brands of helmets."

Melissa scowled, a look almost foreign to her. Even at rest, her face always seemed to be smiling. I knew she was peeved, something else that was unusual for someone so even-tempered.

"Helmets neither cause concussions nor prevent them," she said. "Even helmeted, on impact, the brain slides around like a bowl of Jell-O, twisting and stretching until it smacks into the corpus callosum."

"I know that, other than the corpus coliseum stuff."

"Corpus *callosum*. It connects the two sides of the brain. That's what gets poisoned by the tau proteins of C.T.E." She drained her wine in one swallow. "The study should be run by a neurologist or neurosurgeon. It shouldn't be focused on the engineering of helmets."

I thought that over for a moment. "What's puzzling is that Jeffries has been pushing for higher tech helmets in a way that's overtly critical of NFL safety procedures. So, what sense does it make that you get blackballed because I have a big mouth, but the league turns to this guy, who's also a critic of the league?"

"I have no idea," she said, "but if I know you, you'll find out."

"I'll drink to that." And I did, with a cool swig of the Dutch lager. I made a mental note to look deeper into Dr. Jeffries' background.

She poured herself another glass of Chardonnay. "You're so caught up in Kip's problems and mine, there's something you haven't asked."

I shrugged. My mind was blank.

"Your PET scan, big guy!" she exclaimed.

"I'd forgotten. Completely slipped my ailing mind."

She got down to business. "The scan has been analyzed by three different radiological teams. Ours and the top people at Boston University and UCLA. For the first time, we have a mathematical configuration of the tau proteins in your brain."

She'd already explained the procedure to me in a lecture that might be called "Brain Scans for Dummies." A synthetic molecule called a ligand is used to bind together with tangles of tau protein, the nasty indicator of C.T.E. The scan then quantifies the amount of the protein in order to determine if the levels are abnormal.

"As we suspected, your tau proteins are substantially higher than those in the control group, the non-football players. As for former NFL players, you're almost exactly at the median. As we might expect, the study shows that players with longer careers have larger buildups of the tau."

"So, getting cut by the Dolphins in my prime was a benefit," I said, cheerfully.

When we met, I had told Melissa that my so-called football career consisted mostly of playing on special teams.

"What makes them so special?" she had asked.

"Kickoffs and punts are the only plays where there's a head-on collision at full speed. Which is doubtless why they're also called the suicide squads."

Strangely enough, I loved those hits, the ones you feel in your teeth, the vibrations down the spine. After my unspectacular career, I attended law school at the University of Miami, night division, and hit the books as hard as I ever smacked a fleet-footed punt returner. I had to work my butt off, or I would have flunked out.

Unfortunately, they don't give honors for graduating in the top half of the bottom third of the class. I passed the Bar exam on my fourth try, and the rest, as they say, is history. Or maybe a mystery.

Now, Melissa told me that the new PET-scan gave us a baseline measurement to use as a marker to determine if we're making any progress. Or the opposite.

"It's a perfect time to begin AY-70 treatments." She used the project's bland abbreviation, rather than saying, "to begin the new, experimental, untested protein antibodies that may either help you or turn your cerebrum to oatmeal."

"I know I'm in good hands. Thanks, Melissa." No way would I express the skepticism I was feeling.

☙

Melissa went back to studying test results of patients to whom she was not engaged, and I went back to the Florida Bar office, looking for shady lawyers to prosecute. My email inbox was filled with junk, including entreaties by women from Slovenia who claimed to be young, attractive and available for travel. The snail mail brought a signed order from Judge Gridley, as promised, recommending a public reprimand for Bert Kincaid and his priapic pecker. Later that day, Kincaid popped into my office, unannounced and uninvited. He brought along his brother-in-law, Dr. Eisenberg, the shrink.

They took seats in front of my desk, and Kincaid asked, "Are you going to seek a stiffer penalty?"

"Pun intended, Bert?"

"Aw, just tell me, Jake."

I told him I was fine with the judge's order, and a scolding in Tallahassee should be the end of it.

"Thanks, man! You might have saved my marriage. I had a good talk with Audrey, and I'm not fooling around anymore, no matter how much my lady clients might want it."

"Your self-restraint is a model for us all," I said.

Dr. Eisenberg cleared his throat and stroked his goatee. "I want to apologize, Mr. Lassiter for my diagnosis of sexual addiction." He grimaced at his own words. "I was just trying to help out Bert and Audrey, and there was no basis for..."

"Hey, no apology needed. Family. I get that. In a way, I respect it."

The shrink looked relieved. "Well then, back to my pediatric patients."

He stood to leave. "Hang on a second, Doc," I said. "Can I talk to you about my nephew?"

❧

In the evenings, back in our coral rock love nest, Melissa and I would cook dinner together and share the goings-on of each of our days. Just like old married folks. I told her about the new Bar files that crossed my desk. A favorite was the lawyer who scooted around town in an electric wheelchair, suing restaurants for noncompliance with handicapped access laws, while he was, in fact, a prize-winning marathon runner.

Over dinner one night, Melissa told me about new research involving photobiomodulation, a twenty-five cent word doctors use when a nickel will do. That's red-light therapy meant to regenerate brain cells. Yet another new study showed that there may be a genetic variation that protects some players' brains from C.T.E. damage. No way to tell if I had it, or even if that was a valid theory.

Meanwhile, every three days, I dropped my trousers and Melissa injected AY-70, the new protein antibodies that might cure me or kill me. One evening, as we sat on the back porch sipping vodka and grapefruit juice, I told Melissa about my conversation with Dr. Eisenberg. He said that Kip had adopted a "second family." That's a term shrinks use when an adolescent drifts away from his parents and into the clutches of his peer group. With Kip, the second family was a combination of Shari Ringle's squad of rich kids and her megalomaniac father.

On my visit to California, Shari had told me that Kip was a "clout chaser" who wanted to be part of her "fam," which I took to mean her family. Dr. Eisenberg, better versed in hipster lingo, said the term referred to her closest friends, but like a lot of slang, it had multiple meanings. It could also mean the Ringle family unit. Who can keep up with this stuff?

"What did he suggest about how you get Kip back?" Melissa asked.

"To do anything, I have to get Kip to talk to me. Then, the shrink says to reason with him and avoid outrage and moralizing sermons. When possible, express empathy for the values of the second family, which sure as hell doesn't work when they're a crime family."

Disregarding Kip's instructions several more times, I continued calling the 805 number that I'd memorized by now. Always straight to voice mail. His business tone. "This is Kip Lassiter, president of Personalized Test Enhancement. Please leave a message."

I asked the machine to call me back. So far, nothing but silence, and my fears for Kip continued to grow.

I was in my office a few days after that, reviewing the case of a lawyer who stole money he was supposed to use to pay a client's overdue real estate taxes, but instead bought the property through a tax lien. Just another of my brethren who thought his Bar membership was a license to steal. When the phone rang, I hoped it was Kip. In my fantasy, my nephew said how sorry he was, and let's get our relationship back on track.

Instead, it was State Attorney Ray Pincher. "Jake, I've got Gilberto Foyo snooping around the federal building, his ear to the keyhole."

"Yeah?"

"Grand jury's been in session a couple weeks. I've got nothing official. But Jake, old friend, the sky is darkened with gloom, and there's a shitstorm headed your nephew's way."

CHAPTER TWENTY-SEVEN
Con Air

Pincher had no details for me. Just rumors of indictments in a so-called nationwide college admissions bribery scandal. That night I slept restlessly, dreaming of a long-ago football game in Buffalo, a frigid rain turning to sleet. I tried to tackle a kickoff returner and slid past him with all the grace of a rhinoceros on ice skates.

My cell rang at 2:33 a.m. I tumbled out of bed and grabbed the phone. Melissa stirred, rolled over, and returned to the peaceful, untroubled slumber of the innocent and carefree.

When I saw "U.S. Marshals Service" on caller I.D., I knew who was calling. The shred of good news was that Kip was reaching out to me instead of some mouthpiece provided by Max Ringle. The bad news, of course, was that Kip was in custody.

"Where are you?" I asked, without preamble. I repressed my pain—the feeling of my heart being cleaved from my chest—in order to help the boy I loved.

"I don't know." His voice trembled. "Two FBI agents put me in a car, and I was so stressed I don't even know which direction we went. But then I was put on a bus with no windows with maybe thirty other guys. And now we're at an Air Force base. There are guys in military uniforms with rifles. We're in this Quonset hut, and I'm handcuffed with a chain around my waist. Uncle Jake, I'm so scared I peed my pants on the bus, and this guy with a teardrop tattoo says, 'Wussy make a pee pee.' Now, half a dozen guys are calling me 'wussy.'"

"I need you to stay calm, Kip. And don't say anything to anybody, except the marshals, and then only, 'Sir, may I use the toilet?' Got it?"

"You gotta help me, Uncle Jake. I don't know how I'm gonna get through this."

"I'm here for you," I said. "They'll be flying you out on Con Air." I used the colloquial term for the government's airline, the Justice Prisoner and Alien Transportation System. "The plane will make some stops between California and Florida to pick up and leave off prisoners. When you get to Miami, you'll have an initial court appearance in front of a magistrate, and I'll be there. You get all that?"

"Yeah, I guess."

"Focus on that for the next 24 or 48 hours. You'll see me the moment they bring you into court before a magistrate. I'll get you bail and out of those shackles, and you'll come home with me. You'll shower and shave and have good meal. Are you with me, Kip?"

"Uncle Jake, I'm sorry."

"No time for that now. They're gonna take that phone away from you, so just remember everything I said."

"Okay."

"They didn't arrest Max," Kip blurted out.

Of course not. I'd been right about who would turn on whom.

"We were in his house, and these FBI agents walked into the room," he continued. "They didn't break in. They were...like there already. Max points at me and says, 'That's him.' So icy cold. 'That's him.'"

Kip's voice was filled with hurt. I had warned him about Ringle, but he wouldn't listen. Now, I tried to stifle my anger, not at Ringle, but at my nephew for being so trusting of his boss and so dismissive of me.

Then, Kip said it one more time, with wonder that he could have been so blatantly betrayed. "'That's him.' I couldn't believe it, Uncle Jake."

I knew we would hear the words again. Max Ringle would be on the witness stand and the prosecutor would ask who came up with this nefarious scheme. "That's him," Ringle would say, pointing toward the defense table.

But by then, I would be ready to cross-examine the bastard. And cross him, I would. I would cross him from here to hell.

At the same time, even without reading the indictment, I knew the struggle we faced. Not only would Ringle be on the government's side of the courtroom, but so would many of his clients who would have scrambled like rats off the sinking ship Q.E.D.

Just how would I keep Kip out of prison? The enormity of that task weighed a ton, and I felt like an ant carrying a boulder uphill. I tell my clients that no case is impossible if your cause is just. Even if Kip were factually innocent—and my gut told me he was not—the government's arsenal had me outgunned.

I have long thought that the federal government is a ponderous battleship, weighted down by its own armor and slow to change course. But when it chooses to marshal its might against an individual, the government is a lean, mean, conviction machine. Meanwhile, the defendant's lawyer is a loinclothed Roman gladiator protected by a wooden shield, leather shin guards, and prayers to the god Jupiter. The Constitution promises due process but not a fair fight.

As much as we prize our commitment to the individual and pay lip service to the presumption of innocence, it's the government's courthouse, the government's prosecutor, and the government's judge. Every time you go to trial, you are the Miami Dolphins playing an away game against the Patriots in a January blizzard.

"Is it going to be all right, Uncle Jake?" Kip asked, his voice a whisper.

"Everything I've learned my whole life I will devote to you, Kip. I'll use every experience I've ever had, in and out of court, to defend you."

In my heart, I knew every word was true.

"And hear this, Kip Lassiter. I'm gonna win. I'm gonna beat the United States of America and walk you out of the courthouse a free man, and you'll start your life anew."

My heart also knew that I had just told a lie.

Justice Department Charges 53 in
Nationwide College Admissions Scandal

By Luisa Gomez
Herald Reporter

Miami, FL—Federal prosecutors today charged 53 people in an audacious scheme to buy admissions slots at the nation's most prestigious universities.

Dubbed "Operation Flunk Out," the investigation uncovered bribes disguised as charitable donations, some involving millions of dollars, paid by wealthy parents to secure college admissions for their children. The scheme included falsifying résumés to create fraudulent athletic profiles, bribing coaches who had access to slots in the admissions process, and most brazenly, paying a "ringer" to either take SAT and ACT exams or change incorrect answers to correct ones.

Among those charged today with mail fraud and money laundering were two Hollywood actresses, a billionaire real estate developer, the head of a New York hedge fund, a tech company founder, and various physicians, lawyers, and prominent businessmen.

"We have dismantled the most widespread and insidious college admissions scandal in history," U.S. Attorney Juan Lucayo said in a news conference. "Parents of some of our most privileged students purchased spots for their children at top universities, cheating both the system and honest, hard-working students out of the college education they sought and deserved."

Dr. Maximilian Ringle, 54, of Montecito, CA, who holds a Ph.D. in psychology from UCLA, was named as mastermind of the scheme. Sources indicated that Ringle has been cooperating with the investigation for several months and will likely receive a greatly reduced sentence. Also named was Chester (Kip) Lassiter, 20, of Miami, described by the U.S. Attorney as Ringle's partner and the "ringleader of the scheme's fraudulent test-taking branch." Lassiter is charged with multiple instances of either posing as a high school student taking the exam or working as a proctor and changing students' answers. He is believed to be facing the most serious prison time of those involved.

CHAPTER TWENTY-EIGHT
Operation Flunk Out

Eight days later...

Walking from the parking lot to meet the Assistant U.S. Attorney, there was only one word on my mind: pretrial release.

Wait, that's two words. The one word is "bail."

It would be months before the case came to trial. Today, nothing was more important than getting Kip out of jail.

I had called A.U.S.A. Margaret Bolden, the lead prosecutor, and she told me to meet her at a coffee shop on Miami Avenue half an hour before the hearing. I guess she didn't want to invite me to her office, where there'd be a triangular wall display of photos: Ringle and Kip at the top, then the parents and kids and coaches and proctors, all connected by red Magic Marker, as if they were an organized crime family.

I had yet to see Kip. Con Air did not deliver him within the day or two I had predicted. My inexperience with the federal court system was already showing, and we hadn't even gotten to court. There had been four layovers—Minneapolis, St. Louis, Bangor, and Little Rock—and the aircraft took eight days to reach Miami. From what I could ascertain, there were no onboard movies or miniature bottles of Jack Daniels.

My agonizing eight-day wait was interrupted by the unsealing of indictments. The story, meanwhile, hit the news media with a tsunami of coverage, a frenzy of news, opinions, and lectures on morality. From the bold-face newspaper headlines, breathless television coverage, nasty Twitter storms, and frantic social media posts, you would have thought Allied forces had just landed on Normandy. But this wasn't "Operation Overlord." This was "Operation Flunk Out." Yeah, the government is into branding as much as Gwyneth Paltrow and her lifestyle business, "Goop."

I read all the indictments and every transcript of the taped conversations in which Ringle wrangled admissions from his customers. Some of the colloquies with the filthy rich parents were doozies. "Just so we're clear, Max," a tech company founder said, "You guarantee Yale for my eight hundred grand, right?" Ringle allowed as how that was the deal. "Man, ain't it great being rich?" his client mused. "And don't I feel sorry for those poor slobs who can't work the system? Nope! I do not." Guffaws of laughter from both men.

Reading Kip's indictment wasn't as bad as say, someone driving knitting needles into my eyeballs. Let's just call it heartbreaking.

"United States of America vs. Chester Lassiter aka Kip Lassiter."

If this were a boxing match, it was all fifty states in one corner and my nephew in the other. Three-hundred-thirty-million people against one kid.

The indictment contained 193 numbered paragraphs and 37 counts: 18 of mail fraud, 18 of racketeering, and one for alleged money laundering. Yeah, State Attorney Pincher had guessed right. Only Kip hadn't written lies on postcards from Hawaii. He had taken the standardized tests or corrected wrong answers eighteen times.

I felt physical pain, each allegation a shard of glass jammed into my gut. Sure, I knew what Kip had done after the melee in Montecito where I had landed face down in the rose bushes. But seeing it all spelled out in black and white, paragraph after numbered paragraph, made me woozy, as if from loss of blood.

The indictment laid out all the instances of fraudulent test-taking by place, date, and test score. On taped phone calls with Ringle, Kip discussed his actions in carefree tones. "Yo Max, I can't just go thirty percent higher on the total score for the Martelle kid. I gotta break it down between math and verbal, so one doesn't stick out and raise a red flag."

Ringle secretly had already pled guilty to four counts of mail fraud, money laundering, conspiracy, and racketeering. Judging from the actual extent of his frauds and the millions of dollars that passed through his hands, those pleas represented only a tiny fraction of the crimes he had committed. But that's the advantage of being first in the sprint to the courthouse.

I found Margaret Bolden standing outside the coffee shop, holding two cups. "I hope you like it black," she said, handing me one.

"Thanks. That's the first time a prosecutor has given me anything but a raw deal."

"I thought we'd start out on the right foot."

"I mentioned your name to Ray Pincher. He says you know each other from church. Says you're a straight shooter, meaning you won't lie to me, but if you fire your weapon, it'll be to kill and not wound."

She smiled and said, "I can live with that."

We headed toward the courthouse. Margaret was a petite African American woman in her late forties. She wore a charcoal gray pinstriped business suit and a white silk blouse, the home uniform for female prosecutors on the *Miami Federales*. Recently, she'd been in the news for winning a month-long trial, convicting a dozen members of a ring of car thieves who shipped their bounty on freighters down the Miami River to the ocean and the Caribbean islands beyond.

Because I'm never in federal court and she's never in state court, we hadn't met. Ray had told me that she played the old game of iron fist in a velvet glove. She spoke softly in court, a ploy to make the jurors pay attention by straining to hear her. That was her shtick, along with being an even five feet tall, so that when a lummox like me towered over her, she seemed so defenseless that the jurors wanted to protect her. Then, when she chose to change the equation, she'd raise her voice. The flute player became a full brass band, her volume startling jurors and opposing counsel alike.

"I know why you're treating me to coffee," I said.

"Go ahead, take a shot at it."

"You feel guilty. You went after Max Ringle, Mr. Big, but you ended up flipping Mr. Big on a dozen Mr. Littles. Or in this case, roughly fifty Mr. and Ms. Littles and one Kip Lassiter."

We stopped at a "Don't Walk" sign at the Fourth Street intersection, and she said, "The FBI went to your nephew first. He turned them down and rather rudely. That was a big mistake, doubtless made without your advice. His second mistake was telling Ringle about the FBI's approach."

"A kid. He didn't know any better."

"He blew the lid off the investigation and pissed off the Bureau and my bosses as well."

We crossed the street, and I said, "Let me guess. Knowing he was in the crosshairs, Ringle had one of his fancy lawyers call the Justice Department. He could nail all those rich parents. That would make for an even better press conference than just prosecuting him, an unknown grifter. Oh, he'd also turn on this kid who worked for him. His 'partner,' according to your bosses, so it wouldn't seem as if they were letting all the big fish skate."

"It's an imperfect system, I'll grant you that," she admitted.

"Still the best gosh-darned legal system in the world, with the possible exception of trial by combat. Thirty-seven counts? Don't you think that's overkill?"

"Once it goes over a dozen, does it really matter?"

We walked up the steps of the courthouse, ready to be scanned for contraband. "Before we go in," I said, "I want to talk to you about bail."

"I'm sure you do." She gave me a sad smile. "Unfortunately, my instructions are to vigorously oppose your motion."

"Vigorously? Really?"

"This motion and any others. Those are my marching orders."

Marching orders.

I pictured an Army regiment heading toward me. Marching troops, rolling Jeeps, heavy armor. I furiously dug a foxhole for Kip and placed my body over his in a pathetic attempt to protect him, moments before we were both crushed into dust.

CHAPTER TWENTY-NINE
Brain Matters

Melissa Gold...

At about the time Jake and Margaret Bolden walked into the courtroom, Melissa sat at her desk in the medical complex reviewing the PET scans of the subjects in her new study. Mostly former NFL players, but a smattering of former hockey players and soldiers who'd been too close to IED's when they exploded.

She had told Jake the truth about his condition, but not exactly the whole truth and nothing but the truth. Yes, his build-up of tau proteins was in the median range of those tested. But, in fact, everyone tested had symptoms of brain disease tentatively diagnosed as C.T.E. To be in the middle of that pack was akin to being in a herd of bison galloping full speed toward a cliff. Without a cure, their fall was certain and fatal.

All subjects in the study were taking the experimental AY-70 protein antibodies. Would these curb the growth or reverse the process that had created the deadly tau proteins? It would be months or even years before there would be conclusive results.

Her research needed to yield novel therapies and eventually a cure. Lately, Melissa and her colleagues were looking at re-purposing a leukemia drug known to clean toxic proteins from the brain. It would take government approvals and a substantial grant to try it out.

So much waiting, so many delays, so much frustration.

She'd learned today that her proposed study at the National Institutes of Health was still alive but being slow-walked through Congress thanks to NFL interference. No word yet whether the League had succeeded in cutting her from the team or whether she still had a shot at running the program. Jake was making inquiries about her competitor for the job, the "helmet guy," as he called Dr. Jeffries, the biomechanical engineer. But there, too, no news.

She'd been closely watching Jake for outward manifestations of his brain disease. There had been some bouts of confusion. He'd be thinking of one movie, say *The Godfather*, and say another, *Goodfellas*. He'd misuse words, saying "Interstellar Waterway" when he meant "Intracoastal Waterway." And he'd fumble with the remote, yelling at the TV screen when he forgot the channel number for ESPN, something he knew as well as his own birthday.

His irritability and verbal outbursts also had been increasing. Mostly cursing at other drivers on I-95 and getting angry when discussing Kip and Max Ringle. But he never lost his temper with her. She tried to process that, concluding that whatever mechanism controlled his emotions was tuned to its highest frequency with her.

Melissa called two of her girlfriends who knew Jake longer than she did. Both Victoria Lord and Paulette Pincher-Popkin were hesitant to say anything. Victoria admired Jake, who, after all, had defended her lover, now husband, Steve Solomon, in a murder trial.

"Mostly he seems fine," Victoria said, "but there are moments when he just seems to zone out. You can see his eyes drift off."

Paulette, whose medical skills Melissa respected, said she hadn't spent enough time with Jake recently to answer the question. "But my father thinks it's a mistake for him to defend his nephew. Too much pressure."

Solomon and Lord had the same advice and had offered help as co-counsel.

"I'd rather fly solo," Jake told her. "Just Kip and me at the defense table, Kip looking like a kid, me a little ragged around the edges. At the government table, two or three prosecutors, the FBI agent in charge sitting behind them with a couple investigators. A bunch of support staff and who knows what other worker bees buzzing in and out of the courtroom. It won't look like a fair fight because it isn't."

He sounded reasonable and rational. How could she say he wasn't fit for the job he had taken on, no matter how heavy the burden? She knew the perils of treating the man she loved. Her objectivity had always been a bulletproof vest. But when your loved one is hurting, you, too, feel the pain. She would watch Jake closely as the trial neared. She would give him all the support a woman—and a physician—could give. And she would hope for the best.

CHAPTER THIRTY
Short Leash, Big Dog

I'd never hugged a client in the courtroom. Sure, some of my customers, as I sometimes call them, have embraced me after a winning verdict, weeping their thanks. Others have tried to slug me after a losing verdict. Today, when Kip was led in from a holding cell, I picked him up and squeezed him hard, noticing he'd lost weight. He was five foot eleven and a-buck-fifty tops. So skinny and fragile in an orange jumpsuit, he looked like a 12-year-old dressed as a con for Halloween.

"Uncle Jake, Uncle Jake." His eyes teared up. His face was peach-fuzzed, his hair a matted mess, his face that of a frightened kitten. He must have seen my worried expression. "I look like shit, huh?"

"Nah. But orange isn't your color. You look like a Syracuse cheerleader."

His eyes darted around the courtroom, settled on Margaret Bolden at the government table. I caught the prosecutor's look, and it surprised me.

Compassion. Empathy.

I didn't expect that, given the conversation minutes earlier when Margaret revealed her marching orders. Not just for the initial appearance and the setting of bail, but for trial.

"I have to oppose pretrial release. I can't stipulate to anything except 'good morning.' I can't offer you a plea, and even if I did, it would be so ludicrous, you'd laugh."

"I'm pretty certain I wouldn't find it humorous."

But now, I could see a softness around her eyes. I tried not to give it too much meaning. Ray Pincher had told me that Margaret Bolden never missed a Sunday church service. She and her husband, a licensed contractor, lived in Pinecrest, just a few miles down Old Cutler Road from my place. They had two children: a boy, a senior in high school, and a girl in tenth grade. Is it possible, I wondered, that she looked at Kip and thought of her own son, hoping that he never strayed from the straight and narrow? I made a mental note to try and get as many parents as possible on the jury.

When the case was called, Kip and I stood at the defense table. He wobbled a bit, and I thought I heard his knees knocking, but it was probably my imagination.

The magistrate judge was Selena Vazquez. Unlike federal judges, who preside for life—far longer than we lawyers desire—the magistrates serve eight-year terms. Vazquez, in her forties, was in year three of her first term on the bench.

"Good morning, Ms. Bolden," Judge Vazquez said. "And..." She looked at the court file where my appearance had been filed. "Mr. Lassiter. Welcome."

I bowed slightly. "Nice to be here, Your Honor."

She studied Kip with a look nearly identical to that of the prosecutor a moment before. Compassion and empathy and maybe a question: *What's the kid doing here?* It could be a female thing. I amended my mental note: Get *mothers* on the jury.

Judge Vazquez zipped through the formalities. She noted that Kip was represented by counsel and informed him of his right to remain silent and a few other boilerplate provisions of the law. She then thumbed through the indictment and stated, "You are charged with eighteen counts of mail fraud. I am obliged to inform you that each count carries a maximum penalty of..." She looked toward the prosecutor.

"Twenty years, Your Honor," Ms. Bolden said.

"You are also charged with eighteen counts of racketeering with similar penalties and one count of money laundering for thirty-seven counts in all."

I sensed Kip turning toward me, thought I heard a gurgling in his throat, hoped he didn't hurl on our table.

"Whaaaa," Kip exhaled, his knees buckling. I grabbed him by the elbow and propped him up. Again, the magistrate looked at him sympathetically. Maybe at trial, we could work on him collapsing on cue.

"Is everything all right?" Judge Vazquez asked.

"Your Honor, we ask that the defendant immediately be granted pretrial release secured by reasonable bail and proffer that he's a lifelong resident of Miami-Dade County with deep ties to the community. He's not charged with a violent crime. There's no chance of his repeating the conduct alleged while released, and he's not a flight risk."

Margaret Bolden got to her feet, looking even more petite standing behind the prosecution table in this high-ceilinged courtroom. In a soft, melodious voice, she countered, almost apologetically, "Unfortunately, the defendant is a flight risk. He's facing substantial time, virtually life in prison. He's traveled out of the country on multiple occasions in the last year, and he maintains a bank account with more than $1 million in a foreign country."

"What?" I heard myself ask.

"No way," Kip said.

"Hush, Kippers!" I shushed him.

"Your Honor, we are today filing a motion for a restraining order freezing the defendant's account in the Cayman Islands." Bolden handed a document to me and a copy to the deputy court clerk, who gave it to the judge. "As you can see, there's an account in the name of Chester Lassiter in First Caribbean Bank on Grand Cayman. Current balance, $1.3 million dollars."

Kip was shaking his head. "That's Max's," he whispered. "I don't know anything about it."

I stepped around the table into the well of the courtroom. "Your Honor, this is just another act by the government's star witness and chief perjurer calculated to set up my client. The account is a sham. It's Max Ringle's money, opened without my client's knowledge or consent."

I was winging it. And sometimes when you wing it, you get shot down.

Margaret Bolden handed me another sheet of paper and said, "The government proffers bank documents showing the defendant's signature on the account. These funds are accessible only by him."

Ouch! That stung. But the first rule of the trial lawyer is not unlike that of the football player. Never let them see your pain.

"We demand that this document be examined by a handwriting expert," I said. "And we insist on a bail hearing, and if bail is denied, we demand a speedy trial, by which I mean Monday morning at 9 a.m."

Bolden snickered. "I seriously doubt Mr. Lassiter is ready for trial."

"Really?" I turned to the prosecutor and addressed her, instead of the judge, a no-no in courtroom procedure. I held up a blank yellow legal pad. "I've got this. I'm ready for trial. You've got the burden of proof. Put on your case, counselor! Throw out the first pitch! Let's see what you've got when the cameras aren't rolling, and your boss isn't posturing about the biggest scandal in history."

"Slow down, both of you," the magistrate said. "And get up here, now."

The judge turned her chair toward the empty jury box, and both Bolden and I headed that way for a quiet sidebar conference. When the court stenographer grabbed her machine and tried to join us, the judge said, "That's okay, Gloria. You take five." Then she turned to Ms. Bolden. "Margaret, what the heck's going on here? Are you saying I should keep this kid locked up the next eight or ten months prior to trial? Really?"

I was beginning to like this magistrate judge even more. She was cutting through the bullshit.

The prosecutor sighed. "Judge, I'm on a short leash here."

The judge turned to me. "Translation, Mr. Lassiter. The government is playing hardball, and Ms. Bolden has limited authority."

"I got that, Your Honor."

"Margaret, here's the way I see it," the magistrate said. "The government did a deal with the mastermind of this scheme, so he's getting leniency and a pat on the back for helping make your cases."

"He's forfeiting millions of dollars, Your Honor. And I'm sure he'll do significant prison time."

"Sure, sure," the magistrate said. "And his clients, the parents, are pleading guilty, and they're gonna get slaps on the wrists, maybe a few months at one Club Fed or another. Same with the proctors and coaches. Which leaves you with this baby-faced kid you want me to think is some international criminal on the run."

"Max Ringle couldn't have pulled this off without this co-conspirator."

"I saw your boss's press conference," the magistrate continued. "He said the government had more than 200 agents and lawyers and investigators working this case. Meaning you need at least one trial and one long sentence to justify the millions of dollars that went into this, which after all, is about some kids cheating to get into college. So, be as tough as you want when you get to trial, but we both know that the Eighth Amendment and Supreme Court precedent require bail, so what are we gonna do here?"

Wow. If I weren't engaged to Melissa Gold, I might have asked Selena Vazquez to marry me.

"As I said, Your Honor," Margaret Bolden repeated softly, "I'm on a short leash."

"Then let's get a bigger dog!" I blurted out, frustrated by Bolden's only-following-orders tactic. "Get the U.S. Attorney in here to make his case for pretrial detention. And if Juan Lucayo says he's on a short leash, let's bring down the Attorney General from Washington."

Judge Vazquez smiled at me. "You catch on quick, Mr. Lassiter. Margaret, should we recess for half an hour to get your boss over here? Would Mr. Lucayo like to share his thoughts with us?"

"I think he would be quite irked." She thought things over for a moment and said, "Upon further reflection, the government would not be opposed to a hundred-thousand dollar corporate surety bond, coupled with the surrender of the defendant's passport and the freezing of the Cayman account."

"Sounds reasonable," I said.

"Done," pronounced the judge.

I exhaled a long breath, like air *whooshing* from a punctured tire, as the tension flowed from me. I turned toward the defense table and winked at Kip. He'd be sleeping at my house tonight. While we waited for the court stenographer to appear so we could put the terms of pretrial release on the record, I said to the magistrate. "Judge Vazquez, any chance you can hear the case-in-chief?"

She chuckled. "I'm afraid you'll get a lifetime appointee for that. Margaret, whose division caught the trial?"

"Judge Speidel, Your Honor."

"Ay, Dios!" the magistrate exclaimed. "Lionel Speidel."

I waited for more.

"Well, Mr. Lassiter," she continued. "I wish you and your client good luck. And fasten your seat belt. It's going to be a bumpy trial."

CHAPTER THIRTY-ONE
The Quest for Integrity

I had the top down on the Eldorado convertible as we swung onto the I-95 ramp, heading south toward Coconut Grove. The sun beat down mercilessly, but the rush of air, even humid Florida air, felt cleansing after a morning in court. When your client faces decades in prison, the handsome federal courthouse feels just as oppressive as the county lockup with its rank odors of a faulty latrine.

The massive bench seat of the old Eldo was red velour, suitable for 1980s Cadillacs and 1880s New Orleans brothels. Kip was slouched into the soft fabric, eyes closed. When he'd moved to his Brickell Avenue apartment, he'd left some clothes he hated at my house, so I'd brought to court an old pair of canvas shorts and a Biscayne-Tuttle debate team T-shirt. Dorky, maybe, but compared to the orange jumpsuit, these were designer duds. I shot a glance at him. With his face in repose, Kip looked a 15-year-old, innocent and untouched by the world, which was pretty much the opposite of real life.

"It will be great to have you home, kiddo," I said. "I'm grilling some porterhouses tonight.

Kip opened his eyes. "Getting indicted didn't convert me into a carnivore."

"No worries. Melissa is making that fancy salad you love, the one with fennel and tangerine slices. Plus, something called creamy mushroom kale risotto, which I guarantee you no one on death row ever chose for a last meal."

"That'll be great." He did not sound enthusiastic.

"What is it, Kip?"

"I'm scared, Uncle Jake."

"It's gonna be okay, Kippers. I've got you."

His voice was barely a whisper above the wind. "I'm really, really, really sorry."

"I know you are."

"For letting you down, I mean. You've given me so much. I know how angry and disappointed you must be. That's what I thought about when they hauled my ass across the country. How much of yourself you put into raising me and how ungrateful I've been and how shitty I've treated you this last year."

His words moved me. I'd been hoping for his humanity to appear. His vision of the world had been blinded by the glint of fool's gold. His best qualities—compassion and empathy and honesty—had been buried under all that cashmere and cash.

"I'm glad you're digging deep," I said. "Self-knowledge doesn't come easy."

"You can say it now, Uncle Jake."

"Say what?"

"'I told you so.' You can say it. I deserve it."

"Aw, what good would that do? We've got to look ahead. Prepare for trial."

"But you were right. About Max double-crossing me. About the trouble I was in. I expect a lecture."

"I've never lectured a client. Not part of my job description."

"How about as my..." He thought a moment before saying, "As my dad. How about that job description?"

A warm flood of emotion surged through me. How I had longed for him to say that.

"My dad."

I gave his shoulder a gentle squeeze. "Being your dad is my favorite job."

"Great. But I think I still gotta call you 'Uncle Jake.' Otherwise, it's a little weird."

"Not a problem. Here's my very simple lecture. You forgot one of Granny's rules. 'If you live for money, there will never be enough, and the pursuit will kill you.'"

"I get that, Uncle Jake, but I wasn't doing it for the money."

"Cashmere hoodies, then. It's the same thing."

"No, it's hard to explain, but the money and material things were only...I don't know, the meringue on top the *tres leches*. Does that make sense?"

"What's underneath? What's the cake you hungered for?"

"The thrill. The action. Feeling juiced walking into a testing center as an imposter. Risking getting busted and then, under pressure, nailing any score I wanted."

I thought about it as traffic backed up where I-95 pours into U.S.1, known not so fondly as Useless 1. "We need to find something else that juices you. Something productive and legal."

"A new path in life. I get that."

"If we beat this thing, you can become the hero of your own story of redemption."

He thought that over for a moment and replied, "Like a hero in Greek mythology."

"Like Hercules. Believe it or not, I took a course in mythology at Penn State."

"Really? It doesn't sound like you."

"My mistake. I thought the course guide said 'mixology,' you know, a bartending course."

"In mythology," Kip said, "before the hero goes on his quest, he meets with his mentor who teaches him how to achieve his quest."

"Obi-Wan Kenobi in *Star Wars*."

"Yep. And you're my mentor. I need you to teach me how to seize the sword or find the magic potion or whatever. And I'll listen this time, I promise. I just don't yet know what the quest is."

I reached over and tousled his mop of hair, just like I did when he was ten years old. "We'll work on it together."

We were stopped at the traffic light at Douglas Road, ready to hang a left into Coconut Grove. My cell rang with an 805 number, and I answered with an inquisitive "Hello?"

"Is the creeper there?"

I recognized the shrill voice. Shari Ringle of the gold thong bikini and midnight-blue toenails, and yes, her breasts in my bed at the Miramar hotel.

"He can't talk to you, Shari. He's finished being recorded by the Ringles."

"I'm not recording! And he doesn't have to talk. Just put it on speaker."

I pressed my index finger to my lips, instructing Kip not to say a word, and clicked the speaker button.

"Are you there, Kip?"

"He's listening," I said.

"You ruined my life! USC kicked me out."

"I thought you hated college," I said.

"Hated classes, loved the parties. And that's not the point. Aroma-dot-com cancelled sponsorship of my blog and discontinued my line of perfumes, 'Utopia by Shari.' NoBurn ditched my vlog, and I was supposed to get a reality show called 'Woke and Spoke,' and now everything's gone."

Kip's lips moved a millimeter, and I knew he was going to say, "I'm sorry," but I clamped a mitt over his mouth to keep him quiet.

"Is that it, Shari?" I asked.

"Kip, I hope you rot in prison, you dipdo fricker. You ruined everything! My life is shit!"

"Have a nice day," I said, clicking off.

"Aw, jeez," Kip groaned. "She's really mad at me."

"Dammit, don't you start feeling sorry for Shari Ringle. She's going home to her mansion with an ocean view, and you're going to trial in federal court. You're the one who the government wants to pay for all the sins of the parents, the kids, the coaches, everybody. Even Max Ringle is getting a break. Before you can go on that hero's quest, we have to beat all of them. You understand that, right?"

"I guess."

From Douglas, I turned right onto Kumquat, coming to a stop to let three peacocks cross the street in their slow, waddling, don't-give-a-damn manner.

Kip seemed to be in deep thought. Then he said, "Integrity."

"How's that?"

"Integrity. That's my quest. To be a good person. An honest person. Not to hurt anyone but to help other people. Is that okay? Or is it too vague?"

"No, it's dead-solid perfect."

The peacocks disappeared behind a bougainvillea bush, and I eased the old Caddy to the front of my little coral rock pillbox of a house. I handed Kip my cell phone, and said, "Google something before we go in."

He gave me a puzzled look but sat there, waiting for instructions.

"Plug in the name 'John D. MacDonald,'" I said.

"Your favorite Florida author."

"Yeah, and type 'Travis McGee and integrity.'"

His thumbs were a blur of motion, as any eGames aficionado would be.

"A quote came up from *The Turquoise Lament*," Kip said.

"That's it. Read it aloud. You need to hear it, and I need a refresher course."

"'Maybe all you ever get for integrity is the largest kick in the ass the world can provide,'" Kip read aloud. "'Crime pays a lot better. I can bend my own rules way, way over, but there is a place where I finally stop bending them.'"

He handed me back the phone and said, "I get it, Uncle Jake. It's harder to live with integrity, and maybe there are gray areas, but there's a line you just can't cross."

"I try to live by those words," I said. "I'm not seeking perfection, but integrity requires that the good I do must outweigh the bad. That's why I've always done pro bono work for poor clients. It's why I've mentored junior high kids in Liberty City and lectured in high schools and worked as a volunteer coach for Pop Warner football."

"That slays," he said. "You're my role model, Uncle Jake. I want to be like you."

"Great. Now, let's go in. Melissa is dying to see you, and I'm hungry as hell."

CHAPTER THIRTY-TWO
The Child Emperor

When we walked into the house, Melissa hugged Kip so tightly and so long his face started to turn blue. "I've been so worried about you," she said.

"I'm sorry, Melissa. I really screwed up."

"Hush now and go clean up."

Kip and I both laughed.

"What?" she asked, befuddled.

"You tell her," I said.

"That's what Granny always said when I came in the house. 'Hush now and go clean up.'"

"Mel, Granny rubbed off on you," I added, and the three of us spent a quiet moment thinking about her, gone now the last ten months.

Kip scooted to the shower. Melissa checked on three giant Idaho potatoes that were baking in the oven while I rubbed two nicely marbled porterhouses with salt, garlic, dried parsley, red pepper flakes, coriander seeds, and my secret ingredient, brown sugar. Maybe it was my imagination, but Kip seemed to look longingly at the steaks as he contemplated his creamy mushroom kale risotto.

An hour later, after we'd polished off the meal and a six-pack of Grolsch, saving the pecan pie for later, we were sitting on the back porch listening to the crickets. My cell phone rang nine or ten times before I turned it off. Journalists from around the country, all wanting to interview Kip, or in lieu of that improbability, me. I could see no advantage in our saying a word.

"I read the indictment," Kip said.

I had the hint of a new headache brewing, but I was so damn happy to have Kip home that I dismissed the very notion of pain. "All 193 paragraphs?"

"Yeah. Every allegation is true. I did everything they say." His voice low, his tone regretful. "But the funny thing is, I never really thought I was doing anything illegal. I'm not saying I thought it was okay. I just never thought about it in those terms. Legal. Illegal. Moral. Immoral. It was just...I don't know...just fun."

That stirred a memory. "At Ringle's house, you said that taking the tests was like playing eGames again. The risk of getting caught taking the tests being like the risk of annihilation in the games. And in the car on the way here, you talked about how being an imposter got you juiced."

That caught Melissa's attention, as she poured each of us a shot of tequila. Don Julio 1942, the good stuff. "Is that right, Kip?"

"Both juice me, so yeah, that's it."

Melissa focused her greenish gold eyes on Kip, her voice sliding into physician mode. "Taking those tests gave you the dopamine rush you were missing once you stopped the eGames. You were addicted to the rush, not to *Fortnite* or whatever game you played."

"Just like playing poker gave you a rush before you got busted with the rich kid's credit card in Atlantic City," I said.

Kip gave me a cross look, realizing I'd broken my promise to him about his gambling and credit card problem.

"Yeah, I told Melissa about Penn and Atlantic City, just like you told Ringle. The difference is that Melissa wants to help you, and Ringle used your addiction—"

"I wasn't addicted!"

"Have it your way. Ringle used your hunger for that dopamine rush against you. There's a pattern. You get juiced, you take risks. In the eGames, the risk is your fictional character gets killed. In real life, you get arrested and face decades in prison."

I could tell Kip was processing something. After a moment, he said. "When the twins were chasing me through the Glades in their Maserati, I flashed back to *Road Fury*."

"The road rage game," I said. "I remember."

"I'm not saying it was fun crashing, but...it's hard to describe, the chase lit me up."

Now I was the one with something to think about. "Kip, I want you to see that psychiatrist who helped you kick the eGames habit."

"No way. I didn't like him."

"All right, there's a new guy. Dr. Eisenberg. Treats adolescents. I met him in a Bar proceeding, and he's pretty sharp."

"No shrinks! I'm not gonna do it."

I took a sip of the clear, clean, smooth tequila. I was frustrated and exhausted. If I were driving, I was about to change lanes from annoyance to anger. What the hell had happened? Our mutual quest and our cheery mood on the ride home seemed to have vanished into the evening breeze. Why couldn't Kip see that once in a while, Uncle knows best?

Maybe this is what it means to be a dad. When you try to help a troubled child, he reflexively rears up like a wild stallion, kicking his hooves in your face.

"Kiddo, you admit you did everything they say you did. I'm flailing around looking for a defense. Let me see if an expert witness could be useful."

"I'll talk to Melissa."

"I'm not a board-certified psychiatrist," she said.

"But you're a neurologist who knows more than any shrink about how the brain really works. I'll talk to you. No one else." He stated it firmly and with finality and the brusqueness of a spoiled kid.

I threw up my arms. "The child emperor has spoken."

I felt the first stabs of the ice pick, a migraine, either from the alcohol or stress or the failing synapses in my wounded brain.

"Jake, what about it?" Melissa asked. "Could I testify?"

"Your medical specialty isn't the problem." Fatigue was overtaking me, the last few ounces of fuel draining from my tank. "You can't be an impartial expert witness. You love Kip as if he were your son. You're engaged to his lawyer. Maybe we'll even be married by the time of trial."

"Really?" she asked. "Have we set a date I don't know about?"

I plowed ahead, despite my clanging headache. I wanted to be in bed, curled up with Melissa, welcoming sleep or something even sweeter in her warm embrace. "If you testify, the prosecutor will attack you on bias. It's what I did when Dr. Eisenberg testified for his brother-in-law in a Bar proceeding."

"It won't be a problem if you hang a lantern on the relationship first," Kip said.

"Do tell," I growled, growing more irritated by the moment.

"Make the case that Melissa knows me way better than some quack who's testifying for money and has spent maybe two hours with me."

"So now you're a lawyer!" I snapped. "First an eGames wunderkind. Then a poker player using someone else's credit card. Then an imposter, a cheater, raking in the dough, handing your ass to the government out of your own damn naivete and arrogance. So, sure, tell me how to keep you out of prison for the next thirty years!"

Kip's mouth opened, his face reddened, and his eyes moistened. He looked as if I'd just slapped him across the face, which, of course, I'd never done. I'd never spanked him, never shoved him, never touched him in anger.

"Jake! What the hell!" Melissa got to her feet. "That's not you." She turned to Kip. "Your uncle has moments of irrationality that manifest themselves as anger and rage. It must be shocking to you, but please don't take it personally. His mechanism for impulse control is on the blink, and his damaged brain cells are acting out. That's the only way I know how to describe it."

"It's okay," he stammered, his voice fluttering.

"I'm sorry, Kip," I said, calming down. "Really, really sorry."

"I know," he whispered.

"Let's call it a night," Melissa said.

I took a long, slow pull on the tequila and turned to Melissa with another *mea culpa*. "Maybe I was too quick to dismiss what Kip suggested. Your testifying might work. It would be something novel, that's for sure. We'll talk about it when we set up our war room, by which I mean the kitchen table covered with files."

We gathered our drinking glasses. Somewhere in the neighborhood, a mockingbird was whistling. It was not unpleasant. The moist night air carried the scent of jasmine. We headed inside, shutting out the nighttime sounds and smells.

Maybe Ray Pincher had been right, I thought, as I rinsed the dishes. Maybe representing my nephew would be a disaster. A surgeon doesn't operate on a loved one. And a surgeon with migraine headaches, memory problems, and outbursts of anger might just remove the wrong kidney or stab the patient in the heart with his scalpel. Or maybe just keel over in closing argument, blood vessels bursting in his brain.

Still, I was not willing to trust Kip's fate to another lawyer. I had a stake in the boy's future that no one else could match. If I lost and Kip went to prison, a part of me would die. Life would drain out of me every day that he would be incarcerated. Given my age and medical condition, would I ever see him outside a prison visitors' room? And just how could Kip, this sweet and soft kid, survive life in a concrete cell? Day after day, year after year, locked in a cage and surrounded by brutality. He would snap like a green twig, and I would be a broken man.

While Kip's freedom was at stake, so was my life. Game over for Kip would be game over for me. And while we don't ask lawyers to fall on their swords for their clients, well, I'm the guy willing to do it. If there's blood on the courtroom floor, let it be mine.

CHAPTER THIRTY-THREE
Wild Kip Lassiter and the Unwritten Law

Nine months later...

Actors feel it during endless rehearsals. Football players feel it in August scrimmages. And lawyers feel it during the seemingly endless pretrial process.

C'mon, let's raise the curtain, play the game, try the damn case!

That's how I felt one day before we would select a jury. It was March, and with a cooling breeze coming in from the northeast, kite surfers skipped over the waves just off South Beach. I used to be a windsurfer, but at my weight, I needed gale force winds for the board to plane, so I could hop the chop off Virginia Key.

These days, I was sailing a desk, or, more precisely, the kitchen table, preparing for Kip's trial. The table, the chairs, the floor, and the counters were overflowing with files. Nearly all the other criminal cases stemming from the scandal were over. Parents, coaches, and administrators pled guilty and got stern lectures, fines, and either short sentences—in one case, two weeks—or probation, called "supervised release" in federal court.

Most of the early news coverage had focused on the wealthy parents who happily paid Ringle for his magic elixir of college admission. Then the coverage shifted to examining universities for their ethically shaky practices of admitting students whose families make substantial donations. Now, the spotlights glared on my nephew.

The Miami Herald ran a series of stories describing Kip as the "mastermind's partner" and "young wizard" and "cheater extraordinaire" and "brainiac co-conspirator." Occasionally, the word "alleged" popped up.

The stories overflowed with the frisson of readers' delight. Oh, the comeuppance of such a brilliant young man! Online comments expressed readers' joy that their children weren't "too smart for their own good." For some people, schadenfreude is the most pleasure they'll ever experience.

Through the months of trial prep, I tried to keep Kip's spirits up by expressing optimism about the case.

"The government has the burden of proof."

"The jury will hate Max Ringle and like you."

"The reasonable doubt standard is our ace in the hole."

But, in truth, I knew the government could prove each charge simply by playing its recordings and having Ringle identify Kip as the young man on the tapes. The prospect of losing fueled my nightmares and jolted me awake in cold sweats. It would take creative lawyering, government screw-ups, and a large dose of luck for us to win.

Max Ringle had pled guilty and was as free as the mockingbird whistling in my bottlebrush tree. He would be sentenced after Kip's trial. He had already scored major federal brownie points for acknowledging his crimes, expressing remorse, and forfeiting millions in assets. His biggest ass-smooch, of course, was cooperating with the feds, making cases against dozens of defendants, including his co-conspirator boy genius. Ringle had pledged that, whatever his prison sentence, he would spend each day helping other inmates further their education, and, upon release, devote the rest of his life to community service. What a guy!

At Kip's trial, Ringle would be the star witness, the Big Eye tuna, and I was the sushi chef. If I didn't slice him into bite-size pieces, we would have no chance. I had to show Ringle to be a despicable human being. I am not the best trial lawyer in town. I am not even the best within one block of the intersection of Flagler Street and Miami Avenue. But I am a fearsome cross-examiner, and I had readied myself with sharpened knives for the son of a bitch.

I deputized Melissa as my chief medical consultant and expert witness. Now, with show time a day away, I sat at the kitchen table nursing a cup of black coffee and poring over transcripts of recorded conversations for the umpteenth time. Just after 7 a.m., Melissa padded into the kitchen, wearing a silk sarong with an Asian-inspired print.

"How long have you been up?" she asked.

"Not that long. I wanted to read the wiretaps one more time. I guess I'm hoping Kip would say something different."

"How much coffee?" she asked in full physician mode.

"Only two cups. Maybe three."

"I'll slice some mangoes. Yogurt and toast okay?"

"Fine." Before she could ask how I was feeling, I answered, "Pretty good. No morning headache."

That was basically true, *pretty good* being entirely subjective, and the headache began last night, not this morning. I hadn't told her about the occasional bouts of blurry vision and maybe just a bit of confusion. She hadn't noticed when I missed the exit on I-95 the other night when we were going to dinner in Wynwood. Why make her worry?

The warmth of my feelings for Melissa had only increased with time. So incredibly supportive. So there for me and for Kip, too. How damn lucky was I? If I had to choose between never getting

C.T.E. or never meeting Melissa, well, give me my lover. I'll deal with my damaged brain.

She expertly sliced open a ripe mango, then twisted the pit until it popped out of the fruit. "Any new ideas?"

"Shuffling old ones. It's the part of the game I love, playing poker with ideas, hoping I don't draw a joker after the government deals its hand."

Kip, sleepy-eyed, walked into the kitchen wearing shorts that were actually cut-off jeans—and, according to him, were called "jorts." Once his apartment building had been staked out by the news media, he'd taken up residence in his childhood bedroom.

He looked at my bowl of yogurt and fruit and asked, "Did you know mangoes are related to poison ivy?"

"I'm a lifelong Floridian." I took a bite of the toast. "Of course I know that. Related to cashews, too."

He fished a grapefruit out of the fridge and cut it in half. "Did you see the latest on Shari?"

"You mean the girl whose life you turned to shit?"

Kip laughed. It had become a running joke. In the last several months, Shari Ringle had prospered as a social media influencer. Her father, a guy with his finger on the pulse of our shallow society, correctly ascertained that infamy was more profitable than fame. His PR firm got Shari a sponsored podcast, "Alt-Skool," where she shared career solutions for kids who eschew college. Her Instagram account had exploded from about a hundred thousand followers to more than nine million, and she'd gotten her own cosmetics line, branded with the slogan "Cover-up is no crime."

"I saw online that she's getting a reality show," I said. "I'll ask her about all her deals when she testifies for the government. Same with those twin brothers."

Teague Hallinan, one of the twin nitwits, had been bounced from Wake Forest, but was enjoying success as a hip-hop artist. He launched his new career with the songs, "Git Woke, Wake" and "Git Woke, Not Work." Brother Niles wrote the lyrics, which featured a remarkable number of one-syllable words.

I poured myself another cup of coffee and a fresh one for Melissa. "I'm looking forward to questioning several wealthy parents and, of course, their kids."

Melissa thought it over a moment. "So, you intend to distract the jury by drawing attention to the conduct of others."

"Pretty much," I said. "Especially Ringle. The government's recordings will bolster his credibility. But I can still attack his character. The trick is to make the jury hate Ringle more than they hate Kip. Same with the rich parents who are getting slaps on the wrist, and their spoiled rotten kids who are profiting from their notoriety. I'll appeal to the jurors' sense of fairness, as opposed to the letter of the law."

"And you can do that? Ethically, I mean?"

"I can ever-so-gently nudge the jurors away from the law and toward justice. It's called..."

"Jury nullification," Kip chimed in. "But if Uncle Jake asks them to go against the judge's instructions, he'll get thrown in jail for contempt."

"As my pal Steve Solomon says, a lawyer who's afraid of jail is like a surgeon who's afraid of blood. Still, I'd rather stay in the courtroom and not miss the fun. The jury can do whatever it wants. I just have to walk a tightrope to get them there."

"Does this ever work?" Melissa asked, skepticism in her voice.

"Wild Bill Hickok," Kip said, spearing a piece of his grapefruit.

"Good one, Kip," I said.

Melissa waited for an explanation.

"Hickok got into a dispute in a poker game," I explained, "then killed the other card player in a patently illegal gunfight. Despite the evidence, the jurors acquitted. They said they decided the case on the unwritten law of a fair fight."

"The unwritten law," Melissa repeated. "It sounds so iffy and vague."

"I make my living in the iffy and the vague, the gray shadows of black letter law. And that's what I plan to do for Wild Kip Lassiter."

CHAPTER THIRTY-FOUR
Cut the Crap, Kip

Melissa Gold...

Melissa was worried.

Worried about Kip, of course. Every day and every night. But worried, too, about Jake. He tried to hide his worsening symptoms. She hadn't said a word when he sailed past the exit on I-95 the other night. And she could tell he was in pain from the way he scrunched his eyes when a migraine shot through his skull. Not that he would admit he was hurting. Or occasionally dizzy. She'd seen him stagger a step in the kitchen the other night, and no tequila had been involved.

One positive note, though, Jake's focus on Kip's case invigorated him. He was on leave of absence from his job with the state Bar, and now that he had a case that mattered to him, he was more upbeat. At first, that seemed odd to her because Kip was in such enormous jeopardy. In medical school, she had learned that stress is a negative force, but now she wondered if there might be a positive spin-off. Preparing for the high-wire act of a federal criminal trial carried with it dizzying levels of tension and anxiety. To perform under those conditions required focus and drive, and the resulting work was bringing Jake a sense of purpose and satisfaction.

Still, she could not help but wonder if he was experiencing even more severe symptoms that he was keeping under wraps. There had been one PET scan since Kip's indictment. A small increase in total quantity of tau proteins, statistically insignificant, though she would have preferred a decrease. She continued to administer the experimental AY-70 cocktail that she hoped would begin to show results. Periodically, she checked with researchers at Boston University and UCLA. So far, no one had made inroads.

Now, the evening before the beginning of the trial, Jake was in the kitchen, his war room, scribbling notes. She sat in an Adirondack chair on the back porch as Kip lay in the hammock slung between two palm trees. The air was thankfully free of the soggy humidity that would soon settle in for the six-month summer.

"Let's go over the eGames one more time," she said, opening her notebook. She had been preparing for weeks to testify about Kip's proclivity for fantasy role-playing and the effect of eGames on adolescent brains.

"Again?" Kip protested.

"When you were younger, you played eGames for how long each day?"

"Some days, every waking hour," Kip replied.

"When you went into therapy and tried to stop, what happened?"

He reached a bare foot out of the hammock to push off the ground and started swinging. "Like I told you before, I went cold turkey and felt like I had the flu. Sluggish and no energy. And dreams! Crazy dreams about the games. Pretty much the same thing with playing poker. When I quit, I was a big slug."

"Withdrawal syndrome. Cravings for that rush."

"Yeah. 'Cravings.' That's a good word. That's what I'll say on the stand."

"Kip, I'm not trying to coach you. Just tell the truth."

His hands were locked behind his head, and he was looking straight up, not making eye contact. The hammock swung like a metronome, ropes squeaking. "Sure, sure. I know that."

"Jake said that Max Ringle had eGame consoles in his house, and he limited your playing time to three hours every other day."

"And then not at all a week before I took the exams."

Melissa looked up from her notebook. "How did you feel in those days leading up to the test when you weren't allowed to play?"

"Cravings for the rush. Then, when I was an imposter showing my credentials to get into the test, it was like I was someone else."

"Of course. You were Niles or Teague or whoever's test you were taking."

He stopped swinging, sat up, and looked at her. "No, more like Duke Nukem in *Time to Kill.*"

"An eGame character?"

"Like Duke says, 'It's time to kick ass or chew bubblegum, and I'm all out of gum.'"

"Cute," she deadpanned.

"You know what I think was happening?"

"What, Kip?"

"It's like Max was giving me heroin, then cut me off, and said, 'Go rob that drug dealer' and you can have more. I think he was messing with my adolescent brain and distorting my sense of reality."

She stood, descended the porch steps, grabbed the hammock and stopped it from swinging.

"Whoa!" he yelped.

"Cut the crap, Kip."

"What? What did I do?"

"You've gone through my files, haven't you? You've read the research papers. 'EGames and the Adolescent Brain.' 'Gaming and the Lost Sense of Reality.' Now you're tailoring your testimony to the science."

He looked down at the tops of his bare feet. "Maybe I am. But that doesn't mean I'm lying."

CHAPTER THIRTY-FIVE
The Three Faces of Lionel Speidel

Federal judges are phantoms.

You never see them or their courtrooms on television, and they almost never give interviews. While our state trials have been televised since the Ted Bundy case forty years ago, the federal courthouse remains a monastic sanctuary, hidden from prying eyes and cameras.

Federal judges are kings and queens.

They are appointed for life. No messy elections, no grubbing for lawyers' campaign contributions. They sit on thrones above the lowly members of their kingdom and are served by a royal retinue of law clerks, judicial assistants, court clerks, jury clerks, courtroom deputies, administrators, and, for all I know, court jesters.

Federal judges reign over a palace.

While state court judges are bunkered in a mold-infested building from the 1920s and an obsolete, undersized rabbit warren near the Miami River, federal judges inhabit a modern, palatial tower.

I crossed the plaza toward the federal courthouse entertaining those thoughts, while hauling a trial bag stuffed with files, research, and lunch. The building consisted of twin towers lifted three stories off the ground by massive limestone columns. These could be useful when rising seas turn Miami into Venice, or worse, Atlantis. The towers are connected by an eight-story curved blue-green glass cone that protrudes into space and resembles the bow of a ship. The five-story lobby has slate floors and artistically designed limestone-paneled walls. It more closely resembles a Four Seasons hotel than a federal courthouse.

Kip had arrived separately, checking in first at the Marshal's Office, as part of his pretrial release obligations. Workers were trimming brown fronds from palm trees of the plaza when I heard a booming voice from behind: "Judge Speidel has a warrant out for you, Lassiter!"

Holy shit! Was I late? Federal judges have been known to lock up tardy lawyers.

I spun around to see Ray Pincher double-timing toward me, laughing his ass off.

"Gotcha, Jake! Oh, I gotcha."

"Thanks a lot, Ray. What are you doing here?"

"Meeting the U.S. Attorney. It's that state-federal task force I told you about. Opioid pill mills."

"Let me guess. The feds have all the money but want you to use state resources."

"Same old story. Hey, I tried to poke my head into their war room on your case, but it's cordoned off. About half a floor with restricted access."

"Half a floor just for Kip?"

"They prepped all their college cases there. Lucayo said he had to borrow half a dozen A.U.S.A.'s and even more FBI agents from D.C. From what I saw, they probably have two dozen paralegals and assistants flitting around with iPads and earbuds. Also, an espresso machine, trays of croissants, and pitchers of fresh-squeezed O.J."

"Your tax dollars at work, Ray. You gonna come to court, be my one-man cheerleading squad?"

"Would love to, but I don't want to answer reporters' questions about what the state attorney is doing on foreign soil. I might send Gilberto Foyo over here to keep an eye on you."

We paused in the shade of the building. "I suppose you've done your research on Lionel Speidel," Pincher said.

"Prosecutors call him the 'Lion King' because they think he's kindly and wise."

Pincher chuckled. "Meaning he's government oriented, which makes sense. Every paycheck he's ever gotten was signed by Uncle Sam."

"Defense lawyers call him 'Speed-it-up Speidel,' because he's always pushing them to shut up and sit down. What's your take?"

"From what I gather, Jake, there are three Lionel Speidels."

"How do you mean?"

"You know he's enormous, right?"

"Yeah, Victoria Lord told me he's about six feet five and his weight equals one Lassiter plus one Solomon, which would put him close to 400 pounds."

"Speidel can be charming. Think of Orson Welles in his later years, wearing a black cape, a twinkle in his eye, telling Hollywood stories to Johnny Carson."

"But you're saying there are two others."

"Remember Sydney Greenstreet in *The Maltese Falcon*?"

"Sure, Sam Spade called him 'The Fat Man.' Devious, tricky, and ruthless."

"That's number two. Then, of course, there's King Henry VIII. Had a couple wives beheaded. Prone to anger and throwing his considerable weight around."

The sun glared off the windows of the courthouse, and I shielded my eyes with a hand. "There are state judges who try to bully lawyers. I'm not afraid of them, and I'm not afraid of this guy."

"That's the spirit, Jake." Pincher steadied his gaze at me, and his hands clasped both my shoulders. "Play it the way you always do. Stand your ground. You're damn near an immovable object when you do."

CHAPTER THIRTY-SIX
Brief Briefs and Long Briefs

Judge Lionel Speidel, his enormous black robes billowing behind him, sailed into the courtroom from a rear door and hopped up three stairs to his bench, graceful and light of foot for such a large man. The courtroom was bright and modern with a handsome mix of light and dark woods. The judge's bench was paneled with teak and limestone, and the backdrop was a rich, dark wenge wood.

"Good morning, all!" Judge Speidel boomed, surveying the gallery, reporters filling the first three rows. He plopped down into a high-backed leather chair that, I swear, groaned under his weight.

"Appearances," he said.

"Margaret Bolden, Assistant United States Attorney, for the government." She nodded at the judge, or maybe it was a slight bow, eyes closed, head down for several seconds.

"Jacob Lassiter for the defendant Chester Lassiter, better known as Kip." I nudged Kip, standing beside me in a suit, white shirt, and friendly blue tie. His blondish hair was trimmed short, giving him the look of a studious prep school kid.

Judge Speidel motioned downward with one hand, like the conductor of an orchestra, and we all took our seats. He had bulging pink cheeks that reduced his eyes to slits, their color not ascertainable. His several chins merged into his neck, also pink, as if he had just shaved or his blood pressure was at the boiling point. He had a large forehead and his thinning gray hair was combed straight back.

The deputy clerk, a Hispanic woman in her forties, sat below the judge at a long table with a limestone facing that matched the design of the bench. She stood, turned, and handed the judge the *U.S.A. vs. Lassiter* court file. He put on a pair of wire-rimmed glasses, opened the file, and skimmed several pages.

Without looking up, the judge said, "Margie, I didn't see you or Micah at the club Saturday."

Margie! Assistant U.S. Attorneys, who practically live in the federal courthouse, get buddy-buddy with judges in a way private counsel cannot.

"Micah was taking Justin on a college tour," Margaret Bolden responded, "and I was up to my elbows in trial prep."

The judge chuckled, and his chins jiggled. "Of course you were. Well, I hope to see all of you for the spring picnic this weekend."

As they say, a good lawyer knows the law. A great lawyer knows the judge. Obviously, Bolden had home field advantage.

The judge peered at me over his spectacles. "Mr. Lassiter, I don't believe I've seen you in my court before."

"Maiden voyage, Your Honor. I've spent most of my time in the criminal division of state court."

He coughed up a laugh. "That skid row of justice down by the river! Mr. Lassiter, what's the biggest difference between state and federal court?"

"You have higher ceilings." I pointed toward the unusual origami-shaped wood panels of different heights that formed the courtroom ceiling.

"Ha! Good one." There was a hint of joviality in his voice. So far, he didn't seem sinister at all. "That ceiling gives us opera theater acoustics. Anything else?"

"I haven't been held in contempt yet. But I've only been here ten minutes."

"Ha! Another good one." His laughter caused his bulbous pink cheeks to close the slits of his eyes altogether. "I like a lawyer with a sense of humor. Also, one who stands tall and stands still." He gestured toward the jury box where three nicely dressed young people, two men and a woman, sat taking notes. "Law clerks, pay attention! See the way Mr. Lassiter stands in front of the bench? Perfect posture, feet planted. Solid as an oak. When you start practicing, don't be jumping around like you've got ants in your pants."

Okay, this wasn't so bad. Maybe I was getting the Orson Welles personality.

I glanced at Kip next to me. He seemed relatively relaxed.

"I've visited state court," the judge rolled on, "and it reminded me of my first job after clerking on the Seventh Circuit. I was counsel to the Stockyard Administration in the Agriculture Department. I attended more than my share of slaughter cattle auctions in Oklahoma and Texas. That came back to me over in state court, with all those lawyers and cops and witnesses milling about and chattering while the auctioneer—excuse me—the judge, was calling his motion calendar. Ill-prepared lawyers, shooting from the hip like gunslingers. Both the cattle auction and the courthouse had a stink to them, though I don't remember the lawyers pooping on the floor, if you'll pardon my French."

Spectators in the gallery laughed. Reporters laughed. The prosecutor laughed, so I joined in, wanting to be a member of the club. I knew about the job in the Stockyard Administration. I'd heard the judge got into a jam accepting free sides of beef from some of the slaughterhouses. From the looks of him, he might have eaten the whole damn cow. But in that bureaucratic way of failing upwards, Speidel had landed a job as counsel to the Deputy Secretary of Agriculture. Then, thanks to a friendship with a Florida senator who owned cattle ranches, he was named to the bench by President George W. Bush.

"Now, before we pick a jury, is there any housekeeping we need to do?" the judge asked.

"More like a barn burning, Your Honor," I said.

"How's that?"

"I've moved to dismiss all charges for failure to state a crime. The motion has been pending for three months, Judge."

"Your Honor! Not Judge!" he admonished me. "You're not on skid row down by the river."

"I apologize, Your Honor."

A grating sound came from his throat. "And what do you mean 'pending for three months?' Are you criticizing the Court?"

"Not at all, Your Honor. I was just..." My voice trailed off.

The judge harrumphed, and again, his chins jiggled. I may have already worn out the goodwill I'd created by standing tall and still.

"I've read your motion, Mr. Lassiter, and your memorandum of law in support."

I waited. Margaret Bolden waited. The reporters in the gallery waited.

Judge Speidel riffled through the pleading's binder. "What font is that you're using?"

"Well...I'm...I don't know."

"A carpenter should know his tools. Margie, what font is Mr. Lassiter using?"

"Looks like Comic Sans, Your Honor."

"Aach. Comic Sans." The words dripped with such disgust the judge might have been cleaning pus from an infected wound. "Mr. Lassiter, do you think this case is a laughing matter?"

"Of course not, Your Honor."

"Then tell your word processing department to prepare all pleadings in Times New Roman. And justify your margins."

"I'll text them right away, Your Honor."

I heard Kip, my word processing department, stifle a snicker and hoped that the opera theater acoustics didn't carry the sound to the bench.

The judge was still perusing the motion, maybe looking for misplaced commas. "Also, henceforth please spell 'judgment' without an 'e' after the 'm.' I know English teachers say there's an optional spelling, but not in my courtroom."

"Got it, Your Honor. One 'e,' no options."

This was absurd. He was absurd. I felt heat rising in my chest, an odd sense of growing anger, far out of proportion to having my font and spelling criticized. Without wanting to, without meaning to, I heard myself speaking in a hoarse whisper to Kip, "Do you believe this shit?"

"Shh!" Kip quieted me.

"What's that, Mr. Lassiter?" the judge inquired.

"Nothing, Your Honor. I'm sorry. I was conferring with my client."

Just like that, my anger and my *sotto voce* flareup was over. But what the hell was going on with me?

"Now, I've tanned your hide enough," the judge said, using an expression he may have picked up in the stockyards. "I want to compliment you, and as Margie can tell you, I dole out compliments as if they're gold doubloons."

The judge paused to let us appreciate his wisdom, his kindness, his wordplay.

"Your brief on the legal issues is quite extraordinary." Again, he turned to his captive audience, his trio of clerks, doubtless graduates of the finest law schools. "Pay attention, clerks! Mr. Lassiter's example is to be followed by aspiring trial lawyers."

Wow! I'd used Ray Pincher's idea in my motion. I argued that neither lying in postcards from Hawaii nor lying about your identity at a testing center constituted mail fraud. Was Kip going home a free man?

"Do you know why I liked your brief so much?" the judge asked.

I shrugged. If this were *Final Jeopardy*, I couldn't even take a wild guess. "Sorry, I don't, Your Honor."

"Margie, what do I like about it?"

"It's seven pages."

"Precisely! It's a brief brief, not a long brief. Most lawyers use the full twenty pages permitted by the rule. Why? Are they getting paid by the word? You were concise and to the point, Mr. Lassiter."

I bowed my head in grateful supplication to the Lion King. "Thank you, Your Honor."

"Okay, then. Your motion is denied."

My head jerked up. "Your Honor, don't I get oral argument?"

"Is there anything you're going to say that's not in your seven pages?"

"I'm...well...I don't know...maybe." Sounding like an idiot, even to myself.

"Very well, argue. You have thirty seconds." He pulled a stopwatch out of a drawer and punched the button. "Go."

"You have to be joking!" The anger surged back.

The judge made a rumbling sound in his throat, though his lips didn't move. "Do I look like a man who jokes?"

"Only at executions and funerals," I mumbled.

Kip smashed an elbow into my side, and I shut up.

"What's that, Mr. Lassiter?"

"I understand, Your Honor," I said. "You're not joking."

"Good." He looked at the stopwatch. "You have twenty seconds."

"Mail fraud requires that a victim be deprived of property," I said, rat-a-tat-tat. "Who's the victim? What's the property? We submit there's neither. An intangible admissions slot is not property in the legal sense. It can't be leased or sold or stored in the trunk of a car. You can't place a monetary value on it. In short, there's no victim because no property has been taken. There is no crime because—"

"Time!" announced the judge. "You may take your seat." He turned to the government's table. "Ms. Bolden...?"

"The government stands on its memorandum of law."

"Very well. The defendant's motion is denied. Again. Are we ready to—"

"On what grounds, Your Honor?" I demanded.

The judge's eyes seemed to widen. For the first time, I saw they were spit-colored. "On the grounds I said so, Mr. Lassiter."

I leaned forward over the defense table. That closed the distance to the bench by only a few inches, but some judges find it overly aggressive. "It would be instructive to the defense to know the court's reasoning."

"I'm not here to teach you how to practice law." The judge made a wet, guttural sound. "When your client's convicted and you appeal, I'm sure the government's brief will be highly instructive."

"You mean 'if' my client is convicted."

"That's what I said, counselor. If your client is convicted, I trust the government will have ample reasons why your motion was denied."

I came around the table into the well of the courtroom. The clerk looked up from her table, where I loomed over her.

"Respectfully, Your Honor said 'when.' Spelled w-h-e-n. Same spelling in Comic Sans or Times New Roman."

Judge Speidel banged a meaty fist on the bench and turned to the court stenographer. "Rose, read back our colloquy, please."

Rose, using a computer-assisted transcription stenotype, fiddled with the machine for a moment, then read aloud. "Mr. Lassiter: 'It would be instructive to the defense to know the court's reasoning.' The Court. 'I'm not here to teach you how to practice law.'" She hesitated just a split second before continuing. "'If your client is convicted...'"

"There you have it, Mr. Lassiter," the judge said.

I shot a glance toward Margaret Bolden, who avoided my gaze. She wasn't about to tell the emperor he had no clothes, an image I really didn't want to contemplate. Orson Welles had become Henry VIII. The king can do no wrong, which, after all, is our concept of sovereign immunity.

Thankfully, I felt no surge of anger. My boiling emotions waned, saving me from contempt. "Your Honor, I apologize for my mistake," I said humbly, head down.

"Apology accepted. Now let's pick a jury, and Mr. Lassiter, let's see if you can keep your record intact."

I was puzzled, wondering if the judge knew about the one idiosyncratic record I held to this day. I was the only player in NFL history to be penalized for unnecessary roughness on the opening kickoff, the last play of the first half, and the last play of the game. Two horse-collar tackles and one late hit. But no, the judge had something else in mind.

"You've never been held in contempt in federal court, and I haven't held a lawyer in contempt this year," he said. "Let's both take pains to keep our records intact."

CHAPTER THIRTY-SEVEN
Mansplaining

"Judge Speidel really likes you," Margaret Bolden said.

I almost spit my coffee through my nose.

"He hates me," I responded. "I'm from that skid row of justice down by the river, which reminds him of the cattle auctions where there's cow dung everywhere."

We were standing in the corridor outside the courtroom in recess. In ten minutes, we would start selecting a jury. Or rather, de-selecting. That's what I do, strike from the panel anyone with obvious bias. Or anyone giving my client the evil eye.

"Speidel loved his job with the Agriculture Department," she said. "Someday, when we're in chambers and he's relaxed, he'll tell you about it. He wore cowboy boots, chewed tobacco, and stood there admiring the cattle, one foot propped up on the lower rail of the fence."

"I'm having trouble with the image of Speidel as a Marlboro Man."

"My bet is that he sees you as the embodiment of that. He told his law clerks as much. You're a rugged gunslinger."

"Which he hates. He disparaged lawyers who shoot from the hip."

"That's his cognitive dissonance at play."

I gave her a look, and she explained, "I was a psychology major undergrad."

"Okay, analyze away."

"Speidel's job requires dealing with deep-carpet lawyers who file briefs with footnotes asking for permission to take a leak. But he admires the guys who walk into court with a blank legal pad and say, 'I'm ready for trial.'"

"As I did before the magistrate."

"Speidel read the transcript of your client's initial appearance. He always reads the transcripts."

"Where are you going with this, Margaret?" I took a sip of my coffee. "Or can I call you Margie, like Cowboy Speidel?"

"Margaret will do. The judge admires strength. He bulldozes lawyers he perceives as weak. You impressed him this morning."

The corridor was quiet, neighboring courtrooms dark. If we'd been in the state justice building, bailiffs would be clattering down the hall yelling lawyers' names, hustling their late asses into court, keeping the conveyor belt of so-called justice rolling.

"My advice, just keep doing what you're doing," Bolden said.

That made me laugh. "You're gaming me. You want me to go *mano a mano* with His Majesty, who'll behead me, or at least hold me in contempt."

She shook her head. "Think about it, Jake. Do I want to try this case twice?"

I didn't answer, so she kept going. "Trust me, I really don't want you to have any viable appellate issues."

"So, you're doing what, giving me free advice on how to beat you in court?"

"No way. You have an unwinnable case. Your client did everything he's accused of doing. He has no legal defenses. I'm just trying to be as fair with you as I expect you to be with me."

She seemed sincere, but I never believe a lawyer unless she's under oath, passes a polygraph, and has two corroborating witnesses. Hey, they don't call us sharks for our ability to swim. Still, there was nothing to lose in listening.

"Okay, thanks. What else do you have for me?"

"Just be your own combative self. You'll occasionally win an argument. But choose your battles carefully and don't challenge him personally."

"Like I did this morning. Basically, calling him a liar about 'when' and 'if.'"

"Big mistake. But he's giving you more slack than I've ever seen from him. Just don't push your luck."

I finished my coffee and picked up my trial bag. "I owe you one, and I'm gonna reciprocate by teaching you how to pick a jury."

She chuckled softly. "I've been picking juries for nineteen years."

"But not the Lassiter way."

"Oh, brother."

"I assume you watch the jurors file into the box. Pay attention to their bearing, see who looks like a leader and who's a follower?

"I do all of that. And in the old days, I used to see what books they were carrying. Now, it's just iPads and cell phones."

"Okay, listen up. I'm not gonna give away the secrets of my craft, but if you watch closely when we get started, you'll see I accomplish three goals."

"Why do I think you're gonna number them for me?"

"One, I'll get a few who will actually hold the government to its burden of proof. They're not gonna believe that where there's smoke, my client's ass is necessarily on fire."

"Two...?"

"Two, I will establish the theme of my defense, which is quite simple. The government is attempting to criminalize that which is not a crime. The U.S.A. has kidnapped justice and is hiding it inside the law."

"If you're talking about jury nullification, Judge Speidel might order the marshals to kidnap you."

"And three, I will make friends with the jury. Not all of them. Maybe only two or three. But all I need is one for a hung jury. Shall I tell you how I make friends with strangers who are naturally suspicious of slick-talking shysters?"

"If you must."

"It's not easy. Voir dire requires experience and people skills. You should just watch me, maybe take notes if you wish."

"Oh. My. God." She said it deliberately, emphasizing each word. "It just occurred to me, Jake. I'm being mansplained to by a man with brain damage."

CHAPTER THIRTY-EIGHT
The Ideal Juror

Some lawyers think you win cases in closing argument, jack-hammering the cracks in the prosecution's case into giant crevasses. Some say opening statement, when you tell your story in compelling terms. Me? I don't care if you're a better orator than Abe Lincoln. If you empanel a jury biased against your client by background or experience, or a jury filled with the vindictive and heartless, well, you will lose. To win any case, you must win voir dire.

I stood exactly five feet from the rail of the jury box—not so close as to invade the jurors' space—and inquired, "Ms. Dixon, would you agree that's it's wrong to cheat in school?"

"Why, yes, of course I would."

"So, if I'm a student, if I look over at my neighbor's exam and copy the answers, that would be morally wrong."

"Yes, certainly."

"But should it be a federal crime?"

Dorothea Dixon pursed her lips and thought about it. She was a 44-year-old mail carrier for the postal service. Most defense lawyers are skeptical about seating civil servants who are roughly on the same side as government prosecutors. My view is different.

Government employees know the incompetence, inefficiency, and sometimes pure venality of bureaucrats.

"No, sir. I think that would be a waste of time and money," Ms. Dixon answered.

I nodded and gave her a small, friendly smile. Sending the message: *You got that right, Ma'am.*

"Now let's say I'm the smart student in this story," I said, "hard as that may be to believe." Ms. Dixon smiled back at me, and a couple other prospective jurors chuckled.

Oh, what a warm and friendly puppy of a lawyer.

"I purposely let my friend copy my answers on the test," I continued. "Should I be charged with a federal crime?"

"Same answer, sir," Ms. Dixon replied. "Doesn't seem like that big a deal."

"One more. I'm that same smart student working my way through school. The kid next to me has rich parents, and he offers me money, a lot of money, to copy my answers. What now, Ms. Dixon? Should I be charged with a federal crime for taking money to let him cheat?"

She thought about it. I felt movement behind me, petite Margaret Bolden in her stylish navy pumps, changing position so that my bulk didn't block her view. It's as important to watch jurors' faces and body language as to listen to their answers. I shifted two steps to the left, forcing Margaret to bunny-hop back the other way. Just one of the million games lawyers play.

"The money doesn't change my answer," Ms. Dixon said. "I think both students should be expelled, but neither one should be charged with a federal crime."

"Exactly!" I congratulated her. "What if the government charges me, the smart, poor student, for taking that money? But they don't charge that rich kid who paid me to let him cheat?"

"That's just plain wrong," Ms. Dixon concluded.

"And yet that's the government's case. The United States of America has turned student codes of conduct into criminal statutes. They've chosen to criminalize students' mischief but only charge one of the two mischief-makers."

"Objection!" Bolden sang out.

"Sustained," Judge Speidel replied. "Save that for closing argument, Mr. Lassiter."

"Thank you, Your Honor," I said, as if I had won the objection. Another game we play.

The judge shot a look at the wall clock. "And speed it up, please."

"Of course, Your Honor," I answered, like a good boy.

Margaret Bolden was crisp and to the point when she questioned Dorthea Dixon, my favorite letter carrier of all time. "Ms. Dixon, do you understand that it will be Judge Speidel and not Mr. Lassiter who will instruct the jury on the law?"

"Of course."

"Will you follow the law as instructed by the judge as applied to the facts in this case?"

"Yes."

She had one more question. You could see it coming from the last row of the bleachers.

"Even if you disagree with the law, will you nonetheless follow the judge's instructions?"

"Well, I believe if I'm chosen, I have to take an oath to do that, right?"

"You do."

"There's your answer. I don't swear falsely."

Fine with me. Any other answer, and the government could remove Ms. Dixon for cause. The woman had a heart. I felt it beating when she looked at Kip and I heard a gentleness in her voice when she answered my questions. She was a keeper. And because she was an African American woman around the same age as Ms. Bolden and answered exactly as she should, I doubted the government would exercise a peremptory challenge to remove her.

I turned my attention from Ms. Dixon in chair number four to Manuel Castillo next door in number five. Thirty-seven years old with a shaved head, he wore a black T-shirt and every square inch of each arm was covered in tattoos. For a moment, I wondered if he was a customer of juror number nine, a Sunny Isles tattoo artist. I am old enough to remember when only sailors, prison inmates, and corpses in the morgue sported tattoos.

"Mr. Castillo," I began, "I note on your questionnaire that you are a molecular gastronomy chef. The fusion of chemistry and cooking, right?"

"Yes, changing the form of food for artistic presentations and unique tastes."

"And where do you cook?"

"Catalania on South Beach."

"Aha! One of my favorites. The chicken croquetas have such an unusual burst of flavor."

He nodded, appreciatively. "We inject them with seawater."

"That's it!" I cried out. "Such palatal chaos."

I heard Kip snicker at the defense table. I would have to remind him to clam up when I'm on center stage.

"It's my homage to Chef José Andrés," the chef said.

"Ah yes, at his wonderful Bazaar. Who, in turn, credited Ferran Andriá. Such ingenuity. Gazpacho with no liquid. Ice cream with salt instead of sugar. Chocolate-infused with wasabi. But as far as croquetas go, yours are *más deliciosas*."

The chef beamed at me. People who love their work equally love being told that it's very good work, indeed. I retreated from my position at the jury box to the podium. Not to find my notes because I wasn't using any. I needed to prop myself up.

Vertigo.

It had come on quickly, the jury box tilting to and fro like a dinghy in a storm. The asymmetrical ceiling with its odd-shaped panels spun overhead, resembling animated versions of the Milky Way galaxy. I grabbed the podium with two hands and hung on like a drowning man clinging to a log.

"Mr. Lassiter, please speed it up," the judge told me, his voice echoing so that I heard him twice.

"Of course, Your Honor."

The spinning slowed enough for me to continue. "Mr. Castillo, have you read *We Fed an Island*, José Andrés' book about Puerto Rico after the hurricane?"

His eyes lit up. "I helped him cook there, and I'm reading the book now. In Spanish."

"Of course. *Alimentamos Una Isla: Una Historia Verdadera Sobre la Reconstrucción de Puerto Rico.*"

Maybe I was ladling on the sauce too thick, but the chef smiled at me.

"Mr. Lassiter," Judge Speidel said, "your linguistic skills are duly noted, but please move it along."

"Of course, Your Honor." I moved out from behind the podium and returned to my position in front of the jury box. "Mr. Castillo, based on your experience in Puerto Rico, it seems to me that you want to help other people."

"That is true."

"And would it be true, too, that you appreciate those qualities in others?"

"Yes."

I turned to the defense table and gestured toward Kip. "Then I hope you will carefully listen to all that is said in the coming weeks about my client, Kip Lassiter."

"I will."

When I sat down, Margaret Bolden returned for another round of questioning.

Maybe she correctly guessed that I had never eaten the chef's chicken croquettes. I know as much about molecular gastronomy as I do about nuclear fission, which might actually be involved in some of these modern dishes. My pal, Shifty Steve Solomon, patrolled the jurors' parking lot this morning, surveilling incoming cars. Solomon told me that the chef's Volvo had a parking sticker for Catalania, which gave me his employment, and Señor Google told me about the croquetas on the menu. Clearly visible on the passenger seat was a copy of the Puerto Rico book.

My ideal juror is someone wanting to "stick it to the Man," to use an old expression. I picture a guy driving a 14-year-old Honda with a dented fender and a missing taillight, a bumper sticker reading, "My kid can beat up your honor student," a dozen parking tickets crumpled in the front seat with several Burger King wrappers. Lacking that, I'll take the postal worker who believes cheating on tests shouldn't be a crime and a chef who thinks I adore his cooking. I also like to know what television programs jurors watch. Law shows where defendants are often wrongfully accused are my favorite. And for this trial, I needed a couple of *Star Trek* fans for a gambit I wanted to try in closing argument.

Margaret Bolden kept to her protocol with the chef, speaking quietly and standing as tall as her five foot frame would allow. She'd had the chance to Google the man while I was on my feet.

"Mr. Castillo, you make an appetizer with ibérico ham from Spain, correct?"

The chef smiled. "*Jamón ibérico de Bellota.* Free-range, acorn-fed, cured four years in mountain air. The Beluga caviar of ham."

"And you sell a small appetizer portion for $46, correct?"

"Yes, but one leg of such a ham imported from Spain costs more than a thousand dollars."

"If your supplier, without your knowledge, substituted an inferior ham, an imposter, raised on scraps in a barnyard in Mississippi, would you be upset?"

"Upset! I would be enraged. It would be...a...a..."

"A fraud, perhaps?"

"Yes! And it could ruin my reputation."

I knew the gist of Bolden's next question, and I could object. But I would appear scared of the point she was making. Which I was, but why draw attention?

"So, Mr. Castillo, can you see why elite universities would be upset, even enraged, if they thought they had admitted the Beluga caviar of students and received canned tuna imposters instead?"

Damn, she was good.

"Yes, of course."

The prosecutor thanked the chef, and the judge allowed as it was a fine time for the mid-afternoon recess. He had a hearty snack waiting in chambers. After the jury filed out, I sauntered over to the government table and whispered, "If this were a fencing match, this is where I would say, *'Touché.'*"

She gave me a wry smile. "'Palatal chaos?' What the hell is that?"

"No idea. Pulled it from an incredibly pretentious restaurant review."

"You still got game, you crafty son of a bitch."

CHAPTER THIRTY-NINE
The Boiler without a Safety Valve

Melissa Gold...

Looking drained, Jake walked into the kitchen and plopped into one of the chairs at the counter.

"Hey, hon," she said. "Drink?"

"In a second."

Melissa was about to ask about the trial, but before she could, he announced, "I've got some background on the helmet guy."

"Dr. Jeffries, the biomechanical engineer?"

"He's an expert witness for the football helmet industry. Makes seven hundred bucks an hour testifying for the defense when they're sued by high school players who've been injured."

"I thought he was critical of the helmet industry. Isn't that his claim to fame?"

"This is where it gets interesting." Jake got to his feet, opened the fridge, pulled out a 16-ounce bottle of Grolsch, and sat down again. "Do you know Stuart Grossman?"

"I know of him. Big time plaintiff's lawyer."

"Stuart gave me access to this secret database that P.I. lawyers keep on expert witnesses. I was able to read Jeffries's testimony in a dozen different cases. He always says the same thing. The helmet in every case is 'state of the art,' so it's not defective. Now, get this. He's working on a space-age helmet that will change the state of the art, but they're not available yet."

"I'm confused. What's that have to do with the N.I.H. program, other than the fact that he's unqualified to run it?"

"It took me a while to figure it out. NFL helmets cost between $1,000 and $1,500. He says his space-age helmet will cost double that. If he's running N.I.H. study, it will identify helmets as the culprit in C.T.E. Then, he'll make a fortune when the League throws out the old helmets and starts buying his product."

"But surely the NFL knows that," she said, still puzzled.

"Exactly! They don't care. They'd rather pay a few million for equipment than another billion-dollar settlement for C.T.E. This is their way of sidestepping additional liability."

Her eyes burned with anger. Tampering with scientific research in pursuit of profits was a deadly sin. "The N.I.H. won't stand for this!"

"Then you'd better tell them."

"You bet your jock strap I will!"

Just then, Kip came flying into the kitchen, shorn of suit coat and tie, his trial uniform. "Melissa, you should have seen Uncle Jake today. He kicked government butt."

"It was just jury selection, kiddo," Jake said, his eyes half-closed, as if he wanted to doze off, "and it was pretty much a draw."

"But a draw is a win for the defense because the government has the burden of proof. You taught me that."

Jake let out a long breath and said, "True."

Melissa thought he looked exhausted, with his face drawn. Last night, he had slept restlessly, kicking the sheets now and then and waking her up. She wasn't going to press him to rehash his day in court. She also didn't want to seem overly concerned about him. Jake was a man who soldiered on and played through pain. The stoic male, a throwback in many ways. She would say nothing to make him think he needed a duty nurse.

Kip said, "The prosecutor is pretty tough, though, isn't she, Uncle Jake?"

He nodded. "No pushover."

For a man of many words, tonight he was practically mute. Too tired to talk. She had brought dinner home from Havana Harry's on LeJeune. Vaca frita, shredded beef cooked until crispy with onions and garlic, fried plantains, and, for dessert, Jake's favorite, *tres leches*, sponge cake with condensed milk, whole milk, and heavy cream. But he ate little of the beef and plantains and none of the dessert, which sat in front of him at the kitchen table. Kip had wolfed down his quinoa salad with avocado, sweet potatoes, and beets, but spent a moment inhaling the aroma of the crispy beef.

"Do you want a drink, Jake?" Melissa asked.

"Just coffee. Gotta prep."

Kip seemed unaware of his uncle's condition and just kept prattling on. "I really liked the chef. Especially when he said he wanted to help other people. Before I hooked up with Max Ringle, I did free test counseling for kids from poor families, and now I have an idea to expand it. I'm gonna create SAT and ACT prep courses for underprivileged kids from Appalachia, inner cities, immigrants with problems in English. All pro bono."

"That sounds wonderful," Melissa said.

"I can statistically identify general deficiencies found in those groups, then aim the courses at those weaknesses. What do you think, Uncle Jake?"

"Great idea, Kip."

He said it without any inflection, though Kip didn't seem to notice. He kept going a while, before carrying his own *tres leches* to his room.

"Kip seems upbeat," she said when he was gone.

"Strange as it sounds," Jake observed, "he's not cognizant that he'll probably be teaching his SAT courses to fellow inmates, not kids in Appalachia. He's a little detached from reality."

"Which is part of your defense. Did you get any *Star Trek* fans on the jury?"

"Three." He used a fork to toy with the meringue on top the *tres leches* but didn't eat any. "Three trekkies out of twelve."

"That's good. Did you ask if any of them remember the reality distortion field episode?"

He shook his head. "I didn't want to tip Margaret Bolden to that defense, far-fetched as it may be."

"It's not really a defense, is it?"

"It's more like those rocket ship fins on a 1959 Cadillac," he said. "Showy and distracting, but no real purpose." He barked out a small laugh. "Kind of like my career."

He was worrying her, but she would approach the subject oh-so-gently. "Are you a little down tonight, Jake?"

"Had the adrenaline rush in court. Seems to have sapped my energy. I've got my hands full with Margaret Bolden."

"What's she like?"

"Poised. Confident. Unruffled. She's petite, almost tiny, but she walks across the well of the courtroom as if she owns the real estate. She'll be hard to fluster."

"Will you try?"

He seemed to think about it before replying. "She's too likeable, and I'd look like a big jerk."

"And the judge?"

"Prosecution oriented. Hard-ass. I'm still feeling him out. Not sure how far I can push jury nullification without being held in contempt."

"He doesn't scare you?"

"Nah, but it scares me that he doesn't scare me."

"Meaning?"

"Ninety percent of the time, I can play the game of the obsequious lawyer, kissing the judge's robes, thanking him for letting me breathe. But ten percent of the time, I'm like a hot boiler without a safety valve, nothing to relieve the pressure."

"And how does that manifest itself?"

"Impulse control and a loss of focus. Just for a few seconds. Drifting off somewhere, not hearing the judge or the prosecutor or even my own thoughts. Then I say something seriously stupid."

She kept her demeanor calm, belying her feelings. By any objective standard, Jake's condition was worsening. The symptoms he described were common in the early stages of dementia. She believed more than ever that defending Kip's case was dangerous for him.

"I've been held in contempt a bunch of times in state court," he said.

"I know."

"Once, years ago, a judge yelled at me, 'Mr. Lassiter, I'm gonna send you to a place you've never been.'"

"I said, 'Already been to jail, Your Honor.'"

"And he said, 'Not talking about jail. I'm sending you to law school.'"

She didn't smile and didn't laugh. She just looked at him.

"What?" he asked.

"You've told me that story before. You know that, right?"

He smacked his forehead with his right hand. "Sure, I do."

She wasn't convinced. They had a quiet moment before she inquired, "What else besides impulse control? What about headaches?"

"They come and go, like armies marching in the night."

"Tinnitus?"

"Same, but I'm so used to the sound, it's just background noise. Like jet engines on an endless flight."

"Anything else?"

He took a forkful of meringue into his mouth, then dipped the fork into the sodden cake, which dripped with milk and cream. She handed him a spoon, which was more useful.

"I got a little dizzy in court today, but it passed quickly," Jake said.

Again, she controlled her reaction. Vertigo in patients with traumatic brain injuries usually worsens, especially in times of stress. "On Thursday, you're due for an injection."

He spooned some sugary cake into his mouth. "Gonna skip it until the trial's over."

"Not a good idea, Jake. Nobody quits cold turkey."

Unless they die.

But she didn't say that. Instead, he asked, "How about if we just reduce the dosage?"

"I can't deal with the side effects right now. I need to sleep. I need to focus. I need not to fall down in court."

She could have argued with him, could have said, *"There's no evidence the antibodies are causing those side effects."*

But there was also scant evidence the antibodies were helping, and maybe stopping them would have a reverse placebo effect and he'd sleep better, focus better, and not become dizzy.

"It's your choice, Jake."

He smiled warmly at her, a puff of meringue in the corner of his mouth. "I love the way you give me unconditional love and support."

"Is there a 'but' coming?"

"No way. The opposite. You support me even when you think I'm wrong."

"But I tell you what I think, and then you have to decide. That's the give-and-take of an adult relationship."

With an index finger, she scraped the meringue off his lip and ate it. He laughed and said, "You, Melissa Gold, are the one I never knew I always wanted."

She cocked her head and gave him a sly smile. "That's beautiful, but didn't that come from a movie, some rom-com we watched on Amazon?"

"Of course it did. It was funny as hell, and a wonderful night with you."

She could tell he was just winging it, with no recollection whatsoever. "It surely was," she said.

CHAPTER FORTY
Sorcerer's Apprentice

"This is the story of a very intelligent young man," Margaret Bolden began, "a young man who could have been a success at virtually any endeavor but chose to be a major player in a nationwide criminal conspiracy of deception and fraud. For him, a very lucrative criminal conspiracy. For others, a trail of destruction, criminal records, and shattered reputations."

Bolden turned away from the jury box, walked several paces to the defense table, and pointed at Kip, her pink fingernails a foot from his face. "This is that man. The defendant, Chester Lassiter, also known as Kip. The man who directed the criminal conspiracy and profited from it."

Bolden's opening statement was pretty much what I expected from an experienced, savvy trial lawyer. She didn't cling to the hackneyed structure that begins, "The evidence will show...blah, blah, blah."

She told her story, establishing the theme in the first two sentences. A damn interesting story, I'm sorry to say, that would make a decent movie. It had a hero, an FBI agent named Peter Wisniewski who, with a cast of hundreds, uncovered the villainy and put together the government's air-tight case. It had a villain, the angelic-looking, yet evil Kip Lassiter, an avaricious, manipulative, deceptive young man who preyed on the insecurities of decent parents who only wanted the best for their saintly children.

As in dramas dating back to Aristotle, the villain had an ally, the mastermind Max Ringle. Yes, Ringle was a scam artist, but he finally saw the beatific glow of justice, not unlike Saul on the road to Damascus being bathed in divine light.

Victims? Oh, there were victims galore. The students themselves, some of whom supposedly did not know their parents had paid a ringer to bounce their test scores by thirty percent. I looked forward to cross-examining these entitled brats about their galactic ignorance. The universities, too, were victims, the prosecutor said. They were deprived of their "property," those priceless admissions slots. We were going to hear from university administrators about the damage to dear old Ivy. And yes, I hungered to cross-examine the starch out of those administrators' shirts.

Two other A.U.S.A.'s sat at the government table, a man and a woman, both in their early thirties, each with a laptop. They were typing away, either taking notes or playing solitaire. Behind them, in the row of chairs in front of the railing that separates the gallery from the well of the courtroom—technically the "bar"—sat three more government types. Assistants or consultants or investigative personnel, who knows? They had their own laptops. At their feet were neatly arranged expansion files with color-coded folders.

Oh, bring on your minions. I'm always outnumbered but never outgunned.

Margaret Bolden told the jury that Agent Wisniewski would be the first witness and would give them a tour of the conspiracy. He would explain both the larger conspiracy involving Max Ringle and this particularly devious scheme involving Kip Lassiter. The "exam bribery tentacle," she called it. Agent Wisniewski would play numerous recorded conversations for the jury, each of which would implicate the defendant.

"You will hear the defendant discussing his nefarious actions," she said. "You will see photos and video of him entering and exiting testing centers on the day of exams. You will hear from parents who paid him, and you will see bank records of the deposits of his ill-gotten gains. The proof will be overwhelming that this is an open-and-shut case of fraud, racketeering, and money laundering."

Well, I had to agree. It certainly sounded open-and-shut. But I intended to stick my size 14 cleats through that open door and kick it off the hinges before it slammed shut.

"You will hear from Max Ringle in person," the prosecutor went on. "He may have been the sorcerer, but Kip Lassiter was the sorcerer's apprentice."

Ouch! A deadly turn of phrase. That's what you get when a dozen A.U.S.A.'s and FBI agents hang out in a conference room for months, drinking coffee and eating croissants on the taxpayers' dime.

"Both men are equally guilty in the eyes of the law," Bolden said. "The difference is that Mr. Ringle admits his guilt and expresses remorse. Mr. Lassiter has forced us to bring him to trial at great expense to the government and inconvenience to you..."

"Objection! What the hell!" I was on my feet and just this side of crazy. I wasn't sure what I'd just said or what I'd say next. "That violates the presumption of innocence. It violates Golden Rule by invoking the jurors. It condemns the defendant for pleading not guilty. It's friggin' improper, and Ray knows it!"

The judge pointed a finger at me. "Pipe down, Mr. Lassiter. Your objection is sustained. The jury shall disregard the last statement by Ms. Bolden. Now, up here, both of you."

Next to me, Kip whispered, "You okay, Uncle Jake?"

I ignored him and stumbled a step, making my way to the side of the bench away from the jury. Margaret Bolden followed.

"First of all, Mr. Lassiter," the judge whispered, "who's Ray?"

I pinched the bridge of my nose with my thumb and index finger. There seemed to be a pain somewhere deep in there. "Did I say 'Ray?'"

"You did, sir."

"I guess it's Ray Pincher, the state attorney. I've tried a lot of cases against him, and he always does something to set me off."

The judge turned toward the prosecutor. "Margie, not like you to light a firecracker and toss it under the defense table."

"I apologize, Your Honor. I went too far."

The judge harrumphed and turned back to me. "Now, Mr. Lassiter, did I hear you use an expletive in making your objection?"

"I'm sorry, Your Honor. I lost it there for a second."

He eyed me a moment with a cautious look, as if wondering whether to pet a barking dog. "I Googled you, Mr. Lassiter. Your name came up in a story about that brain disease."

"Yes, sir. Chronic traumatic encephalopathy."

"Is that a bicycle helmet I see on the defense table?"

"It is, Your Honor."

"Is that your head gear in case you keel over? You gonna collapse in my courtroom?"

"Won't happen, Your Honor."

If he pressed me, I thought, I'd have to tell him why the bike helmet was there, costing me a bishop or a knight in the chess game of a trial.

"I've had a lawyer stroke out in closing argument," the judge said, forgetting all about the helmet. "Had a young fellow pee his pants when I struck his pleadings in a civil case. Fouls up my schedule, I can tell you that."

"I'm good to go, Your Honor. Strong bladder."

"Then, both of you, back to your places. Let's wrap up opening statements and take some testimony."

The unflappable Margaret Bolden took her position in front of the jury box. Summing up, she shifted her tone to kind and empathetic, even lowering her voice to that of a trusted friend sharing personal advice. "This is a criminal case, but it is also a tragedy. A tragedy that a young man of such promise could have strayed so far off the path. Perhaps it is a good thing that he is so young so that he will have a chance to redeem himself at some later date…"

Meaning when he gets out of prison.

I didn't know exactly where she was going with this. She walked to the defense table and stood alongside Kip, and then spoke in her soft whispery voice. "As you look at the defendant and see this young man of promise, you might be tempted to feel sorry for him. But the court will instruct you that, and I quote, 'The law does not permit you to be governed by sympathy.'"

She returned to her position in front of the jury box. "Sympathy is a wonderful human emotion, but it has no place in the courtroom any more than vengeance does. All that matters is the law."

Ah, so that was it. Kip's youthful, wholesome appearance worried Bolden. Kip would testify, and hopefully the new, improved, redemption-seeking Kip would appear on the stand, rather than the cocky, cashmere hoodie-wearing smartass.

Of course, when I presented the defense case, I intended to shamelessly appeal to the jurors' sympathy, no matter the jury instruction or the prosecutor's objections. I would invoke Kip's worthless mother, his unknown father, his beloved Granny, and the vicissitudes of his youth. When it comes to my conduct in trials, I have only two rules. I won't lie to the court or let a witness do it. Other than that, batten the hatches, because I sail straight into storms.

Bolden spent a few more minutes talking about the judge's wise instructions and the jurors' grave responsibilities, then thanked them all and sat down.

I got to my feet, nodded to the judge, buttoned my suit coat, smiled warmly, and said my six favorite words in the English language. "Ladies and gentlemen of the jury..."

CHAPTER FORTY-ONE
Too Soon Old, Too Late Smart

"Ladies and gentlemen of the jury." I looked at fourteen faces, a dozen jurors and two alternates. "I love saying that. The jury. The bulwark of our freedoms. Our line of defense against tyranny.

"I represent the defendant, my nephew, Chester Lassiter. He prefers to be called 'Kip.' Because he's still a kid, I sometimes call him kiddo. Or even Kippers. You can call him whatever you want, except one thing. You can't call him guilty because he is not."

I was working without a net, which is to say without notes. Even with my faulty memory, I felt I could do this. There was something purely instinctual about standing in front of a jury and telling a story, and I didn't want to peer down at my notes on the podium, jurors studying the top of my head. I needed to look them in the eye, show them my sincerity

"You are the folks who hold Kip Lassiter's fate in your hands," I continued. "Not me. Not Ms. Bolden. Not even Judge Speidel. What you do sets the course for the rest of his life. So, I'm making sure you realize the heavy burden that's on your shoulders.

"I was thinking about each of you this morning when I walked into this building carrying my coffee past all those reporters and photographers and bloggers and so-called social media influencers.

And I wondered what you thought as you went through security and saw all that commotion that will only build with each day of trial."

I turned ninety degrees to look into the gallery, so the jurors would do the same. They would recognize some local television personalities and a few of the network and cable talking heads, too. The judge would instruct the jurors not to read or watch coverage of the trial. It is an admonition that is never followed.

I spotted Gilberto Foyo from Ray Pincher's office in the first row of the gallery. He returned my look and nodded. As far as I could tell, he was my only cheerleader.

"You've seen the massive publicity. And in voir dire, you each said you can set it aside and decide the case solely on the evidence. But what is it you're thinking? 'This must be a big case.' In this glorious modern building that looks like a giant ship. In this palatial courtroom. Every seat taken. A federal case with a distinguished judge. An indictment charging an astounding thirty-seven felonies. Thirty-seven!

"Are you wondering, 'Is Kip Lassiter some master criminal, some racketeer, some member of organized crime?' Then you take your seats and look at my client. My nephew. The boy I raised. This clean-cut, bright, polite kid; the kind of young man you hope will show up one day to take your daughter to the movies. Maybe you wonder, 'Am I in the right courtroom?'"

Some jurors smiled, and I smiled right back. My demeanor is calculated to say: *I'm a regular guy. Let's chat. You can trust me.*

"A few minutes ago, Ms. Bolden quoted one of the judge's instructions to you. She said your verdict must not be governed by sympathy. Good, because the defense isn't looking for sympathy. We're only looking for justice. And fairness. And equal application of the law. And I'll have a lot more to say about all of those things in closing argument when I talk about who got prosecuted and who didn't.

"By the way, that jury instruction the prosecutor quoted was incomplete. Ms. Bolden left something out. The government does that a lot, shows you the favorable evidence and tosses unfavorable evidence out the window. My job is to stand outside, catch that discarded evidence, and bring it home."

"Objection! That's argument." Bolden was on her feet, glaring at me. "And over the line, even as that."

"Sustained. Mr. Lassiter, let's save it for closing."

"Certainly, Your Honor," I agreed. It was a minor infraction, a five-yard penalty for jumping offsides. "What the prosecutor left out," I continued, "in the very same sentence of the judge's instruction, is that your verdict cannot be based on 'public opinion.' Those reporters, those commentators, and those social media influencers don't get to vote. Only you do.

"Now, here's the government's entire case in a nutshell: Kip Lassiter helped some kids cheat their way into college. That's it. Some might have gotten in anyway, if their parents had just contributed directly to the university, instead of going through Max Ringle's bribery scheme. See, here's the deal. Our elite universities sell admissions slots to children of major donors. Now, the universities might disagree with the word 'sell,' but that's just semantics. And you'll hear the evidence, so you can decide."

Three jurors nodded. Always a good sign, unless it meant they're falling asleep.

"You're going to hear from Kip Lassiter," I went on. "He's going to admit to you everything he did. How wrong he was, how sorry he is. And that reminds me of something I learned when I went to college in Pennsylvania. There's an old Pennsylvania Dutch expression: 'Too soon old, too late smart.' It applies to all of us. How many of us have said, 'If I'd only known then...?'"

I paused a moment and watched nearly every juror nodding, slight smiles on their faces.

"Kip will tell you the worst decision he ever made in his young life was going to work for the con man, the fraudster, the professional liar, Max Ringle. Kip was nineteen when he started working for Ringle. I don't know about you, but I wouldn't want to be judged for the rest of my life on things I did at age nineteen."

Margaret Bolden got to her feet, seemingly considering objecting, but didn't.

"I can't sit down without a word about Max Ringle. I feel sorry for Ms. Bolden and her army of government assistants. Foisted upon them, the hero of their story, is a man who built his career out of a mountain of fraud, lies, and deceptions. How many hours did they spend preparing his testimony and whitewashing his character? Did they hold their noses when dealing with him? He's as crooked and corrupt a man who has ever walked through those courtroom doors."

"Objection!" Bolden sang out. "That is beyond the pale."

"Rein in those horses, Mr. Lassiter," the judge scolded, by which he must have meant, "sustained."

I moved one step closer to the jury box and said, "I'm going to wrap it up now, because I don't want to wear out my welcome. I feel this great responsibility to my client, my nephew, Kip. But in truth, yours is even greater. You are sitting in judgment. In a way, you asked for this responsibility. You could have been excused. But you said you could be fair. I trusted each of you when you said that, and at the end of the case, I will trust in your verdict, which I believe will be not guilty on each and every count. Thank you."

CHAPTER FORTY-TWO
The Perfect Witness

If Peter Wisniewski wasn't an FBI agent, he could have played one on TV. Forty-six years old, undergrad degree in criminal justice from Fordham, law degree from Georgetown— solid Jesuit path that several generations have followed into law enforcement. Five years in the U.S. Army, commendations as a special agent in the Criminal Investigation Command, seventeen years with the FBI, currently the agent in charge of Operation Flunk Out.

Grayish hair trimmed short, grayish suit not too stylish, button-down white shirt, blue-gray tie you wouldn't remember ten seconds after you saw it. He stood a shade under six feet, appeared fit, and exuded competence. If he were a guest in your home and a grease fire broke out in your kitchen, he would put it out while you were wondering whether to call the fire department or douse the flames with baking soda.

My overall impression was that Agent Wisniewski had testified in federal court hundreds of times without ever breaking a sweat. In short, the perfect government witness. As promised in the government's opening statement, he was the tour guide. First stop: Los Angeles.

Quest Educational Development started as a legitimate counseling and coaching service for the children of the well-to-do, Wisniewski said. But somewhere along the line, Max Ringle had devised his "guaranteed acceptance" plan, involving bribes disguised as charitable contributions.

"The conspiracy had many tentacles," Wisniewski said. "Ringle bribed varsity coaches and administrators at elite universities to designate his clients as recruited athletes when they were not. This facilitated their admission because of the relaxed academic standards for athletes. To accomplish this, Ringle arranged for résumés to be falsified, and photographs were doctored to create fabricated credentials. Ringle also created a phony charity to disguise the bribes as charitable contributions. Let's call this part of Ringle's fraud the 'bribery tentacle.'"

"What were the limitations of that part of the fraudulent enterprise?" Bolden asked.

"Ringle could only use the bribery tentacle where he had corrupted university employees. To expand his reach to virtually every university, he needed a way to cheat on the college board exams themselves. That's where the defendant came into the scheme and it expanded exponentially. It's the fraudulent exam tentacle."

"Please describe this fraud for the jury," Bolden said.

"It was brazen, and one might even say brilliantly devious."

A rare editorial comment from the FBI agent.

"Ringle corrupted ACT and SAT administrators at several locations around the country," Wisniewski continued. "He paid them to allow the defendant to take the exams in place of the actual students or to serve as a proctor and correct wrong answers."

Our tour continued in Kansas City, Houston, Miami, and back to Los Angeles, the test locations with corrupted exam proctors who let Kip in the door. Wisniewski recited chapter and verse of Kip's transgressions. The name of each student and date of the test. The student's prior test score and then Kip's score, and the eventual admission of the student to Yale, USC, Texas, Wake Forest, Stanford, UCLA, and Georgetown. Eighteen tests in total, eighteen successful admissions.

Wisniewski identified surveillance photos of Kip entering and leaving the testing sites as well as photos from cameras inside the testing rooms. He called the photos the "smoking gun," although Kip was holding a number-two pencil, rather than a nine-millimeter.

Judge Speidel admitted the photos into evidence and one by one, they appeared on a large screen for the jury to see. The jurors sat up straight, necks craned toward the screen. In the one-picture-is-worth-a-thousand-words department, a single photo stood out: Kip smiling at the proctor who was also on Ringle's payroll. A big, cocky grin, as if one of them had just told a joke. I heard a juror snort derisively. The photo had an impact, and Margaret Bolden knew it.

Next came the tapes, both audio and video. There was Kip on the phone with parents, asking for handwriting samples from their kids for the essay questions. Turns out he was a decent forger, as well as an imposter. More phone calls between Ringle and Kip, matter-of-fact discussions of test dates and target scores. First Ringle, then Kip.

"Don't ever go more than thirty percent above the moron's prior test."

"Aw, Max. Don't worry. I hit within five points of the SAT target every time and you know it. On the ACT, I'll nail it. You want a 34, you got it."

Oh, damn. Kip sounded so cocky, so arrogant. That wasn't the Kip I saw now, the one who wanted to live with integrity and give something back. But Margaret Bolden knew just how to create the impression of Kip the conspirator, the cheater, the fraudster, the criminal.

Next came the audio tape made on Ringle's terrace the day that ended with me face-down in the rose bushes. Belatedly, I had been right. The terrace was bugged with hidden microphones, and the recording was one of the most damning pieces of evidence against Kip. Aware of the taping and buttering the buns of the government's case for his own ends, Ringle had urged Kip not to be modest and tell good old Uncle Jake about his scheme.

The jurors leaned forward in their chairs as the recording began with Kip's voice.

"I've devised two plans. One is to take the tests as an imposter, and the other is to monitor the tests as a proctor. For the first one, I make phony drivers' licenses and assume the identity of the student. That only works with the guys. For the girls, I bribe proctors to get in the door. That's only in a few cities, but I'm working on several more for next year."

Oh, shit on a stick. I could almost see the words "imposter" and "phony" and "bribe" leap from the speakers and lodge in the jurors' minds.

My mood was plunging, but I kept my poker face in place.

Never let them see your fear.

Next to me, Kip fidgeted. I put a calming hand on his arm.

"Was the defendant paid for his services?" Ms. Bolden asked.

"He received between $25,000 and $30,000 per test, plus bonuses for hitting target scores," the FBI agent replied. "The amount of his compensation depended on the total amount the client paid Ringle. The defendant earned more than six-hundred thousand dollars in total, but apparently had an interest in the overall profits of Quest, as opposed to simply being a salaried employee."

"How did you reach that conclusion?"

Yeah, what the hell? I'm wondering the same thing myself.

"We uncovered a bank account of the defendant in Grand Cayman with substantially more money than he had been paid on a per-test basis."

Oh, that.

More documents were produced. Bank account records with Kip's signature on the forms. A total of $1.3 million deposited, none ever taken out.

Kip whispered to me, "I didn't know anything about that."

"I know. I know. Quiet down."

By the time Bolden looked at me and said, "Your witness," I didn't want anything to do with the FBI agent. Not now, anyway. My stamina gone, my energy depleted, I saw little starbursts when I squeezed my eyes shut. When I opened them, the clock on the courtroom wall showed 4:45 p.m.

"Your Honor, noting the lateness of the hour, may I suggest we recess until tomorrow morning for cross-examination," I requested in my polite lawyer voice.

"You may suggest anything you like, counselor, but I don't want to send these good folks out into rush hour traffic. We'll work 'til six-thirty."

I nodded at the judge because that was better than saying, "Shit piss damn."

I braced both hands on the defense table to get to my feet. I felt unsteady for a moment, legs of jelly, and wondered about those two lawyers the judge mentioned. One stroked out. One pissed his pants. I wondered if anyone had done both.

CHAPTER FORTY-THREE
Scienter

"Mr. Wisniewski, we just heard about forty minutes of the government's surreptitious recordings in which Kip was a participant, correct?" I began.

Always "Mister" and never "Agent." Always "Kip" and never "the defendant." Humanize your own client and don't give honorific titles to government witnesses.

"That's about right."

"In those recordings, did Kip ever say that he knew he was committing a crime?"

"Not that I recall."

"How many surreptitious recordings are there with my client speaking?"

He consulted a notepad and answered, "Sixty-two conversations totaling thirty hours and thirty-nine minutes."

"And in how many conversations did my client say anything that would lead you to believe he knew he was committing a crime?"

"None that I recall specifically."

"So he never said, 'If I'm indicted, I'll get the best lawyer...?'"

"Not that I recall."

"Or, 'If I'm indicted, I'll destroy evidence?'"

"Not that I recall."

"Or, 'I'll flee the country or bribe a witness anything at all that would indicate awareness that he committed a crime?'"

"I don't recall your client ever saying anything to that effect."

"To be clear, if he'd said any of those things, you would remember them, wouldn't you?"

He eyed me with a flinty look. "I suppose I would."

"Is it impossible for you to simply say 'yes?' Is that some G-man training I'm not familiar with?"

"Objection, argumentative," Bolden piped up at triple her normal volume.

"Sustained."

"Mr. Wisniewski, you have a law degree, correct?"

"Yes."

"Do you know the meaning of the word 'scienter?'"

"It's a Latin term meaning knowledge of wrongdoing."

"In the law, scienter is synonymous with intent to commit a crime, correct?"

"Close enough, yes."

"Which, as you learned at Georgetown, is an element the government must prove to gain a conviction."

"That's correct. But I might add there are many ways to prove—"

"Don't add anything unless you're asked, sir."

Bolden leapt to her feet. "Your Honor, the witness was not finished answering the question."

"He may complete his answer," the judge instructed.

"I was just saying there are many ways to prove criminal intent," Wisniewski continued. "Usually, defendants aren't caught on tape directly confessing their crimes, particularly in conspiracies like organized crime and racketeering. In my experience, you get leads from the recordings and put cases together from there."

"Perhaps your experience is too limited," I suggested.

He made a scoffing sound. "I don't think so."

At the defense table, Kip looked troubled. I'd cautioned him against any shows of emotion. When a government witness scores a point, it's best not to look like your prom date just stood you up.

"Mr. Wisniewski, who was Gennaro Angiulo?" I asked.

He gave me a crooked smile that said, *Oh, that's where you were going.*

"Angiulo was an underboss in the New England mob. And yes, he had a big mouth."

"Did the FBI record him saying, 'I'm a shylock, I'm a bookmaker?'"

"That and more."

"Did he also say, 'We're selling drugs. We're illegal here, illegal there. Arsonists. We're everything.'"

"Yes, he did, famously. And he ended up doing twenty years in prison."

I glanced at the jurors to get a reading on their feelings. It's good to know if they like the witness or hate the witness or just want to pee. Before I could ask another question, Wisniewski blurted out, "Gennaro Angiulo was an idiot. Your nephew is not."

"What! What! Did I ask you a question, Wisniewski?" I turned to the bench. "Your Honor, would you admonish the witness? Tell him his job is to answer questions and not polish his employer's shoes? The hell!"

"Calm down, Mr. Lassiter." The judge glared at me before turning to the witness. "Agent Wisniewski, you know better than that."

"I'm sorry, Your Honor."

I stomped toward the witness stand, stopping six feet away. Any closer, and I would need the court's permission to approach. My tone became harsh. I'm not sure if I wanted the jury to share in my indignation of the G-man's obvious bias or if I couldn't help myself. Either way, I was louder than necessary.

"You've met Kip Lassiter, haven't you?" I demanded.

"Yes."

"You approached him and told him he was in trouble and should cooperate with your investigation, correct?"

"Not in those words, but that was the gist."

"And what did he say?"

"He declined to cooperate."

I pointed an index finger at him. A crooked index finger that never healed properly after being stomped on by a 310-pound offensive tackle. "Pay attention, sir. I asked a simple question." I spoke slowly, enunciating each word with a snap like a broken twig. "What. Did. He. Say?"

"He said, 'I don't need to cooperate. I don't need immunity. I haven't done anything wrong.' Or words to that effect."

"So instead of saying anything indicating awareness of guilt, my client said, 'I haven't done anything wrong,' correct?"

"Yes. I just said that."

"Thank you, Mr. Wisniewski."

I scratched my right ear, not because it needed scratching, but just to have a moment for the jury to digest that helpful tidbit of cross-examination. Then I walked back to the podium and started up again.

"Let's talk about how the investigation got started. Which of Max Ringle's clients called the FBI?"

"None."

"Which of his disgruntled employees dropped the dime on him?"

"None."

"What about the coaches or the proctors?"

"None."

"Which of those elite universities called the FBI and said, 'Hey, someone is corrupting our admissions system?'"

"None."

"Is that because the universities didn't mind getting all that money funneled through Ringle's company into their athletic departments?"

"I don't know why. Maybe they didn't know what was happening."

"Or were they getting fat and happy off the bribes disguised as contributions?"

"Like I said, I wouldn't know."

"Then just how did the investigation get started?"

"It was a tip from a defendant in an unrelated case. A securities fraud investigation."

"So, much like Ringle, another criminal sought to lessen his own punishment by informing?"

"You could say that."

I paused a beat, hoping my point was getting through to the jury. I would have other witnesses connect the dots and show how the universities profited from Ringle's scheme. Now, I needed to lay the groundwork for my fundamental fairness defense. Call it selective enforcement. It's not a true and lawful defense, but it's appealing to people of goodwill, meaning my jury.

"Mr. Wisniewski, how many parents were indicted as part of Operation Flunk Out?"

"Thirty-eight."

"How many were recorded taking part in either the school bribery or exam bribery schemes?"

"Sixty-four."

"Let's do the math. Why weren't twenty-six parents who paid bribes charged with crimes?"

"You'll have to ask the Justice Department."

"They weren't charged because they never said anything on tape that acknowledged they knew what they were doing was illegal. Isn't that right?"

He shrugged and his tone remained neutral. "I wouldn't know."

"There was concern that the government would be prosecuting innocent people, correct?"

"I'd state it differently. There was concern that those cases were weaker."

"A Chinese billionaire paid five million dollars to Max Ringle to get his daughter into Stanford, correct?"

"Yes."

"By far the largest sum paid as part of the school bribery scheme. And yet he was not charged. Why?"

"He had some very good lawyers who convinced the Justice Department that he had no idea his conduct could be considered criminal."

"I wish my nephew had hired those lawyers." Several spectators guffawed, even the reporters. The jurors did their best to stifle their laughter.

The judge shot me a warning glance, but I plowed ahead. I instructed one of the courtroom personnel to cue up the tape recording of Kip's phone call to me as I drove north on the 101 for that sit-down that ended with me in the rose bed.

The tape began playing, first Kip's voice, then mine:

"You gotta chill, Uncle Jake. Max has an opinion of counsel that says everything we do is kosher."

"Tell me about it, Kippers."

"Max asked the top law firm in L.A. to look at our business. They say it's really ingenious, and even though it's a little hinky, it's not illegal because there are no specific laws covering it."

I turned to the witness. "Apparently, Kip did not think he was committing a crime, correct?"

"Correct, if you just listen to that conversation in a vacuum."

"Okay, let's take it out of the vacuum. Where would you like to put it?"

"Objection!" Bolden squawked. "Argumentative."

"Sustained," the judge said. "Next question."

I paused and tabulated just what else, if anything, I wanted to ask. When you're cross-examining a savvy, experienced federal agent, it's a little like exploring a cave with a torch. You want to get out before the flame is extinguished.

"One more question, Mr. Wisniewski. Are you comfortable with the fact that the Chinese billionaire was not indicted, and that more than two dozen parents weren't indicted, while my nephew is charged with thirty-seven felonies?"

"I have no opinion. You'll have to take that up with the Justice Department."

I turned away, as if disgusted with his performance. "No, I don't, Mr. Wisniewski. I'll take it up with the jury."

I sank into my chair, exhausted and straining not to let it show. With just a note of derision in my voice, I said, "I've got nothing else for him."

CHAPTER FORTY-FOUR
The Texas Verdict

Melissa Gold...

Melissa promised herself she would not ask Jake how he felt. She could tell from looking at him that he was drained. Pale and drawn, he sat at the kitchen table, eating the pan-seared filet mignon with garlic and herb butter she'd made in a cast-iron skillet—plus a baked potato, a dozen grilled asparagus spears, and a pint of Grolsch. At least tonight his appetite was strong.

Kip, still a pious vegan, had already eaten his grilled baby eggplants with a green onion salsa, and was hunkered down in his room, doing his homework. Jake had told him to write a 1500-word essay about where he saw himself in the next several years. Prison was not an option. Jake would use the essay to plan Kip's direct examination.

"Kip seemed upbeat tonight," she said. "He said you were the shit today."

"And that's good?"

"Apparently, '*the* shit' is good. But if someone says, '*you're* shit,' well, that's bad." She handed Jake a slice of garlic bread she'd made from a baguette. "How's his demeanor in court?"

"All-American choirboy, so far. He's taking notes, elbowing me in the ribs when I'm about to throw the water pitcher at the witness. I'm starting to feel optimistic about him. If I can somehow win the case—a very big if,— think he's got a great chance to turn his life around."

"Kip told me you're scoring points."

"I'm like a sniper hidden in the bush. I can pick off the point man of their platoon, but then they bring out a wave of reinforcements." Jake grabbed an asparagus spear with his fingers. "My defense is very subtle, and subtlety isn't my strong suit. I need to persuade the jury to acquit because they think it's unfair to convict, regardless of the evidence of guilt. Some lawyers call it a Texas verdict."

"I've never heard of that."

"In essence, the jury says, 'Not guilty, but don't do it again.'"

She laughed and was happy to see Jake smile in return. They had been short on laughter and smiles in recent days. She reached over and squeezed his shoulder. He seemed to relax, sinking back into the kitchen chair.

"Have you stopped blaming yourself for his...what should I call it? His detour?"

Jake sliced a piece of rare steak and seemed to think about it. "When I look back, there are things I'd change about myself. If I had, maybe he'd have gone in a different direction."

She waited. And waited some more.

Finally, he said, "Long before I met you, when I was single, I might have fallen into patterns that weren't helpful when Kip came into my life."

"You can't stop there, big guy. What are you talking about?"

"Okay, I had younger friends, and maybe a case of arrested development."

He plopped the piece of steak into his mouth and chewed.

"This gets more interesting all the time," she said. "By 'friends,' you mean you hung out with inappropriate women."

"My standards were a little low."

"You had standards?"

"I wouldn't date a woman who had jumped bail. Other than that..."

"What else, Romeo?"

He took a pull on his beer before answering. "This old house was rocking with parties. Now, you might think I would have shaped up by the time Kip arrived. But there he was, at age ten, mixing a dry martini second to none. The Kumquat Avenue mascot, getting his hair mussed by South Beach models. I was drinking too much and was..."

"An aging party animal?"

"*Gawd*, I remember that guy. Really pathetic. Further proof that men are the lower form of the species. Women are more evolved."

"That's your excuse?"

"I've said it before. Men just crawled from the swamp, our webbed feet dripping brackish water, hoping to mate with the first female we saw, or lacking that, a warm patch of mud."

"How enlightening. Maybe you should give a TED Talk on anthropology."

She locked her gaze on his. She wanted to ask something and didn't know quite how. It was not like her to tiptoe around, so she took a hop, skip, and a jump. "That lawyer you prosecuted for having affairs with his clients..."

"Bert Kincaid. What about him?"

"I was wondering about your past, and..."

It took Jake what seemed like several eons to answer. Finally, he said, "I did something worse."

She waited.

"Long time ago, and I'm talking the Jurassic era, I was involved with a client's wife."

Her throat tightened, as if someone were fastening a ligature around her neck. "That's horrible. Why...?"

"Gina and Nick Florio. I knew her before he did, so I figured I was grandfathered in."

"That's not funny. That's not cute. Be real, Jake."

He didn't hesitate. "What I did was unethical, stupid, and reckless. Did I mention that Nick Florio was a killer?"

"Oh my God! I assume you learned from that experience."

"Introspection is a brutal sport. I looked in the mirror, and someone else peered back. I thought of myself as compassionate and caring and ethical, but that bastard in the mirror was cynical and self-centered and soiled."

She shook her head. "But that's not you, Jake."

"Not *now*. I changed through the desire to be a better man and sheer force of will. Which is why I believe in redemption. If I could do it, why not Kip?"

She took a moment to process all of that. "Wow. I'm not sure I would have liked you back in your grandfathered-in days."

"You wouldn't have! Looking back, I don't like me. But now... now, I'm content with who I am and my hard-earned knowledge of self."

"And that knowledge is...?"

"That it's over so quickly. And what we leave behind is as fleeting as footprints in the sand. So, we'd better make the most of our days. We'd better be good to everyone we know, and especially good to those we love and who love us. And knowing all that, these days when I rue the fact that I didn't meet you years ago, well, part of me knows this was the perfect time."

He resumed eating, as if he'd just been discussing the weather and not existential thoughts. It was as if he didn't realize how deep he could go. She considered this man she loved. He was open and honest without thinking about it, and without knowing how rare that was in today's male. Maybe any era's male.

"You're really something, Jake Lassiter," she said.

"Hmm," he mumbled between bites.

"You're very giving, Jake. Do you know that?"

He shrugged. In fact, he probably didn't know that, she thought.

"You would do anything for the people you love," she continued.

"Well, who wouldn't?"

She smiled at his obliviousness. "Oh, you'd be surprised."

Suddenly, he clopped the heel of his hand to his forehead. "I'm an idiot. I've been home two hours and haven't asked about your day."

She had already given him a pass on that. When she was preparing dinner, he was sketching out notes for the next day's witnesses. She knew from the look in his eyes that his mind had been in the courtroom. Sometimes, when he was silently rehearsing questions, his lips moved, like a child reciting the multiplication tables.

"My day was fine," she said. "No word from the N.I.H., but now they know all about helmet guy and his scheme. I hope to hear something soon."

"If justice prevails, you'll get the job," he declared. "And whether you do or not, I'm so damn proud of you. For the work you do, for the person you are. I probably should tell you this more often. Being with you makes me the luckiest man on Earth."

Jake looked away, and she saw that his eyes were moist.

"Aw, jeez. Sorry, Mel. Lately, I've been getting more emotional than usual."

"Just don't try to blame it on brain damage." She gave him a wide smile. "I like you this way."

It took a while to get to know the many layers of this complex man, she thought. Hard bark but a tender heart. She was about to say she loved him, when he turned to her and said, "I love you, Melissa Gold. With every fiber of my being. And for the rest of my days."

CHAPTER FORTY-FIVE
Ali and Frazier

Melissa was asleep. I was in an easy chair in the living room, feet up, scribbling notes. At 11:10 p.m., the phone rang, Ray Pincher calling.

"I knew you'd be awake," Ray Pincher greeted me.

"What's up, Ray?"

"I hate to bring bad news, but you should know. Nick Buoniconti died today."

"Aw, jeez, Ray."

"Yeah. Complications from C.T.E."

"He was my hero."

"How could he not be?" Pincher said. "A Dolphins linebacker who became a lawyer. Pretty much the Lassiter role model."

"You can't even mention me in the same breath. Nick's in the Hall of Fame. Except for special teams, I sat so far down the bench, my ass was in Hialeah. And if Nick hadn't gone into business, he'd have been a better lawyer than me, too. Not to mention raising hundreds of millions for spinal injury research."

"One of a kind."

"Joe Paterno used to tell us to make an impact, and he wasn't talking about a goal-line stand. Well, Nick made an impact that will last forever."

"When did you see him last?"

"Two or three years ago at a Dolphins reunion. He had early symptoms. Memory problems. Unsteady gait. You could look at him and see the future."

My thoughts turned to Melissa, and the importance of her work. Several former Dolphins had been cut down by the horrific disease. Hundreds of former players, maybe thousands, were showing signs of its deadly advance. Hall of Fame members like Nick and Frank Gifford and Mike Webster and Junior Seau and Ken Stabler were already gone. It was well known that Nick had left instructions for his brain to undergo an autopsy by the C.T.E. team at Boston University. Even in death, he would be giving back to society.

I felt a tear trickle down my cheek. There is a strange sensation when a friend dies. Grief, of course. Sorrow and empathy for your friend's family. But just as with a soldier who loses a buddy in battle, there can be an unexpectedly selfish feeling, too.

There, but for the grace of God...

Which is closely related to an inexcusably shameful notion we can barely admit.

Better him than me...

With Nick and me, it was different. His death was a foreshadowing.

First him and then me...

After a moment, I said, "Nick told me he calculated he'd taken half a million hits to the head, from peewee football right through fourteen seasons in the NFL."

"For sure, it's a damn violent sport."

"I loved the game, Ray. The camaraderie. The friendships. The teamwork. Once in a while, the sheer physical ecstasy. But now I'm wondering if all that is worth the toll it takes."

He let me wonder in silence a moment before replying, "I don't know, Jake. It's a changing world. Maybe the next generation will only play football on video games."

While I pondered that, Pincher asked, "How's your nephew's case going?"

"You know criminal trials, Ray. Some days it ebbs. Some days it flows. Some days, a riptide carries you out to sea."

"If you need anything, just ask."

"At long last, you've stopped telling me I shouldn't handle the case."

"Too late to put a tourniquet on that wound. There are more than a hundred thousand lawyers in Florida, and you're the worst one to defend your nephew. But you're still a helluva advocate."

"As are you. Today I inadvertently mentioned your name when I was mad at the prosecutor."

Pincher laughed. "Lawyers come up to me all the time and say our battles in court were like Ali and Frazier."

"I'm Ali," I quipped, "the pretty one. You're Frazier."

"Ha! You're the thrilla in vanilla, white boy!"

We both chuckled at that. Old times. Not always good times, but a mutual respect out of fair combat.

"Hey Ray, I saw Gilberto Foyo in court today."

"He'll be there every day. If you need to post bail, he's got a blank check."

"Don't worry. I'm on my best behavior. Say, did you know the U.S. Attorney didn't charge forty percent of the parents involved in the bribery scheme?"

"No, but so what?"

"Tomorrow morning, I'm going to make a motion to compel the government to disclose their names so I can call them to testify."

"To what end?"

"Get their admissions. 'Did you bribe?' 'Yes.' 'Were you charged?' 'No.' One after the other. A dozen. Two dozen. Make an impression about the unfairness of it all."

"Some will invoke the Fifth."

"That's fine, too. Maybe even better because it implies guilt. The jury will know there are a slew of people who committed crimes and were never charged. So why indict my baby-faced nephew? Selective enforcement."

"Which is not illegal. Not everyone driving above the speed limit gets a ticket."

"But Kip is being unfairly singled out, especially since Ringle is getting a sweetheart deal. No matter what the judge instructs on the law, jurors are guided by an inherent sense of fairness. That's what I'm counting on."

There was silence on the line a moment before Pincher said, "You're going for jury nullification. That's tricky, Jake."

"The only other issue I have is highly technical, and you know how juries react to that."

"What's the issue?"

"That the universities weren't deprived of property so there's no fraud."

"A long shot. Is a plea still out of the question?"

"They never offered one. This is their show trial."

"Is there a number you would take?"

That stopped me a moment. Was the state attorney offering to broker a deal with the U.S. Attorney?

"What are you saying, Ray?"

"Just thinking out loud. Good luck, champ. You're still the greatest."

It wasn't true, but I appreciated the sentiment from my old pal and adversary just the same.

"And you're still Smokin' Joe," I said.

CHAPTER FORTY-SIX
The Law Business, not the Justice Business

Heading north on U.S. 1, an asshole in a Lamborghini convertible—if that's not redundant—cut me off. I leaned on the Eldo's horn, which played the first four notes of the old Monday Night Football theme. *Dun-dun-dun-dunnnnn.* The Lamborghini driver shot me the bird.

I'm not given to road rage, but lately on the highway, I've been impatient and irritable. When we both caught the traffic light at Seventeenth Avenue, I changed into the right-hand lane and pulled alongside him, reaching for my coffee cup.

"Don't do it, Uncle Jake," Kip advised.

I tossed half a cup of black coffee onto the Lamborghini's windshield. Hey, I'm a nice guy. With his top down, I could have dumped it onto his Alcantara suede upholstery.

"You're gangsta!" Kip cheered.

The Lamborghini driver turned on his windshield wipers and sputtered a few expletives. I tooted another horn blast, then headed north on I-95 for the short drive downtown.

It was too early in the day for a migraine, but there it was, an arrow shooting through one ear and out the other. I had a small problem pulling into the parking lot. The arm on the gate seemed to have cloned itself, and I saw two arms, moving up and down like the blades of scissors. Once inside the courthouse, I felt just a touch of vertigo. When I stepped off the elevator, I felt as if I were still moving upward.

I deposited Kip in the courtroom, then poked my head into the judge's outer chambers and told the assistant that I needed ten minutes for an emergency motion before testimony resumed.

Five minutes later, trying to ignore the piercing headache, I was sitting in one of the cushy chairs in front of the judge's desk in his spacious, high-ceilinged chambers. It was a quiet place of light woods and floor-to-ceiling shelves crammed with law books, even though nearly all research these days is done on computers. The judge's three well-groomed law clerks sat on a beige sofa, laptops balanced on their knees. The court reporter was perched in a straight-backed chair, her machine at the ready. Margaret Bolden and her merry band trooped in and occupied much of the open space.

Judge Speidel regarded me skeptically and demanded, "What's your emergency?"

"The defense moves, *ore tenus*, to compel the government to reveal the names of the twenty-eight parents it has chosen not to prosecute," I said.

The judge murmured a quiet *hmmm*. Sitting this close, I saw that his fleshy jowls quivered with every word, not just when he was angry.

"Apparently, Mr. Lassiter intends to argue that because the government exercised its lawful discretion as to whom to charge, his client should go free," Bolden said in a dismissive tone.

"Ms. Bolden, if you're gonna argue my case," I said, "I wish you'd do a better job."

"Mr. Lassiter, just what do you intend to do with these people?" the judge asked.

"Find out why they got a free ride. Do they have any exculpatory evidence helpful for my client?"

"Sounds like a fishing expedition," the judge said.

"I've caught some big grouper that way, Your Honor."

"Counsel is being disingenuous," Bolden said. "Based on his cross of Agent Wisniewski, it's obvious Mr. Lassiter intends to call the non-charged parents and make some frivolous argument about the unfairness of it all."

"Is that true, Mr. Lassiter?"

I tried to focus on the question. My vertigo was gone, but my migraine had become a backhoe and was gouging a hole in my cranium.

"Mr. Lassiter," the judge pestered me.

"I reserve the right to call the non-charged parents, and the government has no right to ask the subject matter of my questions."

Bolden said, "Then counsel should know that if his client took exams for any of their children, we'll be adding additional counts to the charges."

"Well, listen to that." I gave the prosecutor a scoffing laugh. "Margie, you are so darned cute when you make threats."

"Mr. Lassiter! Kindly address me, not opposing counsel," the judge warned.

"You got it, Judge."

"Your Honor! Not Judge."

"Sorry, Your Honor. You're darned cute, too."

The judge's mouth fell open, increasing his chins from four to five. "Mr. Lassiter, are you on drugs?"

"As a matter of fact, I am. Except for the experimental ones, which I stopped cold turkey. My doctor, who I also sleep with, said there might be side effects."

"Jesus H. Christ!" the judge exclaimed.

For reasons I cannot explain, I made the sign of the cross, though I am not Catholic, last time I checked.

The judge was silent for a long moment. Maybe he was thinking about calling the marshals to take me away. Or the guys in little white coats with leather-belted straitjackets.

"All right," the judge sighed. "We're gonna finish this up with no more folderol from Mr. Lassiter. Does the government have anything else to say on the pending motion?"

One of Bolden's assistants handed her a document, which she glanced at, and said, "Under *Campbell vs. United States*, the Eleventh Circuit last year upheld the denial of a virtually identical motion. In an insider trading case, only three of nine persons were charged. Those three sought the identity of the six others. The court reasoned that the identity of non-charged individuals is government work product and also threatened grand jury secrecy."

"Thank you, Ms. Bolden. As usual you are incisive, brief, and on point." The judge turned to me with a scowl so derisive that it would have buckled the knees of most men. But my knees are made of chromium, titanium, and plastic, and while they squeak, they don't buckle. "Mr. Lassiter?"

"I haven't read the case, Your Honor. But by the end of the day, I will be prepared to respond."

"So, Mr. Lassiter, how is it that the government is better prepared to argue your motion than you are?"

"I don't have the entourage Ms. Bolden does."

"Then perhaps you're not capable of handling this case."

"A momentary setback, Judge."

"Your Honor! Not Judge!"

"Right. Right. Your Honor. 'Your Honor' somehow reminds me of 'Your Highness,' which seems excessively royal."

The migraine had hatched baby migraines, and the judge's chambers were spinning. I was seeing double again, so that Judge Speidel seemed to now weigh 800 pounds. It did not make him any more attractive.

"Perhaps if you'd followed the rules and filed a written motion with a memorandum of law, you'd be better prepared," he scolded. "Or perhaps having researched the law, you would have discovered the frivolity of your motion before you filed it."

"Frivolousness," I heard myself say.

"What?"

"You said 'frivolity.' Which means silly or lighthearted. You meant 'frivolousness,' the legal term meaning not worthy of serious attention. If you want, why not have the court reporter read it back? Maybe I'm wrong, and you said *frijoles*."

Judge Speidel's jowls turned pink and quivered like a brook trout struggling to shake the hook. "I'm cutting you every break I can, counselor. I even told my clerks you were a damn fine cross-examiner. No structure but sharp instincts. Then you waltz in here, demanding an emergency hearing. You haven't followed the rules! You don't even know the rules! You don't give a damn about the rules!"

"The rules. The rules. The rules." I sounded like a demented parrot.

The judge's face had turned an angry shade of red. A heart attack was not out of the question. His voice changed timbre as it picked up steam, climbing into tenor range, odd for such a massive man. "I don't know what game you're playing, fella. You want me to hold you in contempt? Declare a mistrial? Lose the case and set up a 2255 for ineffective counsel?"

Not a bad idea. I could hire Marcia Silvers, Miami's preeminent criminal appellate lawyer, to claim I botched the case. Unfortunately, Kip would be incarcerated while that played out.

"Whatever it is," Judge Speidel continued, "you're not getting it! We're gonna try this case to the end by the rules! By the goddamn rules! And when I send this jury home for a job well done, I'll deal with you, starting with a complaint to the Florida Bar."

"Excellent," I said. "I'm a Bar prosecutor. If they let me prosecute myself and defend myself, I'd have a fool for a client, a fool for a lawyer, and a fool for opposing counsel. All things considered, I'd be inclined to offer myself a plea."

"Are you mocking me? Are you mocking the rules?"

"I care about..." My voice trailed off.

"What? Speak up!"

"I care about justice."

"Justice is a meaningless term."

That rocked me. "How can a federal judge say that?"

"And how can you have practiced law so long and not realize that justice is a mere concept? A goal, an ideal, a sweet and fuzzy word like 'spirituality.' But it's just a notion, and your definition of that notion can be far different from mine. It's the law that's real and tangible and nonnegotiable."

He slammed his fist on his desk with a *clomp* and raised his voice even louder. "We're in the law business, not the justice business. And it's the law we shovel from our courthouses like coal from a mine into the hopper. If the application of the law happens to coincide with someone's notion of justice, great. If not, it's still the law. And to that end, the defense motion stands denied."

The judge stood and reached for his robes, which were hanging on a coat rack. "Now, let's get into the courtroom."

Margaret Bolden and her crew of young thoroughbreds exited chambers before I even got out of my chair.

I got to my feet, feeling like an old plow horse with a mangy coat and spavined spine. Too weak to till the north forty, too slow to cavort in the south pasture. I was plagued with the thought that the judge might be right. That I was incapable of handling my nephew's case. And that I knew nothing about the "law business," meaning my career was a sham, and I had as much chance of winning Kip's trial as that plow horse had of winning the Kentucky Derby.

CHAPTER FORTY-SEVEN
The Trap Door

Five minutes after leaving the judge's chambers, with a pit stop for a pee, I sank into my chair at the defense table.

"What's wrong, Uncle Jake? You look bummed."

At the government table, Margaret Bolden and her cast of thousands had set up their tents and were sharpening their swords. Like the Vikings encamped outside York in the ninth century, they were ready to pillage and burn and take no prisoners.

The judge was taking his time getting into the courtroom. Maybe he was telling the marshals to be ready to Tase and cuff me. Or maybe he was simply popping a couple antacids because I gave him indigestion.

I looked at Kip and said, "I hope I don't let you down, kiddo."

"No way!" He put a hand on my forearm. "You're doing great." He studied me a long moment. "I'm really sorry about how pissy I was to you."

"Forget it, kiddo. You've apologized enough."

"At Max's house, I called you an 'old burnout' when you were trying to help me."

"Hey, quit it. We learn. We grow. You and me kiddo, we're cool." His eyes were moist. I lowered my voice to a whisper. "And to tell you the truth, I am an old burnout."

❧

Arthur Kwalick of Greenwich, Connecticut, owned a firm that designed women's clothing, which it manufactured in China and India. He led the hit parade of parents who filled the government's roster today. There wasn't much for me to do but sit and stew and listen to their tales of my nephew, the imposter, taking their children's tests.

Kwalick was the first of five witnesses with similar stories. After first flirting with USC, he was intent on having his son, Craig, attend Yale, his alma mater. Kwalick paid $100,000 to Q.E.D. for Kip to take his SAT exam. From the documents, I knew that Ringle kept $75,000 and gave Kip $25,000. Son Craig got to sing "Bright College Years," the cheerfully ironic Alma Mater, for two semesters before being expelled for his fraudulent admission. His dad was one of the first parents to plead guilty, express remorse, and offer to cooperate. In our system of justice, it is the early songbird who gets the juicy deal.

Kwalick served twelve days at a federal prison camp in Wisconsin. It's called "Papadapoulous time" after the Trump campaign official who served exactly that after pleading guilty to lying to the FBI.

As was her style, so admired by Judge Speidel, Bolden was quick and crisp with her questions. She established that Yale, with a six-percent acceptance rate, was a "reach" school for Craig, though he was a decent student at Phillips Academy in Andover, Massachusetts. Kwalick met personally with Kip, gave him the preppie's handwriting sample, and asked him to get close to a

790 in math and a 760 in English to hit the median of accepted applicants. Kip nailed it, a 1550, and earned an additional $30,000 bonus.

I admired Bolden's abilities. I've long thought that a good prosecutor is a well-trained union carpenter building a sturdy house with shiny tools and freshly hewn wood. She follows blueprints to the letter, makes sure the framing is in plumb, lines up the two-by-fours, and hammers the nails straight. The best courtroom carpenters are Renaissance men and women. They double as bricklayers, installers, tapers, finishers, electricians, and even plumbers. They can build the whole damn house, and it's a thing of beauty that will pass the toughest inspection by city inspectors...or juries.

Until the defense lawyers come along.

We're the stealthy vandals wielding crowbars and spray paint. We tear down door frames, break windows, and spray graffiti on the walls. Our job is to destroy what the carpenters have built and feed it into the woodchipper.

"Your witness," Bolden said, giving me access to the sturdy framing she had built.

I hated the fact that Kip had met personally with Arthur Kwalick. The face-to-face meeting elevated my nephew's status in the scheme, which, of course, was Bolden's goal. I needed to refocus attention on the major sleaze, Max Ringle.

"Mr. Kwalick, who owned Q.E.D., the business you dealt with?"

"To the best of my knowledge, Max Ringle."

"And who pitched you on hiring Q.E.D.?"

"Max Ringle."

"Who guaranteed your son's admission to an elite university?"

"You know who. Ringle."

"Who did you pay?"

"Same guy. Max Ringle."

I walked to the podium with a glass of water, discovered it was empty and walked back to defense table. I opened a briefcase and pulled out an Army canteen, unsnapped the camo canvas pouch, unscrewed the lid, and took a long drink of water. The jurors never took their eyes off me. Refreshed, I walked back to the podium.

"What exactly did Max Ringle say about getting Craig into an elite university?"

"He said there were three doors. You walked through the front door if you're a valedictorian with perfect college boards, and you're building houses on weekends for Habitat for Humanity. The back door meant making huge contributions to the university. The more elite the school, the bigger the contribution. Then there was the side door. That's where the student fabricates his résumé to look like a champion athlete, and the parents give money to the university's athletic program."

"With a coach or other university employee keeping some of that money, correct?"

"I didn't know that, and, frankly, once I wrote the check, I wouldn't have cared."

"Mr. Kwalick, what did Ringle suggest for your son?"

"At first, the side door at USC That's where Craig wanted to go."

"And how was that to be accomplished?"

"Ringle told us to claim that Craig was an all-conference wing on his prep school water polo team."

"Was he?"

Kwalick shook his head. "He can barely tread water. Ringle's staff photoshopped Craig's headshot on top of a water polo player's body."

"Were you concerned about the legality of this plan?"

"Damn right I was. But Ringle said there was no legal difference between paying the university through the back door and what he did through the side door. When I pressed him on it, he said he had an opinion of counsel to that effect."

"Did he ever show you that opinion?"

"He didn't. Max was a salesman and a con man, par excellence." Kwalick scowled. "He told me what I wanted to hear, and I chose to believe it."

"Did Craig apply to USC?"

"No. I was afraid he'd spend four years working on his tan. I talked him into applying to Yale, my alma mater. It's what I always wanted for him."

"And what ivy-covered door did you knock on at Yale?"

He barked a scornful laugh. "Turned out it was the trap door. Like I said to the prosecutor, I paid Ringle to have the defendant take Craig's SAT exam. Craig was admitted and doing fine until this whole thing blew up."

"After Max Ringle was charged in a sealed indictment, he wore a wire and gathered evidence against you, correct?"

"Against me and most of his clients."

"Ringle will testify later in this trial. Would you believe him under oath?"

"Objection!" Bolden was on her feet. "A witness may not opine on the veracity of another witness."

"Overruled. The witness may answer as to his impression of Mr. Ringle's credibility."

"Would I believe Max Ringle?" Kwalick spit out the words. "You're kidding, right?"

"Not at all," I said. "Would you believe him once he puts his hand on the Bible and swears to tell the truth?"

"I'm betting the Bible bursts into flames."

Spectators chuckled, and the jurors tittered.

"Objection!" Bolden called out. "Move to strike as nonresponsive."

"Granted. The jury shall disregard the witness's last statement."

Fine with me. Margaret Bolden had just drawn more attention to Kwalick's colorful and flammable answer.

"Mr. Kwalick, let's try again. Would you believe Max Ringle under oath?"

"I wouldn't believe a word after he states his name. The man is a professional liar."

I thanked the witness and sat down.

Other parents came and went. A local couple, Manuel and Consuela Diaz, who owned a flower-importing business, had both pled guilty and received supervised release and no jail time. Their daughter, Gloria, whose SAT exam Kip had "corrected" while sitting as a proctor, had been politely asked to leave Georgetown, her credits vacated, her transcript erased.

On direct exam, Consuela talked of the humiliation and personal trauma suffered by her family. She was likeable and sympathetic, and I didn't see much use in cross-examining, except for a short exchange.

"Ms. Diaz, did your flower business lose money after news of the scandal broke?"

"No, but there are losses greater than money. There is *reputación*."

"In fact, didn't you get a role on a television show precisely because of your notoriety?"

"You're talking about '*Las Verdaderas Esposas de Hialeah*?'"

"Yes, 'The Real Housewives of Hialeah' on Univision. Didn't I see you in an episode devoted to the scandal where you cried at the injustice of it all?"

She thought a moment before replying. I had the video in case her memory failed her. The episode had a bittersweet moment, a tearful close-up in which she said, "You worked so hard, Gloria, and now my tears of joy are planted with the sugar cane." Okay, my Spanish is rudimentary, so that might not be exactly what she said.

"The show is part of my therapy," Consuela Diaz answered, finally.

"So, you don't get paid?"

"Of course I get paid! It's hard work."

Judge Speidel treated me decently throughout the afternoon, especially given my horrendous conduct in chambers. Just before we hung up our saddles for the day, with the jurors already headed for the elevators, Bolden requested a quick conference with the judge.

"Your Honor might have noticed Mr. Lassiter drinking out of an Army canteen during questioning," Margaret Bolden said.

"I did. So...?"

"Yesterday, Your Honor noted a bicycle helmet on the defense table."

"Yes. Where are you going with this, counsel?"

"Mr. Lassiter also has a book on his table angled so that the jurors can see the title. *Pleasure Times Four*."

"What is that, some kind of porn?" The judge sounded suspicious.

"It's the history of the barbershop quartet in America," I replied.

"I'm lost. Ms. Bolden, what's the beef here?"

That made me think of his Stockyard Administration job all over again.

"In voir dire, we learned that juror number two, Mr. Mauti, is an Afghan war veteran," Bolden said. "Hence, the Army canteen. Mr. Lassiter drank from it while looking directly at Mr. Mauti."

"But I refrained from saluting him," I said.

"Number seven, Ms. Zordich, rides her bicycle over a hundred miles a week," Bolden said. "Hence the helmet. And number eleven, the elderly gentleman, Mr. Prato, sings in a barbershop quartet."

"Hence the book," I helped Bolden out.

Judge Speidel sighed his annoyance but didn't throw his gavel at me.

"Counsel is obviously trying to curry favor with the jury," Bolden said.

"Obviously," the judge acknowledged. "Does this work for you in that skid row down by the river, Mr. Lassiter?"

"Sometimes, but it's challenging finding common ground with every juror. The one that nearly stumped me was a proctologist."

"Enough." Judge Speidel glared at me. "I don't want to hear about it."

"Your Honor, please admonish counsel to cease using props in view of the jury."

"I'll do that if she'll agree not to call Max Ringle, who the government's own witness calls a 'professional liar.'"

"Pipe down, both of you. Ms. Bolden, there's nothing in the rules that covers this. Mr. Lassiter is free to put a lace tablecloth and a silver tea set on the defense table if he wants to. But you are also free in closing argument to comment on his shameless conduct. I won't rein you in on that."

"Thank you, Your Honor," she said.

"I'm down with that, Your Honor," I agreed. "Fighting like hell for my client never shames me."

CHAPTER FORTY-EIGHT
The Parade of the Rich and the Wicked

The next day, I mostly kept quiet as the government drove a little yellow car into the ring, and out tumbled a dozen clowns. Okay, that's not quite accurate. The government paraded a string of wealthy, well-dressed, totally amoral, and thoroughly unlikeable parents into court. Yes, even more folks who paid Max Ringle to swindle their kids into elite universities. They were part of the case because Kip had either taken their kids' tests as an imposter or corrected them as a proctor.

There wasn't a lot of cross examining to do. The parents told the truth. Some expressed remorse, a common theme being, "I loved Dexter too much." Or, "Some parents say they'd take a bullet for their child. I did prison time for mine." That was a dad who served three weeks at a Club Fed and tried to sound like Al Capone in Alcatraz.

But some parents found others to blame, often the ritzy private high schools where their children matriculated or just vegetated. A mother from Los Angeles struck that note, saying, "I paid hundreds of thousands of dollars to Princeton-Eastlake, and they breached their contract to get Nikki into Cornell."

There was the father from Palm Beach who blamed the elite universities for his predicament. "You can't believe the stress they put on my son. Grade point average, test scores, extracurriculars. It's too much. It's too damn much!"

I asked that fellow one question. "Is it safe to assume that you don't know any families whose kids work after school to earn their lunch money?"

"Of course not. What kind of a question is that, anyway?"

The crippling pressure of the admissions process was a common theme, with the parents whining that it was simply unfair. "We're required to lay out enormous sums of money," sniveled a tech mogul from Santa Clara, California. "It's a poll tax on rich white people."

A class action lawyer from New York complained that his daughter broke out in hives during conventional SAT exam prep. Naturally, he planned to file—what else?—a class action against the College Board for infliction of mental distress. The owner of an Internet marketing company sounded off because his son's low score forced him to repeat the ACT, causing the family to cancel a month-long vacation to Bali and forfeit the deposit on a chartered jet.

On cross, I played clips of the government's recordings, choosing highlights that revealed the parents at their most clueless.

"I just want a level playing field, and this is it," said a mother from Scottsdale, Arizona. "This is affirmative action for trust funders."

Whispers of disapproval rippled through the gallery along with the shaking of heads. Even better, several jurors looked appalled.

Many parents complained about a "rigged system" that favored minorities. One mother from San Francisco with her heart set on Berkeley wanted to claim Asian heritage for her daughter because the child's great-great-grandfather had been a missionary in

China. Not an Asian missionary, but rather a Protestant minister from Massachusetts who lived in China. She nixed the plan after learning that one-third of all students at Berkeley were legitimately Asian, and they received no preferential treatment.

I wondered about the effect on the kids when they heard their parents' voices on the tapes or read the transcripts in the news media. Speaking to Ringle on a tapped line, one father laughed heartily and said, "Tell Stanford that Peter will walk-on at linebacker. Don't mention that a stiff breeze could blow the kid over!" Then there was the mother who paid an extra $25,000 to have Ringle's psychologist write a report getting her daughter into the special needs room where Kip would proctor. "I wish Mira really had A.D.H.D., but truth is, she's just plain stupid."

Even Judge Speidel raised his bushy eyebrows at that one.

In my Department of Warped Values, the prizewinner was Harman Fisher of Aspen and Star Island, Miami Beach, a guy who considered himself a genius because he'd had an inside track to buying Apple stock with inherited money when the company went public in 1980. He strode briskly to the witness stand with a sneer on his lips, wearing his arrogance like his tailored Italian suit.

The government recorded him saying, "If a father with the financial wherewithal fails to help his kids this way, he's guilty of child abuse. I did it for both my boys, and I hope they do the same when they're fathers."

I decided to ask the thoughtful guy a question or two.

"What about teaching your kids the value of integrity?"

"Seems to me, Mr. Lassiter, you didn't do such a good job with that yourself."

Ouch! That stings.

I kept my face placid and my tone soft as I tried to spin the insult into something positive. "You're absolutely right, Mr. Fisher, and I hope the jury takes my failures into account when deciding my nephew's fate."

"Mr. Lassiter!" the judge thundered. "Please confine yourself to asking questions, and the witness shall confine himself to answering them."

"I'll try again," I said. "What about teaching your kids the value of integrity?"

"Better to teach them it's a dog-eat-dog world. You can always have integrity after you've made it."

"As you've done?"

His face reddened and he wagged a finger at me. "My integrity is my balance sheet, and it could buy and sell you a hundred times."

A soft *whoosh* swept through the gallery. A couple jurors shook their heads. Unless the witness took a dump on the clerk's desk, I didn't think I could make him look or sound any worse, but I decided to try.

"Now, Mr. Fisher, you're a convicted felon, aren't you?"

"I pled guilty to one count of conspiracy to get the feds off my back." He shot a furious look at Bolden. He was angry at her for bringing him into court and at me for questioning his sterling character.

"You pled guilty because you were guilty, correct?"

"I helped my boys, so yeah, call me a felon. I paid a seven-hundred thousand dollar fine out of petty cash, and I served thirty days at Eglin. The food's lousy, and the tennis courts need resurfacing."

"Not up to the standards of your homes on Red Mountain and Star Island?"

Again, he shook a finger at me. "I get it. I'm rich, and you're not, and the jury's not. So, let's hate the rich guy and his spoiled kids."

An amazingly accurate description of my strategy.

"You seem to believe you did nothing wrong," I said, still trying to provoke him. "But, in fact, you stood in this very courtroom, confessed your guilt, then begged for mercy, correct?"

"I don't beg!" He turned toward the bench. "Judge, do I have put up with this brain-dead shyster?"

A low murmur rumbled through the packed courtroom. One or two spectators laughed.

Calmly but firmly, Judge Speidel replied, "You shall answer Mr. Lassiter's questions unless I sustain an objection thereto."

Fisher cleared his throat and said, "I pled guilty because my lawyers told me to. No one will ever convince me I did anything wrong."

"Would that belief extend to my client?" I asked, as pleasantly as a brain-dead shyster can. "In helping your boys, is Kip Lassiter also blameless?"

Bolden leapt to her feet. "Objection! Irrelevant what the witness believes about the law."

"Overruled. The witness may answer."

Harman Fisher's short fuse was burning down. He leveled a malevolent glare at me. "I think he's a punk kid who ought to do thirty years of hard time, and when he's there, I hope he gets passed around like a candy bar from one gangbanger to the next."

Several jurors gasped, and a wave of whispers rolled through the gallery. A good lawyer knows when to stop. With a pleasant smile and an amiable tone, I said, "Mr. Fisher, thank you for your time and your illuminating answers." Then I turned to Bolden and, with malice in my heart, said, "I tender *your* witness back to you, counselor."

She wanted nothing more to do with him, and we all went home for the day.

CHAPTER FORTY-NINE
Summa Cum Fraud

I was well-rested and focused the next morning when the government put on its hit list of spoiled, rotten kids. Oh, *excuse me*, the "young people who are as much victims of Mr. Lassiter's scheme as the universities themselves." That was Margaret Bolden's description.

Unlike their parents, none of the kids in any of the cases nationwide was charged with a crime. They had all been tossed from their universities, their admissions rescinded, and their credits vacated. Their transcripts disappeared like the biographies of out of favor North Korean officials whose last bus ride was to a desolate coal mine. To heal their wounded feelings, many took European jaunts or went into therapy for, of all things, PTSD. The therapy was mostly at ritzy rehab resorts in Vail and Malibu.

Silly me, I thought that some of these jackasses would be sweating their butts off, pouring hot tar on roofs for AmeriCorps. But I had misjudged just how much the kids enjoyed using their parents' connections for chauffeured rides down easy street.

The young and the shiftless.

Predictably, some had found ways to profit from their perfidy. Contrary to the government's position that daddy's little darlings were victims, I intended to prove that these unindicted coconspirators were making careers out of their academic misadventures.

Craig Kwalick, the young scholar from Yale whose father had testified, turned out to be a pleasant young man with a dark mop of curly hair and an easy smile. He wore black jeans and a burgundy jacket of lightweight leather with a T-shirt underneath. On direct exam, he told Bolden that yes, Kip Lassiter had taken the SAT for him.

On cross, I asked Craig whether he was satisfied with my nephew's services.

He shot a look at Kip and smiled with admiration. "Dude nailed it."

"And subsequently, Yale expelled you and erased the credits you'd earned, correct?"

"Yeah, and I was passing all my courses. It's not like I'm stupid."

"Before you applied to Yale, you applied to USC as a champion water polo player, correct?"

"Yeah."

I asked the judge for permission to approach the witness, then handed him a photo of a muscular young man leaping out of the water, right hand gripping a white ball.

"Is that you, Mr. Kwalick?"

He grinned and said, "Half me. It's my face superimposed on the body of a water polo player."

"Kip Lassiter had nothing to do with that, correct?"

"Right. Ringle's staff photoshopped it."

"Did you have any qualms about fabricating your qualifications?"

He shrugged. "No way, dude. It's a photoshopped world."

A couple jurors shook their heads in apparent wonderment. Good. It's the reaction I wanted.

Just who are these kids? What planet are they from?

"What are you doing now, Mr. Kwalick?" I asked.

"I design and manufacture clothing."

"Just like your father?"

"My stuff's more hip, but yeah, I use his factories in China."

"What's the name of your company?"

"'None of the Above.'"

"Like an answer on a standardized test?"

"That's our hook. That's how we branded it."

"Would you take off your jacket and turn to face the jury?"

"Sure. Always up for free publicity."

Margaret Bolden moved from the prosecution table to get a better angle.

The witness removed his jacket, stood, and revealed a T-shirt in a rich blue with white lettering.

"For the record," I said, "the shirt has an image of a diploma and the words, *'Summa cum Fraud.'* What's that mean, Mr. Kwalick?"

"Seriously, dude? It's a play on *summa cum laude.* But now, instead of highest distinction, it's, you know, the biggest fraud. See, I'm kind of framous for getting kicked out."

"Framous?"

"That's 'famous' in a bad but cool way, so we're playing off that."

"When you walked into the courthouse today, were you wearing that T-shirt?"

"Yeah, without the jacket. There were like a zillion photographers out there and the T-shirt was in every shot. One of my assistants was wearing 'Ivy Be-Leaguer.' I write the logos myself."

"You're good at this, aren't you, Mr. Kwalick?"

"Marketing 101 is my deal, which, by the way, I never took at Yale."

"You're making money at this?"

"It costs me about four bucks each to make a shirt, and they retail for $99. 'Course I got expenses for distribution and advertising, but yeah, I'm dreaming on capitalism, gonna be stanky rich."

After a short recess, the government called the dullard twins, Teague and Niles Hallinan, who testified, as expected, that their families paid Kip to take their tests. Niles had gotten over his anger about Kip double-crossing him with the sky-high score that got flagged by the testing service and kept him out of USC. He didn't end up at Lackawanna Junior College in Scranton, Pennsylvania, as he had feared. Instead, he and Teague, expelled from Wake Forest, seemed to be enjoying their career as hip-hop artists. The twins had a crew of young people on the courthouse steps promoting Teague's latest hip-hop downloads, "Pimpin' the Quad" and "Outta Class, Mah Ass."

Like the Kwalick kid, they, too, bragged about their success. Niles, the Oscar Hammerstein to Teague's Richard Rodgers, said he had just finished writing the lyrics for "Love Me Mah Benjamins," which celebrated the glory of hundred-dollar bills.

Teague had gotten into Wake Forest, thanks to Kip nailing a 1475 on the SAT exam. I had a few questions for the lad.

"Are you telling the truth here today, Mr. Hallinan?" I began.

"Yeah."

"Do you always tell the truth?"

"What do you mean?"

"Your résumé says you were the long snapper on your high school football team."

"Oh, that. Yeah."

"Max Ringle didn't have an accomplice in the Wake Forest football program, so why lie about that?"

"My high school grades were so sorry, my dad was afraid a good SAT score wouldn't be enough. He talked to Ringle, who told him to say I wanted to walk on the football team. Like maybe if it was a close call, that could put me over the top."

"So, you went along with Max Ringle's advice and fabricated your résumé?"

"It wasn't a total lie. My freshman year in high school, I went out for the team."

"Then you must have experience as a long snapper, correct?"

"Some. I mean, I could have walked on the Demon Deacons if I hadn't been expelled."

"What's a long snapper do?"

"Hikes the ball to the kicker."

"You mean snaps the ball to the holder *for* the kicker?"

"Right. But directly to the other kicker. The...you know..."

"The punter?"

"Yeah, him."

I pulled an old football out of my bulky trial bag. Painted on the pigskin was "Penn State 14, University of Miami 10," from the 1987 Fiesta Bowl. Fond memories.

"Mr. Hallinan, catch." I tossed the ball with the underhand spiral favored by game officials. Teague's hands came up late and the ball bounced off his rib cage, but he managed to snag the rebound and clutch the ball to his chest, as you might a crying baby. "Now please come down and stand over there by the government table."

Margaret Bolden got to her feet, eyed me with a bit of amusement, and stayed quiet. I paced off precisely 7.5 yards, which put me at the far corner of the jury box. I got down into the holder's position on one knee.

"Now, get into your stance over the ball."

He spread his legs and held the ball on the floor with both hands in front of him. He teetered unsteadily as he looked at me, upside down.

"Keep your back straight, Mr. Hallinan. Be balanced. You look like a teapot that's going to topple onto your spout."

He adjusted his position, and I said, "Now, a good long snapper can get the ball to the holder in less than seven-tenths of a second. You gotta really whip it and follow through. That's the key. I'm not calling any signals. Just snap it when ready."

"No problem."

He breathed hard and tilted forward, then snapped the ball. As I'd advised, he whipped it with a strong follow-through. Unfortunately, he never let go of the ball and it slammed into his testicles so hard you could almost hear the *squish*.

He emitted a shriek, crumpled onto the floor, and curled into the fetal position, both hands on his groin, whimpering.

"Perhaps this would be a propitious time for a brief recess," I suggested amiably.

⁊

Following the recess, the last witness of the day was Shari Ringle. She wore a silk gray and black wrap dress, cinched at the waist, with knee-high burgundy boots of a soft leather. Her chestnut hair fell to her shoulders. Shari took the oath, sat down, looked straight at Kip, and pursed her lips, as if kissing him. Kip looked back and nodded. A calm, neutral nod that he'd been practicing.

Shari was important to the government because she was "student zero," the first client of the scheme. As Max Ringle's daughter, there was no charge, but Max still paid Kip for proctoring her test and changing her answers.

"Daddy hired Kip to tutor me," Shari said on direct exam. "At first, just plain old tutoring. To make it more fun, Kip would take the practice tests with me, challenging me to beat him, which I never did. Then I noticed he missed the last two questions of every section. Otherwise, he got everything right. I grilled him and he admitted he got those wrong on purpose, so I wouldn't be bummed about my own scores. I told Daddy that Kip's a friggin' genius. He could get a 1600 on the SAT or a 36 on the ACT every time. Then I said, 'I wish Kip could take the test for me.'"

"What did your father say?"

"Daddy was quiet a minute. Then he said, 'Maybe he can.' Which I thought was totally obidiculous."

"Obi...?"

"Obidiculous. Overboard and ridiculous. But Daddy bribed a proctor in West Hollywood to get Kip into the extra-time room as a proctor, and he corrected enough of my wrong answers to get me into USC."

On cross-examination, I started nice and easy.

"Have you been busy since getting expelled from USC?"

"Duh," she answered. "Maybe you heard of my podcast, 'Alt-Skool.'"

"I never miss it. Does it have sponsors?"

"Aroma-dot-com, high six figures and going up. They cancelled me when the scandal broke, then begged to come back when I started making bank on my other projects."

"What else is keeping you busy these days?"

"My cosmetics line. My biggest seller is 'Eraze,' a blemish remover."

"And you have a line of feminine hygiene products, correct?"

"'Change your tampon, not your grade.' I wrote that slogan myself."

"Then there's your nutrition book," I continued.

"It's really a nutrition-lifestyle book. *Count Money, Not Calories*. I didn't actually write it, but I read some of it when the ghostwriter gave me galleys. And my vlog, "Sexting and Blinging," has taken off. So has my reality show, 'Gen Z Nation.'"

"How about your Instagram? Nine million followers, right?"

"Old news. Ten million and powering up from there."

"So, you're really more than just a social media influencer?" I asked.

"I'm a media empire," Shari declared, without a hint of boastfulness.

"How much money did your empire make in the last year?"

"You'd have to ask my accountant, but it's north of eleven million."

I let out an appreciative whistle for the jury's benefit. The judge scowled at me but said nothing.

Then, out of the blue, Shari said, "I met Kim Kardashian at Nightshade."

My look showed my puzzlement.

"Nightshade! Mei Lin's restaurant in L.A. Kusshi oysters with passionfruit leche de tigre."

Oh, that Nightshade.

"I met Kim Kardashian there," Shari repeated. "She knew who I was!"

Shari said it with the enthusiasm Albert Einstein might have displayed when discovering that massive objects distort space-time.

As was my custom, I decided to ask a question without knowing the answer. It's like wandering off a marked jungle trail into an area known for quicksand. But you also should use your instincts. Shari Ringle was all glitz, glamour, and Kushii oysters with passionfruit leche de tigre. But she was not deceptive or malicious. I took the leap.

"Ms. Ringle, when the indictments came down and you were expelled from USC, you were pretty upset with my client, weren't you?"

"Totally. Really aguitado."

"Agitated?"

"Yeah. Bummed."

"And now?"

"Now, I thank Kip for making me what I am today."

Unless the heavens were going to open and rain down milk and honey, this seemed to be the high point of my day.

"No further questions." I felt a measure of joy. I was a poker player who, against the odds, had just filled an inside straight and had won a small pot. But looking toward Margaret Bolden at the prosecution table, I knew that my opponent had a pile of chips that dwarfed my own.

CHAPTER FIFTY
A Bribe is a Bribe

The next morning, I expected the government to call Max Ringle, its star witness. So I was surprised when Bolden asked a woman named Georgina Suarez to take the stand. She was director of Ethical Admissions Compliance at Stanford. It was a nifty new department created in the wake of the scandal, the university building a moat around its castle to keep out the barbarians. Or, rather, "to assure fair and ethical administration of the admissions process henceforth," in Ms. Suarez's words.

Yeah, she said "henceforth."

She was a smart and articulate woman, conservatively dressed in a charcoal skirt and jacket and a gray silk blouse. She had recently moved into the Admissions Department from the faculty, where she taught a course called "Business Ethics and Corporate Social Responsibility."

Margaret Bolden went straightaway to the heart of the government's case. "Did Stanford admit any students whose standardized tests were compromised by the defendant?"

"There was a young woman, a Chinese national, who purported to be a competitive sailor. That was false. Her family gave five million dollars to the university through Max Ringle's company. Because of her difficulties with English, she fared poorly on the English portion of the SAT, so that even had she been a competitive sailor, she would not have been admitted. The young woman then came to Los Angeles where the defendant proctored her exam, or I should say, *doctored* her exam, and her score increased sufficiently to gain admission, albeit fraudulently."

I pulled a file from under the table and found the information regarding the Chinese woman, her family, and the sailing team.

"What is the effect of such a fraudulent admission on Stanford, now that this case and others have been discovered and publicized?" Bolden asked.

"Whoa! Whoa! Objection." I was on my feet, not sure exactly why I seemed to be yelling at runaway horses. "Irrelevant and calls for an opinion."

"To the contrary," Bolden replied. "This goes to the element of the crime requiring that property be taken by fraud."

"Then I object on the ground that the question calls for a legal conclusion."

"No, it calls for facts, which the witness is uniquely positioned to explain."

"Then I object because the government is using the witness as an expert, and under the rules..." I shot a look at the judge to see if he detected any irony in my citing one of his heavenly rules, but he wasn't even looking at me, "the government is required to give me advance notice of all expert witnesses."

"Overruled," proclaimed the judge without favoring us with his reasoning.

"The defendant harmed our university in many respects," Georgina Suarez said. "Securing the fraudulent admission of less qualified students damaged the more qualified applicants who were not accepted. The fraud also hijacked the university's admissions process. Finally, it validated a national cynicism about the process by giving credence to the notion that wealthy families enjoy an unjust advantage."

Wow. My Kip did all of that?

"What property was Stanford deprived of due to the defendant's scheme?"

"The admissions slot was basically stolen by the defendant's actions. We were deprived of filling it in the best interests of the university. We also suffered a reputational loss. The news coverage has portrayed the admissions process at elite universities as corrupt. We strive for fairness, a level playing field, and the defendant deprived us of that ability."

This went on for a while, Margaret Bolden feeding lobs to Georgina Suarez, who smacked overheads into my court like a champion Stanford tennis player. When Bolden turned the witness over to me, I bounded out of my chair—and I don't do much bounding these days. I had no notes; I didn't need them. I stood in front of, not behind, the podium, to create a more imposing presence.

"When you answered the question about the property Stanford supposedly lost," I began, "you didn't say anything about money, did you?"

"No, I did not."

"Because this didn't cost the university a dime, correct?"

"Correct."

"Isn't it true that Stanford actually made money? Millions of dollars funneled to the athletic department through Max Ringle's company, correct?"

"Yes."

"So, there's no real difference in gaining admission through Ringle's bribery and the university selling admissions slots to the children of high-rolling donors?"

"We don't *sell* slots."

"Fine, we'll get back to that. First, let's talk about that level playing field and fairness in admissions. Not all applications go into the same pile, do they?"

"It's all electronic these days, so technically, there are no piles."

"Whether on paper or on hard drives, legacies have a leg up, don't they? Children of alumni."

"Yes, at all major institutions, some weight is given to that."

"Children of major donors get preferential admissions, too. Isn't that right?"

"Again, that's quite standard."

"And athletes get preferential admissions, whether they be football players or women lacrosse players?"

"Yes."

"So athletes, legacies, and children of major donors are routinely admitted with lower grades and test scores than other applicants, correct?"

"As they are at the Ivies and other institutions."

"What's the overall acceptance rate for your applicants?"

"This year, 4.4 percent."

"Harvard, which has a similarly low acceptance rate, reports that eighty-six percent of recruited athletes gain admission. Would Stanford's number be similar?"

"I don't have an exact figure, but that sounds like the ballpark, no pun intended."

"Let's go back to that applicant who claimed to be a competitive sailor. She lived in a landlocked Chinese city about a thousand miles from any body of water, correct?"

"I've since learned that, yes."

"And the young woman wouldn't know a mast from a boom if one hit her on the head, would she?"

"I can't answer that."

"What I'm getting at, Ms. Suarez, is this. Wasn't Stanford negligent in not researching the bona fides of her application?"

"Our process fell short, and my office is taking remedial steps."

"Stanford is very proud of its athletic program, is it not?"

"Indeed."

"Again this year, Stanford won the Directors' Cup, signifying the best overall athletic program, correct?"

She loosened up and smiled. "Year in and year out."

"How many varsity teams does Stanford have?"

"Thirty-six," she reported, proudly. "Second only to Harvard."

"Ah, just as in academics?"

She gave me her first smile. "We can debate that another time."

"How many athletes on those thirty-six teams?"

"Approximately nine hundred."

"The key word is 'approximately,' isn't it? You might have a few more or a few less. It's not a set number, is it?"

"That would be correct."

"So, if the sailing coach has twenty slots, and he comes to you and says, 'Hey, I have a twenty-first person I want,' you give it to him, don't you?"

"Ordinarily, yes."

"Therefore, this notion of a fixed number of admission slots is mythical, isn't it?"

"I'd use the word 'flexible.'"

"Fine. Where legacies, children of major donors, and athletes are concerned, the number of slots is flexible. Correct?"

"That would be a fair statement."

"How many high school students were offered admission to Stanford last year?"

"Roughly two thousand."

"And how many enrolled?"

"About 1,700. Perhaps a few more."

"You're saying 'roughly' and 'about.' So, it doesn't make a lot of difference if you've enrolled 1,700 or 1,701, or 1,799, does it?

"There is room, if that's what you mean."

"Then, as a matter of simple arithmetic and logic, there's no single person who's deprived of an admissions slot because there's always one more, correct?"

"I might quibble with the word 'always.' But yes, it's a flexible number on general admissions, too."

I ignored her quibble and plunged ahead. "If the Chinese family had simply paid five million dollars directly to the university as a contribution, would their daughter have been admitted based on her prior test scores and no claim of sailing ability?"

"It's possible. But if I were to hazard a guess, I'd say probably not."

"Why? Isn't five million enough? What's the price of an admissions slot, anyway?"

Her mouth tightened and she said, "Again, we don't sell them."

"Sure, you do. You've already admitted that. I'm just trying to establish the price."

"Objection! Argumentative." Bolden was on her feet, pointing at me. She seemed genuinely perturbed, not just lawyer-pretending-to-be perturbed.

"Sustained. Mr. Lassiter, please ask a question and don't argue with the witness."

"Ms. Suarez, isn't the problem here that the Chinese family simply bribed the wrong person?"

Her eyes darted to Bolden, beseeching her help, but she got none. "No, I wouldn't put it that way."

"Morally and ethically, what's the difference between bribing the university directly or bribing a coach or bribing an exam proctor?"

"Objection! Irrelevant." Still on her feet, Bolden was ready for battle. "The admissions system isn't on trial here."

"Sure it is!" I raised my voice, so the jury would take heed. "That's exactly what's on trial."

"Sustained. Mr. Lassiter, rephrase your question." He turned toward the jury box. "Please be advised that the court, not counsel, will tell you what's on trial here."

That rocked my boat, but I kept paddling. If there were a waterfall ahead, I didn't want to know about it. "Let's keep it simple. Isn't a bribe a bribe?"

"I don't know how to answer such a tautological question, Mr. Lassiter."

"And I know don't the meaning of 'tautological,' so I'll move on. Instead of going through Max Ringle and the sailing coach, shouldn't the family have just dealt with your admissions and development officers? Shouldn't they have said, 'C'mon, how much is this going to cost us?'"

"That's not the way we do things!"

"No, that's not the way you *say* you do things."

"Mr. Lassiter," the judge called out. "Would you like to rephrase that as a question?"

"No thanks, Your Honor. I think the jury's already heard the answer."

CHAPTER FIFTY-ONE
Too Many *Hocs*

Melissa Gold...

Melissa carried two bags from Havana Harry's down the walking path in South Pointe Park at the tip of South Beach. It was one of her favorite places, and she was meeting her two favorite men. It was Friday, and the judge had adjourned at lunchtime for the weekend break. Jake and Kip were already there, sitting on a bench, watching one of the cruise ships steam out Government Cut toward the islands. The ship was a mammoth boxy contraption that looked like a floating apartment building, and its horn wailed as it cleared the jetty into open water.

Jake had been in good spirits when he left for court in the morning. She had been checking his temperature, as he called it. Asking how he felt, monitoring his moods. He seemed to have gotten into a rhythm with the trial, sleeping better and showing less irritability. She was still worried about him, of course, especially since he'd quit the AY-70 experimental antibodies. But he seemed to be on an even keel, much like the cruise ship, now headed over a light chop in ocean waters.

Kip saw her first, stood, and raced toward her. "Melissa, you should have seen Uncle Jake!" Kip slid to a stop and made a motion as if firing a rifle into the sky. "He was savage! So mint. Totally brill."

"Is that right, Jake?" Melissa asked, approaching the bench and handing him the bags. "Were you totally *brill*?"

"I did okay. Neutralized a government witness, which is about all I can ever do."

"Neutralized?" Kip exclaimed. "I'll bet the prosecutor wishes she never called that snooty Stanford bitch."

"Hey! No misogynistic language, kiddo," Jake said.

"Okay, sorry." Kip dug into a bag and pulled out his vegetarian lunch of black beans and sautéed plantains.

Melissa studied her fiancé. He didn't look tired. He didn't look happy or sad. Or even hungry, for that matter. He simply wasn't registering any emotion. "What is it, Jake?"

"Probably nothing. It's just odd. Margaret Bolden really preps her witnesses well. But today, well, today was different. This admissions director from Stanford was fine on direct but totally unprepared for cross. As if Bolden didn't have time to get her ready."

"Maybe a late addition to the roster," Kip said, between bites.

"Exactly what I'm thinking," Jake said. "What's odd is that a few nights ago, after you two were asleep, my pal Ray Pincher called, asking about the trial. I told him I was going to argue that the universities weren't deprived of any property. Then, today, when Bolden leads me to believe that Ringle was going to testify, she brings in a surprise witness to talk all about the property interests that have been compromised. And, frankly, she wasn't very good at it."

"You don't think Ray tipped off the prosecutor, do you?" Melissa asked.

He shook his head. "Why would he? He hates the feds."

She spent another moment considering this man she loved. He wasn't saying everything he was thinking. He also wasn't eating, which wasn't like him. "What else, Jake?"

"It's just coincidental, I'm sure, but last year, before anyone was charged, Ray and I were talking. I said I didn't see any federal crimes, even if Kip had taken those tests."

"I remember. Ray told you a story about sending postcards from Hawaii," she said. "Postcards with lies."

"Right. In his scenario, which seemed like a joke at the time, the guy who writes the postcards gets charged with mail fraud, racketeering, and money laundering. Well, it turns out he was right. Those are the three felonies Kip is charged with."

"And you think that's a coincidence, too?" she asked.

"Yeah. Otherwise, we're falling into that logical trap. Kip, what's it called when you think one thing causes another because it happened first?"

Kip licked a bit of sweet plantain from his lips and said, "*Post hoc ergo propter hoc.* 'After this, therefore, because of this.'"

"That's the fallacy. Just because X happens and then Y happens, it doesn't mean that X caused Y."

Melissa watched Jake's face. Even though he called it a fallacy, he wasn't entirely sure that X didn't cause Y. "There's nothing else, is there Jake?"

"One more thing." He unwrapped the grease-slicked paper and pulled out his Cuban sandwich but didn't take a bite. "In that call the other night, I told Ray I was going to make a motion the next morning to get the names of the parents who were never charged. When I got into chambers, Bolden cited an Eleventh Circuit case that blew me out of the water. Judge Speidel made a big deal about her being more prepared to argue my motion than I was."

"She's a good lawyer and did her research," Melissa said, not wanting to even contemplate the kind of betrayal Jake thought might have occurred. The two men squabbled endlessly, but more like highly competitive brothers than enemies.

"It was an oral motion," he countered. "There was no time for research."

"Then she knew the case off the top of her head."

"That's what I thought at the time. But thinking back, one of her assistants handed her a photocopy of the decision. Think about it. They had no advance notice of my motion. Even if one of her crew used Westlaw on a laptop while we were in chambers, they had no printer. They must have come to court with the case already printed out." He closed his eyes and squeezed the bridge of his nose with a thumb and index finger. "Five years ago...hell, two years ago, I would have caught that at the time."

They were all silent a moment. Jake exhaled a long breath, and a look of sadness swept over him.

Kip said, "Uncle Jake, do you really think Sugar Ray would sell you out?"

"The question is why. What could be so powerful a force that he had no choice?"

"Uncle Jake, it still could be *post hoc ergo propter hoc.*"

Jake seemed to think it over. "I'm afraid not, Kip. Too many *hocs.*"

CHAPTER FIFTY-TWO
Human Nature

I sent Kip home with Melissa. Thirty minutes after leaving them, I walked through the metal detector into the James Lawrence King Federal Justice Building. I moseyed past two federal marshals sitting at desks and entered the front lobby of the U.S. Attorney's Office. A young woman who sat behind bulletproof glass asked me if she could help. I gave her my name and told her I would like to see A.U.S.A. Margaret Bolden.

"Is she expecting you?"

"We're in trial together. I just need to see her for a moment."

"I'll ring her office."

"Before you do, could I make a call?" I gestured toward a wooden phone booth with a glass window. "My cell has died."

"Dial nine to get an outside line," she advised.

Once in the booth, I dialed a number from my cell phone's contacts list. My well-charged cell phone, to tell the truth. I took a deep breath and exhaled, trying to relax. What I was doing might be legal, and then again, it might not. A gray area.

"Hello?" a woman answered, doubtless looking at Caller I.D., which would have read, "U.S. Attorney."

"Dr. Pop-kin?" I said, disguising my voice with my best Southern drawl.

"Dr. Pincher-Popkin," Paulette said. "Who is this?"

"Doctor, this is Jess Kalartie in the U.S. Attorney's office."

"Who?"

I added a little gravel to my drawl, sounding like a poor man's Bear Bryant. "Jess Kalartie. Ah'm in trial with Margie Bolden in that college admissions case, and Ah'm wondering if ya'll would come down to the office Monday after court adjourns."

"Why?" A stiff and unfriendly question. But not, *"Who's Margie Bolden?"* Or, *"What the hell are you talking about?"*

"Ah'd rather not talk about it on the phone," I said. "And could you bring your son with you? Moses, is it? Like in the Book of Deuteronomy?"

"No, I cannot."

"Ah beg your pardon."

"We're not coming to your office. We've cooperated fully, and the non-prosecution agreement has been signed. My father handled everything. He's Raymond Pincher. Do you know who that is?"

"Hell's bells. Everybody in town knows the State Attorney."

"Ms. Bolden told me personally that our family wouldn't be bothered anymore. No subpoenas. No testimony. And, of course, no charges. We've lived up to our end, so please live up to yours. And that's all I'm going to say."

The phone clicked off. I sat there, still and quiet, paralyzed and mute. I don't know how much time passed. Seconds. Minutes.

Oh, Sugar Ray! How could you have done this? To Kip? To me?

I had misjudged him so completely. Missed all the signs. His over-eagerness to pump me for information about the case. His pretending to give me information about the government's case, which boiled down to their excessively large war room stocked with croissants and coffee. And his faux concern for my health, poured on thick and syrupy.

Ray Pincher pretended to be my friend, but he spied on me for the federal government.

Had I lost my instincts, honed in courtrooms and taprooms and locker rooms? I prided myself on my skill in discerning human nature. My peripheral vision, once sharp as a submarine's periscope in discerning friend from foe, had grown cloudy. Childlike, I had picked up a rock, never dreaming there'd be a snake underneath.

I saw a shadow through the glass. Margaret Bolden was standing in front of the booth, appearing puzzled. I opened the door.

"What are you doing here, Jake?"

"I...I...uh. I had to use the restroom."

She raised her eyebrows. "I hope you didn't use it in there."

I felt claustrophobic, as if the walls of the phone booth were closing in, about to crush me. I stood and exited the booth, my legs heavy, as if stuck in hot tar. It was a narrow space, and I stumbled and nearly fell.

Bolden reached out a hand and steadied me. "Are you okay, Jake?"

I pulled away. "Sure. Absolutely fine."

She looked at me as if she cared. But she didn't, I was certain. All those high-minded slogans carved in granite—"Equal Justice Under Law"—were just bullshit. Bolden didn't play by the rules. Did Judge Speidel know that about his Margie? No, but I'm just the guy to tell him.

Everything was falling into place. The reason Bolden fought so hard to keep the uncharged parents' names confidential had nothing to do with grand jury secrecy or the government's work product. She had a dirty little secret to protect. Paulette Pincher-Popkin was one of those parents. There was a conspiracy of silence to keep Ray Pincher's spying from becoming known.

How could I have not seen this coming? I remembered something Melissa had said the first day Pincher offered me a tidbit about the federal investigation.

"I don't understand why the state attorney is going out of his way to help you."

Her instincts were better than mine. But then, the fossilized remains of a woolly mammoth had better instincts. I felt a surge of heat run through me and started to sweat, misery flowing from every pore.

I realized that Margaret Bolden was speaking to me. "Do you know where you are, Jake?"

"Existentially or geographically?"

"Do you want me to call anyone?"

"Why would I?"

"Are you sure you're okay?"

"Why wouldn't I be?"

"Because you look like you've been crying."

CHAPTER FIFTY-THREE
A Long, Slow Guilty Plea

Ray Pincher lived just off Old Cutler Road in the Snapper Creek subdivision of Coral Gables. I gave my name to a uniformed security guy at the guardhouse, who acted as if he expected me. "Mr. Pincher is around back in the gazebo," he said.

With my tinnitus clanging in my ears like a discordant brass section in a second-rate orchestra, I parked the Eldo in the front driveway. The house had belonged to Pincher's in-laws, his wife's parents having owned a chain of funeral homes catering to the African American community. It was a rambling one-story structure from the 1960s surrounded by a wooden deck with a koi pond running underneath. Tropical landscaping— red bougainvillea, white hibiscus, sweet jasmine—encircled the property, and two small waterfalls poured into the pond. I took a coral rock path around the house where the scent of jasmine gave way to cigar smoke. I followed the smoke to an eight-sided cedar gazebo sitting between two towering palm trees.

Pincher sat in a cushioned chair, a fat cigar in one hand, a tumbler of a dark liquid in the other. "Take a seat, Mr. Kalartie." He motioned me toward a matching chair. "Cigar, rum? Or do we just start arm wrestling?"

I sat down, not because I wanted to, but because fatigue was setting in and my tinnitus had reached the decibel level of a Beaver Stadium whiteout. "Did you think I wouldn't find out?" I said.

"To the contrary. I thought you'd get suspicious of my pestering you about the case. Then I'd confess to you. Maybe you'd slug me or maybe not. In the end, we'd make peace, and I'd start being a double agent, feeding you info."

I shook my head at his audacity. "Do you believe your own bullcrap, Ray?"

He sipped at his rum and said, "You're right. Maybe it was a fantasy."

"How the hell did you let Paulette get involved in Ringle's scam?"

He barked a laugh. "Same way you let Kip. I didn't know because she didn't tell me. She didn't even tell Barry. That sweet *schlemiel* son-in-law of mine wanted Moses to follow in his footsteps at Harvard. Thought the kid might be a basketball player, but that was never gonna happen. Barry didn't have a clue when Paulette paid Ringle to pass off Moses as a tennis player and get him into Georgetown where Ringle had a connection. Fortunately, Paulette came to me when the FBI approached her."

"And you called Margaret Bolden."

"No, I called her boss. If it makes you feel any better about Margaret, she only went along because Juan Lucayo ordered her to."

"You swapped favors with that son of a bitch. Quid pro friggin' quo. He'd protect your daughter, you'd torpedo my nephew."

"That's pretty much it," he admitted.

"The first day of trial, I ran into you on the plaza. You said you were seeing Lucayo about an opioid task force. That was bullshit."

"I'm afraid so."

"And Gilberto Foyo wasn't in court to bail me out if I was held in contempt. He was feeding information to you so you could pump me for my trial strategy."

Pincher didn't say a word. He didn't have to. From somewhere in the yard, tucked into the branches of red bougainvillea, a mockingbird hooted.

"I'm gonna go public, let the *Herald* know about your dirty dealing," I said.

"What's the headline, Jake? 'State Attorney Aids U.S. Attorney in College Scandal.' I can live with that."

"That's not the way it'll play."

"Jesus, Jake, I didn't make their case. Lucayo showed me their evidence, and I saw your nephew was toast. You know what prosecutors call a case like this? 'A long, slow guilty plea.' That's what I was trying to tell you. Get another lawyer, someone objective who could have worked out a plea. But no, Last-Chance Lassiter thinks he can win a hopeless case."

"It's not over," I said, feebly.

"It's your ego that's doomed Kip, nothing I did. Jury nullification? Really? Who do you think you are, Paul Newman in *The Verdict?* 'Look for justice in your heart.' Is that your case? Hollywood endings don't come true, pal."

I leaned forward in my chair, my elbows on my knees. I couldn't look at him. Nagging at me was the notion that he was right about my deficiencies.

"Believe me, I don't enjoy telling you that you've lost it, Jake."

"On Monday, I'm going to file a motion to dismiss for prosecutorial misconduct, and I'll ask the judge to refer you to the Bar for discipline."

"I can't wait to read your motion. You're not known for your written work."

"I'm still working on the adjectives to describe you. Do you think 'scum-sucking, two-faced, shit-eating dirtbag' strikes the right note?"

"Take your best shot, Jake. Two shots. Your whole cartridge belt."

"I want your ticket punched. I want you publicly humiliated and removed from office by the Governor and Lucayo fired by the Attorney General."

"Dream on if it gives you satisfaction." Pincher exhaled a puff of smoke that mingled with the brackish aroma from the nearby marina. "But in the real world, you shouldn't file that motion."

"Try and stop me. I'd like that."

He shook his head and made a *cluck-cluck* sound. "So unlike you to act tactically and not strategically."

"One step at a time. That's all I've got."

"The old Jake would have thought ahead. If I do this, what will Ray do? What will Lucayo do? What will the judge do? But now..."

"What? You're threatening me. You betray me, and that's all you've got? Not even, 'I'm sorry, Jake. Forgive me for being a bigger shit than a ton of manure.'"

"You would have done the same thing."

"The hell I would have!"

He tapped ashes onto the gazebo's wooden floor. "You'd do anything for your nephew, and I'd do anything for my daughter."

"There's a line, Ray. There's a line I won't cross."

"You can't know that until you're standing at the line, jackals nipping at your heels."

I dug out of memory the line I'd made Kip read after he'd been indicted. "'I can bend my own rules way, way over, but there's a place where I finally stop bending them.'"

"I give up. Who said it?"

"Travis McGee."

He coughed out a smoky laugh. "A fictional hero! When did you start believing in fairy tales?"

"When did you become so cynical?"

We were both quiet. When we used to spar, we were each so gassed between rounds that we lost the ability to taunt each other. Now, I felt the same exhaustion, my energy—physical and mental—drained dry. My anger hadn't ebbed, but my ability to exhibit it had melted away.

Without saying goodbye or screw you, I stepped down from the gazebo and started back on the coral rock path. The sun was low in the western sky, and my shadow was elongated. Giraffe legs tapering to a small rectangular body topped by a tiny, ridiculous pinhead, which somehow seemed appropriate.

He called after me. "You don't want to hear it, but I'm telling you as someone who still respects you. Hang up your spurs. Get your medical treatments. Marry that wonderful woman who's oblivious to all your flaws. But give up the law. These days, you couldn't win a jaywalking case if the light was green."

By the time I reached my car, his voice had faded away, and the only sounds were unseen birds in the palms and the ringing in my ears.

CHAPTER FIFTY-FOUR
Speaking with the Dead

Melissa Gold...

Melissa padded barefoot onto the back porch where Jake sat in one of the Adirondack chairs, a tumbler of Jack Daniels on the table, a yellow pad on his lap. It was nearly midnight, and Kip was asleep.

Earlier, when Jake had come home, he told them what had happened at Pincher's house. He seemed dazed, and he spoke with very little affect. He apologized to Kip for letting him down but said that now he had solid grounds to get the entire case dismissed. Kip shot Melissa a look then, as if he didn't believe it. And neither did she.

Jake was off his game, but did he know it? If he did, was he covering it up, protecting her from a deeper knowledge of the depth of his problems? Sometimes, when speaking, he sputtered an unintelligible syllable. She could see in his eyes when he'd forgotten a word—usually someone's name—and he'd try to retrieve it like a man chasing a butterfly with a net.

Jake hadn't seen her approach from behind him on the porch. She paused and listened. Was he talking to himself?

"Of course, Charlie. I know how to cross a cooperating witness," he said, indignation in his voice.

After a moment of silence, he continued, "Cross-exam is just storytelling. My story, not the witness's. If you string all my questions together, there's my story."

Another pause, and then, "No. If I win the motion, there's no cross. Game over. We go to Joe's for stone crabs and hash browns."

He was silent for several seconds. She cleared her throat and walked to the adjacent chair. "Hey."

"Hey, Mel." He looked at his watch. "Whoa, it's late. Sorry."

She spoke softly, gently. "You sounded like you were talking to someone."

"Ah. Well. Yes. Charlie Riggs."

"Uh-huh. But you know Doc Riggs passed away last year."

He shrugged. "I didn't say he was talking back."

"But you seemed to be listening to someone, like a real conversation."

"I'm just imagining what he would say. He taught me so much about trying cases, even though he was the medical examiner, and not a lawyer. For a guy who dealt with corpses, he was remarkably knowledgeable about people."

"What did he say to you about Ray Pincher?" she asked.

"That he'd like to do his autopsy, as soon as possible."

He smiled, and she felt a measure of relief. If Jake needed to talk to Charlie Riggs or even Napoleon, for that matter, that was fine, as long as he was just thinking out loud. Thirty minutes later, they were in bed, spooning, Jake's breath warm against her neck, one strong arm draped across her hip.

She slept a dreamless sleep, awakening with the hope that Jake could reach deep for reserves of strength and resolve and make it through the end of the trial without a physical or emotional breakdown. Then, win or lose, she had a plan she hadn't yet told him about. Four weeks in the hospital for round-the-clock testing and observation. Brain scans with the latest equipment making the most precise measurements of brain functions and dysfunctions. After that, depending on the results, an even more potent array of experimental treatments. Given his condition and her assessment of the future, there really was no other choice.

CHAPTER FIFTY-FIVE
Written Work

On Saturday afternoon, I wrote my "Motion to Dismiss for Prosecutorial Misconduct."

I spent three hours on Westlaw in the morning, which was roughly three hours more legal research than I had done in the last ten years. I came up with several cases in which prosecutors had crossed a bridge too far. Most involved hiding, destroying, or tampering with evidence. Or presenting false or misleading evidence. Or failing to disclose exculpatory evidence. Sometimes, prosecutors were not exactly the guardians of our liberty.

I was following Judge Speidel's beloved rules with a written motion and memorandum of law. Reading the case law as I worked, I dictated and Kip typed on his laptop: "The government is forbidden from planting agents to spy on defense preparations or invade defense work product." I gave him the supporting citation, *U.S. vs. Henry,* a United States Supreme Court case. "Now, put this in quotes. 'The defendant has the right to prepare in secret. The prosecution's intrusion violates both the Fifth and Sixth Amendments.'"

"Good one," Kip acknowledged.

"Now put this into coherent English for me. 'There is an unholy conspiracy between U.S. Attorney Juan Lucayo and State Attorney Raymond Pincher to spy on the defendant's trial preparation. The government's conduct is shocking to the universal sense of justice and violates due process as well as the defendant's right to a fair trial.'"

"Universal sense of justice," Kip repeated. "Love it."

I dictated several paragraphs about Ray Pincher pretending to be "a confidante and ally of defense counsel," when he was, in fact, a government informant.

"The only remedy," I continued, "is dismissal of all charges with prejudice and appropriate disciplinary action against the malfeasors, Juan Lucayo and Raymond Pincher."

"Malfeasors," Kip echoed, apparently liking the word.

Kip printed out the document. I edited and polished. On Sunday morning, I tightened the language even more. In the afternoon, I filed the motion electronically. No more rushing to the courthouse to have a clerk hand-stamp my documents like the Dickensian lawyer Jaggers in *Great Expectations*. These days, you hit a few keys, and *whoosh*, your document sails through the ether and instantaneously appears in the courthouse or in a cloud above it.

Still, I did not expect such a hasty response. Thirty-four minutes after filing, I received a phone call from one of Judge Speidel's eager young law clerks.

"The judge would like you and your team in chambers at eight a.m.," the fellow said.

"I'll alert my team. I assume the judge will be hearing the motion."

"That would likewise be my assumption," he said, noncommittally.

I told Kip, who asked, "Is it a good sign that the ratchet tool is giving us such a quick hearing?"

I gave him the truth. "I have no idea. All I know is that we've got the tool's attention."

CHAPTER FIFTY-SIX
There May Well be a Hanging

At 7:55 a.m. on Monday, an old Mexican proverb popped into my head for no discernible reason: *The week begins badly for the man hanged on a Monday.*

I was sitting in Judge Speidel's chambers, Kip at my side. No judge, no court reporter, no law clerks. The quiet was deafening.

At precisely 8:00 a.m., Judge Speidel, in a light seersucker suit, rather than his robes, waddled into chambers from a side door that led to his private office. Behind him, nearly obscured by his bulk, Margaret Bolden followed. Not a good sign, the two of them huddling. Why did I think they weren't talking about the Sunday evening seafood buffet at their country club?

The judge plopped into his high-backed chair, which groaned in response. "Let's get to it."

"Your Honor, shouldn't we wait for the court reporter?" I asked.

"No reporter. No law clerks. No assistants. And please ask your client to wait in the courtroom."

"I have a right to have every hearing transcribed," I said, "and my client has a right to be here."

The judge exhaled a sigh that rattled loose papers on his desk. "Trust me on this, Mr. Lassiter. It may be hard to believe, but I'm looking out for you."

Kip stirred. "It's okay, Uncle Jake." He got up and left.

"I've sealed the motion to dismiss you filed yesterday," the judge said. "The media and the public have no access to it. If you choose to withdraw the motion, it will never see the light of day."

"I choose not to withdraw it."

"Jesus H. Christ, just hold your horses, Lassiter." The judge tugged at the knot of his tie, pulling it down to half-staff, and two hidden chins jiggled free. "I read your motion and your memorandum of law. Surprisingly, your written work is acceptable."

He said it reluctantly, like a miser forced at gunpoint to give alms to the poor.

"You allege a conspiracy between the U.S. Attorney and the State Attorney," the judge continued. "You claim the U.S. Attorney's office planted a spy in your camp, and you want an evidentiary hearing to put everyone under oath to prove your allegations."

"In front of a court reporter," I said, gesturing to the empty space where she should have been taking down every word.

"Before taking such an unprecedented step, I will inquire of you. Not under oath. No court reporter. Just the three of us. Officers of the court seeking common ground."

He's laying a trap for me. Anyone could see that. But how and why?

"Now, did Ms. Bolden or Mr. Lucayo break into your office or hire someone to do so, à la Watergate?"

"Of course not."

"Did they tap your phones?"

"Not that I know of."

"Hack your computer?"

"I'm not claiming that."

"As for Raymond Pincher, is he your co-counsel?"

"You know he's not. He's a public official."

"And, in fact, a prosecutor, just like Ms. Bolden, though in the state system."

"Ray's also been a friend for decades."

"Don't you mean an adversary, someone you've tried cases against, down by the river?"

"An adversary who became a friend through mutual respect and beating each other's brains out in the boxing ring."

"Did you voluntarily disclose your trial strategy to Mr. Pincher?"

"Yes, on the basis that he would keep it confidential."

"Did he sign a non-disclosure agreement to that effect?"

"No. I trusted him."

"Did you ever say to him, 'Ray, don't tell a soul?'"

"It was understood."

"Did Mr. Pincher rifle through your desk or your briefcase?"

I struggled to contain my anger. "Your Honor, you're missing the point. This unholy conspiracy violated my client's rights because there was a *quid pro quo*. The U.S. Attorney made a secret deal with Pincher not to prosecute his daughter in return for his acting as a spy."

The judge turned to Bolden. "Is that true, Margie?"

"Your Honor, I can categorically state that I made no such deal."

"I didn't say *Margie* made the deal. Her boss did! Pincher admitted it!"

"In writing? Under oath? Do you have an audio or video recording? Will he repeat that admission in court?"

"Let me put the three of them under oath, and we'll find out."

"What next, the Attorney General? Is this another of those Lassiter fishing expeditions where—what did you say?—you've caught some big grouper?"

I felt like I was rowing a dinghy into a headwind and against the tide. The judge was in the bag for the government, and I felt helpless. "Your Honor, I just want a chance to—"

"What it sounds like to me, Mr. Lassiter, is that you were negligent in disclosing confidential information to a third party who had no legal duty to refrain from sharing it with the government. The fact that the third party is a prosecutor only underlines the magnitude of your negligence."

"What are you saying? You're denying my motion?"

"Oh, we're not done quite yet. Margie?"

"Mr. Lassiter makes this motion with unclean hands. Last Friday afternoon, he impersonated an A.U.S.A. on the telephone, in violation of at least two federal criminal statutes."

Ah, so that's where this is going. Had been going, ever since the law clerk's call yesterday and the judge's ex parte tête à tête with Bolden before the hearing.

The judge turned back to me. If I could have seen his eyes through his bulbous cheeks, they probably would have been twinkling. "Good gracious! Your response, Mr. Lassiter?"

Now I knew why that Mexican proverb about a Monday hanging had popped into my head. I must have known, at least subconsciously, that I couldn't get a fair shake from Judge Speidel. A song came to me. Tom Russell's red-dirt classic, "The Sky Above, The Mud Below," where the local deacon was also the sheriff, the judge, the executioner, and the undertaker. *"Someone go and dig a ditch, there may well be a hanging."*

"Mr. Lassiter?" the judge prompted me. "If you desire, you can consult with an attorney before speaking or simply plead the Fifth Amendment."

"Fuck the Fifth," I mumbled.

"What was that?"

"I'll forego the Fifth."

"Then answer carefully, fella, because I'll drop-kick your ass into jail without a second thought."

"Stated succinctly, I did not impersonate an Assistant United States Attorney."

"All calls from our lobby phone are recorded," Bolden said. "We have the audio."

I pointed a finger at her. "Then you didn't listen very carefully. What I said was, 'This is Jess Kalartie in the U.S. Attorney's office.' In fact, I was in your office when I made the call. There is no A.U.S.A. named 'Jess Kalartie,' so I wasn't impersonating him. That's an anagram of my name. I also said, 'I'm in trial with Margaret Bolden in the college admissions case.' That statement is one hundred percent true. I said, 'I'm wondering if you could come down to the office Monday after court adjourns.' That's true, too. In short, I didn't violate any federal statutes. I merely uncovered with very little effort your office's egregious misconduct that the court is happy to sweep under its Persian rug."

For a long moment, no one said anything, and the only sound was the quiet hum of the air-conditioning. In the state courthouse, down by the river, the A/C screeches like angry birds.

Finally, the judge cleared his throat and said, "The defense motion, which shall remain under seal, is denied. Mr. Lassiter, you walked a tightrope in your devious little phone call, but you miraculously live to fight another day. That doesn't mean the court approves of your sharp tactics and slippery conduct. And, assuming your client is convicted, if you think that conduct won't come into play at sentencing, well, you are as ill-informed about human nature as you are about the federal rules of criminal procedure."

"Wait a second! In plain English, are you saying that because I'm an asshole, you're gonna throw the book at my nephew?"

"Did I say that, Margie?" the judge asked, oh-so-innocently.

"Not at all," Bolden replied.

"When this trial is over," I vowed, "win or lose, I'm reporting Bolden and her boss to the Inspector General of the Justice Department. I'm reporting Ray Pincher to the Florida Bar, and I'm reporting Your Honor to...I don't know who I report a federal judge to, but I'll figure it out."

"Try God," the judge said, struggling to get his bulk out of the chair. When he did, he grabbed his black robes that might once have been the mainsail of a pirate ship. Bolden started gathering her papers, but I stayed put.

"I'm probably dying," I told them.

Bolden froze in place, and the judge looked at me, puzzled, before dropping back into his chair.

"At the very least, Your Honor," I said, feeling agitated, my chest a hive of buzzing bees, "I might soon become a burden to people who care about me. I'm not saying this to get your sympathy. Lord knows, sympathy doesn't seem to be part of your DNA."

"What's your point, Mr. Lassiter?" the judge demanded.

"I've got nothing to lose...except my nephew. There's nothing I won't do to keep him out or prison. Your threats don't scare me." I imitated the judge's officious tone. "'I'll drop-kick your ass into jail.' Go ahead! Do it!"

I stood, opened my suit coat, and reached into the inside pocket. The judge looked alarmed. Did I sneak a gun past security? I pulled out a toothbrush with a Mickey Mouse handle.

"I never go to court unless I'm prepared to spend a couple nights in the stockade." I reached inside the other pocket and pulled out Melissa's silk lavender eye mask with white piping.

"Those damn fluorescent lights give me headaches when I'm on the top bunk. What I'm saying, Judge Speidel, is you do what you have to do. I don't give a damn."

"Sit down, Mr. Lassiter," the judge said, quietly but firmly.

I sat, keeping my spine straight and my eyes on His Honor.

"I've cut you a lot slack," he continued, "which you fail to appreciate. Now, we're going to finish this trial, and then we'll have a hearing on your conduct. And, as you suggest, I will do what I have to do. So, keep that toothbrush handy."

The judge kept talking but I stopped listening. I could feel my jaw muscles clenching and my heart beating like a blacksmith hammering an anvil. A hot wave of anger flowed through me. I had told the truth. Jail did not concern me. Bar discipline did not concern me. All I could think of was Kip and how he was getting shafted.

I would keep fighting and would never give up. And sure, maybe at the end of the trial, the marshals will drag me from the courtroom. So be it.

For now, a blinding headache pierced my skull and blurred my vision. The recessed lights in the ceiling seemed to be spinning like flying saucers. And still, the judge was yammering away.

"...Frankly, I have never encountered such blatant rudeness in my courtroom," Judge Speidel said.

Then I heard myself reply, "I'm a rude dude, but I'm the real deal."

"What? What's that?"

"Cocked, locked, and ready to rock. Rough, tough, and hard to bluff."

"Mr. Lassiter!"

"I take it slow, I go with the flow. I ride with the tide, I've got glide in my stride."

"You will cease this...this poetry at once!"

"I don't snooze, so I don't lose."

"Your Honor," Bolden said. "I believe that's a George Carlin routine."

"Who?"

I exhaled a long, slow breath. "I'm hanging in, there ain't no doubt. And I'm hanging tough, over and out."

CHAPTER FIFTY-SEVEN
The Whole Kip and Caboodle

A gaggle of reporters honked and cronked in the corridor like geese around a pond. I cut through the pack, declining all comments. Margaret Bolden followed in my wake. She had one more witness to call, one who was doubtlessly far better prepared than Georgina Suarez had been. The FBI and Justice Department attorneys had spent hundreds of hours with Max Ringle, honing his testimony, encasing him in a knight's shining—if dented—armor. And I'm the guy who had to knock him off his horse.

"Are you okay, Uncle Jake?" Kip asked when I joined him at the defense table.

"Tip-top."

"You look...I don't know...pissed off."

"I'm cool, Kippers."

"The judge ruled against us, didn't he?"

"For now."

"And you're all right?"

"I'm cool," I repeated.

In fact, I had somehow regained my composure. George Carlin's monologue was no longer racing through my brain like a runaway train. My headache had come and gone. The judge had not ordered me shackled and gagged. I had work to do.

Ringle slithered toward the witness stand in black slacks, a gray silk shirt with a black tie, and—what the hell!—a form-fitting, alligator-skin jacket dyed a rusty orange. The jacket was the real thing, not faux reptile, which Kip confirmed by whispering, "Ten grand from a store on Rodeo Drive." Bolden must have told him to wear a coat and tie, rather than one of his cashmere hoodies. Doubtless, Ringle didn't mention that his taste in jackets ran toward the hide of exotic animals. Fine with me if he looked like a Times Square pimp, circa 1972, but what mattered was what he would say, not what he wore.

Ringle appeared ten years younger than when I had met him, argued with him, and tried to strangle him. His hair, once whitish with yellow nicotine streaks, was now a polished brown. He wore stylish wire-rimmed eyeglasses, probably European, with rose-tinted lenses. His face was still bronzed, but the deep crevices in his cheeks were gone, his face now smooth and shiny. The overall impression was of a pampered man whose manse would have a five-thousand bottle wine cellar. When he took the oath, he smiled at the prosecutor with a stiff upper lip.

Botox!

The bastard had probably been hitting the spa for the past eight months.

Bolden's direct examination was by the book. Ringle admitted that he was a scoundrel who had taken his academic consulting business into the netherworld of résumé fabrication and bribery of coaches, admissions officers, and test proctors. Yes, he pocketed millions, most of which would be forfeited to the federal government. Yes, he hired young Chester Lassiter, aka Kip, to take tests for under-performing, over-privileged children of wealthy clients. But once confronted by the FBI, Ringle cooperated and allowed himself to be recorded speaking to his employees, clients, and coconspirators. And yes, he expected that his cooperation would be taken into account at time of sentencing.

Reviewing his business records, he ran through every test Kip had taken or altered and the sums paid to him. The repetition of names, places, and dollar amounts were built into a rhythm designed to make the jurors think that Kip was the major player in the scheme. Which, alas, he was with the fraudulent tests, though the government couldn't resist inflating his part in the overall business.

I sensed Kip squirming in his chair, not from the accusations, but from the pain of Ringle's colossal betrayal. I put a calming hand on his arm, as I had done so many times during the trial.

"What was the defendant's position with the company?" Bolden asked.

"Senior vice president of Q.E.D. and president of the separately incorporated division, Personalized Test Enhancement, Inc. I owned all the stock in Q.E.D. Kip owned all the stock in P.T.E."

"How did it come about that such a young man had a position of such importance in your organization?" she asked.

The jurors shot looks at Kip, sizing him up. To me, he looked like a Boy Scout trying to figure how to make a fire with flint and a piece of steel.

"Let me be honest," Ringle answered, and I smirked at the novelty of such a concept. "It was my train, but Kip was the engineer. He came up with the standardized test scheme, and he had the *cojones* to pull it off."

"What do you mean by that?"

"Walking into the test centers pretending to be someone else, he had to avoid detection and then have the focus to get the score he'd promised. I could never have done it. But Kip has the nerves of a lion tamer and the heart of a cat burglar."

Oh, spare me. The line was so precise, so damaging, so damned perfect, it must been sculpted in rehearsal. And I knew we would hear it repeated in closing argument.

"Did the defendant add substantial value to Q.E.D.?" Bolden asked.

I could have objected to such an obvious leading question, but Bolden would have other ways to get this into evidence, so I stayed seated.

Ringle leaned forward on the witness stand, resting his arms on the railing, looking too damn comfortable. For a moment, I fantasized about strangling him a second time.

"There was a cap on how much we could make from Q.E.D. because we were shut out of many universities," he said. "I simply didn't have contacts in enough athletic departments to grow the business."

"You ran out of people to bribe," Bolden prompted him.

"Exactly. But Kip Lassiter's ability to radically improve test scores opened the doors to nearly every elite university. Once he started masterminding that operation, we had what I like to call 'the whole Kip and caboodle.'"

Yet another phrase they must have worked on over cappuccinos and croissants in the U.S. Attorney's war room.

"So, the defendant was essential to your business?"

Another lob, another leading question, and still, I stayed quiet. I was grinding my teeth, waiting for my turn.

"Q.E.D. might have existed without him but it would not have been nearly so profitable."

"Or so illegal?"

"Objection! Leading." I leapt to my feet, just to remind Bolden I wasn't a potted plant. Also to unwind my aching back.

"Sustained," the judge proclaimed.

Bolden wanted to close it out. Ringle's value to her case had been wearing a wire and furnishing the FBI with incontrovertible recordings. She had already proved her case with Agent Wisniewski. So Ringle's job today was to corroborate the agent's testimony, fill in a few gaps, and not screw it up.

Bolden ended with a series of questions about the Grand Cayman account. Ringle identified Kip's signature on bank documents and asserted that all the money belonged to Kip. Then Bolden sat, clearly pleased with herself and her witness.

At the lunch recess, Kip asked me how I would handle cross-examination.

"Rattle Ringle," I responded. "And then rattle Ringle some more."

Kip looked dejected.

"What is it, Kippers?"

"He's really smooth at conning people. He won't argue with you and get all flustered. He'll just slip and slide around tough questions and then lie to your face."

"Don't worry, kiddo. I'm gonna let that gasbag fill a Macy's Parade balloon with all his lies. Then, I'm gonna puncture the bastard and see what spills out."

Kip didn't look convinced, and, truthfully, neither was I.

CHAPTER FIFTY-EIGHT
The Pied Piper, the Drum Major,
the Leader of the Pack

With the jury well-fed and the gallery packed with news media, social media influencers, and civilians seeking free entertainment, I revved up my engines. I stood, buttoned my suit coat, and walked to the podium. I carried no notes. They're a straitjacket, killing spontaneity and slowing down what should be a machine-gun delivery.

"Good afternoon, Mr. Ringle," I said pleasantly. "Nice to see you again."

He gave me a half-frozen Botox smile. "Is it? Last time, you assaulted me."

"If I do my job well today, twelve people will follow my example."

The judge scowled. "Already, Mr. Lassiter?"

I wanted to say, "He started it," like a fifth grader, but thankfully, my wiser self prevailed. "Sorry, Your Honor."

"Please just ask questions and refrain from this byplay."

The jurors leaned forward, eyes wide, all but licking their lips. Oh, how we all love a fight, whether it's the thuggery of mixed martial arts or the verbal sparring of the courtroom. As Aristotle said—or maybe it was the Joker in *Batman*—"Let the games begin."

"Let's start with something we can agree on," I said. "You're a criminal, correct?"

"While I don't think of myself in those terms, I suppose you're correct."

"You have pled guilty to four counts of fraud, racketeering, money laundering, and conspiracy, correct?

"Yes."

"Because of your cooperation, you have not been charged with what...one hundred additional counts?"

"Oh, heavens, at least that many."

"And yet you still face more than sixty years in prison?"

"That would be the maximum. One hopes for far, far less."

"Far less because of your extraordinary assistance in making the case against Kip Lassiter?"

"I don't know how extraordinary, but yes, I have done my best to honor the conditions of my cooperation agreement."

"Including getting evidence against the coaches, proctors, and college administrators you bribed, correct?"

"Yes."

"And getting evidence against your clients, the parents who paid you bribes?"

"Yes."

"Turning on all of those people who trusted you, correct?"

"Yes."

"In order to lessen your own punishment?"

"Yes."

So far, so good. He admits being a rat.

"Let's talk about your business," I said. "When it came to getting clients, *you* were the Pied Piper, not Kip Lassiter, correct?"

"Pied Piper, drum major, leader of the pack, whatever you like, yes."

"You formed Q.E.D., not Kip Lassiter."

"True."

"And own all its stock?"

"Also true."

"And while you testified that Kip came up with the test-taking idea, are you aware that your daughter Shari testified it was her idea, which she presented to you?"

He made a scoffing sound. "Shari's a sweet girl but frankly not the brightest bulb in the chandelier."

I shot a look toward the jurors. Several frowns told me they didn't like a father belittling his daughter.

"You were the only one with signatory powers on the corporate bank accounts, correct?"

"Yes, except for the Grand Cayman account."

"A company you registered after you began cooperating with the government?"

"Yes."

"Which you did at the FBI's instructions?"

"Yes."

"And you opened that bank account also at the FBI's instructions?"

"Yes."

"You deposited all the funds in that account?"

"Yes."

"Did the FBI tell you to begin paying Kip bonuses to be deposited into that account?"

"They did. I was told to begin treating him as a partner, rather than an employee."

"It seems the FBI was your partner, Mr. Ringle, not Kip Lassiter."

"Objection!" Margaret Bolden leaned over the prosecution table, now covered with her associates' laptops. "That's not a question."

"Sustained. Try to refrain from testifying, Mr. Lassiter."

Fine with me. I'd made my point for the jury.

"Did Kip ever ask for those bonuses?" I said.

"He did not."

"Did he ever withdraw any of the money?"

"Not to my knowledge."

Ringle used a thumb and forefinger to smooth the skin beneath his nose and above his lips, the way some men massage their mustaches. Except he had no mustache. Then I realized he was wiping sweat. Maybe all the Botox in his cheeks was heating up. If I caught a break, maybe his face would melt like those Nazis in *Raiders of the Lost Ark.*

I moved from the podium back behind the defense table. I wanted to be out of the jurors' line of sight so they could focus on Ringle and try to find his eyes behind his glasses. The greater distance also allowed me to crank up my volume without seeming like I was yelling at the witness.

"You made a conscious decision to become a criminal, correct?" I demanded.

"I suppose I did."

"And you have a long history of deception and telling lies, isn't that right?"

"You'll have to be more specific."

"Your Q.E.D. materials state that you were previously an admissions officer at Arizona State. Was that true?"

"Well...more like puffery."

"Meaning false? A fraudulent representation? A lie?"

"Yes."

"You also claimed to have been a vice president of admissions at the University of Miami. Was that a lie?"

"Yes."

"Those same materials claimed that your clients had been admitted to every Ivy League institution, even though you had not even started the business, correct?"

"I suppose it was aspirational and not technically true at the time."

"You lied in written materials, did you not?"

"Yes."

"You lied face-to-face?"

"Yes."

"You lied on the phone?"

"I've also lied to Santa Claus and an ex-wife or two." His voice ratcheted up a notch. "Maybe you want to add those to your list, Mr. Lassiter."

Judge Speidel coughed his displeasure. "Mr. Ringle, please just answer the question. If Mr. Lassiter wants to discuss Santa Claus or his reindeer, he'll tell you."

I paused to let the jury get a whiff of Ringle's anger and absorb the judge's admonition. A two-bagger. Ringle was miffed. Cross-examination reveals the true self under the government's spit shine and the plastic surgeon's Botox.

"You are an extremely intelligent man, correct?"

"It would be false modesty to disagree."

"With a Ph.D. in psychology from UCLA?"

"Yes."

"A skill you put to use in judging people?"

"I'm sure I do."

"Knowing which parents would be open to your bribery scheme and which ones you shouldn't approach because they might blow the whistle?"

He shrugged as if the answer were obvious. "Of course. It requires emotional intelligence to make those decisions."

"Also knowing what young person might be ripe for picking as your fraudulent test-taker?"

"You mean, did I use my knowledge of psychology to choose your nephew? I would have to say 'yes.' And I was right. He was perfect for the job."

"More than that, you knew he would never turn on you. That loyalty was one of his primary traits, correct?"

"Yes, because of a prior incident in his life when he was away at college. Again, I was correct."

"But he was wrong in assessing you as a friend, perhaps even as a surrogate father, wasn't he?"

"Alas, also true. Kip's stratospheric IQ does not encompass an ability to evaluate the personality characteristics of others."

I paused a moment. His answer tickled something in my brain, and I knew I would have to ask Melissa about it. But now, it was time to pick up the pace. Effective cross has a rhythm and a beat. My goal was to have the jurors tapping their toes, as if listening to the Coasters singing "Yakety Yak." Meaning it was time for me to take out the papers and the trash.

CHAPTER FIFTY-NINE
Lies, Lies, and More Lies

Before continuing my cross of Max Ringle, I surveyed the courtroom. The first three rows of the gallery were jammed with journalists. At the prosecution table, Margaret Bolden sat poker-faced. A savvy trial lawyer wouldn't look concerned if her star witness leapt onto the clerk's table, dropped his drawers, and mooned the jury.

At the defense table, Kip was following instructions, sitting up straight with a pleasant look on his face. He occasionally scribbled on a yellow pad, either notes for me or equations in quantum physics.

Judge Speidel looked directly at me and asked, "Do you have anything further, Mr. Lassiter?"

Oh yes, I certainly do.

"Mr. Ringle," I said, "Q.E.D. perpetuated a series of frauds from day one, correct?

"Yes."

"You paid bribes to facilitate that fraud?"

"Yes."

"You lied to keep the fraud going?"

"Yes."

"You lied, despite the harm you were doing to others?"

"Yes."

"Once the FBI uncovered your fraud, you lied to increase others' culpability?"

"Yes."

"You lied to decrease the punishment you faced?"

"Yes."

"You lied to FBI Agent Wisniewski?"

He fidgeted in his chair. "At first, I did. Foolishly."

"Which itself was a crime."

"Correct."

"Did you tell Kip Lassiter that the FBI had approached you?"

"No."

"In fact, when asked, you lied and said they had not approached you?"

"Correct."

"Did Kip Lassiter tell you the FBI approached him, seeking his cooperation against you?"

"He did."

"Did Kip tell you that he refused to cooperate?"

"He did."

"Did you tell Kip he'd better lawyer up?"

"No."

"In fact, you told him you had a legal opinion that the scheme was not illegal, and he shouldn't worry, isn't that right?"

"It is."

"And that was a lie."

"It was."

"A lie intended to encourage him to continue taking tests for your clients?"

"Yes."

"To increase his culpability and assist you in your deal with the government?"

Ringle sank back into his chair, his arms no longer comfortably on the railing. I could see beads of sweat on his forehead. He wasn't beaten, but he was taking painful shots to the kisser. Cross-examination isn't like one of Kip's violent eGames where you use an axe to decapitate your opponent with one swing. Rather, like a boxer with a decent jab, you repeatedly smack the witness, *pop-pop-pop*, snapping his head back, maybe opening a cut over the eye. Knockouts are rare, but winning on points is still a win.

Judge Speidel interjected, "Mr. Ringle, do you need the question repeated? If not, please speed up your answer."

Ringle emitted a long breath. "As I said before, I tried to live up to my agreement with the government."

I could see he longed to get off the stand. But I wanted to keep him there, let the jury watch him twitch and wriggle.

Rattle Ringle.

"Thereafter, you surreptitiously recorded conversations with Kip to elicit incriminating evidence against him, correct?"

"Yes, at the FBI's direction."

"And you increased Kip's compensation after you began cooperating with the FBI and he did not?"

"Yes."

"Having the effect of exaggerating his culpability, correct?"

"I'd say *increasing* his culpability."

"So, in summary, upon learning that Kip would not help the government make a case against you, your response was to help make a case against him, correct?"

He took a deep breath and let it out slowly. "While I'm sure it's of little solace to Kip, who I have great fondness for, I was thinking of my family when I cut that deal. So, the answer is yes."

"You wore a wire and allowed your phone calls to be recorded to help the government prosecute your clients, correct?"

"Yes."

"People you had talked into paying bribes."

"It didn't require a lot of talking, but yes, that's true."

"Then, after you began cooperating, you lied to clients, to coaches, to test proctors, to athletic department employees, and to Kip Lassiter, correct?"

"Yes."

"While gathering evidence against them?"

"Yes, already!" He turned to the judge. "I think I've said that."

The judge ignored him, and I kept going. "So, after you began secretly cooperating with the government, virtually every action you took was intended to minimize your culpability and maximize the culpability of more than fifty other people?"

"Many of my actions were so intended, yes."

"Facilitated by even more lies?"

"Yes! Once more, I've said that."

"On this witness stand, your client, Arthur Kwalick, called you a 'professional liar.' Accurate?"

Ringle wrinkled his forehead, which wasn't easy to do with all that Botox. "As opposed to an amateur liar, yes, I'm quite accomplished at prevarication."

"Then today, you walk into this courtroom, put your hand on the Bible, and swear to tell the truth?"

"I am telling the truth!"

"At this late date, Mr. Ringle, with your history of frauds, bribes, and lies, do you even know the truth?"

"Objection, argumentative!" Bolden called out.

"Sustained," the judge said.

"I'll re-phrase. Mr. Ringle, is it your desire that the jury disregard your lifetime of frauds, bribes, and lies and believe you today?"

Unlike the Nazis in *Raiders of the Lost Ark*, Ringle's face didn't melt like molten wax, but he did look haggard as he said, with resignation, "I don't care what the jury believes or doesn't believe."

"Just as you never cared whether you told the truth?"

"I don't know how to answer that," he admitted.

"Then, I have nothing further," I concluded, sounding satisfied, because I was.

The judge looked toward the prosecution table. "Re-direct?"

Margaret Bolden declined. She wanted Ringle the hell out of the courtroom as quickly as possible. "The government rests," she said.

Judge Speidel cleared his throat and said he thought this was a fine place to stop for the day. Translation: the judge's bladder was ready to burst.

I sat down and looked at Kip, who appeared stunned. He had finally seen the depths of Max Ringle's corruption, and it had to be shattering. In my nephew's naivete, he had revered this man.

Then, with the courtroom emptying, Kip seemed to snap out of it. He rewarded me with a wide smile. "Fan-friggin'-tastic," he whispered. "You made Max look evil and sound evil."

"Nah. He did that himself."

"But you made him reveal his true nature."

I didn't tell Kip what I was thinking. That it's a mistake to get too excited over landing a few punches on cross, especially where the government already has proven its case. And it's also a mistake to get all giddy when the judge would prefer to see both client and lawyer go to jail.

But I would say nothing to ding Kip's confidence. Tomorrow would be the big day for him and the case. He would tell his story. I knew it would be the truth, but I did not know if it would set him free.

CHAPTER SIXTY
Reading People

Melissa Gold...

Melissa watched Jake devour a 16-ounce ribeye, corn on the cob, and creamed spinach. He washed it all down with one Grolsch, one Anchor Steam, and one Negra Modelo. He called it the "international battle of lagers." Holland, USA, and Mexico, finally proclaiming a three-way tie. She was studying him, feeling positive about what she saw. He was focused, alert, and in good spirits.

Ever the vegan, Kip had eaten mint and green pea risotto but seemed to be studying the ribeyes with lust in his heart.

"Melissa, I wish you could have seen Uncle Jake today," he said.

"Me, too," she said.

Jake had explained that she couldn't watch the trial because she would be a witness, so she had to be content with getting daily updates from her boys, as she called them.

"Uncle Jake dug Max a second asshole."

"Watch your lingo, kiddo," Jake scolded. "Mel, is there any Key lime pie?"

There was, and she cut three slices, squirting whipped cream on two of them. Kip took his pie naked. No dairy products, but again he looked toward their plates with envy. Melissa felt sorry for him, but, honoring his wishes, she wouldn't try to convert him.

"Jake, tell me about your cross-exam," she said.

"I scored some points, but that's not the headline. I had one eye on Ringle and one on the jury box. We have at least a couple jurors who want to acquit if we can give them a reason, something to hang their ballcaps on."

"How in the world do you know that?"

"Because I've been doing this a long time. Kip, were you looking at Ms. Dixon, the mail carrier, and Mr. Mauti, the Army veteran?"

"Yeah."

"Did you read their faces?"

"I don't know. Do you mean did I see them smile a couple times?"

"More like their eyes and their body language. I thought you'd notice, because their faces warmed up when looking at you. When they turned to Ringle, their eyes were pinched, their faces registering animosity and disapproval."

"Okay. If you say so."

Kip excused himself and retreated to his room.

Jake's fork was poised above the pie, but his eyes were staring into space.

"I'm reading your face," Melissa said.

"I hope you're seeing the reflection of how much I cherish you."

"Oh, I see that a lot. Just not at this moment. So, what are you thinking?"

He took a bite, savored the tartness, then sighed, "Kip didn't get it. The faces, the body language."

"And you're thinking...?"

"Ringle said something today that's stuck in my brain. 'Kip's stratospheric IQ does not encompass an ability to evaluate the personality characteristics of others.'"

"It's similar to some things you and I have talked about," she said. "Like Kip being better at video poker than the real thing."

"Exactly!" Jake dropped his fork, excited. "When he was working only with numbers and probabilities, he was a superb player. When he got to those tables in Atlantic City with real, live players, he couldn't read them. Did they have a tell? Were they bluffing? Blood pressure rising? Nothing. But they likely read him, and he lost a bundle."

Melissa loved the way he had locked in. Something new in the case, and she could feel Jake's excitement. "Are you looking for the name of a condition?" she asked.

"You bet I am."

"Nonverbal Learning Disorder. N.L.D. It's related to A.D.H.D."

"How would you do a diagnosis?"

"I can pull a couple tests off medical websites and do them tonight. You understand there's no guarantee what they'll show."

"Let's think positive. You're testifying the day after tomorrow. Can you—"

"Be ready?" Finishing his sentences now came naturally to her. "Easily. With a score sheet, the results are almost instantaneous."

He wrinkled his forehead. "These are written tests he takes and you score?"

"Yes, why?"

"And your testimony will also be based on your observations of him."

"Yes. So, what's the problem?"

"Bolden is going to slam us on bias. First, you've got self-reporting bias. Kip will try to answer questions to get the desired diagnosis. Then, you'll be the first expert witness in history who's the fiancée of defense counsel and the stepmom of the defendant. Add the fact that your diagnosis will be based on subjective findings, and...well, you see the problems."

She didn't waste a moment. "You need something objective. Is that what you're saying?"

"Exactly."

"What time does Kip have to be in court tomorrow?"

"Nine-thirty a.m., why?"

"I'll take him to the hospital at seven-thirty and have him in court on time."

"Want to tell me what you're gonna do?" he asked.

"Not yet. After we're done, if that's okay."

"Fine. We're a terrific—"

"Team."

"Yeah."

"Jake, if you can prove objectively that Kip has N.L.D., is that—"

"The peg for those jurors' ballcaps?" He finished her sentence, just as she had done. "I don't know. I never know. I've lost enough times that I don't get seduced by my own rhetoric. But with an objective diagnosis, we've got a chance."

CHAPTER SIXTY-ONE
The Game, Not the Prize

Margaret Bolden and I were standing shoulder to shoulder in Judge Speidel's chambers at 9:05 a.m. the next day. We were waiting for the judge, and the atmosphere was tense. Other than our exchanges in the courtroom, we hadn't spoken to each other since she accused me of committing federal crimes and I threatened to report her to the Inspector General.

"About yesterday," she said. "I want you to know I had nothing to do with Raymond Pincher spying on you. It was way above my pay grade."

"Look, I know it was Juan Lucayo. But you used the information Pincher brought you."

"I did as I was told. What would you have me do, quit?"

"Not my place to give you advice." We were quiet for a moment before I said, "Okay, listen, I'm not filing a complaint against you. But Lucayo and Pincher? I'm out for their scalps."

"Thank you. Can we agree to be congenial when we're out of the courtroom?"

"That's the way I've always played it. Of course, that started with Ray Pincher and look where it got me."

The judge trundled into chambers and said, "Let's get this show on the road. Mr. Lassiter?"

"The government having rested, the defense moves for judgment of acquittal on each count under Rule 29 on the ground that there is insufficient evidence to sustain a conviction."

It was a pro forma motion that almost never gets granted.

"Denied," Judge Speidel said. "There's ample evidence on each and every count. Now, Mr. Lassiter, are you prepared to call your first witness?"

"Locked and loaded, Your Honor."

"Fine. Let's try to keep the questioning brief, shall we?"

"What! You never said that to the government."

"That's because Margie knows the protocol in my courtroom. I do not consider 'Speed-it-up-Speidel' a derogatory term."

"I'm sure Ivan the Terrible felt the same," I said, the words flying out of my mouth like wasps from a hive.

"Oh, Jesus, here we go."

"Respectfully, Your Honor..."

"Beginning a sentence with 'respectfully' does not make it so, Mr. Lassiter."

"Fine. My questioning will be no longer or shorter than it needs to be, and I ask...no, I demand, that you don't interrupt me. If you do, the jury will believe I'm doing something wrong when it's Your Honor who mistakenly believes that due process means fast process."

The judge wrapped one meaty hand around his forehead and massaged both his temples. "You gallop into my chambers like a wild mustang pissing all over my carpet. I don't know if it's your brain injury or the fact that you're defending your nephew, or if you're just naturally defiant in the face of authority, but why do you insist on making this so difficult?"

"Probably all of the above, Your Honor."

He let out a long, whispery sigh. "You exasperate me, Mr. Lassiter."

"I'm sorry, Your Honor."

"Your cross yesterday was first-rate. I told my clerks that. Precise and to the point and with a consistent theme. Margie, wasn't it first-rate?"

"I don't think I should opine on that," she replied.

"Of course. Let's get into the courtroom and ride this pony to the finish line."

⁂

Five minutes later, I was at the defense table waiting for Kip. The jurors were in their box. The reporters were in the gallery. Judge Speidel was drumming a pen on the polished wood of the bench. It was 9:29 a.m., and when the minute hand hit thirty, Judge Speidel said, icily, "Either call a witness to the stand or rest your case, Mr. Lassiter."

"Your Honor, may I request..."

The door flew open and Kip hustled in, his suit coat unbuttoned, his tie flapping over his shoulder.

"The defense calls Kip Lassiter," I announced, with pride in my voice.

Kip never broke stride and hopped onto the witness stand, skipping both steps, and took the oath before sitting down.

"Please state your name for the record," I instructed.

"Chester Lassiter. I prefer Kip."

He sat with his back straight and his hands folded in his lap. His white shirt was an inch too big around the neck, at my instructions. It gave him a frail look, a child pretending to be a grown-up. His suit was a friendly brown plaid, the tie picking up the brown with some yellow. No navy blue or charcoal grays, power colors. His blondish hair was neatly trimmed.

"How old are you, Kip?"

"Twenty."

"Let's talk a bit about your childhood. Who's your father?"

He cocked his head and looked at me, puzzled. Last night, when he asked whether we were going to prepare for today, I had said, "Listen carefully to the questions and answer honestly."

"Aren't you going to tell me your questions?" he had asked.

"Nope. I want spontaneity. In fact, I might want to surprise you."

Now, I repeated, "Who's your father, Kip?"

"I don't know. Mom didn't know. So, she gave me her father's name, Chester, the guy your mom ran off with after your dad was killed in a bar fight down in the Keys."

Excellent summary of the trailer trash clan known as the Lassiters.

"Who's your mother?" I asked.

"Your half-sister, Janet."

"Where is she now?"

He shrugged. "Try a drunk tank or a county jail. I dunno."

"How'd you end up with me?"

"When I was nine, Mom dropped me at your house. She was going to jail on her seventh or eighth shoplifting charge, and the state was gonna dump me in a foster home."

Kip's eyes grew watery. I wouldn't have gotten that if we'd rehearsed.

"Were you with your mother when she was arrested that seventh or eighth time?"

"I was always there. She'd make me drink hydrogen peroxide, then we'd go into a Target or Wal-Mart, and I'd throw up in an aisle, and while security came running, she'd start stuffing merchandise down her sweatpants."

I gave the jury a moment to process that, to visualize it, to feel it.

"How old were you when this began?"

"Five or six, I can't remember exactly."

"Where were you going to school in those years?"

"I wasn't."

"Home schooled, then?"

He shook his head. "Home was a V.W. van. If Mom had money for gas, we kept moving."

"Your mother was not employed?"

A sad little smile, and he said, "I went with her to the welfare office once. She filled out a form and where it asked for occupation, she wrote, 'Gypsy.'"

Before I could ask another question, he blurted out, "I don't like talking about this stuff."

"I know that, Kip. I'm almost done with this line of questions."

"No, I'm done! What more do you want? I ate Cheetos for dinner. Okay? One night, Mom cooked raccoon over a campfire. A raccoon we ran over in the van. I vomited that night without any hydrogen peroxide. Is this what you want, Uncle Jake?"

He sniffled and used a knuckle to wipe away a tear.

Yep, that's what I want. Shameless? Hey, I would bleed for this boy. The least he can do is cry.

I sneaked a look at the prosecution table where Bolden's assistants were fluttering about like flies on that roadkill raccoon, fingers dancing across keyboards. Probably researching how to stop a defendant from crying.

I signaled one of the courtroom personnel, and she wheeled a poster board into the well of the courtroom. An old-fashioned board with sheets of white paper. These days, lawyers use video screens with digital displays for their demonstrative evidence. So, my courtroom helpers had to dig into a storeroom in the garage to find the poster board. Call me old school. I don't care.

I angled the board so that it was visible to both the jurors and Kip and used a thick black marking pen to write on the top sheet:

$$\text{If } y = x^3 + 2x + 5, \text{ and } z = x^2 + 7x + 1,$$
$$\text{what is } 2y + z \text{ in terms of } x?$$

"What is that?" I asked.

"It looks like a basic math question on the SAT."

"What's the answer?"

"You're supposed to give me four multiple choices and some scratch paper."

"Are you saying you can't do it in your head?"

"Sure, I can. It's pretty simple."

"What's the answer?"

He stepped down from the witness stand and grabbed the marker. "What's the point of this?"

"I have my reasons, Kippers."

"Mr. Lassiter," the judge called out, and both Kip and I turned to face him. "Not the defendant. Jacob Lassiter. Why are you arguing with your client?"

"It's the way we communicate, Your Honor. The Lassiter way."

"Well, let's do it the Speidel way. You ask a question. He answers. Move on."

"Will do, Your Honor."

While we were talking, Kip had scrawled on the paper beneath my equation:

$$2x^3 + x^2 + 11x + 11$$

According to my answer sheet, that was correct, of course. "Well done, Kip," I said.

"No big deal, Uncle Jake."

At the prosecution table, Bolden cocked her head and studied me, wondering where I was going with this. Nowhere just now, but I could use it in closing argument as a counterpoint to Melissa's expert testimony. Basically, Kip was smart in some ways, clueless in others. Book smarts versus street smarts.

"Don't be modest, Kip. How'd you do that?"

"I substituted polynomials into an expression and then simplified the resulting expression by combining the terms."

"I'll take your word for it," I said, and the jurors smiled. "Kip, when you were applying to colleges, what score did you get on your SAT?"

"Pennsylvania Avenue."

"A 1600? A perfect score?"

"So they say."

"Did you take one of those courses to prepare for the test?"

"No."

"How did you spend your time in eleventh grade when you weren't at school?"

He shrugged. "I played video games. *Left 4 Dead, Red Dead Redemption, Call of Duty, World of Warcraft.*"

"How many hours per week?"

He shrugged. "I don't know. A lot. Sometimes I'd start after dinner and play until bedtime. Then, after you fell asleep, I'd get up and play until time to go to school. When you found out, you made me see a shrink who said I had an addictive personality. I thought he was a dweeb with a very average IQ."

"But you stopped playing?"

"I stopped to prove to you that I could."

"Then you tried out for high school football?"

"I stunk. At wide receiver, at cornerback. It's where coach put the skinny kids."

"Did you play?"

"Coach cut me. Said to come back when my arms and legs moved in the same direction at the same time."

"You were a little clumsy?"

"A total spaz."

"Why'd you try out for the team?"

"Duh! Did you notice when I was little, I wore your old Dolphins jersey everywhere, even to bed? I wanted to be like you."

Of course, I had noticed that number 58 jersey with permanent grass stains and dried blood. It hung down to his knees, and Granny had to tear it off him to toss it into the washer.

"Funny, Kip," I said, my eyes tearing up, "I wanted you to be better than me."

"Mr. Lassiter!" the judge called out. "Please save the family counseling for after hours."

"Sorry, Your Honor." I pulled myself together and asked, "Kip, when did you take up video poker?"

"In college, where you couldn't stop me."

"Were there similarities between those earlier video games and video poker?"

"Not in the games themselves, but they gave me the same feeling. Juiced me."

"What's that mean?"

"A rush. Pleasure. Satisfaction. Probably the way you felt when you made the perfect tackle, drove the runner backward and dropped him on his butt."

"Seldom happened. What about the money in video poker?"

"I won some money, but that wasn't much different than being the last one standing in Battle Royale."

"So, it wasn't the money that juiced you?"

"No, it was *winning* the money! My cravings were for the game, not the prize."

"Let's talk about the Atlantic City escapade."

I took him through the whole story, the borrowed credit card, the disaster at the poker table, taking the rap as if he'd stolen the card from Taylor, the rich kid. And being bounced from Penn. If I didn't do it, Bolden would do it herself on cross. It's always better to shine a light on your client's blemishes before the prosecutor can.

Then I moved to the meat and potatoes of the case. "How'd you get started taking those tests?"

"Max Ringle hired me to tutor his daughter Shari. I helped improve her score, but not enough to get into USC. Max got a doctor to say she had ADHD and needed special accommodation, so her test was in a separate room with no time limit. Max bribed the proctor to let me sit in, and I corrected her answers. That became the template for the business."

"How'd it feel that first time?"

"A rush. Like winning the biggest poker pot or being John Marston, the gunslinger in *Red Dead Redemption*, blasting bad guys with a sawed-off shotgun."

"Did you tell Max Ringle that?"

"Yeah, and then he bought professional video consoles for his house, the kind the big-name players use in tournaments at eGame arenas."

"So, he encouraged you to play?"

"Three hours every other day until a week before a test, then he cut me off."

"Did he say why?"

"He said he wanted me thirsty."

"Thirsty," I repeated. "What do you suppose Ringle meant by 'thirsty?'"

"Objection. Calls for a conclusion." Bolden was on her feet.

"Sustained," the judge called out.

That was fine with me. I had just wanted to say "thirsty" a couple more times so the jury would recall the word when I ran it up the flagpole in closing argument.

"How did you feel between the time Ringle made you stop playing the eGames and when you took someone's test?"

He closed his eyes and bit his lower lip. "It's hard to explain. Kind of scratchy and I don't know...it's almost like I had a cold."

"And then when you took the tests...?"

"Just like the first one for Shari. Just like the eGames. A rush."

"Were you concerned about the legality of what you were doing?"

"Max said he had a legal opinion that it wasn't criminal. I believed him."

"And now, looking back, how do you feel?"

"I'm sorry for what I did. Really sorry. I realize now it wasn't a game. And I promise I'm going to be a better man. My plan is to create SAT and ACT prep courses for underprivileged kids from Appalachia and the inner cities. Pro bono."

"Why?"

"To seek redemption. To live a life with integrity."

I paused a moment. I'd gotten what I needed for Melissa, the first couple rungs on a ladder she would build.

"Let's step back and look at the overall picture, Kip. Did you take all those SAT and ACT exams for Max Ringle's clients, as alleged in the indictment?"

"Every one. And I changed the answers on the others when working as a proctor, just like the indictment says."

"And were you paid the sums set out in the indictment?"

"Yes."

"That's a lot of money, Kip. Now, be truthful with the jury. Is that why you did it?"

"No way. It was never about the money. I did it for the rush. I did it because it was fun."

CHAPTER SIXTY-TWO
No Victim Except the Law

Judge Speidel called a fifteen-minute recess to give the jury a break before cross-examination, and my nephew expressed a similar notion to one I have heard from clients over the years.

"Do you even know what you're doing?" he asked.

"I'm laying the groundwork for the medical defense. And you're doing just fine."

He looked at me skeptically. I've seen that plenty of times, too.

"Did you intend to make me cry?"

"Let's say I had my hopes. Say, how'd it go at the hospital?"

"They did a brain scan, and it took longer than they expected. Is that a good sign?"

"No idea. What did Melissa say?"

"Nothing. She was talking to a couple specialists when I ran out to get an Uber. The driver wouldn't go near the federal buildings because he was afraid of being deported. So, I ran all the way from Flagler Street."

"You did well on the stand."

"I feel like such a wuss for crying."

"Nobody thinks that. You seemed honest and regretful. All I hoped for. But now, we're gonna get our bumps and bruises."

We were standing at the end of a corridor, a triangular glass-enclosed space that resembled the forecastle on a sailing vessel or maybe a spaceship. The view was to the south and east, over Coral Gables, Coconut Grove, and Biscayne Bay, where about twenty white sails were visible. Sailors racing solo in A-Cat catamarans, moving swiftly on a broad reach. Oh, wouldn't it be grand to be cruising in one of those with Kip in another? Sails crackling in a stiff easterly, water spraying our faces, one pontoon high out of the water. Nephew and uncle, free as the wind.

My cell phone rang, and the daydream disappeared into the mist. Melissa calling.

"Hey, Mel. Do you have the brain scan results?" I asked.

"I think it's just what we're looking for. I'll know for certain by the time I see you tonight."

"Great."

"Something else. I got a call from Bethesda. The N.I.H. just told Congress it won't do the C.T.E. study if you-know-who is running it."

"Helmet guy?"

"Right. Which leaves two other candidates and me. And since the program will be based on my grant request and précis, you'd have to figure..."

"That you're the favorite coming down the stretch."

"Let's hope. How's Kip doing?"

"Great on direct. Now come the fireworks."

"Wish him luck for me."

We clicked off, and Kip said, "Is the prosecutor going to be really harsh?"

"She won't come on strong until she gets to a point she wants to emphasize, or she catches you in a lie. Then she'll carve out your liver."

"I'll tell the truth, Uncle Jake."

"Make sure you do. It's crucial. Jurors sense evasions, embellishments, and most of all, lies. We round up twelve strangers, all rather ordinary, throw them together, and it's as if each one's IQ is added to the next. Individually, they're dullards. Together, they're a genius."

☙

Margaret Bolden put on her courtroom smile, said hello to Kip the way a teacher might welcome a new student to her classroom. Then she got down to business.

"Let's talk a bit about your childhood," she began.

He winced and said, "Okay."

"Your life improved quite a bit when you moved in with your uncle, didn't it?"

"A whole lot."

"Is your uncle a good father figure?"

"The best."

"And he provided you with a warm, nurturing environment?"

"Totally."

"You were well fed, well clothed, and you attended a prestigious private school that he paid for, correct?"

"Yes." Kip started to say something more, then stopped, probably because I told him to just answer the questions and not add salt to prosecutor's stew. But then he added, "One of the reasons I feel so bad is that I let Uncle Jake down."

"Because you know what you did was wrong, correct?"

"Yes, I do now."

Her voice louder now, the tone disapproving. "Now, Mr. Lassiter, you didn't just discover that what you did was wrong, did you?"

Kip weighed his words before answering. "I always knew it was shady. But I didn't know it was a federal crime."

"Did you ask to see the legal opinion Max Ringle allegedly told you about?"

"No."

"Did you do your own research?"

"No."

"Did you call your uncle and ask his opinion?"

"No."

"Is it possible you didn't want to dig too deeply, that you simply chose to believe Max Ringle, rather than learn the truth?"

"Max said no one would ever complain, and it made sense. The parents and kids were happy. The proctors and coaches and universities were all making money. There were no victims."

"No victim...except the law?"

"I don't know what that means. I think it's up to the jury to determine that."

A pretty good answer, kiddo.

"So that there's no mistake, you admit you did each and every one of the acts laid out in the indictment?"

"Yes."

"You cheated on Shari Ringle's exam?"

"Yes."

"You cheated on Teague and Niles Hallinan's exams?"

"Yes."

"You cheated on Craig Kwalick's exam?"

"Yes."

This went on for the next fifteen minutes. Every single exam, followed by the amount of money Kip collected. Bolden's intention was to burn into the jurors' minds the notion of multiple illicit activities. As if to say, "*Hey, if the kid did this once, it was a lark and no big deal. But he's a racketeer, a serial offender, a one-man crime wave.*"

"In one year, you made six hundred thousand dollars as senior vice president of Q.E.D. and president of Personalized Test Enhancement, Inc., correct?"

"Yes, but those were just titles Max came up with. We joked around about them."

"But the money was no joke, was it?"

"I didn't do it for the money."

"Right. You said that on direct. But you lived in a four-thousand-dollar-a-month apartment on Brickell Avenue, didn't you?"

"Max provided it."

"And you bought a Tesla SUV that cost in excess of one-hundred and twenty thousand dollars, correct?"

"Max thought I should have nice ride for meeting wealthy Florida clients."

"And your credit card records show you bought several Italian cashmere sweatshirts for, what was it, over two thousand dollars each?"

"Max encouraged me to dress well."

"Max. Max. Max. Is Max to blame for your having committed all these crimes?"

"Objection!" I sang out. "Argumentative. Calls for a legal conclusion. Invades the province of the jury."

"Anything else, Mr. Lassiter?" the judge inquired.

"Also...I wanted to stretch my legs."

"Overruled. The witness may answer."

"I don't blame Max. I blame myself for trusting him. I blame myself for not listening to my uncle. I blame myself for being what Granny Lassiter used to call a 'dang fool.'"

Bolden spent the next ninety-four minutes playing audio recordings of Kip discussing the scheme with Ringle and their clients. She replayed the recording from the day I visited Ringle's home, just in case the jury had forgotten those excruciating admissions. The one that begins, "I devised two plans..."

Having scored all her points, Bolden sat down. Judge Speidel declared that the sun had set on today's festivities and gave the jury the usual admonitions not to discuss the case or read about it.

I had known that Kip would take a lot of incoming fire today, and he had. I pictured one of those B-17s in World War II, returning to England after a bombing run over Germany. One engine missing, wings peppered by flak, tail shot to hell, stabilizers shredded, and still, somehow it lands. The crew would live to fly the next day, and we, too, would be back tomorrow. I gathered my files and my nephew, and we headed home for our final War Council, bloodied but unbowed.

CHAPTER SIXTY-THREE
The Dopamine Rush

I watched Kip, who was sprawled in the hammock with his eyes closed. Melissa nudged me in the ribs and whispered, "Who's that remind you of?"

"What do you mean?"

"The way Kip locks both hands behind his head when he's resting. That's you. He's picked up a lot of your mannerisms without either of you being aware of it."

We were on the back porch, nursing our margaritas. I watched Kip for a moment, my heart filled with warmth, my mind overflowing with dread.

"You haven't told me how it went today," Melissa prompted.

"Pretty much as expected. Kip was very good on direct, and he got dinged on cross. If the trial had ended today, we would have lost. But we have one more day and one more witness."

Before replying, she took a long sip of her cocktail. "Well, that doesn't put much pressure on me, does it?"

"Face it, Mel. You have to save two lives. Kip's and mine. Tell me again about Kip's brain scan. I don't understand why you had to do it twice."

"To double-check the imaging. The first one just didn't seem right."

"And...?"

"Well, you have to understand. It's complicated."

☙

The next morning, Melissa wore a double-breasted navy skirt suit on the witness stand. Her fitted jacket had gold buttons, and her skirt fell below the knee. Her reddish-brown hair was pulled back into a half ponytail. Tortoise shell reading glasses were perched on her head in case she needed to review documents. The impression she conveyed was one of quiet stylishness and professionalism.

I spent several minutes qualifying her as an expert witness. Undergrad degree from Columbia. Masters in neuroscience and a doctorate in molecular science from Yale, M.D. from Duke, board certified in neurology and neuropathy. A couple fellowships, a bunch of papers with titles like "Cerebellar Cognitive Affective Syndrome: Implications for Neurology and Psychiatry." Former Director of the Center for Neuroscience at UCLA, currently head of the Concussion Project at the University of Miami, in contention to be the first director of the brand new C.T.E. research program at the National Institutes of Health.

"Dr. Gold, how are you and I acquainted?"

She smiled. "You took my deposition in a civil case. At dinner that night—lamb shank for you, gnocchi with Dungeness crab for me—you stood up, recited the names of several deceased football players and collapsed. That night, I became your treating physician for your traumatic brain injury."

"Excellent memory. And besides being my doctor...?"

"I am your fiancée. We are engaged to be married."

A murmur swept through the gallery, and several jurors smiled. Everyone likes to see love in bloom.

"Do you know my client, Kip Lassiter?"

She looked at Kip with care in those pale green eyes. "I've known him for three years. For two of those years, we all lived in the same house."

"Are you an impartial observer when it comes to Kip?"

"No, but I'm a medical professional. I can render objective medical opinions, just as I do when treating you. The fact that I love you, that we are to be married, does not interfere with my medical judgments."

"Then let's get to it. What's the first thing you noticed about Kip when you met him three years ago?"

"Several memories coincide. How bright and inquisitive he was. How warm and caring he was with you." A cloud crossed her face and her words became more reluctant. "And then some things off-key. I remember trying to read a note he left for me on the refrigerator. He had a child's messy handwriting. Then, I noticed he had difficulty buttoning the sleeves on a shirt, and, finally, that he was somewhat clumsy with scissors when opening one of those sealed plastic packages. Batteries, I think."

"Leading you to conclude...?"

"A deficit in fine motors skills. Not a huge deficit, but enough to be noticed."

"Anything else stand out?"

"In social situations, I noticed he had difficulty processing nonverbal cues. Body language and facial expressions. Sometimes, he didn't know when someone was joking because he missed those cues and took everything literally."

"In preparing for your testimony, did you give Kip any written tests?"

"Yes, the Grossman Learning Assessment."

"And what did you find?"

"Considering both my observations of Kip and the written test, I diagnosed him with the brain affliction known as Nonverbal Learning Disorder."

"What are the major characteristics of this disorder?"

"Generally, a weakness in personality judgment, assessing another person's behavioral characteristics. Missing the nuances and subtleties of conversation. Specifically, in Kip's case, an overly trusting nature stemming from an inability to tell when someone is lying."

"How do the rest of us make those judgments?"

"We constantly use nonverbal cues to assess other people. If someone avoids eye contact or sweats profusely or bites their lower lip when speaking to us, we might conclude they're lying. Kip would not. Call it a childlike naivete."

At the defense table, Kip frowned and shifted uncomfortably. He seemed more upset being called naive than a master criminal.

"If Max Ringle told Kip there was nothing illegal about taking tests for other people...?"

"Kip would be more likely than most people to believe him."

"Are there hallmarks of N.L.D. we'd consider positive?"

"Several." She glanced at Kip, gave him a small smile. "Excellent vocabulary, exceptional memory and auditory retention, extremely high intelligence."

"Good traits for taking standardized tests?"

"Obviously."

"As you know, Kip had a problem with video games beginning in his early adolescence. What do you make of that?"

"An overindulgence or even addiction to video games is consistent with the personalities of many young people who suffer from N.L.D."

"Do you have any special expertise on the effect of excessive gaming on the young brain?"

She nodded. "At UCLA, my department led a study in changes in brain patterns and long-lasting effects of overindulgence in gaming. We established a gaming detox center because the addiction is as real as drug, alcohol, or gambling addictions. We treated teenagers who wore diapers when they played so they would never have to leave their games."

A couple jurors appeared appalled at that. They were watching and listening, and they liked Melissa. Well, what's not to like?

"What are the effects on the brain of excessive gaming?"

"Surges in the release of dopamine, a neurotransmitter."

"And the effect of those surges?"

"It's quite profound. The brain binges on those surges and elevates dopamine to the same levels experienced by drug users on ecstasy."

I paused a moment to let that sink in. The courtroom was quiet as a tomb, Melissa holding everyone spellbound.

"And what's the effect of repeated elevations of dopamine in the brain?"

"Addiction, because the surges create a craving for even more dopamine."

"And if someone who's addicted to gaming gets cut off from playing?"

"He'll crave it even more. This is particularly true in adolescents whose brains are not fully formed."

"Kip has testified that he feels a rush playing the games, that he gets 'juiced.'"

"Yes, of course. That's the dopamine surge."

"And the effects long-term?"

"A hyper-reactivity to gaming that numbs the pleasure response for virtually everything else. It's either gaming or a new substitute. There can be positive substitutes, like exercise or satisfying work, or negative substitutes."

"Kip testified he got juiced taking other people's tests. How does that fit the equation?"

"The test taking, unfortunately, was a negative substitute. The risk-reward of the tests replaced the risk-reward of the games. If he aimed for a 1500 on the SAT and got it, the effect on the brain is identical to winning in eGames."

"Is it your medical opinion that Kip's addiction to the dopamine rush of gaming primed him for the rush of the fraudulent test taking?"

"Yes, that is consistent with my findings."

I had one more issue, the big one. The brain scan, our only objective evidence supporting Melissa's diagnosis. I felt confident it would make an impact with the jury. But if I dared leave it out and baited Bolden into asking the question on cross, well, the impact might be a hundred megatons greater.

Will Bolden take the bait?

If I didn't present the brain scan on direct, would she wander into my trap by hammering Melissa for her purely subjective findings? If so, *ka-boom!* Melissa would haul out the scan. The risk was that Bolden wouldn't venture into that area, and I would then be foreclosed from getting into it because re-direct cannot exceed the scope of cross-examination.

I weighed the probabilities, realizing this would be my most important decision of the trial. The cautious choice would be to present the evidence myself. And if I thought we were winning, that's what I would do. As it was, I thought we were getting close to having a couple jurors on our cheerleading squad. Just not quite there yet.

One last thought went into my decision. A trial is part legal proceeding and part theater. In *Phantom of the Opera*, they could have just turned out the lights on the chandelier, but crashing it to the stage in an explosion of glass and flames packed a far more powerful punch.

Hell yes! I'll take the risk. If it blows up in my face and Kip is convicted, his best bet would be claiming ineffective assistance of counsel.

"Your witness, Ms. Bolden," I said, cordially, masking my fears with an amiable smile.

CHAPTER SIXTY-FOUR
In the Eye of the Beholder

Margaret Bolden gave me a sideways glance as she strode to the podium. I could read her face, too. Happy, confident, maybe even a little relieved. She knew, absolutely *knew*, that she could neutralize any points we'd scored on direct.

"Dr, Gold, I didn't know that you and defense counsel were engaged and living together," Bolden said, and miraculously, her nose didn't grow a foot.

Hah! She probably knows what we ate for dinner last night.

"Congratulations," Bolden continued, and I sensed just a hint of sarcasm.

"Thank you, Ms. Bolden," Melissa replied evenly.

"So, would it be correct to say that you are the defendant's *de facto* stepmother?"

"That sounds a little legalistic, but I suppose you could say that."

"Let me ask it this way," Bolden said. "You admit that you're not objective, correct?"

"I admit that I have feelings for Kip, but I can still exercise independent medical judgment."

"Subjective judgments?"

"Some are subjective, and some are objective."

"We'll get to that..."

Jeez, don't forget. That's our ball game.

"But first, Dr. Gold, you testified that adolescent brains aren't fully formed."

"That's correct."

"And yet the defendant at age seventeen was able to score a 1600 on the SAT, correct?"

"Yes, competing against other teenagers."

"Still, compared to other teens, he was quite advanced when he first took the exam and also when he was paid to take it for others, correct?"

"I believe you're confusing his intelligence with his maturity, or lack of it," Melissa said, shielding her criticism with a polite tone. "You must know the *Miller* case, where the Supreme Court struck down mandatory life imprisonment sentences for juveniles."

"I do, but we're talking about—"

"The court found that adolescence is marked by 'immaturity, impetuosity, and failure to appreciate risks and consequences,'" Melissa stormed ahead. "That takes on greater meaning, given Kip's Nonverbal Learning Disorder."

Touché. Oh, she's good!

I wanted to cheer. Last night, I'd told her about *Miller vs. Alabama*, and now Melissa had found a way to shoehorn the court's quotation into her testimony.

Bolden's shoulders stiffened, but her face gave away nothing to the jury. She was pissed and would sharpen her knives for the remainder of cross. I knew Melissa could handle herself, so that wasn't my worry. I just didn't want Bolden to change her plan. I needed her to stay on that two-lane highway of subjectivity versus objectivity.

"Part of the reason you concluded that the defendant suffers from a learning disorder is that he's clumsy with scissors and buttoning his shirt, correct?"

"A small part, yes."

"That's a subjective conclusion on your part, isn't it?"

"Yes."

That's it. Go, baby, go!

"Someone else might conclude differently?"

"It's possible, of course."

"How about your conclusion that the defendant fails to pick up body language, facial expressions, and the nuances of conversation? Also, subjective conclusions?"

"Yes."

"His weakness in making what you called 'personality judgments.' Also, subjective?"

"Yes."

Keep on trucking. Bolden couldn't know it, but this is just where I wanted her headed. But she wasn't there yet.

"The Grossman Learning Assessment is a self-reporting test, isn't it?"

"Yes."

"Dr. Gold, what's 'self-reporting bias?'"

"It refers to people's tendency to try to present themselves in the best light."

"So that, when asked for their heights and weights, people tend to exaggerate their height and minimize their weight, correct?"

"Yes, the classic example. But when I administered the test, Kip didn't know I was testing for N.L.D."

"Really?" Bolden grabbed a folder passed to her by one of her army of assistants. "Here's one of the questions. 'Do you have difficulty holding a pen, tying your shoes, or holding small objects?' Now, Dr. Gold, don't you think that this brilliant young man knew exactly what you were looking for?"

"Even if he did, I told him to answer truthfully."

Bolden gave the jurors a wry smile, a smile that said, *I hear this bullcrap every day.*

"Your entire testimony hinges on your diagnosis of the defendant having N.L.D., correct?"

"I'm not sure I understand what you mean by 'entire testimony,'" Melissa replied.

"Well, isn't the house of cards propping up the defense simply that N.L.D. caused—"

"Objection, argumentative!" I got to my feet and stayed there.

"Sustained." Judge Speidel gave Margaret Bolden a sideways look, which was probably as peeved as he ever got with her.

"I'll rephrase," Bolden said, as if she had a choice. "Doctor, if I understand your testimony, it's a three-step process. First, you conclude that the defendant has a learning disorder that made him susceptible to gaming addiction as a young teen, correct?"

"Yes."

"The same disorder made him susceptible to believing Max Ringle's false statements, correct?"

"Yes, there's a direct connection."

"And it also caused him to substitute the illegal test taking for his gaming addiction?"

"Clearly, it was a contributing factor."

"My, but that N.L.D. is a powerful force to cause all that, isn't it?"

"Objection, argumentative. Also, overly sarcastic."

Judge Speidel shot me a scolding look. "Overruled. The witness may answer."

"The disorder is related to everything you mentioned," Melissa said.

"Therefore, if you're wrong about what you claim is his Nonverbal Learning Disorder, aren't you wrong about everything else?"

Saying "what you claim..." in such a dismissive tone. Nasty, Margaret Bolden.

"I wouldn't characterize it that way, but yes, the N.L.D. is the building block of my conclusions." She paused a quick beat and continued, "And it's the stumbling block of Kip's life."

Bolden leveled a sharp look at Melissa, as if to say, *"You just couldn't resist, could you?"*

Bolden gathered her notes from the podium and headed back toward the prosecution table. Maybe it was a pause for effect, before she ended with a flourish, perhaps a roll of drums and blare of trumpets. Or was she finished?

Hey, don't sit down yet! We need you to pitch the big fat hanging curveball you think is a wicked slider.

Still on the move and facing the gallery, Bolden said, "Concerning your diagnosis of N.L.D., isn't beauty in the eye of the beholder?"

Getting closer... C'mon now.

Melissa shrugged. "Meaning?"

Like an actor on a stage, Bolden whirled ninety degrees to face Melissa. She raised her voice just a notch, added a bit of spice to the tone and said, "Meaning that your findings of N.L.D. are based solely on the defendant's self-reporting and your own observations, all of which are subjective?"

Yeah, baby! Oh, yeah!

"Not solely," Melissa said.

"What then...?" Bolden stopped, mouth agape. If she were a cartoon lizard, her tongue would have flicked into the air and retrieved those two fleeting words.

"There is the abnormal brain scan," Melissa said. "That is quite objective."

Oh, God, how I love this woman!

For a moment, Bolden stood paralyzed, like Lot's wife, a pillar of salt. "You...you didn't mention any brain scan on direct."

"Mr. Lassiter must have forgotten to ask. He's been having memory issues."

Bolden shot a look at me that could have left third-degree burns. She had two choices, neither one appealing. If we were on one of those cattle ranches Judge Speidel used to visit, she could stroll into the corral blindfolded and hope she didn't step in anything squishy. That is, she could continue asking questions to which she did not know the answers. Or, she could belatedly lock the barn door—that is, sit down and hope the judge would keep me from letting out all the horses, chickens, and traveling salesmen.

"Nothing further." Bolden took her seat with dignity and a rigid backbone. No way the jury could feel the fire that had to be burning inside her. She was a pro, and I did admire that.

"I assume the defense has re-direct," Judge Speidel said.

"Indeed," I declared, a word I seldom use.

I got to my feet and floated on air to the prosecution table, where I handed Bolden copies of the brain scan and the related radiologist's report. Had I done this on direct, Bolden would have found a different avenue of attack, rather than lash herself to the mast of a sinking ship, the *S.S. Subjectivity*.

I spent four or five minutes with foundational questions to establish that the scan was done yesterday morning at the University of Miami Hospital. Bolden objected, but Judge Speidel admitted the documents into evidence. And hurrah, we were off to the races.

"Dr. Gold, what were the results of the brain scan?" I asked.

"Kip has a significantly smaller splenium than would be considered normal," Melissa began. "That's the part of the corpus callosum that facilitates communication between the left and right sides of the brain. Also, the nerve fibers of the mesolimbic reward pathway are abnormally thin, and there are signs of weaker connections there among brain cells."

"What's the significance of those findings?"

"The smaller splenium is a hallmark of Nonverbal Learning Disorder. The mesolimbic reward pathway is a deep brain circuit that assists in socializing skills. Deficiencies there are consistent with both autism and N.L.D."

"Are these findings subjective or objective?"

"Nothing could be more objective. You can see the abnormalities."

Melissa then walked the jury through Kip's brain images projected on a screen, comparing them with the scan of a young person without his abnormalities. She wielded the laser pointer expertly, highlighting pathways and callosi, reminding me of Joe Paterno diagraming football plays with X's and O's.

When we were finished with the show-and-tell, I inquired, "And your ultimate conclusion, Dr. Gold?"

"Kip Lassiter suffers from Nonverbal Learning Disorder, which made him susceptible to the dopamine rush of both gaming and the improper test taking and also susceptible to being easily misled by Max Ringle."

I told the judge I had nothing further, and Bolden did the same. Then, having fired every arrow in my quiver and praying that a few had crossed the moat and landed inside the government castle, I concluded, "The defense rests."

CHAPTER SIXTY-FIVE
The Night of All Nights

Melissa Gold...

Boys will be boys, Melissa thought, and Jake was the biggest boy of all.

Sitting on the back porch, flimsy clouds scurrying across a full moon, Jake and Kip were whooping it up over pizzas and beer. She thought Jake should be preparing his closing argument, but the boys kept praising her testimony, recounting the day's events at such an excessive decibel level that at any moment, the City of Miami police might rappel down from cop choppers.

"Miller vs. Alabama!" Kip yelled.

"Oh, that look on Bolden's face!" Jake exclaimed.

"And my poor, immature, impetuous brain," Kip moaned.

"Subjective, my ass!" Jake harrumphed.

"Okay, guys," she said. "All I did was tell the truth."

"And we love you for it," Jake declared.

Melissa had thought Jake's trial strategy had been too risky. But hiding the ball had baited Bolden into banging "subjectivity" like a steel drum. Then, certain she knew the answer, asking the ultimate question—*it's all subjective, right?*—and getting gobsmacked.

But really, just how much had been gained?

Melissa didn't know, and Jake wasn't saying. The government still had overwhelming evidence of guilt. Maybe that alone had justified Jake's risky maneuver, but to Melissa, it had felt desperate. To use one of Jake's football analogies, a Hail Mary.

"You gotta be fearless in court without being reckless," Jake had told her one night earlier.

But these days, did he know one from the other?

So, she chose her words carefully and spoke them gently. "Shouldn't you be preparing your summation?"

"Darlin', I've been preparing since voir dire. In fact, I've been preparing all my life."

She gave him a puzzled look.

He pointed at his right temple. "It's all up here."

"Are you planning something for the three Trekkies on the jury? Will Dr. Spock make a cameo appearance?"

"No spoilers. And, I don't want to over prepare. Bolden goes first. I have to be flexible enough to respond."

"Okay, then."

She held eye contact with him, and after a moment, he asked, "What?"

"Ray Pincher called. He said he's been leaving you messages, but you haven't responded."

"Did George Washington return Benedict Arnold's calls? Did Jesus reply to Judas's emails?"

She rolled her eyes. "Ray said he had some information for you."

Jake grunted his disinterest.

"So, what now?" she asked.

"I'm gonna watch some TV."

"Really?"

Melissa pictured Margaret Bolden and her team of young lawyers and paralegals hunkered down in their conference room deep into the night. Pitching ideas, choosing vicious verbs and pithy adjectives that could be shoveled onto Kip until he was buried under a pile of calumny. Gravediggers!

So why wasn't Jake working? Shouldn't he at least be scribbling notes on a legal pad?

"I just want to relax," Jake said. "Trust me. I have a method."

Ten minutes later, Jake and Kip were sprawled out in the den, watching a documentary about stand-up comics. From the kitchen, she heard George Carlin's voice: "Think of how stupid the average person is and realize half of them are stupider than that."

Both her boys laughed uproariously.

How could Jake be so loose and lackadaisical on this of all nights!

Closing arguments were tomorrow morning. Then she realized what was happening, what Jake was thinking, and she felt tears welling. This could be the last night for years that uncle and nephew could drink beer, eat pizza, and watch television together. Given Jake's condition, perhaps forever. Jake wasn't going to spend this night scribbling notes on a legal pad. He was going to spend it enjoying life with the boy he'd raised as his own son.

CHAPTER SIXTY-SIX
Play it Again, Bolden

Margaret Bolden spent a few minutes thanking the jurors for leaving their jobs, their families, their pets, and their hobbies to fight Miami's abysmal traffic and do their civic duty as responsible citizens. Smiling warmly, Bolden conveyed the impression that they were the best gosh-darned folks in town and stopped just short of inviting them all home for dinner.

Bolden told the jury that this was the most important of all the cases stemming from a "nationwide criminal conspiracy that wreaked havoc on our system of higher education."

I thought that was a bit overstated, there being roughly fifty cheaters out of sixteen million college students.

"This is a story about two men," she explained. "One, Max Ringle, is the sorcerer. The other, the defendant Chester 'Kip' Lassiter, is the sorcerer's apprentice. The sorcerer has already pled guilty to his crimes. Today, his apprentice must be held to account for his criminal conduct."

Then, for what seemed like an eternity but was actually twenty-three minutes, she replayed highlights of the government's most damning surreptitious recordings. Oh, how the government loves recordings. FBI agents are born eavesdroppers and federal prosecutors are born tattletales. There was Ringle on tape saying that Kip was the "brains of the operation, the mastermind," and Kip not denying it. There was Kip, going on about the different ways he took exams as an imposter. And there were parents telling Kip just what score they needed for young Chad or Brandi, afflicted with their fabricated diagnoses of ADHD.

Listening to Kip—in the prime of his unrepentant, arrogant, smartass, cashmere hoodie phase—was just as brutal this time around. A punch in the gut for me, and the most damning evidence against Kip. If you include opening statement, this was the third time the jury had heard the recordings. Bolden apparently believed the old saw about trial practice: Tell them what you're going to tell them; tell them; then tell them what you've told them.

She summarized Agent Wisniewski's testimony, the parents' testimony, and the Stanford admissions director's testimony. She spent twenty minutes hitting the high points of Ringle's testimony, including his insidious statement that Kip had "the nerves of a lion tamer and the heart of a cat burglar."

Bolden then took a detour to avoid the sinkhole of her star witness's character. "You're going to hear defense counsel attack Max Ringle. Sure, I wish we could have brought a priest or a rabbi or the Nobel Peace Prize–winner to testify. But that's not how criminal cases are made. I could recite hundreds of major trials involving organized crime, or terrorism, or the Ku Klux Klan that were won only through the testimony of coconspirators."

Then she focused her sights on our defenses. "What do you do," Bolden asked, looking toward me, "when your client admits committing each and every act alleged in the indictment? You say, 'Yes, but.'"

She waited a beat, then continued. "Yes, but he had a rough childhood. Yes, but he got addicted to video games. Yes, but he fell under the influence of Max Ringle. *Yes, but* he's really the victim here."

Another pause to let the jurors consider the weakness of our excuses.

"What defense counsel is saying is, 'Yes, he did all these crimes, but feel sorry for him.' But the court will instruct you that you must not let your feelings interfere with your judgment. In my opening statement, I told you that you cannot let your verdict be based on sympathy, and I remind you of that now.

"Defense counsel has done little more than appeal to your kind natures. The defendant had no father and a lousy mother. I'm sorry, but so have a lot of young men who didn't become criminals. And you know what? The defendant caught a lucky break the day his mother left him with Jake Lassiter. I asked the defendant if Mr. Lassiter was a good father, and he said, 'The best.' And do you remember what else he said? 'One of the reasons I feel so bad is that I let Uncle Jake down.' That's an acknowledgment of guilt. He told you he was guilty!"

Kip squirmed in his seat, almost imperceptibly. I silently clamped a hand on his forearm.

"The defendant had the good fortune to be raised by defense counsel," Bolden went on. "He had the good fortune to attend the prestigious and expensive Biscayne-Tuttle school. Maybe you've seen their sailing team boats in the bay. The defendant lived a life of privilege in a stable home with love and support and was given every chance in the world.

"He had the good fortune to be blessed with a special mind, and with that comes a special obligation. Do something positive with your God-given gifts. He was admitted to an Ivy League university, all expenses paid. But the defendant blew that opportunity. He got in trouble, got expelled. The defendant is not a victim, but rather a very fortunate young man who has no one but himself to blame for the trouble he is in today."

Bolden turned to face Kip at the defense table. That brought the jurors' eyes along, too. Kip sat impassively but had one involuntary motion, his jaw muscles clenching. Well, who could blame him?

"Now, I don't know if the defendant has some obscure learning disorder," Bolden continued. "But I do know that he's way too smart to have been tricked into criminal conduct. Would a reasonable person, a person of even average intellect, have believed Max Ringle when he said that bribery and fraud were lawful? And shouldn't we hold this brilliant young man to, at the very least, the standard of a reasonable person? Would such a person believe that defrauding universities of their admissions slots was just fine with law enforcement? Of course not.

"Then there's the excuse that the defendant craved that dopamine rush. Well, that doesn't justify a drug addict robbing the corner grocery and it doesn't excuse the defendant in this case. Dopamine rush? Oh, please! How about a cash rush? That's what the defendant was all about.

"Millions of kids play billions of hours of video games and don't end up as conspirators in a crime ring. *Fortnite* and *Red Dead Redemption* are not the villains here. Video games did not commit these crimes. The defendant did.

"Kip Lassiter became a criminal freely and knowingly, and, judging from the recordings, quite happily. You heard him boasting about his illegal actions, as if he were playing a trick on the world. Yes, Max Ringle was the sorcerer, but Kip Lassiter was the sorcerer's apprentice."

That being the government's theme, in case we'd forgotten.

Bolden ran through a few of the instructions the jury would hear from the judge and closed with a salute to the flag, amber waves of grain, and bombs bursting in air.

"Under the laws of this nation," she said, solemnly, "this defendant was entitled to have his day in court. He got that. He was entitled to have a fair trial by an impartial jury. He got that, too. That's all he's entitled to. And since the government has proven his guilt beyond and to the exclusion of every reasonable doubt, the United States of America is entitled to guilty verdicts on each and every count. Thank you."

CHAPTER SIXTY-SEVEN
Rewrite, Get Me Obit

With fifteen minutes left in the lunch recess, I paced the corridor, gathering stray thoughts for closing argument when I heard my name called. I turned to find a young man in an ill-fitting brown plaid sport coat over a green T-shirt, faded jeans, and dirty sneakers. He had a pen over one ear and held a small notepad in one hand. "Mr. Lassiter, I'm from the *Miami Herald*."

"Really? I thought it might be *GQ*."

"You probably don't remember me. Rudy Schulian."

"Rudy! You're the intern who thought I was going to die after the Thunder Thurston murder trial."

"No, sir. I merely wrote your obit. We do that in advance for prominent Miamians."

"Are you here to see if I drop out of that category? Or just drop dead?"

"Now I cover federal court, state court, the city commission, the zoning appeals board, South Beach nightclubs, and I'm the weekend deputy city editor."

"No delivery route in Opa-Locka?"

"We've had some cutbacks. As for your prominence, this trial raises your profile. I predict a front-page obit."

"Now there's something to look forward to. What do you need, Rudy?"

"Is it true you used to spar with State Attorney Pincher at the gym?"

"Why are you asking?"

"It's a neat metaphor. Boxing in the ring, fighting in court. In the old days, I mean."

"You want a metaphor? Pincher used to hit me in the nuts."

"I'll take that as a confirmation."

"Are you writing his obit, too? He's an asshole, and you can quote me."

"I don't think I'll do that, sir." He thumbed through his notepad. "I need to confirm a quote, something you supposedly said to a class at F.I.U. law school."

"Florida International has a law school?"

He studied me a second to see if I was serious, decided I was, and answered, "Since about 2000 or so."

"Hah! Who knew the new century dawned with Miami needing more lawyers?"

"Do you remember speaking to students there a couple years ago?"

"Let's say I do. What did I allegedly say?"

"The professor quoted you as saying, 'I lose most of my cases. That's true, even with the big-name lawyers. If our customers knew our real winning percentage, they'd either cop a quick plea or jump bail and flee to Argentina.'"

"I regret saying 'customers.' But it sounds about right. Say, Rudy, have you been watching the trial?"

"Every day, except when I had to cover the commission vote on the new sewage plant."

"What do you think about my chances?"

"Hard to say. The government has all the evidence. But you're known for your summations. There are young lawyers lined up outside to see you."

"Really?"

"I heard one of them say you always have a strong theme and you repeat it several times for emphasis."

"Either that, or I forget I've already said it."

"Someone else said you're always flirting with contempt."

"I don't flirt, Rudy. I take her all the way."

Schulian scribbled something on his pad.

"Take a stab at it," I said. "What's the jury's going to do?"

He shrugged, helplessly. "No idea. What happened to your posse, those retirees who follow you from courtroom to courtroom?"

"The courthouse gang," I said. "No longer with us, Rudy."

I missed my old friends who dispensed advice and complained about the air-conditioning. Marvin the Maven. Cadillac Johnson. Teresa Toraño. All gone. As were Doc Charlie Riggs and Granny Lassiter.

Rudy wished me luck and left me standing there, feeling old and tired and weighed down by responsibility. I wondered if I was up to the task before me. All I had in the world were Kip and Melissa, and it seemed inevitable I would lose one to prison and leave the other a young widow. In short, I was not in the best frame of mind when the courtroom deputy strode into the corridor and advised everyone that court was about to resume.

CHAPTER SIXTY-EIGHT
Smart Kid, Dumb Kid

My pants were belted, my tie knotted, my suit coat buttoned, and yet I felt naked standing in front of the jury. Ordinarily, summation is my favorite part of every trial. Unshackled from the formality of the Q & A, it's a chance to soar with the ghosts of courtroom lore. Clarence Darrow comes to mind. "You can only protect your liberties in this world by protecting the other man's freedom. You can only be free if I am free."

Today, my hands were moist and my temples throbbed. I am never nervous in court. What the hell was going on? I hoped the jury would not see the flop sweat threatening to pour down my face.

Breathe in, breathe out. Repeat.

Standing five feet from the jury box, I exhaled a long breath and began in my friendly neighbor tone. "How can someone so smart do something so stupid? I've asked myself that a thousand times, but I needed this trial to learn the answer."

The jurors waited, expectantly. They wanted to know, too.

"Sometimes, the smartest kid in school is the dumbest kid on the street. That's my nephew. That's Kip Lassiter."

I pointed at him and shook my head, letting the jury feel my disappointment, and letting my theme sink in. I hoped the parents would relate to my anguish. I hoped they would worry about their own kids going astray. I hoped they believed in second chances.

"Kip is living proof that a perfect score on a test doesn't help you navigate the river of life, doesn't protect you from those deadly rocks and those treacherous rapids. And it surely doesn't give you the skills to deal with a sociopath like Max Ringle. That's right, a man without a conscience who only cares about himself. If you're on a raft with Ringle and you both go overboard, he'll pry your fingers off the hand strap and climb over you to save himself. He's the cockroach who will always survive."

I paused again. Like an actor delivering a soliloquy, a lawyer uses pace to propel the story and emphasis to pound home the theme.

"You saw Kip solve that SAT math problem. He didn't need a calculator or scratch paper or multiple-choice answers. He did it in his head. Something in his brain works differently than yours or mine. His synapses crackle and pop at the speed of light. How I wish he could read people the way he solves equations! Sometimes, the smartest kid in school is the dumbest kid on the street."

A couple jurors nodded. If I kept repeating the line, I wondered how many more jurors might join in.

"The prosecutor told you this was a 'nationwide criminal conspiracy that wreaked havoc on our system of higher education.' Was it? Fifty young people cheated their way into college. My nephew helped some of them. None of those fifty—zero—were prosecuted. Were they any less culpable than Kip? Many of them have profited from their cheating. Advertising contracts and clothing lines and music deals. And yet Kip Lassiter is on trial, and they are not. What about fundamental fairness?

"Look at Craig Kwalick and his clothing line. He got 'framous' with an 'r' because of the scandal. Look at the Hallinan twins and their hip-hop careers. Look at Shari Ringle and her eleven million-dollar business. What did she say about my client? 'I thank Kip for making me what I am today.'

"These young people are enmeshed in a strange new culture that I barely understand. They want the easy road, even if it is the low road. They worship not only money, but also celebrity. And in their world, infamy gets you more Twitter followers than achievement does.

"It's a world I find bewildering. In a society without shame, where faking it is making it and deceit trumps virtue, integrity is for losers and cheaters win. Fairness? Forget about it! A meritocracy? In your dreams! Earn your diploma? Why bother, when you can buy it?

"Is this the message we want to send to the young? That the vapid and vacuous and amoral achieve happiness. And yet, I think there's hope for those young people whose values are so foreign to me. Why? Because they are *young* and still learning. And they haven't been charged with crimes that will destroy their lives. The government has chosen to let them mature and grow wiser with age. What about Kip? What about fundamental fairness? Will you let him have that same opportunity?"

I paused and tried to be inconspicuous as I gave my head a little shake, as if clearing water out of an ear. My tinnitus was kicking up with the sharp staccato beat of a snare drum, irritating but not so loud as to drown out my thoughts. My headache, too, was still in the moderate zone.

"How about those parents who got slapped on the wrists? You saw some of them. What about Harman Fisher, the guy from Star Island who could buy and sell me a hundred times? Max Ringle and Harman Fisher—what a quinella! The two faces of the prosecution's case.

"Ringle is a fraudster, a con man, a cheat, a professional liar, a scam artist, and a low life. To make his fortune, he needs the Harman Fishers of the world. Greedy, arrogant, avaricious, immoral, vicious...and those are his best qualities."

The jurors rewarded me with chuckles and small smiles. Oh, they remembered Fisher. They probably raced home that night and, in violation of the judge's orders, excitedly told their spouses about the wealthy asshole who said he hoped Kip would be sexually assaulted in prison.

"I asked Fisher if he should teach his kids about integrity. Remember his answer? 'Better to teach them it's a dog-eat-dog world.' Now, there's a role model! Speaking of fathers, how about Ringle? Remember what he said about his daughter Shari? 'She's not the brightest bulb in the chandelier.'

"A vote to convict my nephew is a vote for these two men. Ringle has secretly pled guilty, and his sentencing awaits the outcome of this trial. He's praying for a conviction to help his own cause. He's the one prying Kip's fingers off that hand strap to save himself as the raft heads toward the rapids. What about fundamental fairness?

"Ringle expertly preyed on Kip's weaknesses. He rationed the video games. Why? To make Kip thirsty for the dopamine rush. When up against Ringle, Kip never had a chance. You heard the testimony of Dr. Melissa Gold. Objective evidence. The brain scan proves that Kip has Nonverbal Learning Disorder. He misses personality cues and fails to read faces and body language. Kip is a lot smarter than I am, but I can spot a phony and he can't. He has what my granny used to call 'book smarts.' But he lacks 'street smarts.'"

I waited a moment before delivering my theme a third time, and I spoke slowly to convey the importance of the words. "Sometimes, the smartest kid in school is the dumbest kid on the street."

A beat, and then I continued. "Now, a word about those surreptitious tape recordings. Altogether, they have Kip recorded for thirty hours and thirty-nine minutes in sixty-two different conversations. Agent Wisniewski admitted that Kip never said anything that indicated he knew he was committing a crime. Of course, he didn't know. Ringle, master liar, told Kip he has a legal opinion that there's no crime. And what does Kip say when Wisniewski approaches him to cooperate in the investigation against Max Ringle? 'I don't need to cooperate. I haven't done anything wrong.' What does Ringle do when he's approached by the FBI? Knowing full well his guilt, he races to inform on the parents, kids, coaches, proctors, admissions officers, and, of course, my nephew. What about fundamental fairness?

"Now, this is going to surprise you..."

I paused. No one would fall asleep with that bait dangling in the air.

"Maybe Max Ringle was right. Maybe inside all his lies was one kernel of truth. He didn't have a legal opinion, but maybe it's not a federal crime. And you're the ones who get to decide that. Not the government. Not me. Not even Judge Speidel. So, what am I talking about when I say maybe it's not a crime? Well, I have a confession to make."

Again, the jurors waited. They seemed to be enjoying each little mystery.

"Despite my gray hair and membership in AARP, I've never been lead counsel in federal court before. I never tried a mail fraud case. So, I asked a state prosecutor, 'What the heck is mail fraud?'"

A couple jurors smiled. Maybe they had the same question. Or maybe they liked a lawyer who confessed he wasn't a legal eagle.

"And this prosecutor says—"

"Your Honor," Bolden interrupted. "This is not proper commentary on the evidence."

"Overruled. I've always allowed a little storytelling."

"The prosecutor says that mail fraud is what the feds use when they don't have anything else. See, there's no statute saying, 'Thou shalt not cheat on the SAT exam.' So, they use this catch-all mail fraud statute. The state prosecutor gave me an example. 'Assume I go to Hawaii, and I send you a postcard saying I'm having a wonderful time, wish you were here. But I'm lying. I'm having a lousy time, and I don't want you here. The feds would say that's mail fraud.'"

Four out of twelve jurors laughed. So did a healthy percentage of spectators. It would be supremely ironic if that bastard Ray Pincher inadvertently helped me win. But I couldn't get too carried away with my own—or Ray's—imagery. I knew that in her rebuttal, Bolden would tell the jury that Judge Speidel, not some state prosecutor, would deliver instructions on just what constitutes mail fraud.

"This splendid courtroom in this magnificent courthouse has seen the worst humanity can dish out. Colombian drug cartels, human traffickers, sex slavers, terrorists bent on mass murder, billion-dollar Medicare fraudsters...and now this case: some teenagers cheating to get into one college instead of another. When I was a snot-nosed kid and would fuss about something, my granny would say, 'For crying out loud, Jake, don't make a federal case out of it.' And today, I say the same to you.

"You heard the testimony of Georgina Suarez. The admissions process is broken and corrupt. Those admissions slots, treated as holy artifacts by the prosecution, are traded like pork bellies in the real world. If you're an athlete, if your family donates millions, if you're a legacy, welcome aboard! It's not a level playing field, and it was ripe for plundering by the likes of Max Ringle.

"What happened here? The parents bribed the wrong people. They should have gone straight to the development departments. Fund a scholarship and get junior into college."

My tinnitus had gone up in volume and lower in pitch. The snare drums had turned into bass drums, reverberating with deep sonic booms each time the mallet struck. The headache that had begun in my temples now enveloped my head, as if a torturer were hammering rivets into my skull. I needed to move swiftly.

"You also heard about the twenty-six parents who weren't charged. One was the Chinese billionaire who paid a five million-dollar bribe to get his daughter into Stanford. Why wasn't he indicted? Agent Wisniewski said it was because the man didn't know it was crime. Well, neither did Kip Lassiter! What about fundamental fairness? It's time to answer that question. This prosecution has been tainted from the outset. They charged Kip Lassiter and let others equally culpable go free. You may consider all of that in reaching your verdict."

"Objection! Objection!" Bolden must have been serious, or else why the repetition? "That's an incorrect statement of the law, and a blatant attempt to urge the jury to violate Your Honor's instructions."

Translation, that shyster is shooting for jury nullification, a major no-no.

"Sustained. The court will determine just what the jury may consider in reaching its verdict."

"Let's go back to Max Ringle for a moment," I said, as if leading a tour group through the Louvre and wanting a second look at the Mona Lisa. "How did he pull this off? How did he convince parents and kids and coaches and proctors and admissions officers to dance with him? I don't know how many of you are fans of *Star Trek…*"

Okay, that's a white lie. I know from voir dire that three of my dozen are Trekkies.

"You may remember an episode where aliens from the planet Talos create a reality distortion field, where illusions are indistinguishable from reality. They could make humans see things that weren't there. Ladies and gentlemen, Max Ringle is a Talosian. He created a reality distortion field that fooled a lot of people, including Kip Lassiter.

"The prosecutor told you to hold Kip Lassiter to the standard of a reasonable person. Let's consider that. Max Ringle, a man who can conjure mythical worlds out of thin air, told my young, inexperienced nephew that his actions did not constitute a federal crime. I submit that Kip was reasonable in believing the man's lies."

I waited a moment and closed my eyes. Either there was a thunderstorm inside the courtroom, or my brain pan had decided to slam itself against the inside of my skull. I needed to wrap this up before the jury mistook my pained facial expressions for fear.

"Years ago, in state court, I represented a client from South America who was unfamiliar with our justice system. He asked me, 'Who owns this courthouse?' I told him the government. He asked, 'Who pays the judge and the court staff?' Same answer, the government. 'Who pays the prosecutors and their investigators and the police?' The government. Not surprisingly, my client seemed worried. But I explained that no one owns the jury. The jury is independent, and that's what guarantees a fair trial. Ladies and gentlemen, no one owns you. No one can question what you do in this case. Today, you are the law.

"I will close with this. At the Justice Department in Washington, there's a sign over the entrance that reads, 'The government of the United States, the people of our country, never lose a case, despite a not guilty verdict, so long as justice is done.'

"In this case, the government has not proved guilt beyond a reasonable doubt. Rather, the government has proved that Kip Lassiter, the smartest kid in school, was the dumbest kid on the street. A verdict of not guilty on all counts will satisfy the government's own standard that justice be done. Thank you."

CHAPTER SIXTY-NINE
Lunch Date

Margaret Bolden's rebuttal was uneventful. The jurors, some of whom had been perched on the edge of their swivel chairs when she spoke the first time, now settled back into the cushions. They had already made up their minds, but in which direction? I had no idea.

The jury's attention picked up when Judge Speidel read his instructions in a perfect judicial monotone. "For you to find the defendant guilty, the government must prove beyond a reasonable doubt that the defendant devised a scheme to defraud or obtain money or property by means of false or fraudulent pretenses, and..."

I didn't need to listen to the rest. Thankfully, the caissons rolling through my skull seemed to have come to a halt, the soldiers setting up camp for the night. When the judge was finished, he released the jurors for the evening with instructions to return at 9 a.m. sharp to begin deliberations. As the courtroom emptied, Judge Speidel bellowed, "Lead counsel, in my chambers, now! No one else."

Already? I wondered if the judge's law clerks had polished the blade of the guillotine.

I gave Kip keys to the Eldo and told him to drive home if I didn't reappear in fifteen minutes. Also, to check with the federal marshal's office to see where I was being held.

Bolden was already there when I walked into chambers shooting glances left and right to see if I was going to be mugged, or at least handcuffed. Judge Speidel had removed his robes and settled into his high-backed chair, his hands resting on his massive belly, fingers twined.

"Well, well, Mr. Lassiter," he drawled. "Are you still packing?"

I opened my suit coat and drew out the toothbrush by its Mickey Mouse head. "I never leave home without it."

The judge barked a laugh. "Well, put it back. You won't need it. By Jove, I have to thank both of you!"

By Jove?

"For what?" I exhaled a long breath, and the tension drained from my shoulders.

"Tell him, Margie."

"Judge Speidel always thanks the lawyers if he's enjoyed the trial."

"This was a spellbinder," the judge said. "My last two cases were a social security disability appeal and a maritime dispute over a shipload of spoiled mangoes. Thank you both for providing first-rate lawyering and entertainment."

I nodded, which was the least I could do after the kindly king called off my beheading.

"Oh, you two!" the judge enthused. "What a spirited battle. But always respectful of each other. Mr. Lassiter, I misjudged you."

"Oh. Well. Thanks. I thought you hated me."

"No! Never! I like to baptize newbies with a little fire and brimstone to see if they can take it. And even though you've got the gray hair, as you told the jury, you're a newborn babe in my courtroom. But damn, you can take it and dish it right back! Right to the edge of the precipice, didn't he, Margie?"

"He's a fighter," she agreed.

"Now these young lawyers," the judge said, "be they prosecutors or public defenders, well, they're too...Margie, what's the word?"

"Sensitive," she ventured.

"Exactly. They have..."

"Tender sensibilities," I said.

"Right you are." He stared off into space a moment, then said, "Say, Margie, what was your favorite moment of the trial?

She gave a wry smile and replied, "It would have to be Jake's closing when he talked about, what was it, the reality *bullshit* field?"

"Hah!" The judge laughed so hard his massive belly shook, not like a bowlful of jelly, but maybe a fifty-five-gallon drum of marmalade. "*Star Trek!* Oh, Jesus. That was rich!"

The whole experience was becoming surreal, but the Lion King was in such a jolly mood, it was hard not to smile.

"For me," the judge continued, "it was that wealthy jerk from Star Island who went after Lassiter. 'Brain-dead shyster!' Hah!"

"Harman Fisher," she said, with an unhappy sigh.

"How the hell did you let him off the reservation, Margie?"

Bolden shook her head. "I prepped him, Your Honor, but something about Jake got under his skin."

"I have that effect on people," I said.

"And you, Lassiter? Any favorite moments?"

"It hasn't happened yet, Your Honor."

They both understood but kept quiet. Neither one thought the jury would bring me that moment.

"Say, Lassiter, I'm taking some time off next week," the judge said. "How would you like to spend a day showing me around the state justice building?"

"Down by the river?"

"Unless it's moved."

The surreal had become utterly bizarre. "You and me? Hanging out."

"Hell, yes. You'll give me a tour. We'll wander from courtroom to courtroom. Find some cases we don't get over here. Homicides. Armed robberies. DUI hit-and-runs. Is there any place to have lunch over there?"

"You like Cuban?"

"Jesus, look at me. I like everything!"

I was still stunned. But spending a day with Judge Speidel was surely preferable to thirty days behind bars. "Okay, sure. We'll catch a couple trials. Have lunch."

"Say, Lassiter, one more thing, and I hate to ask it." He looked at me gravely.

"Yeah?"

"Are you really dying?"

"Aren't we all?" I answered.

CHAPTER SEVENTY
We, the Jury

An empty, darkened courtroom is a forlorn place. A circus tent without the ringmaster, the animals, and the children with painted faces. Not even a lone pigeon fluttering high among the quarter poles. The lights were dimmed and the courtroom empty when I entered at 8:50 a.m. the next day.

Our ringmaster, Judge Speidel, sat in chambers with his clerks, reviewing motions and memoranda of law in other cases. Margaret Bolden was in the U.S. Attorney's office. One of her lower ranking soldiers would remain at the prosecution table during deliberations. A courtroom deputy—we used to say "bailiff"—would guard the door to the jury room. I would stay at the defense table because I always do.

Judge Speidel wanted lawyers within shouting distance if the jury came back with a question...or a verdict. Melissa was taking the afternoon off from work and would bring Kip along later to keep me company. I was at peace in my solitude. Thinking back, I wouldn't have done anything differently. I fought as hard as I could without breaking any furniture.

I still believed what I told Melissa early in the trial. If I could walk Kip out of the courthouse a free man, I was optimistic about his future. He seemed changed, which is to say, back to his old self, the kid I had raised. It almost felt as if he had caught a virus from Typhoid Max, something that had poisoned his character. Now, thankfully, he seemed to be cured.

If only we can win...

Court assistants and deputy clerks and random journalists occasionally opened the courtroom door, poked their heads inside, then left. Nothing to see here.

Melissa and Kip arrived just before noon, and just as they sat down, I heard a *knock-knock* from inside the jury room. It had to be a question, or a plea to turn down the frigid air-conditioning, or a request for lunch. It could not be a verdict. The courtroom deputy, the centurion at the gate, had been dozing in the jury box. He leapt to his feet, opened the door and went inside the jury room. A moment later, he scurried out, heading for the judge's chambers.

"Arturo!" I yelled at him. "What's up?"

He waved me off and disappeared out the back door of the courtroom.

Ten minutes later, Margaret Bolden and her band of *federales* hurried into the courtroom. Five minutes after that, Judge Speidel, robed and flush of face, took the bench and nodded to Arturo, who opened the jury room door.

They filed into the box, these dozen citizens, good and true. None looked me in the eye, usually a bad sign, but then they didn't look at Bolden, either. I was getting no reading. Juror number five, Manuel Castillo, the South Beach chef, held the verdict form, meaning he was the foreperson. That was fine with me, not that I had a choice.

"Has the jury reached a verdict?" the judge asked.

Castillo stood and said, "We have, Your Honor."

Castillo handed the verdict form to the deputy clerk, who handed it up to Judge Speidel, who read it silently. His mouth twitched slightly, jiggling a chubby cheek. Was that a smile, or just some nerve endings firing? He handed the form back to the clerk and told her to "publish the verdict."

This would take a while. There were thirty-seven counts. But I would know with the first mail fraud count if we had won or lost. It was an all-or-nothing game. Either Kip was guilty of every count or none of them.

We stood side by side, my big paw wrapped around his elbow to keep him from toppling over if the news was lousy. Melissa sat just behind us in the row of chairs that back up to the railing separating the well of the courtroom from the gallery.

A deputy clerk, a petite woman in her forties, stood and read aloud from the verdict form: "United States of America vs. Chester Lassiter aka Kip Lassiter. As to count one of the indictment, we, the jury, find the defendant..."

By the time she finished that sentence, tears streamed down my cheeks. Then, inexplicably, I laughed and cried at the same time, as if the sun were shining through the rain. I realized my knees had gone weak, and Kip was holding me up, not the other way around. The skinny kid couldn't manage it. Melissa leapt from her seat and steadied me from the other side. Damned embarrassing!

The clerk kept reading. I didn't need to listen. I knew. But I listened anyway. Were any words in our language so sweet?

"As to count five of the indictment, we, the jury, find the defendant not guilty. As to count six of the indictment, we, the jury, find the defendant not guilty. As to count seven..."

You were smiling, Judge! I misjudged you, too. Yeah. This is it. My favorite moment of the trial!

CHAPTER SEVENTY-ONE
We Are Family

In our coral rock house on Kumquat Avenue that evening, there were hugs and there were kisses. There was music and there was dancing. There were stone crabs with mustard sauce and champagne with caviar. There was laughter mixed with tears.

Melissa was making a vegetarian risotto for Kip, but he was eyeing the stack of stone crabs, shells expertly cracked.

"I don't want broccoli cheddar risotto," he said.

"Really?" I asked, surprised.

"I want what you two are having, Uncle Jake."

"You sure?"

"And tomorrow, let's go to Dairy Queen and get a couple Blizzards."

I whooped and hollered, "Welcome home, Kip!"

The three of us danced to Sister Sledge's "We Are Family." Melissa, in a blue and gold halter-top sleeveless sun dress, was the most graceful, her hips keeping perfect time with the beat. Kip was the most energetic, a frenzied dance solo. And I was, well...I was the aging guy with bad knees who danced as if my feet were stuck in wet cement.

"We are fa-mi-ly..."

My lack of rhythm and grace didn't matter. All that mattered was that Kip was free, and the three of us were together.

"We're giving love in a family dose..."

When exhaustion caught up with us, we sank into chairs, breathing heavily. We finished the champagne and I found another bottle in the refrigerator. Then, Melissa brought me up to date. "Some news from N.I.H. today."

"Yeah?"

"No celebrating yet, but I've been named interim executive director of the C.T.E. program."

"Interim? Is that like being a little bit pregnant?"

"That's the rub. The appropriations have been held up till the next fiscal year."

"Ah, jeez."

"But it's going to happen. And they're giving us a partial grant for more research and clinical trials here. You're 'Subject One' when we start with the new protein antibody. And I want you in hospital for four weeks of round-the-clock testing and observation."

"Sure. Always a pleasure being your guinea pig."

"Really? I expected some resistance."

"That's the old me. Now, I go along. I get along. Life is short, but oh so sweet."

She hugged me and said, "I love the old you and the new you."

Hanging out on the perimeter of the kitchen, Kip blurted out, "I have news, too."

"Yeah?"

"I'm going back to college. Penn State."

"You mean Penn," I said.

He laughed. "Bad memories. *Not* Penn. Penn State. Your alma mater."

"This isn't a joke? A twist on those T-shirts I made?"

"Nope. Penn State has an excellent IST program."

"Sounds like a subway line."

"Information Science and Technology. Joint major in data science and entrepreneurship and innovation. Plus, they've recruited me for their eSports team."

"What the hell is an eSports team?"

Melissa broke in. "I've read about it. There are college and professional leagues, and they're even building arenas for spectators."

"People pay to watch other people play computer games?" I asked.

"As they do football," Melissa informed me.

"More people saw the last League of Legends championships than the NBA Finals," Kip said. "Anyway, Penn State is giving me a full scholie."

"EGames? Again?" I was dumbfounded by deja-friggin'-vu.

"Don't worry, Uncle Jake. Playing a team sport with coaches and other students is different than being holed up in my room. Besides, my focus won't be on the games. I'm channeling my energy into coding and game creation."

"For your classes?"

"And a career. I'm going to create a start-up to develop and market eGames. By playing on the team, I'll be hanging out with other techies and sampling different games. It'll help the development process."

"This is a lot to digest." I let out a long breath. "What happened to your idea about helping underprivileged kids with the SAT and ACT?"

"I'm getting to that. Remember the *Road Fury* game?"

"Sure. You flashed back to it when you were being chased through the Everglades."

"My first eGame will be *Road Test*, an exam prep course, but really fun. The kids compete against the median test score of successful applicants at the college of their choice. They start on Founding Fathers Parkway, the history course, then drive through Trigonometry Falls..."

"Math," I groaned, "my Achilles heel."

"Then through the Valley of Irony, which is the pathway into the English section, ending at the Science Suburbs. They'll see if their score will get them in, and if not, where they would be admitted. They can race countless times on different courses to improve their skills, competing against new applicants, including their friends, or kids from China, if they choose that option."

"I love it," I said.

"And it's all free. Totally pro bono."

"This is wonderful," Melissa cried. "You have a direction and a worthy goal."

I felt a soothing sense of peace, and it wasn't from the champagne. I felt optimistic about Kip, about Melissa and me, and about the future. In short, I felt blessed.

"Kippers, when do you go to Happy Valley?" I asked.

"Summer session. Mid-June."

I turned to Melissa. "That doesn't give us much time."

"For what?"

"Wedding plans. How does the first week of June sound?"

She threw her arms around me, and we kissed long and slow, sweet and deep. I didn't think anything could disrupt the mood, the warm flood of emotions like an incoming tide on a Caribbean island. Then, just before 10 p.m., there was a knock at the front door.

CHAPTER SEVENTY-TWO
Friendship Like a Bamboo Bridge

"What the hell are you doing here?" I demanded, blocking the doorway.

"I wanted to congratulate you." Ray Pincher stood on the front step, a bashful grin on his face.

"Get off my property, or I will throw you from here to Dixie Highway."

Pincher raised both hands as if surrendering and said, "Open my briefcase."

I looked down, saw his soft leather case on the ground and did nothing. "I don't feel like playing games."

"C'mon, Jake. Just look. Then I'll leave."

"What the hell." I stepped outside into the muggy night air. I grabbed the briefcase and pulled out a thin manila folder. Inside was a State Attorney's office investigative report with Gilberto Foyo's name on the cover. "Yeah, so what?"

"Jeez, just open it."

I opened the folder. Three typewritten pages with a photo of two men standing on a seawall, a giant, gleaming white boat behind them. "What is this?"

"Either of those two guys look familiar?"

"No. Should they? Wait a second. Is that Harman Fisher? Rich jerkoff from Star Island."

"And his 125-motor yacht. The other guy is a Miami Beach zoning inspector."

"So, what?"

"Fisher tried to bribe the zoning inspector to approve dock space for his 125-foot yacht when he was limited to 100 feet. We've got video and audio of the hand-to-hand transaction, fifty grand in cash."

I shrugged. "Other than being a prick on the witness stand, the guy means nothing to me."

Pincher reached into his pocket, withdrew a cigarette lighter, clicked the wheel, and in seconds, the report and photo were black ash, which he dropped into my planter of equally moribund Impatiens.

"I don't get it."

"C'mon, Jake. Think about me as the link between you and Fisher."

It took another moment. Then it all came at once. Gilberto Foyo wasn't sitting in the gallery every day to bail me out of jail. He was seeing how I was doing. Checking if I needed help, which I did. So, Ray Pincher gave it to me.

"You sleazy son of a bitch!" I yelled.

"I'll take that as a 'thank you.'"

"You extorted Fisher. You forced him to be the biggest asshole in the history of government witnesses, and that's a rectum the size of the Lincoln Tunnel. You told him you'd shitcan the bribery charge if he torpedoed the government's case."

"He couldn't guarantee the result, but he agreed to play a role. World's most obnoxious zillionaire, which, frankly, was typecasting. Hey, did you like 'brain-dead shyster?' That was my line."

"Jeez, Ray. This taints my victory."

"How? There's no way to know if Fisher turned the jury. He was a minor witness, and Gilberto said you were outstanding. As good as ever. I wish I could have seen you. Here I thought you had one foot in the grave. But you come off the bench like Michael Jordan with the flu, dropping thirty-eight on the Jazz in the finals. You're a champ."

Suddenly, I was exhausted. "I feel old, Ray. And behind the times and...I don't know...like the merry-go-round keeps spinning faster, and I'm hanging on for dear life."

"You'll get over it. Your adrenaline's spent, and you've got the post-trial blues."

"This seems different."

"C'mon, you're the Jakester. You may be the lion in winter. Your fur may be matted, your gait unsteady. But Jake, you are still the lion."

We were quiet a moment, and I heard a police siren in the distance. From somewhere in the trees, an unseen bird trilled.

He picked up his briefcase. "Are we good, Jake?"

I shrugged. "I don't know. Give me some time."

He clopped me on the shoulder and headed toward his car.

Moments later, when I opened the bedroom door, I saw Melissa, wearing a black negligee, sitting up in bed, reading a book. She looked at my face and said, "Oh, if you're too tired..."

"No! Never too tired."

She cocked her head coquettishly, if that word is still used in an era where colleges give scholarships to play eGames. "Did I hear Ray Pincher's voice at the front door?"

I undressed as I told her the details of our conversation. She seemed astonished, but who wouldn't be? "What about Ray's question? Are you okay with him?"

I slid into bed next to her, moved close, felt the warmth of her thigh against mine. "Basically, he's asking for forgiveness."

"Do you have it in your heart?"

"If not today, when would I? And given what I do for a living, believing in redemption, how could I not?"

"So, you and Ray are friends again?"

"Our friendship has always been like one of those hanging bridges made of bamboo. It shakes and shimmies in the slightest breeze, but it can withstand an earthquake."

I thought about the ebb and flow of friendship and the challenges of loyalty. I had told Pincher that I wouldn't have double-crossed him as he did to me. Regardless of my love for Kip, I wouldn't have turned against him or his daughter. But how do I know? I'd never been faced with the choice.

"Mel, if it's okay with you, I'd like to invite Ray to our wedding."

She smiled and nuzzled her cheek against mine. "I always knew there were a thousand reasons I loved you. Now, there are a thousand and one."

We kissed, and she said, "A thousand and two."

We kissed some more, and she purred, and my hand slid the strap of her negligee off her shoulder, and she continued, "One thousand and three."

My kisses descended from her lips to her neck to her breasts, and she said, "Keep going, big guy. I'm really good at math."

#

ALSO AVAILABLE

JAKE LASSITER SERIES

TO SPEAK FOR THE DEAD: Linebacker-turned-lawyer Jake Lassiter begins to believe that his surgeon client is innocent of malpractice . . . but guilty of murder.

NIGHT VISION: After several women are killed by an Internet stalker, Jake is appointed a special prosecutor and heads to London and the very streets where Jack the Ripper once roamed.

FALSE DAWN: After his client confesses to a murder he didn't commit, Jake follows a bloody trail from Miami to Havana to discover the truth.

MORTAL SIN: Talk about conflicts of interest. Jake is sleeping with Gina Florio and defending her mob-connected husband in court.

RIPTIDE: Jake Lassiter chases a beautiful woman and stolen bonds from Miami to Maui.

FOOL ME TWICE: To clear his name in a murder investigation, Jake searches for buried treasure in the abandoned silver mines of Aspen, Colorado.

FLESH & BONES: Jake falls for his beautiful client even though he doubts her story. She claims to have recovered "repressed memories" of abuse . . . just before gunning down her father.

LASSITER: Jake retraces the steps of a model who went missing eighteen years earlier . . . after his one-night stand with her.

LAST CHANCE LASSITER: In this prequel novella, young Jake Lassiter has an impossible case: he represents Cadillac Johnson, an aging rhythm and blues musician who claims his greatest song was stolen by a top-of-the-charts hip-hop artist.

STATE vs. LASSITER: This time, Jake is on the wrong side of the bar. He's charged with murder! The victim? His girlfriend and banker, Pamela Baylins, who was about to report him to the authorities for allegedly stealing from clients.

BUM RAP: Defending Steve Solomon in a murder case and fighting his growing feelings for Victoria Lord, Jake find a missing witness—a stunning Bar girl—before she's eliminated by the Russian mob.

BUM LUCK: "Thirty seconds after the jury announced its verdict, I decided to kill my client." Is Jake suffering brain damage from all those concussions? And will he really resort to vigilante justice?

BUM DEAL: Appointed special prosecutor in a high-profile murder case, Jake vows to take down a prominent surgeon accused of killing his wife. There's just one problem...or maybe three: no evidence, no witness, and no body.

SOLOMON & LORD SERIES

SOLOMON vs. LORD: Trial lawyer Victoria Lord, who follows every rule, and Steve Solomon, who makes up his own, bicker and banter as they defend a beautiful young woman, accused of killing her wealthy, older husband.

THE DEEP BLUE ALIBI: Solomon and Lord come together—and fly apart—defending Victoria's "Uncle Grif" on charges he killed a man with a speargun. It's a case set in the Florida Keys with side trips to coral reefs and a nudist colony where all is more—and less—than it seems.

KILL ALL THE LAWYERS: Just what did Steve Solomon do to infuriate ex-client and ex-con "Dr. Bill"? Did Solomon try to lose the case in which the TV shrink was charged in the death of a woman patient?

HABEAS PORPOISE: It starts with the kidnaping of a pair of trained dolphins and turns into a murder trial with Solomon and Lord on *opposite* sides after Victoria is appointed a special prosecutor, and fireworks follow!

STAND-ALONE THRILLERS

IMPACT: A Jetliner crashes in the Everglades. Is it negligence or terrorism? When the legal case gets to the Supreme Court, the defense has a unique strategy: kill anyone, even a Supreme Court justice, to win the case.

402

BALLISTIC: A nuclear missile, a band of terrorists, and only two people who can prevent Armageddon. A "loose nukes" thriller for the twenty-first century.

ILLEGAL: Down-and-out lawyer Jimmy (Royal) Payne tries to reunite a Mexican boy with his missing mother and becomes enmeshed in the world of human trafficking and sex slavery.

PAYDIRT: Bobby Gallagher had it all and lost it. Now, assisted by his twelve-year-old brainiac son, he tries to rig the Super Bowl, win a huge bet . . . and avoid getting killed.

PRAISE FOR PAUL LEVINE

TO SPEAK FOR THE DEAD

"Move over Scott Turow. *To Speak for the Dead* is courtroom drama at its very best."
—Larry King

"An assured and exciting piece of work. Jake Lassiter is Travis McGee with a law degree . . . One of the best mysteries of the year."
—*Los Angeles Times*

"Paul Levine is guilty of master storytelling in the first degree. *To Speak for the Dead* is a fast, wry, and thoroughly engrossing thriller."
—Carl Hiaasen

NIGHT VISION

"Levine's fiendish ability to create twenty patterns from the same set of clues will have you waiting impatiently for his next novel."
—*Kirkus Reviews*

"Sparkles with wit and subtlety."
—*Toronto Star*

"Breathlessly exciting."
—*Cleveland Plain Dealer*

FALSE DAWN

"Realistic, gritty, fun."
—*New York Times Book Review*

"A highly entertaining yarn filled with wry humor."
—*Detroit Free Press*

"A dazzler, extremely well-written and featuring so many quotable passages you'll want someone handy to read them aloud to."
—*Ellery Queen's Mystery Magazine*

MORTAL SIN

"Take one part John Grisham, two parts Carl Hiaasen, throw in a dash of John D. MacDonald, and voila! You've got *Mortal Sin*."
—*Tulsa World*

"Recalling the work of Carl Hiaasen, this thriller races to a smashing climax."
—*Library Journal*

"Wonderfully funny, sexy, and terrifying."
—Dave Barry

RIPTIDE

"A thriller as fast as the wind. A bracing rush, as breathtaking as hitting the Gulf waters on a chill December morning."
—*Tampa Tribune*

"A tale involving drug smuggling and murder, windsurfing and murder, multi-million-dollar thievery and murder. The action never stops."
—*Denver Rocky Mountain News*

"One of the best mystery writers in the business today. The story fairly leaps with enthusiasm toward the finale. *Riptide* is Paul Levine's finest work."
—*Ocala (FL) Star Banner*

FOOL ME TWICE

"You'll like listening to Jake's beguiling first-person tale-telling so much that you won't mind being fooled thrice."
—*Philadelphia Inquirer*

"A fast-paced thriller filled with action, humor, mystery and suspense."
—*Miami Herald*

"Blend the spicy characters created by Elmore Leonard with the legal expertise and suspense made famous by John Grisham and you have Paul Levine's *Fool Me Twice*."
—*Lake Worth (FL) Herald*

FLESH & BONES

"The author keeps the suspense high with innovative twists and touches of humor that spice up the courtroom scenes."
—*Chicago Tribune*

"Filled with smart writing and smart remarks. Jake is well on his way to becoming a star in the field of detective fiction."
—*Dallas Morning News*

"A well-focused plot that stresses in-depth characterization and action that is more psychological than macho. The author keeps the suspense high with innovative twists."
—*Atlanta Journal Constitution*

LASSITER

"Since Robert Parker is no longer with us, I'm nominating Levine for an award as best writer of dialogue in the grit-lit genre."
—*San Jose Mercury News*

"Lassiter is back after fourteen long years—and better than ever. Moving fast, cracking wise, butting heads, he's the lawyer we all want on our side—and on the page."
—Lee Child

"Few writers can deliver tales about sex and drugs in South Florida better than Levine."
—*Booklist*

STATE vs. LASSITER

"Blend the wit of Carl Hiaasen with Elmore Leonard's dialogue and throw in John Grisham's courtroom skills, and you have State vs. Lassiter."
—Amazon Review

"Lassiter's narrative, which oscillates between self-deprecating and wiseass, is so entertaining and the story so deftly plotted that you will want to read more of his adventures even before you are through."
—*Bookreporter*

"Lassiter is likeable and a character that stands tall like Jack Reacher, Travis McGee or Spenser. Levine's only problem is he isn't prolific enough. I want more Lassiter!"
—*Pick of the Literate*

BUM RAP

"The pages fly by and the laughs keep coming in this irresistible South Florida crime romp. A delicious mix of thriller and comic crime novel."
—*Booklist* (starred review)

"Levine effectively blends a puzzling crime, intelligent sleuthing, adroit courtroom maneuvering, and a surprising attraction between Victoria and Jake in this welcome-addition to both series."
—*Publishers Weekly*

"Ebulliently seamless melding of Levine's two legal-eagles series."
—*Kirkus Reviews*

BUM LUCK

"A one-sit, must-read novel full of memorable characters and unforgettable vignettes. Levine's pacing is perfect as always, and the pages just fly by, even as he juggles multiple plots with his own unique aplomb."
—*Bookreporter*

"A gripping and often quite an amusing thriller with a surprising climax, all of which is built around an intriguing cast of characters as it achieves an almost flawless rhythm."
—*Book Pleasures*

"Paul Levine continues his trademark brisk pacing with timely storytelling and well-placed humor. 'Bum Luck' is elevated further by teaming Jake with Steve Solomon and Victoria Lord. The trio make an unstoppable team—concerned about the law, but even more about people."
—*South Florida Sun-Sentinel*

BUM DEAL

"Any book with Jake Lassiter is a drop-everything, read-it-now for me—and this one has Solomon & Lord too. Bum Deal is fantastic."
—Lee Child

"Fascinating, fully developed characters and smart, well-paced dialogue keep the pages turning. Levine manipulates the expectations of the reader as skillfully as Jake manipulates the expectations of the jury"
—*Publishers Weekly* (starred review)

"Bum Deal is the real deal. Jake Lassiter at his smart-talking, fast-thinking best. A funny, compelling and canny courtroom thriller, seasoned with a little melancholy and a lot of inside knowledge."
—Scott Turow

SOLOMON & LORD SERIES

SOLOMON VS. LORD

"A funny, fast-paced legal thriller. The barbed dialogue makes for some genuine laugh-out-loud moments. Fans of Carl Hiaasen and Dave Barry will enjoy this humorous Florida crime romp."
—*Publishers Weekly*

"The writing makes me think of Janet Evanovich out to dinner with John Grisham."
—*Mystery Lovers*

"Hiaasen meets Grisham in the court of last retort. A sexy, wacky, wonderful thriller with humor and heart."
—Harlan Coben

THE DEEP BLUE ALIBI

"An entertaining, witty comedy caper with legal implications . . . sparkles with promise, humor, and more than a dash of suspense."
—*Blog Critics*

"A cross between *Moonlighting* and *Night Court* . . . courtroom drama has never been this much fun."
—*Fresh Fiction*

"As hilarious as *The Deep Blue Alibi* is, it is almost possible between the cleverly molded characters and sharp dialogue to overlook that the novel contains a terrific mystery, one that will keep you guessing."
—*Bookreporter*

KILL ALL THE LAWYERS

"A clever, colorful thriller . . . with characters drawn with a fine hand, making them feel more like friends than figments of the author's imagination. Levine ratchets up the tension with each development but never neglects the heart of the story—his characters."
—*Publishers Weekly* (starred review)

"Levine skillfully blends humor, a view of Miami, and the legal system into tidy plots."
—*South Florida Sun-Sentinel*

"Another successful fast-moving, highly entertaining mystery. Irreverent to juveniles, judges, and the judicial system, but does it all with a wink. Encore . . . encore."
—*Reviewing The Evidence*

HABEAS PORPOISE

"Steve Solomon and Victoria Lord are smart and funny and sexy in a way that Hollywood movies were before comedies became crass and teen-oriented."
—*Connecticut Post*

"A *Moonlighting* crime novel. Great fun."
—*Lansing State Journal*

"Entertaining and witty with lots of laughs."
—*Mysterious Reviews*

STAND-ALONE THRILLERS

IMPACT

"A breakout book, highly readable and fun with an irresistible momentum, helped along by Levine's knowledge of the Supreme Court and how it works."
—*USA TODAY*

"Sizzles the Supreme Court as it has never been sizzled before, even by Grisham."
—F. Lee Bailey

"A masterfully written thriller, coiled spring tight. The plot is relentless. I loved it!"
—Michael Palmer

BALLISTIC

"*Ballistic* is *Die Hard* in a missile silo. Terrific!"
—Stephen J. Cannell

"It's easy to compare Levine to Tom Clancy but I think he's better for two simple reasons—he's a better storyteller and his characters are more believable, good guys and bad guys alike."
—Ed Gorman

ILLEGAL

"Levine is one of the few thriller authors who can craft a plot filled with suspense while still making the readers smile at the characters' antics."
—*Chicago Sun-Times*

"The seamy side of smuggling human cargo is deftly exposed by the clear and concise writing of the Edgar Award–nominated author. *Illegal* is highly recommended."
—*Midwest Book Review*

"Timely, tumultuous, and in a word, terrific."
—*Providence Journal*

PAYDIRT

"In the tradition of Harlan Coben's thrillers, Paydirt is a sizzling caper with spine-tingling suspense, laughs, thrills, some football, and a touch of romance!"
—*The Daily Review*

"This book is great for mystery lovers, suspense lovers, and even those loving the good ol' All-American pastime and those who play while being true to themselves. A heartwarming story with lots of twists and turns."
—Amazon Review

"Paydirt is one of those books that has characters that stay with you long after the book is finished. The story was a fast and engaging read. I loved the way Levine built up the suspense about the Super Bowl while still keeping the story believable."
—*Vine Voice*

ABOUT THE AUTHOR

Photo by Doug Ellis

The author of twenty-two novels, Paul Levine won the John D. MacDonald fiction award and was nominated for the Edgar, Macavity, International Thriller, Shamus, and James Thurber prizes. A former trial lawyer, he also wrote more than twenty episodes of the CBS military drama *JAG* and co-created the Supreme Court drama *First Monday* starring James Garner and Joe Mantegna. The international bestseller *To Speak for the Dead* was his first novel and introduced readers to linebacker turned lawyer Jake Lassiter. He is also the author of the critically acclaimed Solomon & Lord series, featuring bickering law partners Steve Solomon and Victoria Lord. Levine has also written several stand-alone thrillers, including *Illegal, Ballistic, Impact,* and *Paydirt.* A graduate of Penn State University and the University of Miami Law School, he divides his time between Miami and Santa Barbara, California. For more information, visit Paul Levine's Amazon Author Page at www.amazon.com/Paul-Levine/e/B000APPYKG/ or his website at www.paul-levine.com

Made in the USA
San Bernardino, CA
09 January 2020